The Drum Tower

Books by Farnoosh Moshiri

The Drum Tower
Against Gravity
The Crazy Dervish and the Pomegranate Tree
The Bathhouse
At the Wall of the Almighty

The Drum Tower

Farnoosh Moshiri

Black Heron Press
Post Office Box 13396
Mill Creek, Washington 98082
www.blackheronpress.com

Jacket art and design © 2014 by Bryan Sears.

An earlier version of *The Drum Tower* won a 1999 Barbara Deming Award for a writer "whose work speaks of peace and social justice." A short excerpt from that version was published in the Winter/Spring 2007 issue of *Gulf Coast*.

ISBN: 978-1-936364-06-0
ISBN ebook: 978-1-936364-11-4

Black Heron Press
Post Office Box 13396
Mill Creek, Washington 98082
www.blackheronpress.com

To the loving memory of Fereydoon Moshiri (1926-2000),
people's poet of Iran.

....

The battle of Good and Evil
Which had broken out
From the Primordial Dawn
Is now sunk in a deep long night.

The Good has fled to another land.
This is its warm blood shrouding the earth
Wherever we set foot.

....

Fereydoon Moshiri

An excerpt of "From Silence" translated by Ismail Salami

Acknowledgments

In 1999, a year before his untimely death from a long illness, and on his last reading tour in the United States, I spoke with my uncle, Fereydoon Moshiri, about my then immature plan to write a novel with the central imagery of the Simorgh, the legendary bird of Persian mythology—the Bird of Knowledge. I remember that he was delighted and encouraged me to begin the novel. After he returned to Iran, he sent me a kind letter with useful references. He did not live to see the finished work, but his encouragement kept me going throughout the years of drafting the novel.

For his dedication and support, I'd like to thank my publisher, Jerome Gold, who appreciates serious literature and is always ready to take a risk and go against commercial trends.

Special thanks to my friend, Jane Creighton, who read a very early draft of this novel years ago and encouraged me to go on.

And finally, for their love and encouragement, I thank my husband, David, and my son, Anoosh, who are the foundations of my life.

Why isn't anything going on in the senate?
Why are the senators sitting there without legislating?

Because the barbarians are coming today.
What's the point of senators making laws now?
Once the barbarians are here, they'll do the legislating.

From "Waiting for the Barbarians" by
C. P. Cavafy
Translated from the Greek by Edmund Keeley
and Philip Sherrard

Book I

The Bird of Knowledge

I sense the oncoming winds through which I must survive.

—Rilke

The House of Drums

When I was crazy and the winds of the world blew in my head, I lived in the basement of our old house, Drum Tower. My grandmother's ancient parrot, Boor-boor, sat in a gilded cage behind the window, guarding my room, and Uncle Assad's watchdog, Jangi, paced in the courtyard, panting. In those days, the *chek, chek, chek* of the parrot's hard beak cracking sunflower hulls was the only sound I heard day and night, unless a stranger passed behind the tall walls or someone descended the stone steps approaching my room; then Boor-boor shouted, "Boorrrr!" to alarm my grandmother.

From wherever she was—with her father in the depth of a dark, camphor-scented dream, or in the dim rooms of the house, roaming with her stiff legs, searching for her lost playroom—my grandmother, whose real name was Khanum-Gol, Flower Lady, but almost everyone called her Khanum-Jaan, Dear Lady, rushed to the courtyard to see who was going to my room. If the visitor was my sister Taara, she didn't let her go—she pinched her arm, pulled her ear, or prodded her into the house. If it was our old maid, Daaye, she checked the tray to make sure the soft-hearted woman wasn't sneaking sweets to me. "Sugar stimulates her nerves!" she said. But if Uncle Assad was heading toward my room, Khanum let him go.

"Go Assad, go! But don't stay too long!" she shouted after him. "Crazy enjoys the company of the crazy," she said to herself. "Go, but don't bother the poor thing!" she yelled.

Walled in, isolated from the world in my subterranean confinement, guarded by a noisy parrot and a nasty dog, in those long-ago days I was "the poor thing."

When I heard the *lek, lek, lek* of Uncle Assad's plastic slippers scraping the courtyard's brick floor in his lame way of walking, I rushed to my closet and hid there among my smelly clothes. Uncle came in, calling me, "Talkhoon! Talkhoon! Where are you?" knowing very well where I was. Assad, who knew I wouldn't come out of the closet, made himself comfortable in the middle of my messy room and fumbled with my things.

In those days, the chaos in my room was the image of the chaos in my head. Clothes, socks, shoes, books, and papers, chewed-up pencils (I'd eaten them in fits of anger and anxiety), dirty plates and cups, filthy stuffed animals (presents left after each visit of my absent father), and many other strange objects for which I could not find a name or a function, were piled on and around the bed or on the old dirty desk. A thick layer of dust sat on everything and spider webs connected one old object to another. Daaye was not allowed to clean my room.

"Let her clean her room! If you do it for her, she'll never recover," Grandmother warned the old woman.

From the little hole I'd made in the closet door to breathe and watch, I saw Uncle Assad picking up my underwear, smelling it, looking around, then squeezing it into his pocket. I let him touch my stuff, steal a pair of panties, a hairpin, a broken comb, and leave me alone. Once or twice, when I wasn't quick enough to hide in the closet, Uncle Assad walked toward me, like a zombie, and the more I stepped back, the more he moved forward, until he pressed me against the wall and rubbed his big belly against my chest. I screamed and punched him on the back. Boor-boor shouted, "Boorrr!" Jangi barked, and Khanum-Jaan rushed down, calling, "Assad! What happened?"

"Nothing, Khanum. She's acting up again. I'm coming."

This was my life in those crazy days: the mad parrot's commotion was my peaceful time and the alarming sound of Assad's slippers was my disturbance. If I caught a glimpse of my sister's legs swinging out from the porch above my room while she sat memorizing a long poem for her literature class, my day was made. I gazed at her black polished shoes, white socks, and shapely calves. My heart pounded crazily, and I felt content. But when Khanum-Jaan called Taara inside, I felt lonelier than before.

So I sat behind the narrow, dusty window, looking up at the brick floor of the courtyard where the dusk lingered before creeping into my room. In a short while, from her rooftop room, Taara's tunes rose in the air— she played her setar way into the night. I held my breath and listened, knowing she wasn't looking at her notes, but making her own music. In these sad, tranquil moments, the winds didn't blow in my head but turned into a caressing breeze. Taara's melodies and the soothing silence between them rippled in my dark head like the repeating wavelets of a calm sea.

My room was never locked and I was free to go upstairs, but Khanum-Jaan had made sure that this would never happen. She knew that I was afraid of at least five things—first, her old parrot and her screeching cries which scratched my brain cells, announcing each coming and going; second, Jangi, Assad's long-fanged dog who threatened me with his evil way of panting, circling around me, barking and slobbering thick saliva; third, Uncle Assad himself—his zombie walk, his rude way of breaking into my room and pushing me against the wall. If I survived the parrot, the dog, and the uncle, the ghost of Khanum-Jaan's mother, who had been wandering around in her rusty wheelchair for half a century, scared me to death. If I could ignore the ghost and find my way upstairs to the house, my fifth fear awaited me, and that was the house itself. Yes, I was afraid of the dark, decaying Drum Tower. So there was no need for Grandmother to use locks and bolts, chains and cuffs to keep me inside; she had no doubt that the "poor girl" would stay where she belonged.

And I stayed in my basement room most of the time. Only once a month when I knew that Uncle Assad, Daaye, and Grandmother had gone to the central bazaar for their one-day shopping trip, or once every few months when all of them were invited to a party at the aunties' house, did I dare leave my room. On these occasions, I bribed the unfriendly watch dog with my lunch and let the parrot scream her lungs out and I left my room. First, I strolled in the garden before going upstairs to visit my grandfather.

Ghosts don't exist, ghosts don't exist, I whispered to myself while walking under the weeping willows around the pool. But still I heard the squeaking noise of that old rusty wheelchair approaching me from the depth of the garden. So before I could see the dark-haired, white-gowned woman, my great grandmother Negaar on her wheels, I ran to the stone steps and climbed them up to the building.

In front of a window that framed a blazing, birdless sky, in his threadbare green recliner, half-sitting, half-lying down, Baba-Ji was left to himself. Poor Grandfather was in a deep sleep, but I spent most of my time in his room, combing his silky hair, or stroking his old hands stiffened with dried veins. I pushed his recliner forward and adjusted the pillows under his head, just in case he'd open his eyes. I wanted him to see the street and the vendors sitting on the sidewalk selling fresh walnuts. Then I sat at the foot of his chair, asking him about the bird's feather.

I held my breath and listened to hear what he had to say, but there was no response. I pressed my ear to his chest and heard a vague sound, a dying drum far away in the depth of a remote place. I leafed through his old books in his tall bookshelves covering all four walls of the room, but I couldn't find the sapphire feather of the bird.

"Where is the feather, Baba?" I asked him, and repeated my question many times. But my grandfather's lips were sealed.

When Baba-Ji could still talk, when he was writing the last chapter of his book on a lap-desk with a fountain pen filled with green ink, when I still had a room next to my sister's on this same floor—in those old days, the bird's days, when I wasn't treated like a bastard child, when Assad wouldn't fumble with my things—every night Taara and I sat with Baba before bedtime and he told our fortune.

Baba-Ji sat cross-legged on his cushion with the thick book, *Classical Poems*, in his hands. Slowly, he brought it close to his mouth and whispered a prayer: "O' you holder of the secrets of the world, O' you knower of the riddles of the wise, cast a glance upon us, show us the open horizon, pour a light on our future, we plead you—" Then he kissed the book gently, as if kissing a woman's cheek, and blew softly onto and around it, like blowing out many candles with one breath. At last, after this long introduction, he opened the book.

All the while, Taara and I, who had to keep our eyes shut, cheated and watched Grandfather from the crack between our eyelids. We had to make a wish now. When Baba said, "Open your eyes, your fortune is ready!" we opened our eyes and sat still to hear our poems. With his deep but shaky voice, which trembled more when a phrase was beautiful, Grandfather recited the poem on the right page and that was the answer to our wish. Taara's wish was always about Father. Was he coming soon? What would he bring for her? How long would he stay? But most of the time her poem was the story of Leili and Majnoon, the crazy lovers. Baba-Ji glanced at the page, sighed, and shook his head, "Taara, my child! You're going to be a lovesick girl!"

I don't remember ever wishing for anything but the Simorgh, the Bird of Knowledge. Because I thought that the bird had hidden my mother in its scented nest and I wished to hear something about it. When Baba opened the Simorgh poem for me, and recited the epic, when he described the bird's majestic wings and its powerful beak, I stared at the page, mesmerized, and studied those claws that were bigger than human fists. Now Baba told us how the Simorgh saved Prince Zaal, the white-haired child, who was abandoned on the mountaintop by his father, the king. When he reached the passage where the Bird of Knowledge picked up a live leopard with its powerful talons and took it to her nest to feed the white-haired child, I closed my eyes and imagined that the bird fed my mother in the same way, with the meat of wild animals, and protected her inside its fragrant nest.

Baba-Ji lost himself in ecstasy when he recited the Simorgh poem. He stretched his voice at the end of each line and moved his hands in the air to make the epic more exciting. At the end, when he read the closing lines and his voice fell, we raised our heads and saw Uncle Assad's dark shadow squatting outside in the dim corridor, peeking through the crack of the door. He was listening to the tale of Simorgh. We could not tell if Baba-Ji knew that Assad was hiding in the dark hallway, but Taara and I, who saw him hiding and eavesdropping, didn't invite him in.

Now, thinking back, I realize that the years of the bird, the years before the winds in my head, Uncle Vafa's divorce from the family and devotion to God, the years before Taara's elopement and Baba's descent into silence— all the years before I was sixteen, were the best of my life. It was in those days that Grandfather retired from his teaching job at the University of Tehran and worked on the book sixteen hours a day. Every few weeks, when a chapter was ready, he called the three of us in and read his writing aloud. Most evenings, Taara, Vafa, and I helped him copy the manuscript. Taara, who had the best handwriting among us, copied the last version with black ink and my uncle, Vafa, who was the strongest and could press hard on a thick stack of paper, used three carbons and made copies for the files. I put the notes in order and organized them alphabetically. Our work took many hours of each night.

I liked the atmosphere of Baba's study, the sound of pens scratching paper, Vafa whistling a tune in a low pitch, Baba-Ji's breath wheezing as he wrote. Sometimes, he put one of his old, heavy records on the record player. The tunes of a symphony filled the room—Schubert's "Unfinished," Berlioz's "Fantastique," Korsakov's "Scheherazade." But his favorite was "The Firebird," which had a strange, mesmerizing mood and was about the Simorgh. When the strings went crazy, Baba lifted his head from his manuscript to see how we reacted. Once, Taara, unable to stand the excitement of the Simorgh music, jumped to her feet, whirled around the room, leapt and flapped her arms like the Firebird's wings. Her curls disheveled, her long skirt twisted around her body, she laughed wildly, as if drunk. Baba-Ji smiled with delight and shook his head with admiration.

"We've neglected your dancing talent, Taara. You could've become a ballerina!"

All through "The Firebird Ballet," I stared at the large tapestry covering one of the walls, showing the rainbow-colored bird opening her four wings. Two of the wings were strong and majestic, two were soft and silky, like extended ends of long scarves, or the hanging braids of a woman sweeping the earth. The Simorgh, the Bird of Knowledge, flew toward the Tree of Knowledge, embroidered with meandering shades of blue and green on the left side of the tapestry. In the top branches of the legendary tree, the naked Prince Zaal sat. The prince's hair was snow white like an old man's and he had extended one arm forward to greet the Simorgh that had brought him fresh meat for nourishment.

After the bewitching music ended, Daaye tiptoed to our room with a tray full of delicious snacks—halva, walnuts, feta cheese, and hot, freshly brewed tea which she poured into three small, narrow-waisted glasses for us and into a tall, fat glass for Baba.

I raised my head now and then from my book, looked at Baba-Ji and sighed with relief. He was well and alive! What else did I want in the world? Baba-Ji, a Simorgh himself, glowed with knowledge and spread wisdom around.

It was hard then, and it's harder even now to decide if my grandfather was going insane, if he really believed that the Simorgh existed. Baba-Ji might have been playing with us and amusing himself when he felt exhausted after a long day of work. Or, he might have been half-serious, or even dead serious, pursuing a goal. He might have begun with collecting the legends and facts, but gradually came to believe that the bird was real. All I can say now is that in his massive book, my grandfather was trying to prove that there was no evidence to indicate that the enormous bird ever became extinct.

The happiest moments of those years were our regular picnics under the dryandra tree. When he was deep into his research on the Chinese version of the Simorgh, Baba frequently took us to the garden. We sat in the shade of the umbrella-like branches of the dryandra and Taara played her setar. Ancient Chinese believed that if someone played a string instrument under a dryandra tree, Feng Huang, who was a male and a female bird in one, would appear.

There were always the three of us, Vafa, Taara, and I. My sister played the setar, Vafa and I held our breath and listened. We knew that it was all a play-game, but we had a secret hope that if we listened wholeheartedly, we could hear the flapping of the Simorgh's majestic wings from far above.

The picnic culminated in a delicious lunch of bread, cheese, and herbs that Baba provided from his small herb bed. He picked basil leaves, tarragon twigs, mint and leeks and made us cheese and herb sandwiches. Now he told us how every thousand years the Simorgh flew over the earth, dropped the seeds of knowledge, and spread her wisdom around. We looked up, absentmindedly, to check the sky.

When Baba-Ji was working on the Angha, the Arabian version of the Simorgh, he encouraged us to steal cinnamon sticks from the pantry room. We took all the sticks and powdered cinnamon to the tower and mixed them with dry twigs of willow and left the scented mixture for the Simorgh to make her nest with. Angha, or Cinomolgus, made her nest from cinnamon, as Baba's research had proved. So, on hot summer afternoons, Taara, Vafa, and I tiptoed to the pantry, stole handfuls of cinnamon sticks and ran to the tower. Baba, in his blue pajama pants and white undershirt, red in the face, sweat running down his temples, waited for us in the damp tower. Talking in whispers all through the work, as if the bird were hidden somewhere nearby and would fly away if she heard us, we helped him make the nest.

The Indian version of the Simorgh, Garuda of the Mahabharata, was a bird whose beak had holes like a flute and who played music each time she took a breath. Baba had found the evidence of the bird's existence in Attar's *Conference of the Birds*, a twelfth-century mystical book he used as one of his sources. I remember that Taara and I had memorized the lines about the Indian bird and chanted them while hopping around the dryandra tree:

> In India lives a bird that is unique
> The lovely phoenix has a long, hard beak
> Pierced with a hundred holes, just like a flute
> It has no mate, its reign is absolute.
> Each opening has a different sound; each sound
> Means something secret, subtle and profound

But the most colorful memory of my bird days belongs to the ritual of the sapphire feather and this happened three times during the last year of Baba's wakefulness. Khanum-Jaan, who had tolerated the setar-playing under the dryandra tree and hadn't raised much hell about the cinnamon theft, now screamed her lungs out, called her husband a wizard and told him that in his old age he had gone out of his mind.

"Have you lost your mind? Are you driving these children crazy, too?" she shouted at Baba. "Instead of making a fool of yourself, put that damn book together and try to sell it. How long should I wait for this cursed book of yours to end?"

But Baba, as was his lifelong habit, ignored his wife's sharp tongue. He held the sapphire feather in one hand, a match in the other, and headed toward the tower. Taara, Vafa, and I followed him like a file of geese rushing behind their mother.

I remember that Baba-Ji took his portable record player to the tower and we all sat in that small, square space, listening to "The Firebird." Baba turned up the volume and that eerie music with the explosion of its many strings echoed in the garden. It was twilight, when Baba believed the bird would choose to appear. When the last bangs of the percussion ended the music, Baba plucked one barb of the feather and burned it with a long matchstick. We sat, held our breath, and gazed at the indigo sky. The smell of burned feather in our nostrils, the volcanic music in our heads, and the orange of the clouds blending into the darkest blue in front of our eyes, we sat motionless waiting for the bird's descent.

But, of course, the bird didn't descend, and maybe Baba-Ji knew it wouldn't. So he said, "Well, I think we have to wait until the next time. We still have plenty of these blue barbs left on the feather. But we didn't lose anything, did we?" We all shook our heads. "We listened to fantastic music, enjoyed the sunset and meditated a little, too, didn't we?" We all nodded.

Once, in his youth, Baba traveled to England to see the thirteen-inch egg of the Rukh in the British Museum. Rukh was the seventy-foot bird Marco Polo had heard about in Madagascar. The natives had sworn they had seen the bird preying on elephants, snatching the gentle beasts in their talons, lifting them into the sky, dropping them and feeding on them. Wasn't the Rukh the same Simorgh of the Persian epic who carried leopards in her talons to feed the king's albino son? Wasn't the Rukh the same multicolored beast-bird of the Arabian Nights from whose claws Sinbad the Sailor hung? Baba raised such questions in his book.

But my grandfather's enormous book which contained the scientific, the mythical, and the literary aspects of the bird and included folkloric tales, paintings and their interpretations, analyses of ancient works of literature, photographs, charts, graphs, statistics, and a massive bibliography (itself the size of a book), was destined to remain unfinished. Baba's rough draft, written in his tiny archaic cursive in green ink, was missing most of the last chapter, as was the revised copy, which he had begun when our father was in high school, copying for Baba, and had been continued with Taara's handwriting in black ink, and the carbon copies in Vafa's handwriting.

Chapter thirteen, which was supposed to contain the conclusion, and to create a finale for Baba's long symphony, was never completed. It was as if our grandfather had spent all his life weaving a vast carpet with pure silk threads, but had never been able to put in the last touches, to give the carpet a shape and make it into something usable. His bird, whose origin was so carefully sought, was transfixed in midair, unable to fly. Baba had never decided if the Simorgh was pure legend, a shared symbol among nations, a bird that was still around, or the Savior.

I remember that finally the copies in the binders and the manuscript in the box, each containing twelve chapters and one small section of the thirteenth, sat idle, the pages yellowing, the ink fading. The marvelous words of the book died slowly as the memory of the joyful work vanished in time. "The Firebird," uncovered on the record player, was left to gather dust, and the sapphire tail feather, with its many barbs still unburned, was forever lost.

Grandmother's Companion

I kept telling Taara that Khanum-Jaan had hammered nails into her slippers' heels to annoy us, to let us know that she was in every single spot of the dark house, spying on us. But Taara never liked the joke. She loved our grandmother.

Click, click, click, click... Khanum's golden slippers sang something like,

"I'm here, here, here, here... I can see you, see you, see you, see you..."

Uncle Kia had sent her these tiny strapped slippers from Paris and she wore them day and night, roaming around the house, doing her endless chores, complaining that her feet ached.

These were the chores Khanum had created on purpose to torment herself, but mostly to annoy us. After she walked for hours, climbing three stories many times, taking inventory of her antique objects, the lost ones and the existing ones, she lifted up her legs at the dinner table, to show her swollen ankles and her spider web veins. She pressed her joints hard, traced the strange purple lines with her fingers and moaned from pain. She complained of her chores and lamented the poverty and misery that awaited her in old age. Then she sulked because of her family's lack of compassion and appreciation, and became quiet.

In old times, when Grandmother hadn't stopped going to her husband's room, she took her complaints to Baba-Ji's study, interrupting his work, showing her swollen ankles, whining. We heard Baba's calm and serious voice telling her, "Don't work, Khanum! Just stop working! Why are we paying half a dozen people in this house?"

When she sat with her sisters, she said, "Didn't I have a room for myself? I don't mean our big bedroom where Mademoiselle Marie stayed with us, what I'm talking about is my own play room, the one with a train set Papa had brought me from England. Remember?"

One of the aunties would say, "Oh, you mean the sun room, the one attached to our parents' bedroom, where they played checkers together."

"It wasn't called the sun room, Puran, it was called the almond room and it was my own play room. You two were older and spent most of your time in the study with your tutors; the almond room was mine. The red locomotive ran around and around, passing all these little houses, trees, and small people. It whistled too. I remember the whistle very well. What happened to my almond room, huh, sister?"

When Grandmother wasn't with her sisters, reading Turkish coffee grounds, spreading tarot cards around, looking at astronomy charts, studying each other's palms, gossiping and reminiscing, her companion was Assad. Assad and Khanum-Jaan always took a break on the porch, had tea together, chatting and enjoying the gurgle of the small fountain in the middle of the square flowerbed. Since she had raised the wall between herself and the garden, all Khanum could see from the porch was the courtyard and a small flowerbed any low-class family could manage to have. Assad planted a dozen marigolds in the autumn and a few pansies in springtime. And this order never changed.

Grandmother sat on her folding chair—an old sun-washed beach chair—took off her golden, strapped slippers, and rubbed her sore feet. Assad limped and scraped his plastic slippers on the floor, carrying a small tray with two glasses of maroon-colored tea, a china teapot, and a saucer full of thin, coin-shaped honey candies, and sat on the lower step of the porch, rubbing his bad leg. They always spoke about the same subjects, as if they had never talked about them before.

"Tell me, Assad, how much does it cost to fix the garden, huh?"

"A zillion, Khanum," Assad said with a fake indifference. "Don't even think about it. If I were you, I'd level the garden and build apartment houses here. That's where the money is."

"Nonsense!" This was Khanum's favorite word. "I haven't fallen this low! Have I? You're expecting the daughter of Hessam-Mirza Vaziri, the Minister of War, the descendent of a dynasty of ministers, to become an innkeeper? A slum lord?"

Assad chuckled and shook his head. Khanum's case was hopeless.

"Don't laugh, Assad. I'm serious, how much does it cost to fix the garden? The pool smells, the water storage houses snakes, the tower is about to fall. How can we get rid of this ugly tower, Assad?"

"The house of the Simorgh?" Assad said teasingly.

"What nonsense! The Simorgh! That damn bird and her endless story—."

"You're jealous of the Simorgh, Khanum, because Baba spent all his life with her!" Assad teased her again.

"How can I be jealous of a damn bird that remains invisible? It's not jealousy, Assad, its hatred! I hate the monster's guts! She choked my husband in her claws!" Saying this, Khanum made crooked claws with her stiff fingers, and shook them in front of Assad's face.

Now she began telling Assad for the thousandth time how when she and Baba married, she was only eighteen, an orphan girl who didn't know better. The man was already married to his books. He took long trips to the mountains and came back all bearded, with bags of papers.

"Tons and tons of them, Assad. His books and papers covered the bed. I had nightmares, seeing myself under an avalanche of them. And then, before you knew, he lost his appetite for any kind of earthly pleasure. At age forty-five! And how old was I? Only thirty!"

"My father is a saint!" Assad said and filled his mouth with salted chickpeas.

"A saint!" she mimicked him. "The books ate him up. The dark books. He broke from real things, and went inside those pages. The unreal world."

Although Assad had heard all this and Khanum had said all this, they took new pleasure each time they repeated the conversation. These were Khanum-Jaan's main topics: Baba-Ji neglecting her; her sons, Sina, Kia, and Vafa, abandoning her; Sina's wife (our mother), the crazy bitch, taking her son away from her; and finally, the stars not lining up in the sky for her.

They sat on the porch during the mild autumn days, breezy spring days, summer evenings, or sunny winter afternoons. They talked and when Khanum raised her voice to curse, the old parrot, Boor-boor, screamed from the bottom of her lungs and Assad laughed, and in this way the strange bond between the woman, the servant, and the parrot became stronger as time passed and they repeated the same stories.

But if you'd tell Khanum-Jaan, You've made your husband's son a servant of the house, she'd shake her head so hard that the dyed ringlets around her face would quiver, and then she'd tell you that the boy wanted it. Assad wanted to do the chores.

"I sent him to school, bought him books, even tutored him myself. But he wasn't interested. Assad's head was full of chalk, if you want to know. Nothing went through. Clay and chalk! I told my husband, Let's send him to a trade school, let him become a carpenter, a roofer, a plumber or something, but Anvar was always too busy to think about anything outside his books. He neglected him."

But Daaye, who had been in the house even before Khanum-Jaan was born, said that Baba was the one who insisted that Assad should go to school. When Khanum argued that she needed him around the house, he suggested the night school. And this was when the boy was already twelve years old.

I overheard Assad many times saying to people that he was twelve when they sent him to night school. They were all grown-ups in the class and he felt embarrassed to sit with them. That's why he quit after a few months.

Then Baba taught him the alphabet, and he read at the third-grade level with difficulty and wrote clumsily and that was all the education he received in the house of Professor Anvar Angha, the well-known scholar.

But who could deny that Assad was a compulsive worker? We always saw him fixing the broken faucets, scrubbing the algae from the pool's walls, stirring Daaye's seven-herb soup, or ironing Grandmother's silk blouses. He did tough and delicate jobs equally well. His thick, callused fingers, greasy after repairing the car's carburetor, could hold the thinnest, tiniest needle and stitch Khanum's skirt hem. He was the one who pickled small cucumbers and herbs in tall, glass jars and made cherry and quince jam for the winter. He was a perfect housekeeper and Khanum-Jaan needed such a capable worker in Drum Tower. Daaye was getting old, her hands shook and she forgot to add salt to stew and sugar to jam.

Three Theories of Soraya's Disappearance

"She vanished in a wink!" Daaye said when I was still living upstairs in a room next to my sister's. She snapped a green pod, took out three lima beans, and dropped them in a bowl. She sat cross-legged on the carpet with the bowl of beans in front of her and I sat on the bed, still in my pajamas, a plate of rice pudding on my lap.

Daaye couldn't read or write, but she'd learned how to spell one word. On the golden, smooth surface of my rice pudding she'd written ALLAH with powdered saffron. I dipped the big spoon into the pudding, dug out a quivering chunk of cool dessert with all the letters of ALLAH, and put it in my mouth. The heavenly thing melted at once.

"No one had ever known someone to vanish like this," she said. "I went up to their room to tidy up, as I did every morning. The bed was untouched." Snap, snap. Lima beans in the bowl, empty skins in the tray. "She must have left sometime during the night, before even going to bed." Snap. "You were a week old, in your crib, next to your parents' bed. You were whining. Hungry for your mother's milk. Your sister, Taara, was one and a half, baby-walking around the house, falling, crying. But your mother had vanished. Just like this!" Snap.

"Where was my father?" The pudding was gone. I cleaned the edge of the bowl with my finger, licking it.

"As usual, in the rose arbor. Whenever they quarreled he sat on a bench amid the roses, drinking and smoking. Then Assad joined him and they got drunk together. He was there that morning."

"Why did my mother disappear, Daaye?"

"Do you want me to tell you the truth?"

"Nothing but the truth!"

Daaye lowered her voice so that no possible eavesdropper could hear her, and then, in a whisper, said, "She hated the house! She said Drum Tower was alive, breathing and even talking to her, like a person, a monster. She wanted your father to take her out of here. But you know that your father couldn't leave his mother."

"But he finally did."

"Too late, though. Not when his wife was around. Once, when he mentioned leaving the house and renting an apartment for himself and Soraya, your grandmother had one of those famous fits. But this time when she passed out she didn't come to for an hour. Then your father stopped mentioning the apartment. Your mother insisted some more, then threatened your father that she'd leave him. But he didn't believe her. They loved each other a lot, you know? But their love was poisoned."

"Still, I don't understand why she left."

"She was scared of this house. She set herself free."

Daaye snapped some more beans in silence, then stopped and just sat rocking herself gently to right and left, as if she had a baby in her arms. Her eyes had a hollow gaze, looking at nothing.

"I don't blame Soraya a bit," she said. "I'd do the same if I were her.

We're born only once!"

Uncle Assad never knocked. I heard him scraping his slippers on the
corridor's tiles, dragging one foot. He opened the door, came in and sat
down in the middle of my room, looking around. He looked at my clothes
scattered on the bed, at my schoolbooks and toys. He fumbled with my
things, picked up a doll, looked at it carefully, pulled up its tiny skirt and
investigated what was underneath. He chuckled to himself and put the
doll aside. Now he took a fistful of salted chickpeas out of his pocket,
stuffed his mouth and, while chewing, told me his own version of Soraya's
story.

"Your Mommy is in Bandar. My friends have told me. The Big Sheikh's
men kidnapped her and took her to Bandar. The Arab fell in love with her
at the coronation ball and had his men kidnap her. If you want to know
where your Mommy is, I'm telling you, she's in Bandar. She's the Sheikh's
last wife.

"Khanum kept telling her, 'Don't walk alone in the streets at night.
You're pretty, something bad will happen to you! She didn't listen, and
this happened to her. She ruined your father's life altogether. Ruined your
life, Taara's life, and above all, Khanum-Jaan's life."

You lie, Assad! You lie! I wanted to scream and throw him out, but my
voice didn't come out.

"Maybe you think I'm lying," he said, as if reading my mind. "But why
should I lie? Huh? How do I benefit in all this? I'm just trying to solve the
mystery for you. Maybe you'll feel better if you know the truth about your
mother. You're growing into a sad child, Talkhoon. I keep telling Khanum,
let me take Taara and Talkhoon to Bandar and show them where their
mother lives, maybe they'll feel better. But she doesn't listen to me. She
constantly consults her papa's ghost and the ghost says, 'Leave the bitch
alone!'

"You know where Bandar is, don't you? It's a harbor town. On the
Persian Gulf. The deep south. The end of the country. Soraya is the old
Sheikh's last wife. Safe and sound. The flower of his harem."

Khanum sat on her folding chair on the porch while Taara and I played quietly behind the dusty maple that had grown by itself next to the brick wall. Our dolls were sleeping on their spreads next to a small set of cups and saucers. We were waiting for the girls to wake up and have their afternoon tea. Whenever people came out and sat close to where we played, we talked in whispers and played quietly in order to eavesdrop.

Khanum-Jaan knew we were behind the maple, but she didn't lower her voice. She and Assad were talking about our mother.

"I warned Sina, didn't I, Assad? You must remember how I warned him. I told him this girl didn't belong to our class. She didn't have good blood. I could tell just from looking at her. She was pretty, all right. But she was dark-skinned, like a servant girl, and she was a bit crazy. Weird. Wasn't she, Assad?"

"She sure was, Khanum," Assad said from the flowerbed. He was digging the earth, taking pebbles out. "She was wild like a stray cat, and stubborn too. Didn't listen to anyone. Her skin was dark. You're right," he said, panting a little.

"She wasn't a pure breed. Her father was a Baluch, her mother a Kurd, or the other way round. She could never become a lady. She hadn't been brought up the way we had. I warned my son when I saw these signs, but I wish I'd known earlier that she was loose. Had I known she was loose, I'd never have let that marriage happen."

"Now you're hurting your nerves again, Khanum! Didn't the doctor tell you to take it easy and not think about the past? Why bother about the dead and gone?"

"Dead and gone? No one is dead and gone, Assad. I'm left here alone to raise their brats. Am I not? He comes and goes every two years, as it pleases him. He's gone mad; he's ruined and lost. He is a majnoon, a wanderer of deserts! And she's not dead, either. Didn't you say she's married to an Arab emir?"

"That's what people say, Khanum. People have seen her in Bandar."

"Well, let me tell you what I've been thinking all these years." Khanum bent forward and lowered her voice to a whisper. "Soraya wasn't kidnapped against her will, Assad. She went with the Sheikh. At that damned coronation ball, the Sheikh fell for her and she, who was itching for an Arab, went with him. She betrayed Sina and left her babies behind. Even the second one, who was probably not my son's—"

"Hush, Khanum! The girls are behind the tree," Assad said, and shoved a pansy into the dirt.

"But how could the second one be my son's if they hadn't slept together for more than a year?" Khanum tried to say this in a whisper, but it was loud enough for us to hear. "Didn't Sina sleep in his old room after the first one was born? Do you remember, Assad?"

"I remember, Khanum. Everybody remembers. We were all under one roof. But let's not talk about it now."

"If she hadn't gone with the Sheikh, she would have ended up in the streets. She'd have become a prostitute and then how could we raise our heads? But the big emir is like a shah. Richer than the Shah, or maybe as rich. I swear to my God that all these years whenever a relative asked me what happened to your daughter-in-law, I said, Well, they divorced, like many young people do these days, and thank God she's married to the Big Sheikh, the emir of Bandar. You see how I try to save face?"

"You do the right thing," Assad said wiping his sweaty forehead with his sleeve. "We have to keep our faces red, as they say, even if we need to slap our own cheeks once in a while!"

"But the crazy bitch took my Sina away from me. I wish she'd die and the curse would be removed. Sina—the flower of my sons—the kindest, the handsomest, the light of my eyes." She wiped her tears and added, "I dreamed, Assad, I dreamed…"

Uncle Vafa

In the absence of our father, who was a wanderer of the deserts, as his mother said, and Uncle Kia, who was abroad all through our childhood, Uncle Vafa was the only young man around. Taara and I neither saw Assad as a man nor considered him an uncle. He was always there, but we never counted him as family.

I was seven years younger than Vafa and when I was between three and eight, I spent long hours playing with him. The list of our mischief is long and these are just the highlights: We burned a silk Persian carpet while setting fire to plastic soldiers that we were pretending were the army of Alexander the Great. Trying to study history for his sixth grade finals, Vafa had arranged the whole war scene on Grandmother's antique carpet. Neither of us received allowance for one full year, but this wasn't even one thousandth of the price of Khanum-Jaan's carpet.

We broke into the storage room on top of the tower one summer afternoon to see if it was so that there were real drums stored there from hundreds of years ago. It was true—we saw the dusty war drums with our own eyes, banged on them and tore a couple. We awoke the whole neighborhood from their afternoon nap and Khanum locked us up in our rooms for twenty-four hours.

Once, angry with Grandmother who didn't allow us to watch TV, we broke into the guestroom where the set was locked up. Khanum-Jaan was hospitalized for an appendectomy and the key (the set had sliding doors) hung on her neck. We broke the lock and watched television for four consecutive nights, five hours a night. We began with the cartoons, watched grown-up shows, a couple of black-and-white American movies, the news, a late comedy show, the Quiz Show, and then passed out in front of the oak set when the National Anthem announced the end of the evening programs. When Khanum was released from the hospital, we accepted our punishment with grace and without much fuss.

And there was more. We ran the two hundred thirty-five stone steps of the brick tower up and down many times a day to check the hollow space and see if the Simorgh had nested there. We stole fresh meat, bread, and pastry, and left it for the bird, but it all rotted and Assad had to clean the tower, and of course tell on us. We peered through the dark hole of the water storage tank to see if it was true that human skeletons were at the bottom of the abandoned pool. We played with the ghosts. Vafa made ghost sounds to call them, and when we heard the squeak of the wheelchair under the weeping willows, we screamed and ran for our lives. Once, escaping from Grandma Negaar's ghost, Taara fell in the pool and almost drowned. Assad was the only grown-up around, but he was lame and didn't know how to swim. Vafa dived into the slimy pool and fished her out.

"Talkhoon and Vafa are the devils," Khanum announced at the dinner table. "They bring my poor Taara into their schemes."

But what we shared the most was the Simorgh. We repeated Baba-Ji's stories for each other and added our own imaginary ones. We sat for hours in Vafa's room, cracking sunflower hulls (stolen from the old parrot), and made up Simorgh stories. Taara preferred to practice her setar. When the weather was pleasant, we sat under the dryandra tree, Taara played, and Vafa and I wove fantastic tales for hours. Baba-Ji saw us from his window, came down and sat with us. He admired our tales and encouraged us to weave more.

When he was fifteen, Uncle Vafa outgrew the Simorgh stories. He stopped copying for Baba and being a friend and playmate for me. He left our work-play team unnoticed. But before he replaced the Simorgh book with the Book of God he went through a long period of silence. He stayed out after school and crept into the house at dusk. He locked himself in his room with the lights out. He hardly ate. He didn't answer Khanum's questions when she interrogated him, and didn't react to Daaye's pleadings to eat. He didn't go to Baba's room when he called, and stopped walking with Taara and me to school. When I asked him to read to me or play with me, he gave me a faint, distant smile and patted my head as if he were an old man and I were just a baby. He dismissed me in silence.

At seventeen, Uncle Vafa became a stranger in the house. Khanum and her sisters sat around the oak table, searched for their fortunes in cards, looked inside coffee cups, and read astronomers' charts. They even called Sayyed Mirza, the ghost man, for a séance. Grandpa Vazir's ghost appeared and told Khanum that Vafa was possessed by evil forces from outside the house. Daaye prayed to her favorite holy one, Imam Reza, that if Vafa would become himself again she'd cook saffron rice pudding for one hundred beggars who sat in the courtyard of the Imam's Mosque. Neither Khanum's fortune telling and séance nor Daaye's vow brought Uncle Vafa back.

One Friday morning Baba-Ji came out of his study and went straight to his son's room, knocked on the door and, before hearing anything, entered. Taara and I ran barefoot out of our rooms to eavesdrop. Baba had never left his study to go to anyone's room before. From behind the tall Indian vase containing peacock feathers, we saw our young uncle lying on his back, his sunken eyes wide open. Baba said, "Son, if you want me to tell you that I don't need your help with my book anymore, I'm here to say so. You've done your job, as your older brother did. He left—you may want to leave too. You're free. You don't believe in my book? Find your own book, or write one. But don't hurt yourself and your family. Get up, eat, and live again."

Soon after Baba's visit, Uncle Vafa took the Koran to his room. This was the fat, hard-covered black Koran with golden letters and a faint smell of rose water rising from between its pages. No one had ever read this book for the simple reason that the only believers in our house were Daaye and Assad—the first, illiterate, and the second, half literate. So the Holy Book was used only once a year when Baba-Ji and Khanum-Jaan placed fresh bank notes between the pages to give away as New Year presents.

Vafa taught himself Arabic and read the thick, black book day and night. Like a Chinese monk, he grew a thin beard with a few long strands hanging from his chin. Five times a day, he adjusted himself diagonally toward the corner of the wall (facing Mecca) and prayed aloud. He was still quiet and somber, but he ate with the family and kept his door unlocked.

In the month of Ramadan—so far observed only by Daaye and Assad (who stopped drinking vodka for the whole month)—Vafa fasted with them. At four in the morning we heard the three of them eating in the kitchen, whispering and praying. Daaye, who now believed that Vafa was the only saved soul in the family, cooked the promised saffron rice pudding, and on the last day of the month, the Sacrifice Day, Assad drove her to Imam Reza's Mosque and they distributed the food among the beggars who were scattered in the courtyard with their empty alms bowls.

Now, gradually, Uncle Vafa's friends came for meetings. In his room, they recited Arabic prayers, interpreted them and discussed the political events of the day. Once, I caught Khanum-Jaan eavesdropping behind Vafa's door, pressing her ear against the cold wood to hear what her son and his friends were saying. Noticing me, she pretended that what she was doing was absolutely justified.

"Just reading books," she whispered. "I thought they were drinking liquor or something. But they're just reading! You stay behind this door, Talkhoon. When the boys are about to leave, run and call me. I want to look at them and see who they are. One glance and I can tell if they're vagabonds."

Soon Vafa finished high school and left the house. He lived with the same friends in a rented room and, before long, joined a religious organization under the leadership of a young doctor. He became an anti-government activist. Baba-Ji, who believed in myths and legends more than religions, or thought that religions were no more than myths, had secretly hoped that Vafa would return to him. Now he lost hope, became sulky, and didn't perform the Simorgh rituals anymore. Khanum-Jaan, who associated all political activity with the lower classes, cursed her son and banished him.

Uncle Vafa's banishment lasted for five years. We never saw how he changed from a boy to a man and how his thin beard thickened. His room stayed untouched—a seventeen-year-old's room. Daaye was forbidden to clean it, but I sneaked in once a week with a damp rag and wiped the dust off every single object. I cleaned his football trophies, his toy soldiers, the stuff on his desk and his books in the bookshelf. Khanum never found out that I cleaned Vafa's room.

I kept telling Taara that one day Vafa would stop us on the way to school just to see us and say hello. This never happened.

When he was twenty-three, a graduate student of theology, he came to Drum Tower, kissed his parents' hands and asked permission to get married. He was tall and lanky and had a bushy beard. In the kitchen, Assad told Daaye that Vafa was not the type of person who needed anyone's permission to do anything; he had come back for a reason. What reason? Daaye asked. Khanum was getting old, Assad said, the boy wanted to be mentioned in her will.

"Who is the girl's family? What's their last name?"

These were Khanum-Jaan's first questions, of course. When she realized that the girl's last name was obscure and her father was in the grocery business and not a member of the aristocracy, she cursed and swore that she'd never let such a marriage happen.

Baba-Ji was weak and weepy those days. When he saw that his son was back, he wiped his tears and blessed him. He had neither the mental energy nor the physical to argue with him. But Khanum-Jaan, in her black silk, sat at the head of the oak table and rested her bony fingers in front of her like a raven's claws. She was ready to take Vafa's eyes out.

"You'll have to step over my dead body to take this girl as your wife. Once was enough. I let Sina marry that rotten whore and look what happened to us. Over my dead body!"

But the wedding happened without Vafa stepping on his mother's corpse. I was sixteen then and this was just a few months before the winds in my head blew hard and commanded me to dive from the top of the tall tower.

Since Vafa's visit, I felt a sickness in my chest, a grip that nearly choked me. It was as if a net were entangling my lungs and imprisoning my breath. I was gloomy all the time and didn't take any interest in anything. I stopped studying and pretended I had a cold and missed school. Twice in math class I held my breath, thinking that if I'd stop breathing for too long, I'd die. Either because of lack of oxygen or the power of suggestion, I really passed out, disturbing the class. Our math teacher was a gray-haired, soft-spoken old man. I was so pleased to open my eyes in his arms that I closed them again and passed out for the second time. My old angel knelt on the floor, held me in his arms and stroked my hair. The principal called home and I soon found myself lying on the back seat of the black Cadillac. Assad, noisily chewing chickpeas, drove me home.

Doctor Shafa, our family physician, suspected asthma and visited me twice a week with a balloon for me to blow into and a big inhaler to take medicine into my lungs. After a few weeks he asked me how I felt. I said someone was breathing inside my head—it sounded like a mild breeze or a secret told in a whisper. The doctor stopped asthma treatments and didn't visit me anymore.

The memory of Uncle Vafa's wedding is foggy and blurred. Clouds wrap and unwrap around faces and voices. I remember a commotion in the house, but I'm not sure if someone reported this to me, or I was present. Khanum kept screaming, "Over my dead body!" and opened her arms wide like a bat. She blocked Baba's door, not letting him out. Baba in his tuxedo and red bow tie, the same old suit he had had since his youth and hadn't worn since his last attendance at a university ceremony, stood confused, then covered his ears with his palms so as not to hear his wife's screams. Assad held Khanum from behind and tried to calm her down. "Now, now, now—you're hurting your nerves again." Daaye cried and pleaded, "Khanum-Jaan, I beg you! Let me see my son as a groom!" Taara, half-dressed, barefoot, long hair disheveled, was sobbing. Baba fell into his recliner, held his forehead, and waved his hands. "Leave me alone! Leave my room, please! I just want to be alone!"

I remember Assad calling Uncle Kia for help. After twenty years residing in Europe, he had returned with his wife and twin daughters a few months earlier and was now a counselor to the War Minister. He was constantly in meetings and conferences and barely had time for family matters. He was a counselor by nature, cold and remote, and of course he thought that his great stature put him above the family. But he was the only person who could calm Grandmother and he knew that, so he came.

An hour-long conference occurred behind the closed door of the guest room. We were all half-dressed, waiting for the result. Finally, Uncle came out with his faint diplomatic smile, and announced with a tinge of French accent that we could all go to Vafa's wedding, but Khanum-Jaan wouldn't go with us. He and his wife couldn't go, either—they were expected at the Minister's house.

Now we had to hurry to get ready. Daaye fixed Baba's crooked bow tie and Taara and I rushed to our rooms to rinse our red eyes and finish dressing. Daaye wore her mothball-smelling black chiffon dress, permanently creased from long years of lying folded at the bottom of her trunk. Assad in a double-breasted, gray suit, now out of fashion and too large for him (it belonged to my father once), sat in the driver's seat. We all crammed into the shiny black Cadillac and headed toward Uncle Vafa's wedding, which was held in his father-in-law's garden. We left Khanum-

Jaan alone in the dark Drum Tower to feel sorry for herself and mourn her evil luck.

My old playmate was in a black suit, smiling, but did not notice me at all. Instead, he looked deep into his bride's eyes and the photographer took pictures of them in front of the fountains, the trees, and a tall, three-tiered cream cake. Now they invited us to pose with them. But Baba-Ji was blowing his nose in a big handkerchief, pretending he had a cold. It turned out that my uncle's father-in-law owned a chain of grocery stores, not just one, and was quite wealthy. But we all knew that even this news wouldn't change Khanum-Jaan's mind. She'd say, "They're shop keepers, commoners. No good blood." Or, "Their name is a made-up name. No roots!"

The wedding, as it happened, was the turning point of Taara's life and, in a way, of mine, too. At seventeen, Taara's beauty was blossoming. She was like a camellia that had taken a long time to bloom, but was gorgeous now in each stage of its slow growth. She played her setar that night and mesmerized more than a hundred young men who immediately fell in love with her. It was no secret now that Taara was unique. In her long, white, beaded dress, she seemed more a bride than the bride herself, and like a sun, wherever she sat, she attracted a party of men who rotated around her like small planets.

They took turns dancing with her. A tall, young gentleman with a large, bony nose was the most arrogant of them. He took others' turns and danced with Taara the rest of the night.

"He is General Nezam-El-Deen's son," women whispered, and watched the couple with envy.

Until that night I'd never compared myself to my sister, but now for the first time I realized I could never even remotely compete with her. Taara was heading toward pure perfection. But it was I who looked like our mother, not Taara. I heard this from the aunties who whispered to each other and ran their eyes over my developing body the way men do. I heard this from Assad, who stopped me in the dark corridors, blocked my way with his stocky body, and whispered, "Soraya!" his smelly breath assaulting my face.

I didn't hear anything from Khanum-Jaan, but I felt her resentment. The more I matured, the less she liked me. Once in a while, without any reason, she stopped talking to me, even frowned when we bumped into each other in a corridor. She found fault with the way I dressed, read, ate, walked, and almost everything I did. While she went to Taara's room to scold her for something she'd done wrong, she never came to my room. Instead, she sent warning messages through Daaye or Assad about the rude way I'd behaved in front of the guests, or the wrong way I'd held the drumstick at the dinner table. The day finally came when my grandmother stopped looking at me altogether.

"Soraya's ghost has entered her body," I heard Auntie Puran saying.

"Nonsense!" Khanum told her sister. "What ghost? The bitch is not dead yet."

"How do we know? Huh? Maybe she has died and her ghost has possessed the girl's body," Auntie said. "Have you ever seen such a resemblance? She lies flat on her stomach, legs up in the air, reading story books for hours, exactly the way her mother used to do. Remember, sister? Do you want us to call Sayyed Mirza and talk to Papa?"

"The bitch is still alive!" Khanum said. "I'd know if she'd died. The curse would be removed from my poor son!"

Now the more they said I resembled my lost mother, the more I became obsessed with her. I went to the master bedroom where I knew my parents once slept. I sat in front of the tall oak dressing table, the ancestral vanity my mother used. I touched the shiny silver set of brushes, mirrors, and powder boxes. These items had originally belonged to Grandma Negaar and Daaye polished them carefully.

I picked up the heavy crystal jar of green perfume, held it in front of the lamp and shook it. The liquid was so old that a layer of thick sediment, like moss, had gathered at its bottom. I looked at the feathery green particles in the jar and squeezed the puffy sponge. The scent of all the grasses of the world, of long forgotten springs, of unknown and nameless wild flowers filled the room. I was certain that this was the perfume my mother had used on her wedding night.

"Soraya!" I whispered, and looked around. Then I lay on the wide bed that smelled of dust and mildew and closed my eyes. I tried to envision her, to draw her body in my mind. She was transparent, luminous, and seamless. When she called me, her voice was a breeze, soothing like the tunes of Taara's setar. When she lay her moist palm on my forehead, her fingertips smelled of the red and yellow blossoms that grew around the pool, whose names no one knew.

I lay on that bed for hours, daydreaming, weaving images and stories, catnapping, until Grandma Negaar's dark, piercing eyes commanded me through the tall picture frame on the wall to leave the room. I tiptoed out, walking barefoot on the cold tiles, my heart pounding with fear until I reached my room. Like my mother, I was afraid of the house. I could hear its heart beating and its large lungs breathing inside the walls.

The Last Wednesday of the Year

Taara played with the four strings of her instrument. She didn't strum them hard, but tickled them gently, murmuring a poem she'd just made, then humming the lyrics with the music she was trying to compose. We never closed the door between our rooms; I could see her sitting on the floor, one leg bent into her chest, the other stretched out, the setar in her lap, as if sucking milk from her breast.

> On the balcony of the tower I play my setar and listen
> Under the dryandra tree I play my setar and listen
> On the roof top room I play my setar and listen,
> No flutter, no scream
> The bird is not coming today

On the porch and farther down in the courtyard there was a commotion. It was the last Wednesday of the year, "Fire Wednesday." Khanum-Jaan and Assad were setting the long table for the party. The weather was mild for March and Khanum wanted the celebration to be outside in the courtyard.

"I won't have any party in the guest room until I can afford to wash those carpets and paint the walls. We sit outside. If anyone feels cold, he can wear an extra jacket!"

Assad had splashed water on the brick floor and was now setting the Polish chairs around the table. The small piles of dry twigs were set in a row along the flowerbed. Later, at sunset, Assad would pour kerosene on them and light the fire. The guests would jump over the flames and pray for good health. Boor-boor sat in her gilded cage, hanging from the fig tree. She observed all this with a serious look on her face.

Khanum-Jaan brought the china set herself. She didn't let anyone else handle it. The stack of plates, saucers, and serving dishes were heavy. *Click, click, click,* she went up and down the steps, panting, grumbling behind her lips, then gradually cursing louder.

"Why don't you call someone to fix this damned elevator, Assad?" she yelled from the courtyard. "With these swollen legs, I have to go up and down a million times!"

"No one will fix this kind of elevator anymore," Assad said, holding Baba-Ji's arm, helping him down the porch steps. "You have to install a new one and it costs a zillion!"

"Why are you bringing Baba down? Nothing is ready yet."

"But he is ready and wants to be down here in the courtyard. Isn't that so, Baba-Ji?" Assad hugged Grandfather and kissed him on the cheek with a loud munching sound. "Look at your husband, Khanum! Isn't he handsome?"

"His tie is crooked and he's wearing too much cologne! Yuck! He's washed himself in the damn thing."

"Your jam is burning, Assad!" Daaye screamed through the kitchen window.

"Coming! Coming! Don't you see I'm helping Baba down the steps? Just turn the thing off, can you?"

Khanum and Assad placed Baba-Ji at the top of the table by the fountain. He was quiet and passive, letting people carry him around, pet him, button his shirt, tuck him into bed. Since Uncle Vafa's wedding less than a month ago, he had become strangely remote. When he looked at us, he didn't see us anymore, he saw through us. He woke up every morning and went to his desk and sat there dutifully until noon, but didn't work much. He didn't work in the afternoons, either. He lay in his recliner and fell asleep, a book open on his chest. It was as if a wire had come loose in his brain.

Once I caught him sitting at his desk, holding his forehead in his right hand, covering his eyes. He heard me next to him, but didn't remove his hand. Gently, I lifted his hand and looked into his eyes. They were wet.

Now in his navy suit, white starched shirt and black tie, he sat at the head of the table, motionless. His silky white hair was slicked back with water and Vaseline. He still combed his hair himself, with great care. He didn't forget his cologne either, which he splashed on his shaved face generously, spilling some in the sink. Khanum approached him and fixed the knot of his tie. She told Assad to bring a white kerchief for Baba's pocket.

From where I peered through my window, Baba-Ji was only a white head and I knew that, like my own head, it was full of cries.

When I heard the aunties laughing and descending the steps to the courtyard, I closed the window and moved back. I was not going down tonight.

"So where is your music, Assad?" I heard Aunty Puran saying. "What kind of a party is this without music?"

"Where is your Turkish coffee, Assad?" Aunty Turan asked. "I want to look at everybody's cups before it gets dark. It's the last fortune telling of the year!"

Soon a rhythmic music filled the air and covered over Taara's melancholy tunes. She put her setar down and stood next to me, looking out the window. We both gazed at the top of the brick tower in silence. It swam among the waves of orange and blue clouds. The sun was setting.

Now we smelled the wood burning. Taara opened the window and bent down. Assad had lit the twigs; long tongues of red flame stretched outward. We could hear children in the street screaming with joy. They had their own flames on the sidewalks and were jumping over them. Firecrackers exploded like gunshots.

"Taara! Taara!" Khanum called and looked up at the window. We pulled back and hid in the shadows of the room.

"Don't you want to jump over the fire, sister?" Aunty Turan asked Khanum. "It brings bad luck if you don't. Get up!"

"No. I'm not doing it this year. It's all nonsense. Nothing will change. I get older every year, and sicker and weaker. What's the point?"

"Ancient tradition," Baba explained, but more to himself.

"Ah! What a spirit!" Aunty Turan said, and passed one leg over a low flame. "My yellow is yours, your red is mine!" she addressed the fire.

"Fire, water, wind, and earth," Baba said. "The four elements! Firebird is the Simorgh. Russians used the same name for both birds. So they must be one. In the Indian tradition, as well as in the Chinese—"

No one listened, but Baba went on lecturing, as if addressing his students. The Aunties had pulled their sister to the flames and were forcing her to pass at least one foot over the fire. Assad suddenly grasped Khanum's narrow waist, lifted her up and carried her over the fire. She screamed and kicked her small feet. Her sisters laughed with joy. The parrot hanging from the fig tree cried, "Boor-boor—" and made a commotion. Assad threw firecrackers in the flames. The rattle and smoke scared the bird—she screeched and fluttered her wings.

"Taara! Taara! The flame is dying! Come down!" Khanum called.

"Talkhoon! Where are you?" Assad looked up at my window.

We both withdrew into the shadows.

More guests arrived. Uncle Kia's wife and twin daughters came down the steps; Doctor Shafa and Uncle Kia followed them. Behind them there was another man.

"Vafa!" Taara whispered.

"No!"

"Yes. That's Vafa. And his wife, too. What's her name?"

"Zahra."

"The doctor has brought them," Taara said.

A scene was taking place down in the courtyard. Doctor Shafa and Uncle Kia held Vafa's arms and led him to Khanum-Jaan, who was now sitting solemnly on a chair, frowning.

"Mother, Vafa wants to kiss your hand and apologize!" Uncle Kia said.

Khanum-Jaan remained quiet.

"Khanum, forgive the young man. He is here to kiss you and be accepted into the family again," the doctor said. "You are older and wiser, he is young and—"

"Young and stupid," Khanum said. "Is his wife here too?"

"They're both here, Khanum, to pay respect. The New Year is coming; it's not good to end the year in gloom. Forgive them," Doctor Shafa said.

"Doctor Shafa is right," Aunty Puran said. "It's New Year. Time to forgive and forget."

"Come, Vafa, kiss Mother's hand," Uncle Kia pushed his brother toward Khanum's chair.

The bearded Uncle Vafa bent and kissed Khanum-Jaan's large emerald ring. Taara and I held our mouths to keep from bursting out laughing.

"Oh my God! What a show! He's really doing it!" Taara said, swallowing her excitement. "And kissing the ring, as if she is a queen!"

"His wife is bending too."

"It's not for Khanum's inheritance," Taara said. "Khanum is broke and everybody knows it. All that is left is Drum Tower. And besides, the girl's father is rich. They don't need Khanum-Jaan's old, rusty jewelry."

"So, why—?"

"Why? He loves his mother!"

"Nonsense!" I said, and I realized that I sounded like my grandmother. We burst into wild laughter.

We watched the party from the window. Colorful food was brought in in many trays and dishes. Assad, with a kitchen rag on his shoulder and one tucked into the waist of his pants, limped up and down the porch steps; Daaye, panting and sweating, handed him heavy trays of saffron rice, pomegranate stew, eggplant stew, and cutlets. The guests all ate and drank and joked and jumped some more over the dying flames. Aunty Puran took her little lap drum—the *tunbak*—and held it under her arm as she played. Her sister, Turan, wriggled her shoulders while still sitting, then rose and began to dance. In her shimmering orange dress, a version of her sister's red one, but a shade lighter, and her Cleopatra wig, she whirled, shook her bosom and moved her butt in all directions. Everyone clapped and snapped their fingers. Now they all insisted that Khanum should join the dance.

"Oh, no," Taara said. "Khanum-Jaan cannot dance with that little hump on her back!"

"Do you remember when we were little, we'd ask Khanum what was hidden under her blouse?" I asked Taara.

"If she was in a good mood, she'd say, my jewelry-purse."

"And when she was in a bad mood, she'd chase us out of the room."

Grandmother didn't dance. Instead, she pulled the twins' hands and lifted them up from their chairs. But Uncle Kia's girls screamed, ran away, and hid behind the bushes. Their mother said the children were still new here and hadn't learned the Persian dance.

When everyone had danced and had eaten homemade pistachio ice cream and pudding as dessert, they needed calm, soothing music to go with their vodka drinking, reminiscing and gossiping, and they remembered Taara and her setar. In a minute Khanum-Jaan was in my room, scolding Taara for hiding herself all night.

"What does this mood mean, anyway?" She asked, raising one eyebrow. "Bring your setar down and don't keep the guests waiting. I don't want to come all the way up here to call you again!" She left, but then she came back and said, "And if your sister is coming down, she'd better change and comb her hair. And tell her to say good evening to all the guests and kiss their cheeks."

"Are you coming with me?" Taara asked.

"No. I'll watch from here."

"Come!"

"No. I don't feel like changing. You go! Play the tune you made up this afternoon. I like it."

"It's called 'On the balcony of the tower.'"

"Play it."

"For them?" She paused, thinking, then said, "No. That's for you. I'll play it just for you, some other time."

It was past eleven. With my chin resting on my hand and my elbow on the windowsill, I was dozing off. I'd heard Taara's performance and the guests' occasional applause. She'd played almost all of her repertoire.

Now most of the guests were drunk. Assad, carrying up the empty dishes, swayed a little and walked in a funny way.

"Are you talking about this system? This down-to-the-roots corruption?" Uncle Vafa's voice rose above the guests' murmur. Everyone became quiet.

"Vafa! There is no need to bring this up here," his wife advised him.

"It's corrupt down to the roots. The monarchy is breathing its last breath!" He announced.

"Wishful thinking!" This was Uncle Kia, who sat next to him, holding a glass of cognac in his hand. He didn't drink vodka. "The monarchy is as stable as it was twenty-five hundred years ago. No one can shake its foundations!"

"This system is rotten, I say! Its stink is rising to the sky!" Vafa repeated again. "The army of Islam is gathering power, but most of us are blind, we don't see the upcoming jihad!"

Something was about to happen and I was all alone in the dark room. I wished Taara were here with me, holding my hand. I looked at my favorite uncle, my old playmate, Vafa, and couldn't recognize him. He was an arrogant, angry man with a bearded face and a hoarse voice. Was this really Vafa?

"Don't argue with him, Kia!" Doctor Shafa advised Uncle Kia.

"The laws of the prophet will be restored again!" Vafa announced, moving his forefinger in front of his older brother's face.

"It's Nineteen seventy-eight, brother, wake up! How can you run the country with backward religious laws?" Uncle Kia asked in a calm tone. "The Shah is raising the country's valor to the level of the European countries. Tehran is another Paris, another Geneva!"

"And the people of the southern slums are starving while Americans are stealing our oil," Vafa said.

"Nonsense!' Khanum said. "The people of the slums had better pull their pants up and go to work!"

"Maybe there are no pants left on them to pull up," Uncle Vafa's wife raised her voice. "And where is work? Do you know the unemployment rate?"

Now everybody was silent. No one had ever dared contradict Khanum-

Jaan. Zahra didn't know the rules of Drum Tower.

"Now, now, now!" Aunty Puran said, and banged on her *tunbak*. "Let's dance again! Assad, put that record on!"

"No, we're not dancing anymore!" Khanum-Jaan announced. "No one raises her voice in my house!"

"No one raised her voice, Khanum," Doctor Shafa said. "They're just discussing politics. These days, in every house I go in, people talk about politics."

"Not in *my* house!" Khanum said. "I'm not fond of this imbecile Shah of yours, Kia, nor of his father who ended our dynasty. But I want to tell you one thing, young man!" She addressed Vafa. "No one can shake the strong roots of the monarchy in Iran. Understand? Only a powerful king, like Nader, can control the rioting, ignorant peasants."

Now she stood up and said, "I've heard that you've changed your name, Vafa! You can change it to whatever you want, but there is one thing you can never change, and that's your blood, your family tree, your ancestry. You're the grandson of Hessam-Mirza Vaziri, the War Minister of this country at the time of the old Shah, and the son of five generations of ministers before him, back to Nader Shah's time, and you cannot change this fact even if you change your name one million times. Go now. See if you can change your blood!"

Saying this, she walked away from the table to climb the stairs. Her posture was wooden and the small hump on her back looked larger. Doctor Shafa and Uncle Kia rose to pay respect. The aunties became emotional and wiped the corners of their eyes and sighed. Everyone was silent, waiting for Khanum-Jaan to finish climbing the stairs. Now Kia's French twins burst into tears and Boor-boor screamed in her cage as if sensing a disaster.

In a minute Taara was up, embracing me from behind, whispering in my ear. "Did you see everything?"

"I did."

"They're leaving."

"The party is over."

"Khanum won't see Vafa anymore."

"If he wanted to argue with her, why did he come to kiss her hand?"

"Strange," Taara said and yawned, heading toward her room. "And Baba didn't say a word, as if he was asleep all the time."

"Taara!"

"What?"

"Nothing." I wanted to tell her that small winds whirred and people cried in my head, but I didn't.

The guests left and Assad took Baba's arm and helped him up the stairs. For a second I felt an urge to go to my grandfather's room, to help him undress, to put him in bed and spend the rest of the night at his bedside. But I kept sitting, listening to the sounds in my head and watching the reflection of the moon in the fountain and the parrot that was a green ball, hiding her head inside her feathers.

Now Assad came back and stamped on the fire to make sure it was out. He took the parrot out of the cage, kissed her, and put her on his right shoulder. He sat at the top of the table, fingering the desert dishes one by one. He ate from this dish and that, and put a candy in the parrot's mouth. He poured some more ice-cold vodka for himself and drank it fast. Then he noticed Uncle Kia's cognac bottle, poured some and emptied the glass down his throat. Now he munched pickled garlic and burped. He said things to himself, laughed and shook his head. He hadn't changed for tonight. He was in his dirty house pants, stained shirt, and plastic slippers. *Lek, lek, lek,* he limped to the other end of the table, picked up a ring, and looked at it under the light of the lantern hanging from the post. This was Aunty Puran's large ruby ring; she had taken it off to play her tunbak. Assad examined the ring for a long time, then put it in his pocket. Now he hummed a song for himself, "Bibi lost her panties! Bibi lost her panties..." He fed the parrot more candies and slowly cleaned up.

Father in the Pantry Room

After Father came and hid one night in the pantry room and then left at dawn, Baba's brain failed. This was the day before Norooz, four days after Fire Wednesday.

We had all gathered in Baba-Ji's room, preparing a small Norooz table.

This year, Khanum-Jaan didn't want to receive visitors in the guest room. "Not before I paint the walls!" she kept saying. But we all knew that she was upset with Uncle Vafa and our father for not showing up even for the New Year.

As we did every year, Taara and I painted the smooth surfaces of the hard-boiled eggs. Baba, with his shaky hands, helped us, but his eggs were ruined and he ended up with yellow and red stains on his pajamas. Khanum, who had stopped talking to us since Fire Wednesday (as if we were all Vafa's secret allies), placed fresh bank notes inside the pages of the old Koran to give away as Norooz presents. But the notes were not hundreds, as in every other year; they were tens.

Daaye and Assad came in and out of the room, carrying dishes of home-baked baklava and rice cookies. Assad placed a pot of the purple hyacinth in the middle of the table. The cool scent of the vanishing winter filled the room.

Around dusk, the power failed and we heard random shooting. Assad brought candles and a portable radio and we all sat in the dim light, held our breath, and listened to the sounds of the disturbed street. This went on for a long hour, but the radio kept airing regular programs. There were no announcements.

"These are the Moslem rebels," Khanum-Jaan said with disgust. "Vafa's slum gang."

"No one knows, Khanum. Let's wait and see," Assad said.

"Call Kia, Assad, he must know what's going on," Khanum said. "Then call the Power Company. How do they dare leave people in the dark? Imbeciles! Can't they catch a few thieves?"

"The telephone is disconnected," Assad said.

Now someone banged on Drum Tower's oaken double door and we all held our breaths. *Bang, bang, bang, bang.* Jangi barked in the garden and Boor-boor shouted on the porch. Assad rushed down to the gate and the rest of us sat in panic. A minute later, the door opened and in the dim light of the flickering candles, Father stood like an apparition.

"Sina—" Khanum covered her mouth as if she'd uttered a forbidden word.

Father was tall and dusty, his thick curly hair, salt and pepper. His coat, maybe black once, was gray and wrinkled; his shoes were old, beaten and crooked. He fell on his knees, and with his long arms embraced all of us at once. Baba-Ji was shocked, couldn't say a word. Khanum kept repeating, "Sina—" Taara and I, who hadn't seen our father for two years, held each other tightly and wept.

It turned out that Father was not here to stay. He'd come just to hide for the night. For the first time, Taara and I realized that our father was a fugitive, an outlaw. Not the kind of rebel that Uncle Vafa was, holding a job and living his life, but much worse, the kind that had to hide. But hadn't Grandmother said all these years that our father was a crazy wanderer in search of his lost wife? What we saw now was an aging man who looked tired and wore old, dirty clothes. True, he could easily be mistaken for a vagabond, but when he talked, he sounded as eloquent as a younger Baba lecturing in the university hall.

Two years ago, when father had come and stayed for a few days, Taara and I hadn't even thought about these matters. We were younger, and naïve. But now all these questions were raised in our minds—who was our father and what was he doing in this dark night?

Father explained the political events to his parents. He talked about the upcoming revolution, freedom, the republic, justice. Our hearts pounded in our chests. We were waiting for Khanum to shout at Father to throw him out. But she sat motionless, listening. Father was her favorite son. Also, he had a calm voice and didn't argue the way Vafa did. So he talked for a long time and used a vocabulary that we didn't quite understand. This was neither the language of Baba-Ji's Simorgh book, nor Vafa's language of Jihad. Father seemed to be a different kind of rebel.

Khanum closed her eyes and rocked like a pendulum, as if her suffering had gone beyond words. Baba-Ji listened with worried eyes, tears welling up behind his round lenses. It didn't take long for Father to realize that Baba was not so well. He changed the subject and talked about a city on the eastern border where he'd stayed with his brother-in-law for a while, visiting a Baluchi tribe.

Late at night, while sporadic shootings kept breaking the silence of the city, Father said he had to rest, not in a bedroom, but in the pantry behind the kitchen where he would be hidden. This precaution, he said, was in case the Guards broke in to search the house. Now he embraced his parents and urged them not to get up at dawn to see him off. Assad and Daaye took Father to the pantry and Taara and I stayed with our grandparents who were pale and still, as if turned to salt.

"Am I dreaming?" Khanum asked. "Am I dreaming, Anvar?"

"No, Khanum. He came and he'll leave before dawn," Baba said.

"What is going on that's beyond my understanding, Anvar? You never talked to me when I was young. Your talks were in your books, and later you spent more time with your children than you ever did with me—now tell me what the hell is going on in this country that I cannot understand? Why have two of our sons lost their way? Why have we lost them? What have we done to fail them? Did we neglect them, Anvar? Did we bring them up wrong? What did we do that they've turned against us? Against their own country? The Grandsons of Hessam-Mirza Vaziri, the War Minister of the old Shah, turned rebels? Did you see his clothes, Anvar?"

"All I saw was his gray hair," Baba said. "His hair has turned whiter than mine!"

"What do your books say about all this, Anvar? What is going on?"

"My books are not about humankind, Khanum. They're not about this rotten world."

In this way Baba-Ji and Khanum-Jaan whispered to each other and sighed shakily. Then Khanum rose to give orders to Daaye to prepare a good dinner for Sina. Candle in hand, Khanum went in and out of the pantry, taking food to Father. Her hump looked larger, her body smaller. At last Father urged her to go to bed. He said he wanted to see his daughters for just a short while.

It was past midnight when Taara and I went to the pantry. Father was surrounded by burlap sacks of rice, large cans of cooking oil, boxes of spices and jars of homemade pickles. He was lying on his side, his head resting on a rice sack. He was exhausted. His black socks had holes in them and the tips of his toes showed. He ate his dinner slowly and sipped cold vodka. Daaye had prepared him a pitcher with slices of lemon floating in the ice.

Father asked Taara to bring her setar and play for him. He wanted to see how she'd progressed in two years. When Taara left, he poured some vodka, drank a little, and put a black olive in his mouth. Now he looked at me as if seeing me for the first time.

"You've grown tall, Talkhoon," he said. "How is your schoolwork? What grades are you making?"

My face burned. Whatever I'd say would sound wrong. So I didn't say anything. I just dropped my head and avoided his eyes.

"Is everything all right?"

I nodded and didn't say a word. I could have told him about Grandmother's unkindness, the net gripping my heart and the winds blowing in my head. I could have told him about passing out in my math class, not wanting to live. I could have told him about the way I looked, so plain and dark, without hope that I would ever become pretty and fair. I could have said that I feared Drum Tower, the dense garden, and the ghost of Grandma Negaar wheeling among the willows or watching me through the picture frame. I could have confessed that I despised Khanum's parrot and Assad's dog, that Assad had recently looked at me in a way that frightened me. I could have told Father that Baba-Ji couldn't write his Simorgh book anymore and the bright days of the bird were gone.

But I didn't say a word and silence deepened between us. Taara came with her setar and played her tunes. Father closed his eyes the way one does when the spring breeze caresses one's face. Taara played the tune she'd said was mine and that she'd play only for me.

On the balcony of the tower I play my setar and listen
Under the dryandra tree I play my setar and listen ...

Father kept drinking and I squeezed myself farther away, almost hiding behind a barrel of pickled garlic. In this way the night passed, and around two in the morning Khanum came and chased us out so she could have her son to herself for a while before he left. Father embraced us, fished in his pocket and pulled out two gold chains. From Taara's chain a small setar the size of a pinky fingernail hung, and from mine a tiny bird holding a flower in its mouth.

"Happy New Year," he said. "Be good. Help your grandmother."

We were at the door of the pantry when he called Taara back. I stood in the dark corridor and held my breath to hear.

"Taara," he said. "There might be one or two old masters who can play the setar better than you, but your style is unique. Practice your art! When our country finally sets herself free, which won't take long, I want to see you in the spotlight on a big stage!"

I stayed up all night, eavesdropping behind the pantry's closed door. I wanted to hear Father's voice. I wanted to store it in my head. He talked with Grandmother for a long time and at the end asked for money. I heard Khanum-Jaan's softest voice, the voice she used only once in a long while when she called Taara "the light of her eyes."

Now Father went to the garden and drank some more with Assad in the rose arbor. The rest of the night I sat on the windowsill, looking out and listening. All I could see was the top of Father's head and his fingers running through his salt and pepper curls. I couldn't hear the conversation, but at one point Assad broke into loud laughter. Now there was silence, and a minute later Father recited a poem. I sharpened my ears, but the night breeze took his words away, leaving only the music behind. The lines all ended in long "a"s: baa, raa, saa, maa, daa.

When dawn broke, I ran to Taara's room to see Father through her northern window. Assad hid him under a blanket on the back seat of the Cadillac and took him away in the foggy twilight.

The day after father's visit, a few hours before New Year's Eve, Taara and I put on our new dresses and headed toward Baba-Ji's room to help him to get ready. We knew he couldn't button his shirt or knot his tie.

Taara's dress was emerald velvet and it changed the golden specs in her eyes into pure green. Mine was cherry-red velvet, a bit too long and too large in the shoulders. Our dressmaker, Madame Abulian, had confused my measurements with Taara's. My dress looked like a borrowed one. We both wore our gold chains, held hands as we did when we were little, and went to our grandfather's room.

When we entered Baba's study, we found the lights out. Baba sat in his recliner, his back to us, facing the window that framed the blue-purple dusk. We turned on the light and approached him. He had fallen asleep. We called him, but he didn't answer. We touched him; he didn't wake. We listened to his heart—it pumped. We shook him, but he didn't respond. We realized that our grandfather's soul had moved somewhere else, somewhere cold, shady, and remote.

I ran out to the garden, a scream rolling in my throat, but not rising. Boor-boor saw me running and shouted, and Jangi barked his loudest bark. I ran to the end of the garden where the tower was and climbed the stone steps to the balcony with four portholes on the sides. Facing the evening sky, I screamed from the bottom of my lungs, shouting words that had no meaning. I made unknown sounds, sounds beyond language. I thought I was calling Baba, calling him to the tower to play the Simorgh game with me. I thought I made sense and that this shouting would work, this made-up language would bring my grandfather back. I thought these utterly meaningless sounds would bring a miracle.

Soon Assad came, lifted me in his arms, and carried me to the house. Doctor Shafa bent over Baba's recliner, feeling his pulse. Khanum-Jaan, Daaye, Taara, and Assad circled around the doctor and my sleeping grandfather. Daaye sat me in a chair, rubbed my neck, and murmured prayers under her lips. The doctor said that neither he nor any doctor in the world could bring Baba back. He had to return himself. Now he injected something into my vein and I fell asleep, my head resting on Daaye's arm.

I'm not sure how long I slept, but when I woke up my head was full of cries, sometimes faint and confused, sometimes loud. When the cries became louder, I had to cover my mouth with my hands so as not to let the sounds out. If someone were to approach me, he would hear muffled moans rising from behind the wall of my throat.

Lying in my room, I saw my sister through the open door standing by the window, hitting her head against the hard wooden frame. *Taara, don't! Taara, stop!* I wanted to urge her, but no sound came out.

This was when I sensed the oncoming winds blowing sand in the air, twisting and approaching our house, rippling among the now useless branches of the dryandra tree, whistling in the hollow brick tower. Doctor Shafa called my condition "shock and depression," and recommended rest and strolls in the garden.

Every day I walked around the pool where the willows grew tiny lettuce-colored leaves. I no longer feared the ghost of my great grandmother Negaar. That night on top of the tower, I had screamed out all my fears. I sat on the cold bench inside the rose arbor under the dried twigs of the crawling bushes, waiting for the winds to come. I didn't go to school anymore. A few times a day, Assad visited me, bringing a jacket or a cup of warm tea. He sat next to me, smoothed my hair, and talked sweetly.

"It's cold, Talkhoon. Come in and eat something. I've made you cabbage soup. The kind you love! Guess what I've dropped in it?" He paused for a second and said, "A big bone full of marrow and a huge chunk of meat sticking to it. Red pepper to spice it up! Yummy! My mouth waters!"

I didn't respond, but Assad kept talking. He reported that Grandmother had locked herself in her room, not eating, not speaking a word. Doctor Shafa was concerned about her nerves. The aunties, he said, had taken Taara to their house because her final exams were approaching and she had to study hard. Daaye and he took turns sitting next to Baba's bed just in case he moved his body or began to talk. They fed him liquids with a small spoon, as they would a newborn baby. But the doctor believed that if he kept sleeping for too long, he would have to be connected to a tube.

"Let's go home, Talkhoon," Assad insisted. "It's cold here and my soup is steaming."

Diving in the Dusk

A while passed—I have no idea how long. Taara came back from the aunties' and moved to the only room on the vast asphalted roof. This small, square room was built by the first Grandpa Vazir for his armed watchman, and a watchman occupied it until the Vaziri dynasty collapsed. It was Khanum-Jaan who stopped hiring a guard. She installed barbed wire on the walls to protect the house.

In spite of everything that had happened in the house, Taara had to take her final exams in May to graduate from high school. In two subjects she didn't need much work, in the other two she needed tutors.

Soon Khanum freed herself from her self-imposed prison and came out to take inventory of the household furnishings. She said she had dreamed that in her absence the grand piano had disappeared. So, *click, click, click—* she roamed around the house and took notes with a red pencil in her black notebook. The piano was there, but a pair of gold candlesticks and a gold-framed mirror with carvings around the rim—Great Grandmother Negaar's wedding set—were lost.

In this way life in the Drum Tower went on.

In April a long season of rain began. The storm I'd foreseen approached and pushed the flood's yellow water madly against the oak door. Strong winds blew in my head and I lay on my bed and held my head to keep it from spinning. When the winds calmed, Taara's music dripped from her rooftop room. She played for long hours, day and night, and her books remained open, unread. It was as if she protected herself with her songs. She didn't want to hear, to think, or to remember.

It rained every morning and Taara in her black and white school uniform came down to her old room beside mine, looked out the northern window and smiled. I could read in her glowing face that something behind the curtain of rain filled her with joy. Now she came to my room, kissed my cheeks, and said good-bye. I stayed in bed, listening to the sounds in my head. I didn't have a desire to scream anymore, nor did I want to roam in the wet garden. People who came to see me and talk to me and those who avoided me were all shadows—obscure and unreal.

Khanum-Jaan didn't talk to me anymore. After Father and Grandfather left us, her silence became absolute. She knew I was not well and had stopped going to school, she knew I was taking medication, but she never came to my room. In the last seance Grandpa Vazir must have finally removed her doubts about my origin. He must have announced that I was not her son's daughter. Assad sat by my bed and nursed me the way he had when I was a baby and my mother had disappeared.

So every evening, between the glare and the gloom, when the rain stopped and a rainbow appeared above Alborz Mountain, while Daaye prepared dinner and Assad fed Baba and Khanum sat in her nun's cell, writing a letter to her dead father, the winds howled loud and wild in my head and I played with the thought of climbing to the roof of the tower where I could see the whole world. But what would I do next? I did not know.

At last, one evening, unable to stand the sweet smell of the purple hyacinths, the New Year's blossoms with which Assad had decorated my room, I gave in to temptation and rushed to the garden. I walked through the thick dusk barefoot on the wet ground, and climbed the tower's stone steps as light-footed as a ghost. I looked at a city I did not know—the turquoise minarets, the blue domes of the mosques, and tall buildings with glass walls glaring in the last rays of the sun. I saw the fresh green of the spring trees glowing in the fading light. I looked at the darkening garden and the winds told me to jump. A curtain parted a crack—Taara looked out and sighed. Behind the kitchen window, Daaye bent to lift a heavy pot. Assad turned the lights on and in the darkest moment of dusk, the house's presence gripped my throat. Jump! the winds commanded. The city lights turned dim, the garden sank in darkness, and the winds prodded me. With a vague memory of Taara and myself as small girls wading in the pool, flat torsos naked, I held up my arms like a diver and, head first, I dived toward the ground.

Confession

Because I hit the feathery branches of the dryandra tree instead of the garden's hard ground, Daaye announced the Almighty's miracle, wore her mothball-smelling black chiffon dress, covered herself with her rose-water-scented chador, and walked all the way from College Intersection to the Shah's Memory Square to her favorite mosque. She threw her savings in the dead Imam's purse and walked all the way back, muttering prayers. Now she cooked sacred halva and saffron rice pudding and fed the beggars of the College Intersection who sat in all four corners.

Khanum-Jaan, who hadn't taken my sickness seriously at first, was alarmed and afraid. She sent me to the basement room so that I wouldn't be alone with Taara. Doctor Shafa injected me with something that filled my head with puffy, white clouds and consoled Khanum by saying that I was not the only adolescent who had developed certain "conditions" after a family trauma. But Khanum saw everything in the only way she could.

"Bad blood runs in her veins," she said. "Her mother was crazy too. If dirty blood starts acting up, there is nothing any doctor can do about it. She tried to kill herself, didn't she? No one, ever, in the Vaziri family, has attempted suicide. Trace our family tree back to the first Vaziris and see for yourself. We've always been brave and resilient. This is her dirty blood. And she's going to hurt herself or someone else again. Now wait and see!" She said this and forbade Taara from visiting me in the basement room.

But at least three times a day she sent Assad to check on me and keep me company. When he approached, I heard his plastic slippers scraping the courtyard's brick floor. He limped to my room with a tray of food, a cup of warm tea, or a few wet pansies plucked from the flowerbed.

"Go, Assad, go!" I heard Grandmother's voice from the porch above my room. "Go, but don't stay too long. Your jam will thicken!"

Dizzy and numb with Doctor Shafa's pills, I lay in my bed, looking at the long, narrow window that stretched almost to the ceiling. Boor-boor whose gilded cage was right behind my window, cracked sunflower seeds patiently and made little hills of husks on the cage's floor. Now and then she sharpened her hard beak on the iron bars or hung upside down like a monkey, staring at me from this strange position.

Lek, lek, lek—I heard the sound of Assad's plastic slippers, closed my eyes and wished he'd vanish. But I knew he was bending over the flowerbed to pluck pansies for me. Jangi barked at him, demanding food. I heard Assad kick the dog and curse him. When he came to my room, he put the tray on the table and lay the moist blossoms next to my pillow. He sat, sighed, and rubbed his thighs like an old woman. Now he talked about this and that, reporting the news of Drum Tower.

Taara's young tutor, an engineer fresh from America—the same man who'd danced with her at Vafa's wedding—had fallen in love with her. Khanum had eavesdropped behind the study room and heard him proposing.

"Khanum is excited, Talkhoon. She approves of the boy's family. She says it's time for Taara to get married and bring some good blood to the family." He lowered his voice to a whisper and added, "And, of course, some money! The boy's father is one of the Shah's top Generals. What do you think? Huh?"

I kept looking at the ceiling, wishing Assad would vanish. But he stayed and laid his hand on my forehead to see if I had a fever. He touched my cheeks with his rough, kerosene-smelling fingers, sighed and said, "Poor girl, what would you do without me?"

I pretended to fall asleep, closed my eyes and breathed deeper. But he continued to sit and talk, now in a different tone.

"Talkhoon," he whispered. "Talkhoon! Do you know who named you? You were three days old and your parents fought so much that they forgot to name you. Daaye was busy in the kitchen, so she sent me to change your wet diapers, to rock your cradle and put the pacifier in your little mouth. I held you in my arms, girl, and rocked you. You were a tiny, brown thing and you had a grassy smell. You were thin and delicate like the skinny leaves of a green herb, like a leaf of tarragon.

"So I went back to the kitchen one day with you in my arms. I told Daaye, 'You know what this little baby's name should be?' She said, 'What?' I said, 'Talkhoon!' She said, 'What nonsense! Talkhoon is an herb, like mint or basil. Here, I've picked some from Baba's herb bed and I'm rinsing them for his lunch.' I said, 'Yes, I know, Daaye, look at the thin, needly leaves of this bunch of tarragon! This is how this baby is and she smells of the herbs, too.' Daaye said, 'You love this baby, silly boy!' and laughed.

"So I named you and fell in love with you when you were in your crib. Your mother vanished and then your father left, and Khanum kept busy with Taara, who was a year and a half old and as pretty as a little doll. She talked baby talk with her sweet tongue and took all of Khanum's time and attention. Daaye cooked all day and I was left alone with you. I fed you, rocked you, and called you Talkhoon until everybody else called you Talkhoon, and this is where your name came from.

"Now let me tell you that no other girl in the whole world is called Talkhoon. You are unique, and it's all because of me. Now you're sleeping and you can't even hear me, but I still love you, child. When you dropped from the tower and I carried you all the way home in my arms, my heart banged against my chest like a huge drum and I wanted you in a crazy way—a way I've desired only one woman in my life. And that was very long ago. So they sent you down here and this made me happy. Because now I could nurse you as I did when you were a baby. No, I don't want you to be sick. I want you to be healthy and come out of this basement room, but now that you're sick, you're all mine. You little girl—you tiny, needly, tasty, tarragon leaf."

He crept under my blanket, sniffed me all over, jerked in a crazy way, and panted like a dog.

After that I stopped pretending to be asleep and avoided taking my pills, so as not to feel numb. I stayed alert and tolerated the tearing winds in my head. Assad came to my room and called, "Talkhoon! Where are you?" Knowing very well where I was. I was in the closet watching him through a hole I'd made in the door. He thought hiding in the closet was part of my craziness and he didn't force me to come out. He sat in the middle of my messy room, chewed salted chickpeas, and fondled my things. He thought I couldn't see him.

"So you like to be in the closet now? Okay, I can wait. I'll wait till you come out. I'll wait till you recover. But I'll wait for what? You may ask. I don't even know. I'm going crazy too. Am I really your uncle? Are you Sina's daughter? Am I Baba's son?"

He mumbled these things, touched my underwear, and left. But the next day he came back again, and I ran into the closet and heard him talking to himself. I had no doubt that it was Assad who had gone out of his mind, not me.

In Search of the Sapphire Feather: The Tea Room

In my windy mind, Soraya and the Simorgh were somehow connected. If I found the bird's feather, if I burned a barb, my mother would appear. So once a month when everyone went on the day-long shopping trip, I left my room in search of the sapphire feather.

In front of the window, on his threadbare recliner, half-sitting, half-lying, Baba-Ji was left to himself. A transparent tube connected a hanging bottle to his vein. They didn't feed him real food anymore.

I gazed at Baba's pale face and saw a shadow lingering above it. I pressed my fingers to the thick vein in his neck—it pulsated. I took a comb and brushed back his white hair, the way he liked it. I sprayed his favorite cologne on him and fixed the crooked collar of his pajama coat. Now I pushed his recliner forward, closer to the window, and adjusted the pillows in case he opened his eyes. Outside, at the bus stop, Taara and a girl talked. A man in a white raincoat craned his neck to see her.

I talked to Baba-Ji the way I did when he was awake.

"Where have you hidden the tail feather, Baba? Huh? Please! Just one word. Where? In the pages of your *Golden Book*? Your *Tales of the Beasts*? Your *Conference of the Birds*? Where is the sapphire feather, Baba?"

I cleaned the Firebird record with alcohol and gently laid it on the gramophone. I turned the volume up. "Let the ghosts get disturbed. Damn them all. Damn Grandmother and her ancestors' ghosts! Am I not right, Baba-Ji? Damn the damned ghosts. Let them get disturbed."

The strings went crazy and I remembered that Taara had once opened her arms and danced the bird dance. I tried to move, leap, turn and hop, but I couldn't. I wasn't a dancer.

"I could never dance, Baba. I've never hummed a song, either. I don't know how to whistle. 'You're a sad, sad child,' Assad tells me. 'Talkhoon is a bitter herb,' Assad says. 'You're sharp and bitter.'

"'Talkhoon is originally two words,' you said once, 'talkh' and 'khoon.' Talkh means bitter, khoon means blood. 'Bitter blood.' That's what my name means.

"Assad named me bitter blood. This was when everybody was busy and didn't have time to name me. They were fighting, or talking to the ghosts. You were writing the book of the bird. Why didn't you name me, Baba? You'd find a bird name for me, wouldn't you? Rokhy, Anka, Garuda, Oshadega—

"You didn't name Taara, either. Grandpa Vazir did. His ghost, I mean.

He said to Khanum, 'Name her Taahereh, for purity!'

"No one was around to name me. Assad took me to the kitchen in his arms. I'm sure his shirt smelled of onions and his mouth stank of vodka. I was named in the kitchen, above Daaye's cabbage soup. Talkhoon. Tarragon. Bitter blood.

"Where is the feather, Baba?

"I looked inside all your sources. 'My sources,' you used to say. 'Organize my sources, Talkhoon. Write their names on these cards.' I did all that when I was only six. Remember? I learned to read by reading your classic poets—Nezami and Attar, Hafez and Rumi. I can't find the sapphire feather, Baba. You lost it!"

Now I walked barefoot through the house, roamed the rooms, stepped on cold tiles and slippery marble until a chill ran up my spine. I walked on soft silk carpets, opened doors, closed doors, and breathed in the scent of the lost ones. No one dusted Vafa's room after I stopped. His football trophies were under a layer of dust on top of his bookshelf. The pages of his books were yellowing. The pencils he wrote with were in a cup full of dust.

No one had cleaned my room, either. Since I'd been banished to the basement a thick layer of gray powder sat on everything. I was among the unwanted, the ones Khanum didn't like or had liked once, but now resented. She took revenge on us by not dusting our rooms, by letting our rooms decay. She left the objects alone to die. Nothing was worse than being buried under the dust. She knew it so well.

My parents' bridal bed. Their closet. My mother's hats, shoes, dresses. Father's suits. All hanging. Khanum-Jaan didn't give things to charities. Didn't help the beggars. Didn't donate them to thrift shops. Objects stayed where they were, for years, centuries, buried under the white dust. Objects aged and died a natural death. Khanum wanted to see their decay. She wanted to see Sina's suit dying, Vafa's tennis shoes dying, my ninth-grade books stacked on the desk, dying.

I wanted to wear my mother's long soiree gown—a dark blue color. She must have worn this at the Shah's Coronation Ball, because this was the fanciest dress in the closet, with shiny beads all over its wide collar. But I changed my mind. I was not pretty. My hair was thin and short. I didn't even have breasts. Instead, I put on Father's suit—navy blue with white stripes. I posed in front of the tall mirror and frowned like an angry man. Too large and too long. I rolled up the bottom of the trousers and roamed around the master bedroom. Satin lining felt slippery and soft. Now I was invisible. No one could see me.

I stood in front of Great Grandma Negaar's portrait. As usual, she had a reproachful look. *Silly girl! How silly you are, Talkhoon. Take off that suit!* But I didn't listen. *Damn you! You're a ghost. But how real they've painted you, Great Grandma!* I touched her white gown. It felt real, rough and bumpy, like lace. But now something happened. Something strange. Who could imagine Grandma Negaar's tall picture would be a door and would open?

I stepped into an L-shaped room. It was carefully furnished. The best furnished room of the house. The floor was covered with a silk carpet— soft green with cream-colored aigrettes all around. A large tapestry covered the wall: The story of Leili and Majnoon, the legendary lovers. His torso naked, love crazy, Majnoon with his long hair hanging down to his waist cried in the desert. Leili's father had married her to another man. Miserable lions and leopards sat around Majnoon, weeping with him. Leili was in the right corner, in a long wedding gown, her hair wavy and dark, sweeping the floor. She wept for Majnoon. Two maidens fanned her with wide peacock-feathered fans. They wept too.

This room was cozy and fancy at the same time. The best room of Drum Tower had been hidden from all of us. Cushions lay against all the walls—each cushion cover, a needlework made by a tasteful ancestor. Low tables were set in front of the puffy mattresses. A polished silver samovar sat in a corner surrounded by gold-rimmed tea glasses and a china sugar container full of sugar cubes. The samovar was filled with water and dry tea leaves were ready to be brewed in the china teapot. Someone had prepared everything for a tea party.

In the short extension of the L there was a round oak table and five chairs. There was no dust in the room. This was the tearoom, where children had never been allowed. *Oh, Vafa, what fun we could've had in this room, if we'd only discovered it! We could've toppled the samovar and burned this silk carpet too. We could've done mischief.*

I turned on the electric samovar to make some tea for myself and searched the room for the sapphire feather. But why would Baba-Ji hide the feather here? He might not have stepped into this room at all. This secret place belonged to Khanum's ghosts.

I gave up searching and sat on the cushions, looking out a wide glass door. This was a greenhouse. Large, pink, Damascus roses and miniature rose-shaped eglantines were surrounded by green, feathery ferns. English Ivies hung from the ceiling of the greenhouse. Water gurgled in a small turquoise fountain. A canary sat in a golden cage. But the bird was still and quiet.

Water boiled. I made some tea, poured a glass and left it to cool. But now I heard voices from behind the wall. My heart pounded in my throat. In panic, I ran to the greenhouse and hid behind the flower pots. Soon, the tapestry-covered wall rotated and Khanum-Jaan, the aunties, a pale-looking woman, and Sayyed Mirza in his black suit and red fez entered. My grandmother led her guests to the oak table and went to the samovar to prepare some tea.

She saw the water boiling, the tea ready, and one glass already poured. She screamed and clenched her chest, as if to keep her heart from bursting. The women gathered around her, fanned her and talked at the same time.

"Papa Vazir is here. My father is here!" Khanum mumbled in tears. "He knew we wanted him today, and he came even before we called him."

The aunties wiped their tears and talked at the same time.

"He's poured himself a glass of tea," Aunty Puran said and wept.

"We came in and scared him. He must have left," Aunty Turan said.

Now Sayyed Mirza urged the ladies to calm down and sit. The black tassel on top of his red fez dangled when he talked. The women sat. They all held hands and murmured something. Khanum-Jaan wept all through the prayers. She was beside herself.

Hiding behind the tall, crawling roses, crazy winds loose in my head, I saw how the top of the oak table turned like a wheel and the women cried.

A while after the séance, after Khanum and her sisters talked to their dead father and the pale lady shook and shivered, foamed at the mouth and spoke with the ghost's thick voice, a long time after they all left, I went back to the tea room and collapsed on the cushions. Although I knew it was I who'd made the tea, not Grandpa Vazir's ghost, the effect of the whole ritual had shaken my weak nerves.

It was dark outside. Any minute now, Daaye would go to my basement room with the dinner tray to find me missing. Any minute now they would realize that I was lost. In haste, I ran to the wall and pressed the tapestry, but nothing happened. I pushed every single spot of the picture and it didn't move. A long time passed and I became dizzy from hunger. I ate all the sugar cubes and drank cold tea. Now I needed to pee. But there was no toilet around. I peed in the fountain and tried to find a way out again. At last I heard voices rising from behind the wall: "Talkhoon! Talkhoon! Where are you?" But soon the voices faded away.

I lay down on the cushions and through the glass door of the greenhouse followed the moon's slow motion, floating in the lavender sky. The winds blew in my head and I covered my ears to keep from hearing them, but they grew louder. Now the sky became darker and I feared the ghosts. What if Grandma Negaar in her wheelchair rolled down here to visit her husband? What if they saw me and got mad at me for entering their territory?

Ghosts don't exist! Ghosts don't exist!

I wept and the people of the tapestry wept with me.

The next day, I made some tea. I had nothing to eat and the tea was all I had to drink. No one called my name anymore. I held my breath and heard the house breathing quietly. I daydreamed all day and the winds blew in my head. I touched and studied every single object carefully. The greenhouse canary was made of painted wood. The ivies, roses and ferns were all made of silk and plastic. Khanum-Jaan's greenhouse was a fake.

The fountain bubbled real water. I peed in it.

At the end of the second day, the wall rotated and Khanum came in. She found me in my father's suit, sleeping under the picture of the crazy lovers. Sugar crumbs and tea stains had ruined the embroidered cushions and the empty samovar had heated almost to burning. The plastic leaves were plucked and the fountain gurgled yellow, smelly water. One shout was enough to wake me up.

She grabbed my right ear and lifted me in the air. I hunched over in case she wanted to beat me, but she didn't. She cursed my mother and said if I was really crazy I belonged in a crazy house. Now she took me to the garden through a door in the greenhouse (which I hadn't noticed because it was concealed by a fake fern). We walked among tangled trees and dark passages in silence. Khanum's slippers got soiled when we stepped in a puddle of muddy water and she cursed again and prodded me. We reached the walled courtyard. She took her key chain in her hand and searched among the many keys. It was dark and her eyes were bad. At last, she opened the narrow wooden door and we entered the courtyard. She pushed me down toward my basement room and waited for me to change and give her back my father's suit. She grumbled some more because the bottoms of the pants were muddy.

I knew why she'd taken me to my room from the garden and not from the tapestry-covered door. She didn't want my sister to see me. She protected her little Taara from the crazy one.

The same night she sent Uncle Assad to my room to watch me. I stayed in the closet the whole night. I watched Assad, instead of him watching me. Through the hole of the closet door I saw him stealing my underwear, stockings, and hair ribbons, and shoving them into his pockets. Now he played with my childhood dolls, caressing their plastic hair and smelling their rubber bodies. At last, he fell asleep on my bed and began to snore loudly. I dozed in the closet, but every few minutes I opened my eyes in panic. All through the night I watched the room through that narrow hole.

In Search of the Sapphire Feather: Khanum-Jaan's Closet Room

At the end of a spacious bedroom in which neither of my grandparents slept, a door opened to a walk-in closet. No one remembered when exactly Khanum began to use this small, windowless storage room as her solitary confinement.

In her cell, my grandmother slept on a narrow bed covered with a woolen gray blanket, the kind soldiers use. Next to the bed stood a small table on top of which rested a large, black marble box, almost as wide as the table. A closet with sliding doors extended along the right wall. There was nothing more. No mirror, no window, no flower pot, no radio, no shaded lamp, no bottle of cologne, no clock, no calendar. Nothing. This was a soldier's temporary residence, a poor student's dormitory. A nun's room.

On my second trip in search of the sapphire feather I looked around Khanum's room, then opened her closet. Black silk blouses and black crepe skirts hung in a row like a dozen headless mourners on the way to a funeral. There was no color other than black in my grandmother's closet except for a long, gray, fur coat (probably her mother's) at the very end, wrapped tightly in a plastic cover full of mothballs. On the floor, identical black shoes sat in a row, all flat soled, ugly and gloomy. Only one pair of golden slippers with three centimeters of iron heels glowed among the mourning shoes.

I wore a silk blouse and a crepe skirt and wished I could arrange my hair in ringlets, the way Khanum did when she had company or was invited somewhere. Now I sat on her narrow bed and set the heavy black box next to me. The box didn't have a lock, so I opened the lid. As if I was about to see a severed head, my heart hammered and almost broke out of my chest. I was searching for the sapphire feather, I told myself. But would Baba ever ask Khanum to hide it? And if Khanum stole it, wouldn't she destroy the instrument of sorcery, as she'd always called Baba's research material? So I knew the feather was not here or anywhere in Khanum-Jaan's room, but still I opened the box. What had Grandmother hidden here?

Stacks of envelopes. Five stacks. Neatly organized and tied separately by narrow red ribbons. Under each stack and in between, dried rose buds scented the letters. The buds, once red, had faded to yellow and turned to powder when touched. There was nothing more. No sapphire feather, no Simorgh's yellow egg, no priceless family gem, no severed head, no mystery. Just stacks of white envelopes, dried rose buds in between.

These five stacks were divided by decades. On the first envelope she had written with red ink, "1933-1943," on the second, "1943-1953," and so on. I wished I could read every single letter, but I didn't have enough time for even one stack. So I decided to read the first letter of each stack to satisfy my curiosity.

Letters to a Dead Father

Tehran. Drum Tower. Summer 1312 AH. 1933 AD.

It was in this ominous season, this summer of burnt star jasmines and loose ghosts in the garden that you left me. You left me with the burden of your loss and the weight of this old, decaying house on my narrow shoulders. Now, at the end of summer, all I can write to you is the account of your death. You died in a hellish heat that choked your jasmines before they could ever bloom. The dry garden smelled of burned leaves those days and the house was a furnace. You were perishing, Papa.

So we set the tent—your mosquito net—on the porch and the girl sat behind the transparent wall with that wide bamboo fan in her hand. You rested on a narrow canvas bed, listening to the sounds of the garden, moaning or whispering something inaudible. You never cried; you didn't curse the pain, or your bitter fate. You bore your anguish majestically, like a prince, Papa. But I knew your agony and felt it in the marrow of my bones. I burned with fever and shivered with chills with you.

I sat on the edge of the narrow bed that night, held your hand, and listened to the sounds of the garden and your faint moans. The girl behind the net fanned you, switching hands or using both. Her face had no expression. The girl's face was always as blank as a wall.

You opened your eyes, squeezed my hand and brought it to your cold lips. But you did this with much effort, as if lifting solid stone. You kissed my hand gently, as you always did, then you whispered to me to go to bed and rest; you said you were fine. But you were not fine, Papa. You were dying and I sat with you as long as I felt your pulse under my fingers.

The house was empty at that time. Daaye was in the village, trying to find a husband for her daughter, and I was alone in the house with the girl and the ghost of my mother who roamed around in her squeaking wheelchair, knowing that you were going to join her soon.

You remember all this, don't you? Can you remember things in that realm, or is it all oblivion there? You remember that I was alone with you all summer; my sisters were in Europe with Mademoiselle Marie and they didn't even know that you had fallen ill. Their letters came once a week, but I never wrote them of your illness, because I didn't want them to return. I wanted you all for myself; the girl didn't count. How could she ever be counted—Daaye's daughter, a servant, a child barely fourteen, an ignorant, peasant girl who walked barefoot around the house in her cotton pajamas, with her callused feet and unwashed hair? That hair, hanging down her back like a long, thick rope, sweeping the floor, became the everlasting image of my nightmares, Papa.

I never blamed you for what happened. So there was no need to forgive. But in the last minutes, just before dawn, just before the dim light of the sun penetrated the transparent net, you whispered, "Forgive me, flower!" I laid my hand lightly, like the caress of a feather, on your mouth to silence you. I didn't want Hessam-Mirza Vaziri, the Minister of War and the son of many ministers back to the Great Nader Shah, to ask forgiveness from his eighteen-year-old daughter for something that was a common practice for a man of his status. Who sought forgiveness from anyone? From his own child, for that matter? So you whispered into my warm hand as if I were not your daughter, but your beloved wife, Negaar, and as if she, Negaar, not I, had seen you from the crack of the pantry door, on the rough burlap sacks of rice, lying half naked, unbraiding that twisted rope–that boa–to cover the girl's small body with a blanket of unnatural hair—that mass of hair that became the torment of my dreams in the dark nights of my future life.

"Forgive me" was the last thing you said before you left, and believe me, Papa, at that exact moment, the moment of your departure, the restless, wandering wheelchair stopped squeaking under the willows and dawn invaded our tent like an unwelcome guest.

All I wanted was peace and darkness, but the ruthless sun sent its arrows down from the top of the tower as if a war was breaking out. The girl stopped fanning and stood. She felt it. She saw me bending over your body, heard me weeping, and stood outside the tent like a shadow, round in the middle, small and spent, at age fourteen—a question mark with no phrase before and no comment after, a vague thing, a shade. I wept for a while over your cold body, closed your lids with my fingers gently, so as not to disturb your peaceful departure, and left the tent.

"He's all yours now," I told her. You know the rest.

Tehran. Drum Tower. Summer 1322 A.H. 1943 AD.

Look what has become of me, Papa! Of me and of the house. I'm only twenty-eight and my hair is graying. I've lost all my French and the grand piano hasn't been opened for a decade. The key is lost and no one calls someone to make a key. But even if they open the piano, who will play? Who, in this house of gloom, can remember the happy tunes of the days gone?

My hair is graying, Papa, but thank heavens I still have it. My heart is barred in a cage, but I'm light-footed like a deer, and healthy like a village girl. I can work in your house like a hired maid.

Don't feel sorry for me, Papa. Don't say that my flower is working like a servant girl and no miracle will ever happen. There is hope. There is always hope. I sold that half crown with rubies around the rim, the gift from Akbar Shah of India to your ancestor. I sold it a few months ago in an auction. I had to do this when the university reduced my husband's teaching hours. We've lived on this money ever since, and it will last us for a few more years. There are more things to sell in Drum Tower and I'm not worried at the moment. The day that the last sellable object leaves the house, my life will end, Papa, unless our fate turns between now and then, and something unexpected happens.

But I don't have any hope that my husband's income will ever increase. He's not a man, Papa, I didn't marry a man. Do you know this? So what is he? you may ask. Why is he so aloof from our lives and our pressing needs? Why does he reside on a mountaintop half of the year and return with a sack of papers, a bird's feather, or a pair of dried talons? Have I married a man or an otherworldly creature? A ghost? A bird? Or maybe an angel who doesn't know human needs?

I curse the day you enrolled me in the university to be the first woman in our family to attend higher education. I curse the day you sat me in this man's class to learn literature and philosophy. What did I want all this nonsense for? If knowledge is meant to remove one from real life, it's unnecessary and even destructive.

But the past is past and I'm not blaming you for my marriage. Didn't I have my own brain and my own heart, my own womanly instincts, to realize that this professor was not made to be a husband for me or for any girl, for that matter? Couldn't I see his detachment from the tangible and his occupation with the strange, the nonexistent? Couldn't I break the engagement that very first month, the very first week when he carried a bag full of papers with little green scribbles on them, like live worms, to the restaurant where we sat in candle light? He didn't even touch his food, or notice the candles and the roses. He didn't hear the violins playing for us on the terrace. Instead, he read long passages from his damnable manuscript that turned into the nightmare of our lives. He read for me as if I cared how many cursed poems were written on the subject of a bloody bird that had talons as big as human fists, lifted live elephants, lived one thousand years, and didn't even exist.

No, I won't let you feel sorry for me, Papa. It was meant for me to become unhappy. It was meant for all of us. It was the way the stars were patterned and the planets were aligned when we were born. It was meant to be that the damned Shah, that illiterate peasant with the borrowed English crown, would take your seal and confiscate your lands. It was fated for our fortune to turn its back on us. That Mother must die and leave you alone in your old age. The garden, your paradise, must burn in ruthless summers and then you must perish under a mosquito tent on a folding bed, leaving me with two half-sane spinster sisters, an insane husband, an ignorant maid, these boys, and the torment of the girl's hair which was all that remained of her, floating, floating like strange sea weeds that could choke—

And now, sitting here, on this porch, in the dark, I look at my sons on top of the tower. Their kites rise in the evening sky, and the boy, one year older than my oldest, stands at the foot of the tower, watching them.

I swear to all the sacred ones, to your dear soul, Papa, I swear to my mother's innocence, that I've never forbidden this boy to join my sons' games, to mingle with them like a brother, to eat and sleep with them, but it is as if he feels something, senses something unsayable. He is a strange boy, Papa—clever, cunning, and calculating. He knows where his place is. He stands at the foot of the tower where he belongs.

Tehran. Drum Tower. Summer 1332 AH. 1953 AD.

I made a high wall, finally, to keep from looking at the bottom of the tower. I told them I couldn't bear to see the garden dying—a lie. I'd seen the garden dying since I was twelve. I could go on witnessing its decay. What I couldn't bear to see was the foot of the tower, that fresh, smoothed soil, that small area between the tower and the honeysuckle bushes, where nothing grows.

For twenty years, Papa, as if I'd lost my wits, or was under a strange, stupefying spell, I sat every single evening on this porch, faced the tower and the fresh brown soil at its foot, watched the honeysuckle blossoms falling, covering the earth. I sat like someone hypnotized, and it never occurred to me that I could raise a wall and conceal the earth at the foot of the tower.

Now the bricklayers are laying bricks on top of bricks, raising the wall, hiding the garden. Your boy is twenty now. He doesn't look like anyone in the world. I can't describe him the way you expect me to. He is lame—born lame—but he is strong and hard-working, like a mule. He has rolled up his sleeves and the bottom of his pants, has jumped on top of the half-built wall and is helping the mason. Again, no one has asked him to do this. He wants to work, without caring about the purpose of the job. This must be his peasant blood. Is he stupid? Oh yes, he is, but then no, he is not. I've said this before. He didn't stay in night school, he can't read and write well, but he is not ashamed to talk. He is oddly opinionated and capable of taking care of himself— unlike my sons.

My husband is away again. He is writing chapter eight or nine of his cursed book on top of one of his mountains. Except for small excerpts published once in a while here and there, in magazines that normal people never read, nothing of the manuscript is published, and he is thinking about retiring from the university to be able to speed up his work.

Sina helps him. He sits in his father's study, sometimes till morning, copies the chapters, and listens to his endless, insane lectures on the subject of the bloody bird. I'm worried for my son. When he leaves the house, he mingles with the vagabond youth that gather in the corner cafes, discussing cheap politics. No plan for the future, no interest in a career. He scribbles meaningless poems on cigarette papers and matchboxes and then loses them. I collect these square pieces of wrinkled paper from all around the house. I force myself to read what is written on them, but they don't make any sense. He is my first born, Papa, my dearest, handsomest, kindest son. He has your delicate ways, your gentleness, and your gallantry. He has your tall and erect posture, your wide shoulders, your dark, calming eyes. But at eighteen he is vain, absent-minded, and fragile, like the stem of a fresh eglantine. I don't understand my son, Papa; his head is wrapped in blue clouds.

At the end of the second decade following your death, Papa, I have no good news for you, except that Kia, my second one, might win a government scholarship and go to France to make something of himself and save us from future misery. He is the ambitious one. Studies day and night and teaches himself French and German. He plans to pursue the family trade—court politics! Imagine! He says he wants to become Prime Minister one day, and by God, he is so capable. But all I want from him is to pursue his studies in France and get a respectable job. I must have someone sane to support me in my old age, someone reliable. Am I wrong, Papa?

The condition of the house: long ago I dismissed the gardener and his wife. The woman would just sit around in the kitchen with Daaye, gossiping and creating all sorts of horror stories about Drum Tower. I got rid of the couple, mostly because of the woman. If the garden is dying, no gardener can save it. So once a month I hire someone for a day to pull the weeds and trim the bushes and I feed fewer mouths.

I closed up the whole third floor, finally. It was a waste of time and energy to keep it clean and Daaye is getting old and slow. I emptied the rooms, brought some of the furniture down, and auctioned off the rest. I noticed that certain objects were missing. Didn't we have an hourglass, Papa—a gift from the minister of somewhere? It's lost. And the gold-framed oval mirror is missing too. If anything small is lost, I'm not aware of it. But how could these objects leave the house?

And the last news: I'm five months pregnant and not ashamed. I look at least ten years younger. But how did this happen? Did I invade the saint's study while walking in my sleep one night? Or, like Holy Mary, was the seed of God planted in me when I was drifting in my nightmares? My third will be like a child to its older brothers, Papa. This was meant to happen. This child is destined to save us all.

Tehran. Drum Tower. Summer 1342 AH. 1963 AD.

I hate to ruin my anniversary letters, Papa, with the report of my ongoing misery. But how can I not talk to you? Who else do I have?

That lunatic left a week ago and I'm relieved but unhappy. How can I ever feel happy, seeing my son melting like a candle inside that rose arbor with his package of cigarettes and a bottle of wine? Didn't I tell him three years ago, when he brought this loose woman to my house, that she was not his kind? One glance was enough for me to see through the girl. My son could pick any of this type on the grounds of the university campus and he picked the worst of the kind. A weed among flowers, an unknown, unnamed wild grass that grows at the edge of the gutters in any rotten alley of this infested city. He brought this soft-brained trash to my house as his wife, so what could I do when the deed was done?

But you know the rest, Papa; I've written to you many times. I've written about her night walks, her wild cries, loud laughter and wine drinking, her Gypsy dances and her long conversations with herself, as if she'd been raised by fiends or demons. And she has left two girls, one a year and a half old, running in the long corridors, screaming and calling her mother, the other just a few days old, starving in the crib, no voice rising from her weak lungs. The first one might very possibly be my son's, but I swear to your dear soul, Papa, that the second cannot belong to us. How could she? The whore stayed out of the house every night, or if she was inside, she didn't let her husband share her bed. Since the first one was born, Sina has been sleeping in his old room.

But can I throw the two orphans out, Papa? Would you do this if you were in my place? I know you wouldn't and I won't. Didn't I keep your boy in Drum Tower? I'll shelter the girls too. This is my destiny, to run an orphanage in my ancestral house.

And Kia is not coming back. Four years of studies at the Sorbonne turned into ten years of wandering in Europe, and now he has a hybrid wife I've never met. He phones me from the Alps or other frozen mountains and his voice is as cold as the countries he's calling from, and as remote as it could be. With a tinge of an accent, he tells me that he'll come only if the Ministry offers him a high-level job. How did I ever assume that this one was going to protect me in my old age?

The old man is lost on top of Mount Ghaf, buried under hundreds of pages of his Chapter Eleven. The bird has finally taken over. There is no hope. The Simorgh will sooner or later devour him. Now he is using the tiny hand of my nine-year-old Vafa to copy his chapters for him. Sina gave up long ago, realizing only too late that his mad father had wasted his time.

From where I'm sitting on my accustomed place on the porch, in the exact spot that I set your mosquito tent thirty years ago, I can see the tall wall that conceals the garden. Most of the tower is hidden and only the top is visible. The servant boy is up there with a long broom, sweeping the dry leaves and cleaning the balcony, as if the drummers were going to come and beat their drums to announce the time. Thirty years have passed since you abandoned me, Papa, but it is as if you are dying in my arms now.

Tehran. Drum Tower. Summer 1352 AH. 1973 AD.

I dream, Papa, I dream. I take my dreams to dream interpreters and they don't make head or tail of them. But I know my own dreams better than any dream reader. I see myself on top of the brick tower, not in the hollow balcony where the drummers used to stand, but on the very top, on the roof of the tower where no one ever climbs. I see myself bending down, looking at the earth below, at that patch of perpetually fresh earth in which nothing grows, and on which only the dead blossoms of honeysuckle fall and rot. I bend down, looking at that patch of earth, and it opens a crack. Then it opens more; the crack widens, and some strange, sucking power, gravity a hundred times intensified, pulls everything inside the earth's dark womb. It wants to suck in the whole tower. I feel myself falling, being pulled into the earth, but with a very slow, lingering motion, as if it will take me all my life to get there, yet I have to witness my fall, suffer and bear every second of it, a lifelong fall from the top of the tower into the dark crack of the earth in which someone else is lying, and I know who she is. And why should I sink into the same spot? I reason this way with myself but this reasoning does not change anything at all.

Now something strange happens, Papa, something that takes even me by surprise. While descending, I look up for a split second, and in the indigo sky I see the Simorgh, as large as a passenger plane, each of her talons the size of a big man's hand. She is sapphire blue, glittering in the last rays of the sun, her rainbow-feathered wings hanging long like a woman's hair, extending to the earth. She hovers above me as if wanting to lift me up. In my dream I wonder if she is here to save me, and I wake up somewhere between the earth and the sky, my fate undecided.

It's madness. I know. It's sheer madness. My insane husband has driven me mad too. Sina is gone, Vafa is gone, Kia has not returned, my sisters are gone. They've all left me. I'm here in Drum Tower with the old man, the maid, the orphan girls, and the lame one who is my sole companion now.

The girls live their school life together and spend most of their time with their grandfather. They resent me and they don't hide it well. Now they copy the bird pages and sit all night listening to this eternal madness. Meanwhile, the lame one and I rest on this porch each day at dusk, crack sunflower seeds like the old parrot, and chat like washerwomen squatting by the stream after a long day of hard work.

The key to the grand piano remains lost. My French vocabulary is lost. I search the abandoned third floor and I don't find my playroom—the almond-shaped room. That red locomotive and all the little houses are lost.

This is forty years after your death, Papa. And I'm still falling.

Reunion in the Tower

It rained, the wind shifted from west to east, and hail hit my window like small pebbles. If it wasn't for the rain, I could hear everything, but the sound of the storm and Boor-boor's constant screams covered the voices of the house. All I could hear was Khanum shouting, Taara crying, Assad saying something, and Khanum screaming again. Then, above my head, I heard Taara running onto the porch, then down the steps to the courtyard. For a second I thought she was heading to my room to throw herself into my arms and cry on my shoulder, but she ran out of the courtyard to the dark, wet garden, toward the tower.

"Stay up there all night, you ungrateful brat," Khanum screamed on the porch. "Is this the way you appreciate what I've done for you? Why did I raise you? Why did I sacrifice my life for you? Who obliged me to bring you and your sister up? To feed you, to keep you warm and give you love? And now when it's your turn to show love and respect, to think about my old age, you betray me, you stab me in the back. You want to lose this once-in-a-lifetime chance and ruin us all! Am I trying to marry you off to an old, toothless man? To a cripple? Or to a young, handsome, noble man? Who do you want as a husband, anyway? Huh? A vagabond? A street person? A good-for-nothing? Go to the tower and stay with the birds and bats! I wash my hands of you, as I did with Vafa! Go!"

She banged the door but kept shouting inside. Her voice was muffled now and most of her words were lost among Boor-boor's screams, Jangi's angry barking, and the rain that hit the windowpanes like small rocks.

Neither Daaye nor Assad brought a dinner tray for me and I realized that upstairs it was still stormy. So I waited for the lights to go out, then picked up a flashlight and an old blanket and left the room. Boor-boor was a wet ball of shabby feathers, shivering in her gilded cage. Busy with the commotion upstairs, they had forgotten to cover the bird—something they would never forget on other rainy nights. But I didn't feel sorry for my prison keeper. Let her catch cold and die! Let the damn parrot perish!

It had been a while now that Jangi became friendly with me. All those untouched meals I'd fed him had done their work. He was even fond of me, wagging his tail to get my attention, to please me. So I squatted in front of the huge gray dog and stroked his wet, wooly hair. I put a sugar cube in his mouth; he chewed and licked my fingers greedily. I told him, "Jangi, go to your crate!" He obeyed.

I held the blanket over my head and walked through the wet garden, following the flashlight. *Ghosts don't exist, ghosts don't exist.* I chanted Baba's phrase. When I found myself at the foot of the decaying tower guarded by the bushy dryandra, I felt more secure. Nothing would happen to me by the Simorgh's tree.

One hundred and thirty-five stone steps. As a child I'd climbed these steps many times, alone or when playing with Taara and Vafa. But now I breathed heavily, my knees buckled, and I felt shaky and weak. Months of medication, lack of exercise, and feeding my meals to Jangi had weakened my body. I held my hand against the cold, mossy wall and climbed the steps to the tower's balcony. Taara sat holding her legs in her arms, gazing at the moving clouds. She was not weeping.

For a while I stood and watched her. She couldn't see me in the dark. The wind whirled in the hollow space, picked at locks of her long hair and whipped them into her face. But, unaware of the wind, she remained motionless and serene. This was my own sister, the sister who had been so close to me. But since Khanum-Jaan had banished me to the basement, she hadn't even once come down to visit me. She was forbidden, true, but did she have to obey? Couldn't she, like Daaye, hidden from Grandmother, come down and see me? Hadn't she missed me? But she had her own worries—serious ones. Grandmother wanted to marry her off.

She sensed a presence, looked up and saw me. For an instant I thought she was afraid of me, of my madness, and I prepared myself for her scream. But she said, "What are you doing up here?" in a calm voice, as if we were still lying in our beds in our adjoined rooms, chatting through the open door.

"I brought you a blanket. It's cold." I opened the folds of the blanket and spread it over her legs.

"Sit," she said.

I sat. She let me slip under the blanket and covered my legs. Then we squeezed close to each other and listened to the wind.

"I hear them in my head sometimes," I said.

"Hear what?"

"The winds. My head is the house of winds—like this tower." I laughed.

"What do you mean?"

"They cry in my head and then they whirl and whistle."

She listened with her eyes wide open, tears rippling in them like the waves of the sea. Were the tears for me? Or did the wind burn her eyes?

"You'll be fine, Talkhoon. Fine," she said, squeezing my hand.

"If the winds leave, I will."

"They'll leave. They'll leave."

"I heard you crying, Khanum screaming—"

"So you know."

"Not everything."

"Talkhoon, I'm in trouble. You understand? I love this other person. A sad man, a lonely, handsome man, a man with blue eyes and nothing else but thin blue sheets of paper filled with depressing poems. I see him every day and we've started talking. We go to this pastry shop to read poems and talk. I can't marry anyone now. Not now."

"You haven't passed your exams, either."

"To hell with the exams. I can't love someone and marry someone else. If this man, this suitor, this general's son, had come a few months before, I'd have married him right away—without love, but without worry. Cold, like this brick wall. Passive. You know what I mean? I'd marry him to help Khanum-Jaan. But I can't do it now. I'm involved. And I can't tell this to Khanum. I know I'm betraying her and I feel sorry for her. She is not forcing me to marry an old, ugly man, like some parents do. She thinks she has found the best match for me and maybe he is; I mean he could be, if I were not so involved. But how can I ever—? What about Vahid?"

"Don't, Taara! Don't cry. We'll find a way out. There must be a way. Maybe Father will come—"

"Ha ha! Or maybe the Simorgh will appear! Or maybe Baba-Ji will wake up. Or, who knows? Maybe our mother will return after sixteen years."

"Taara, do you know where Baba-Ji's feather is?"

"No. Why?" she asked, then burst into wild laughter. "Don't tell me you want to burn a barb?"

"Not for the Simorgh to come."

"You don't think the bird will ever come?"

"She'll remain in Baba's unfinished book, Taara. All versions of her. The Rokh, the Feng Huang, the Firebird—"

"You have to try to forget, Talkhoon. Forget the Simorgh. Forget Baba-Ji."

"I can't." I wept and Taara wept with me. Now we pulled the blanket over our heads like old times, when we were little and afraid of the sounds of the house. We both cried, loud and hard.

"Do you know what is the worst of all?" Taara removed the blanket.

"What?"

"Assad has seen me with Vahid. He stopped me in the dark corridor the other night and whispered into my ear, 'I know who you're seeing everyday, Taara. Do you know what will happen if your grandmother finds out?'"

"What did you tell him?"

"Nothing. What could I? He has followed me. He knows Vahid. He knows about our letters—everything. Then he said, 'If you do something for me, I'll keep your little secret in my chest and I may even be able to postpone this engagement party that's worrying you so much. I'm not saying I can change Khanum's mind. But I may be able to postpone—.'"

"What does he want, Taara? What does he want?"

"He wants Khanum-Jaan's letters."

"Letters to her dead father?"

"The letters she writes in her room and hides in her marble box. Assad says they're in five stacks. He has seen them, but hasn't been able to read them. He wants me to bring one stack at a time. Five nights in a row."

"No! She'll find out."

"He says if I bring just one stack at a time, she won't find out. She may not write letters these days anyway, she may not even open the box. She is too busy shopping and cleaning the house for the General's visit."

"Why does he want Grandmother's letters?"

"Maybe he is after her will—wants to know if he is included. If he is not included, then he'll need time to get himself included."

"How?" I asked.

"How would I know?" Taara said and brushed her hair away from her eyes. "More than anyone in the world, Assad knows the way to Khanum's heart. But if he is looking for the will, and if the will is in one of these envelopes, he'll find out that he is included. That's what I think. I think Khanum will give more to Assad than to anyone else."

"But she may not even have a will. She's not that old."

"She's not?" Taara asked, surprised.

"She must be around sixty-five. She is healthy. Except for her nerves, of course. And the spider veins on her legs."

"Now I'm going to mess up her nerves in a bad way, Talkhoon. In a major way."

"Don't worry now. We'll find a way."

So we sat on top of the tower, close to each other, and the wind wrapped us in a bundle. I was happy and anxious at the same time. My anxiety was for Taara and my joy for our strange reunion in the dark. Clouds passed swiftly behind the small portholes and gathered for more rain. Preoccupied, shaky, and excited, I tried hard to concentrate on Taara's problem, to find a way out of Assad's threat and out of the marriage with the General's son.

"Taara—"

"Hmmm?"

"I have an idea. Listen. Tell Assad that you'll get him the letters. Tell him to postpone the engagement."

"How can I get the letters? Do I dare go to Khanum's room? Do I dare open her box?"

"I'll get the letters for you."

"No, Talkhoon. Never!"

"Listen to me. I've already opened the box. I've even read some of them."

"You have?"

"Just a few. Try to take her and Assad out for a few hours every day. Take her shopping for five days. Pretend you've changed your mind. Tell her if she wants you to court the man, you'll need new clothes, shoes, hair cut, manicure—. I'll get the letters for Assad. But he has to promise to postpone the engagement."

"And after that?"

"After what?"

"After Assad postpones the engagement, if he does? Eventually the day will come that I'll have to get engaged."

"We'll think of something by then. Who knows? You'll have time to know Vahid better. To see if he is serious about you."

"Talkhoon, who said you were crazy?"

We laughed and hugged each other tightly.

"You have to go now, Talkhoon. They'll find you here."

"Taara, what if Assad is not after the will?"

"Then what is he after?"

"The Simorgh's feather."

"Nonsense!"

"Don't you remember how he used to hide behind the door, in the dark corridor or in the shade of the trees to hear Baba-Ji's bird stories?"

"Yes, but he was young then. Now he knows that the bird doesn't exist."

"Maybe he believes that it exists, otherwise why should he have a Simorgh on his belly that flutters its wings for him?"

"What?"

"A Simorgh on his belly—"

"Talkhoon! Has he told you this?"

I wanted to tell Taara about the day I pretended to be sleeping and Assad slipped under my blanket and pressed himself against me, but I didn't. I just said, "He talks to me sometimes. But I hide in the closet. I don't want to be in the room when he talks."

"Oh, poor Talkhoon. You have to come back upstairs again. I have to do all I can to bring you back to your room."

"Let's get the letters first. Don't forget that you have to take Khanum shopping for five days in a row. Now I'll go."

On the landing I showed Taara the small wooden door on the right. "Do you remember this storage room?"

"This is where the drums are. You and Vafa once broke into it."

"Some day I want to look at them again."

"I don't think they're drums anymore. They've been sitting here forever; their skins must be loose, or even turned to powder."

"One day I would like to open this door and look at the big drums."

When I reached the courtyard, the sky brightened; it happened so suddenly that I thought someone up in the heavens had turned the lights on. I raised my head to see the morning light, but instantly the sky shadowed again. This was either the shadow of an enormous cloud or a pair of wings flapping soundlessly in the false dawn.

"Simorgh!" I whispered to myself. "Do I really believe you do not exist? Or do I pretend that I've lost faith?"

"Boorrrr!" The parrot screamed with her annoying voice, as if ridiculing my thoughts.

The Big Theft

All day thunder cracked and small whirlwinds lifted the street trash and carried it to the courtyard. The winds grew stronger the next day and debris hit my window. Boor-boor, threatened by a scream louder that her own, opened her stony beak and shouted all day, "Boorrr ... Boorrrr...," but no one came to her rescue. I heard Khanum-Jaan and Assad locking the doors and windows upstairs and securing them with tape.

Late that night, Daaye came down with a thermos and a bundle under her umbrella. She had brought me enough tea, bread, cheese and walnuts for as many days as the storm was going to last. She said the radio had predicted twisters and she couldn't come down until it was over. Rain slashed her umbrella and the wind tried to lift her off the ground, so she ran upstairs without noticing the poor bird's uncovered cage.

On the third day, the strongest whirlwind uprooted Boor-boor's cage and carried the parrot to the sky. Through the tides of water running down my windowpane, I saw the bird's cage spinning, then flying among the black clouds. Anxious and confused (I wasn't sure what to feel about the bird's loss), I sat nibbling a cheese sandwich and sipping hot tea. I waited for the wind and rain to stop. At dusk on the third day, when they finally stopped, I heard setar melodies trickling down from upstairs, like dew drops on the calm surface of water.

Taara had been playing all these days, fighting with the winds.

Your fingers are bleeding, Taara. I know. I know.

Four days after my visit with Taara in the tower, Daaye came down with a bowl of warm chicken soup, some fresh bread and a small note under the plate. "We'll go shopping today. The house is all yours! T."

Daaye had caught a bad cold the other day and her temper was sharp. She sniffled, sneezed, and told me that Taara had agreed to the engagement and Khanum was the happiest she could ever be.

"She is beside herself," Daaye said and sneezed again. "She's acting young. She's spoiling the girl, taking her out to buy her fabrics, then to the dressmaker for measurements. But first they're going to the pawnshop to pawn Khanum's old emerald earrings. Unbelievable! The earrings from her emerald set! She's gone mad with joy; she wants to spend like old times, but she is short of cash."

"Is Taara happy?" I asked.

"The other night when they fought, I wasted my tears on her," Daaye said, and blew her nose in a handkerchief the size of a headscarf. "She wants to marry for money. Let her. I don't care anymore. I wash my hands of her." She said this and left the room, coughing an old person's cough. But then she came back and added, "I can't read what she's written to you, but I warned her not to write another letter, or I'll tell on both of you!" She said this, sneezed, and dragged herself upstairs without noticing Boor-boor's absence.

Less than a minute after the black Cadillac left the garden, I was in Baba-

Ji's room, pushing his recliner closer to the window. I knelt next to him and lay my head on his bony lap. He had lost all his flesh. This was the skeleton of my grandfather. Outside, the sky was gray and raindrops dripped from the top of the stores' awnings. I couldn't see the street sweeper, but I could hear his long broom brushing the debris off the sidewalk. I lay my head on Baba's chest, listening to his heartbeat. His body was warm.

"But why are you so still, Baba? Why don't you move at all?"

I combed back his white hair. The strands felt dead and dry like the hair of my childhood dolls. "Baba-Ji, wake up, while I'm still here—please!" But he remained motionless. I kissed his cheeks and left the room.

In Khanum-Jaan's room I took the first stack of her letters out of the black box and spent the rest of the day searching for the sapphire feather. In each lost person's old room, I looked for the feather, and when I didn't find it I put on their clothes and looked at myself in the dusty mirrors. I wore my Father's suit again, then my mother's blue soiree gown, a huge cashmere robe of one of the aunties, Daaye's rose-water black veil—the one she only wore to visit Imam Reza's Holy Shrine.

In Uncle Vafa's room, I stole a cotton shirt and a pair of khaki pants, rolled them up and carried them away under my arm. I thought maybe some day I'd need these boys' clothes. But this was a passing thought—I just enjoyed the thrill of stealing. I'd steal more things if it wouldn't endanger my main plan. Then I looked into the old, rusty elevator, but didn't dare to step inside. I was afraid of getting trapped in it. I climbed the dusty stone steps to the third floor. Except for a few carpets and heavy velvet curtains, the rooms were empty. I looked behind the curtains and under the carpets to see if, by any chance, Baba-Ji had hidden the feather there, but all I found were dust balls, mothballs, and spider webs. Now I entered Grandpa Vazir's bedroom and saw the skeleton of a huge brass bed with brass posts erected on the four sides. I imagined a transparent gauze tent covering the bed, Khanum's parents sleeping under it. When I heard a rattle and clatter and strange hissing and sighing sounds, I thought Grandpa Vazir and Grandma Negaar were in their old bed, making love. I rushed down the three flights, ran to the basement, and hid in my closet. I shook with fear until I heard the black Cadillac pulling in the garden.

For five consecutive days, Taara took Khanum and Assad on shopping trips and walked them through covered and uncovered, ancient and modern bazaars until they collapsed. Taara complained that she didn't have anything to wear, and if she was going to be engaged to the General's son, she needed this and that. Meanwhile, Daaye stayed in bed alone, burning with fever. She had caught the flu when she brought food for me the other night.

For four consecutive days, I went upstairs, took a stack of letters out of the black ivory box and handed it to Taara in the evening. She was now allowed to bring my tray down. In a dark corridor she handed the stack to Assad, and he read the letters in his slow way. These days I didn't see Assad at all, but his light was reflected in the courtyard's fountain every night.

On the fifth morning, I made the mistake of roaming the rooms for too long, and leaving the theft for the last minute. I was just putting the fourth stack in the box and picking up the fifth, when I heard the Cadillac pulling in. Jangi barked, and Khanum's voice rose above the dog's, echoing in the main lobby.

"I'm not paying a black coin to this stupid woman anymore. I'm not going to let her touch my hair. Look what she's done to me. She's burned all my hair!"

With choking panic, I closed the box, dashed out of Khanum's room, passed the large bedroom and Baba's study, and ran down the steps into my basement room. Only then did I realize that I hadn't taken the fifth stack of letters, the one that belonged to this half decade.

Fearing that Assad wouldn't keep his promise and Taara would get engaged to the man she didn't love, and blaming myself for my stupidity, I covered my face in my hands and sobbed.

On the morning of the sixth day, a weekend when everyone was resting, I heard the *lek, lek, lek* of Assad's slippers in the courtyard. He was coming down. I rushed to hide in the closet, but tripped over a pile of clothes and fell. When I stood, he was in the middle of the room. He moved forward and I stepped back, unable to scream, wishing that Boor-boor were here to shout and call someone down. But the parrot was gone and Assad kept approaching. His breath smelled of vodka.

He pressed me against the wall and placed the flat of his palms on either side of my head next to my ears, and caged me in with his body. Now he rubbed his big belly against my body and grinned. With that prickly beard and the large beads of sweat that bubbled on his skin, his face looked dirty. But he didn't kiss me; all he wanted was to press his belly against mine and move it in a circular way—clockwise and counter-clockwise. He grinned more and showed his yellow teeth and at last he let me go. I ran into the closet, closed the door, and sat in the dark, thinking that he'd come just to do this and now he'd go. But he didn't. I stayed in the closet, looking through the hole. He sat on my bed, fumbled with my things and talked to me. But each word seemed to have a huge weight in his mouth and slipped off his tongue and was drowned in a pool of sadness that rippled in his voice. I saw him picking up my sleeping gown, holding it toward the window and gazing through it for a long time as if seeing the world through a thin, blue glass. He said things he'd never said before.

"I wish I'd never read the woman's letters to her fossil father, Talkhoon! I wish I hadn't read them. Fuck me! What a good life I had before I read the damn letters of the crazy, old hen—what a good, carefree life I had just a few days ago.

"You may ask me, why did I want to read the witch's dirty, damnable letters in the first place, huh? Is this what you want to know? The whole thing was for you, baby, just for you. I mean for me and you—for us. To see if we could, or if we could not—you get me? To find a clue. Where have I come from? Who the fuck am I? And you. To see if you're Sina's child, if Sina is my brother.

"Sometimes I get mad at the old man for keeping it a secret. Where have I come from? Why does nobody tell the truth for a single minute in this fucking house? Do they want me to believe that I'm Baba's child? Do they want me to believe that Baba cared for a woman at all? He was a man who even in his youth could barely satisfy his own wife, not to speak of having a mistress, or messing with a village woman. He went to the mountains to find his fucking bird, if you ask me, to see that gigantic damnation of the Simorgh that he was so obsessed with. So, do they want me to believe that he went to the mountains and there was a village woman on the peak of Ghaf, or Alborz, or Black Death Mountain, or wherever he went, and he planted his seed in her and I was born and he brought me in a bundle down to Drum Tower and handed me to his wife? Do they expect me to believe that he handed me to the witch and asked her to raise me like her own sons? Do they expect me to buy this fairytale? And Khanum—the old turkey, the hell-raiser, the head witch of the tower—wouldn't she kick her husband's ass for bringing a bastard baby into her crumbling ancestral house? No, I've never bought this, although they've fed me this tale since I was a child. Not him—he never talked. So he didn't lie. She did. She sat her fucking bony ass on her folding chair on the porch, sweet-talked me for as long as I was a child and told me that Anvar, her beloved husband, had brought me in one cold winter when I was burning with fever because I had a disease called polio and that Doctor Shafa had cured me but that my leg had stayed crooked, and so on, and then she raised me with my half-brothers like her own son.

"Like her own son? Do you see the lie? Be my judge, girl, for once. Do you call this, 'like her own son'? They didn't even send me to school until I was this tall. I was twelve years old and illiterate like a village boy, doing fucking hard errands around the house. I was a kitchen boy, Daaye's assistant cook, the gardener's hand, the garbage collector, the mail boy, the errand boy, the shoe polisher—name it. Then one day the old man said, *Oh, my God, I've forgotten to send the poor boy to school!* Do you buy this? And this was when Sina and Kia (their little brat, Vafa, was not born yet) wore starched blue uniforms everyday and went to this fucking French school. What do you call this, huh? *Like her own son?*

"So what I'm asking is, who am I and where did I come from? I wouldn't ask this if I weren't in love, Talkhoon. I want you, because I saved you when you were an abandoned baby and I named you and now I claim you. You're mine and I want to marry you and make everything legal in the house of God and in the court of law. But I want fucking evidence to show that I'm not their son, and have never been—so where have I come from?

"That 's why I wanted the letters. I knew the old hen had been writing for years, saying everything to her long dead and rotten father. I wanted to see if there was a story about me somewhere in these letters. Or a document, a birth certificate, anything saying that I was not Anvar Angha's son. Or maybe I was hoping to find proof that you, Talkhoon, were really a bastard, your mother's daughter but not your father's, as Khanum claims. But there was nothing about you or me. So what do I find instead? Treason and lies. Fake pride. Things that make me want to kill the woman with my own hands. All those 'Assad is this and Assad is that. He is the cane for my hand, my only loyal son—' was bullshit. You hear me? The way she talks about me in her damn letters is the real way she sees me. She calls me 'the servant boy, the lame—.' She says, 'Who are my companions, Papa? Cooks and servants. Daaye and the lame boy.'

"Oh, worse than this, worse. She calls me filthy and dirty and dumb and condescends to me all through the letters. Not even once, not once in the whole four fucking stacks does she call me by my name. She doesn't say 'Assad,' she doesn't say 'son.' She has more respect for Daaye, who has come from the backwoods, than for me who is supposed to be Professor Angha's son!"

Assad talked and talked, squeezed my nylon sleeping gown and wiped his tears with it until night fell and Khanum, from the top of the porch, called, "Assad, where are you?" He rose and left my room without a word.

I opened the closet door and saw him passing outside the window, scraping his plastic slippers on the brick floor—*lek, lek, lek, lek*—his back stooped like an old man's.

Proposal

A short while before the guests arrived, Taara, in her new turquoise outfit, came down to the basement room to get me ready. Her dress was too short, as the new fashion dictated, and when she sat her skirt slipped up and showed her thighs. Her honey-colored hair hung down like a wavy curtain to the small of her back, and a white belt curled around her narrow waist. White shoes with delicate openings in the front showed her pedicured, red toenails—little shiny radishes. She said that Khanum-Jaan wanted me to sit with the guests, smile, and carry on a polite conversation. Then she searched the closet to find something nice for me to wear.

The guestroom was scented with freshly cut gladiolus and tuberoses, but you could still smell the mothballs which had remained under the carpets and in the cracks between the couch cushions. Khanum had finally agreed to open the room and uncover the furniture, but with much embarrassment about the dirty rugs and dusty chandeliers. I sat on a chair and prayed no one would talk to me.

On the wall of the guest room, opposite the double oak door, Grandpa Vazir, the War Minister of the old Shah, stood erect in his red tuxedo, medals and decorations hanging from his pocket. His right hand, adorned with four large rings—two rubies, one jade, and one emerald—rested on a cane with the head of an elephant carved out of ivory at its top. He frowned and smiled at once. The frown was for his inferiors—the clerks of the Ministry and his house servants. The smile was for his wife and daughters, and of course for his superiors—the Prime Minister and the Shah himself.

The General, tall and square, with as many medals and decorations as Grandpa Vazir's, sat under the tall painting of the long dead minister. He didn't take off his dark sunglasses, and when I said good evening, he nodded. His son, who had a bony nose dividing his face like a wall, didn't even see me, or if he did, ignored me. The boy's grandmother, a skeleton of a woman with flaming red hair freshly dyed for the occasion and set in the shape of a cabbage above her head, smiled at me and I smiled back. No one said a word and I was grateful for not being obliged to talk with them.

Taara came in and served tea in a silver tray. Small, gold-rimmed tea glasses jingled in their crystal saucers as she walked, and when she bent slightly to offer sugar cubes, her skirt slipped up and revealed her shapely upper thighs. From where I sat, I saw how the General's eyes, concealed behind the dark lenses, penetrated Taara's flesh.

From the numerous bottles of perfume sitting on her dressing table, Taara had picked a sweet, hot scent that smelled of overripe tropical fruits, burned opium, and sheer madness. When she moved, her legs rubbed against each other, silk caressed silk with a swish, and that crazy scent rose into the air. The men went out of their minds, lost their judgement and insisted on a date even earlier than May eleventh—what everyone had agreed on. But Khanum refused. May eleventh was the earliest she could manage. She had to prepare the house. At last they agreed on the eleventh and offered to buy a diamond ring for the future bride.

In the absence of our grandfather and father, Uncle Kia was supposed to act as the patriarch of Drum Tower. But apparently he was stuck in the Ministry and showed up only when the guests were leaving. Khanum reported the date of the engagement to her son and he announced his agreement, as if it mattered at all. At the door, he and the General exchanged a few polite words and boasted about their sensitive positions in the government. Now the general kissed Khanum-Jaan's hand, and the red-haired skeleton kissed her cheeks, as if she was already a close relative. Before leaving, the old lady pulled Taara to her bony chest, whispered something in her ear, and shoved a large gold coin into her palm. "Buy yourself a beautiful gown for the ceremony, my jewel!"

The young man held Taara's hand for too long and gazed into her eyes and I stood behind everyone, feeling awkward but grateful that the proposal was over.

The minute the door was closed behind them, Taara ran down to my room and I followed her. She dropped onto my bed, put a pillow over her head and cried. Not having been able to give Assad the last stack of letters, she was sure he would not cancel the ceremony.

"They liked me! They liked me!" she repeated and wept. "Vahid will never make up his mind in ten days. We've just started seeing each other. We need more time. But these people liked me. I could tell!"

"Couldn't you wear something longer and uglier, Taara?" I asked. "Why did you put on that crazy perfume?"

But she ignored my questions, sobbed and talked about Vahid. "Most of the time he's dreamy and doesn't say anything." She sat on my bed and wiped her tears. "Then he wants me to listen to his poems and when I talk about my life in Drum Tower, he looks at me with empty eyes and I know he's not listening. No, I don't think in ten days I can bring him to listen to anything serious like this. I need time, Talkhoon, I need more time. Assad won't do anything to postpone the engagement, and the old, fat man liked me even more than his stupid son did."

"Taara, come up!" Khanum called from the porch. "Your Uncle Kia wants to talk to you."

"Who is this Uncle Kia, anyway?" Taara said with anger. "I haven't seen this man more than three times in my life, and now he is acting as the family's counselor!"

"Khanum pretends she is a weak woman and needs a man's advice," I said.

"You're talking nonsense, Talkhoon! Do something instead of blabbering. The party will happen in a week and they'll buy me a diamond ring—"

"Taara!" Khanum screamed.

"Coming!" she screamed back. "Damn you all," she cursed and left.

Now the week of lunacy began. Khanum-Jaan, overwhelmed with joy, wanted to make the impossible possible. Any work that had been postponed, neglected, or simply forgotten for the past decade needed to be done. She didn't want the ugly brick wall to separate the courtyard from the garden anymore. She wanted it removed, and when Assad argued that the garden would then have to be made presentable, she wanted a gardener to fix the shrubbery that had been neglected for fifty years. All in one week!

"Get the Shah's gardener for me, Assad. Call the Marble Palace and tell them you want that Italian gardener."

"Are you joking, Khanum? Or maybe you're out of your mind?" Assad asked. "That was half a century ago when those Italian guys came to trim your pines. Your Papa was a minister then. Who knows us anymore?"

"Who knows us anymore, huh? I'll show them!"

Khanum was out of her mind.

And she wanted new clothes for all of us (even for herself!). She wanted all the dull, dirty gold, silver, and brass to be polished, the walls to be painted—all in one week. She wanted to throw an engagement party that would restore her family's lost status and forgotten reputation. With empty pockets, she wanted to recreate the glorious past. So she pawned more ancestral jewelry, humiliated herself and borrowed money from stingy Uncle Kia, or Uncle Counselor, as we referred to him—to repair and adorn the house, its furnishings, and the people of the house.

For a whole week, Madame Abulian, the Armenian dressmaker, and her seamstress girls, three men from the carpet-cleaning company, the gold and silver shiners, the pool cleaners, the mason and his laborers, the wall painter's crew, the gardener and his men (not from the Marble Palace, though), the ancient man from the clock repair shop, and several other workers—whose function remained unknown—came to the house early in the morning and stayed until sundown.

Assad and Daaye were busy in the kitchen, cooking a week ahead for the party and feeding the army of workers. Every day Khanum clicked her slippers and walked herself nearly to death, giving orders, writing inventory, and calling long-forgotten acquaintances to get their addresses for invitation cards. For hours in the middle of the night, she sat at the dining table and signed the stack of cards with the picture of red roses and nightingales. One hundred cards were mailed out.

One early morning, all of the house's three clocks, having slept under a layer of dust for decades, awoke at the same time, rang, chimed, cuckooed and shook the walls of Drum Tower. Now I heard Grandmother's clicking heels on the porch steps and saw her passing through the courtyard where the mason and his men were busy tearing down the wall. Since she'd found me in her tearoom and cursed my mother, she hadn't talked to me, and that was a long time ago. She had talked about me, and behind my back, but not to me, and in such a friendly tone.

"The poor parrot is lost, Talkhoon," she looked at the window behind which she'd planted Boor-boor's cage. "This stupid Daaye didn't take the bird in and she was washed away with the flood—God knows where. I'm sorry for the poor thing. That was my own parrot, Talkhoon, a gift from the Ambassador of India who was our guest one time when I was a little girl. The parrot was a chick when this turbaned Indian Ambassador brought it to our house. A servant carried the gilded cage and walked ceremoniously behind the Ambassador. Papa said, 'This parrot is for my little flower, hang it in the almond room.' So they hung the cage in the almond room and I started to teach the bird to talk. But, as you know, the poor, dumb thing never learned a word, except to scream, 'Boor!' So we called her 'Boor-boor.' I think the bird had learned the Hindi language earlier and when we taught her our own language she became confused and lost her tongue altogether. Anyway, she lived a long life in this house and never talked. Then I gave her to you to keep you company in your sickness. Well, I hope the winds have taken her back to India! Who knows, huh?" She said all this in one breath, without looking at me, then glanced at the courtyard where the mason and his boy were breaking up the wall.

"Now, thank God, you're much better, Talkhoon. What a nightmare it was! And what a good time to feel better. Madame Abulian is here. I want her to make you a couple of new dresses. The hairdresser is coming tomorrow just for you, so you won't have to go all the way to her salon. This is a new hairdresser, not that bitch who burned my hair with her smelly stuff. You definitely need to trim your hair, my dear—it looks wild. It's your sister's engagement party and you have to look good."

She looked around the room and sighed. "You don't want to clean up your room? To start a new life? Bad days are gone, Talkhoon, good days are coming. We're making the house nice and new like the old times when my Papa was alive. Clean up your room, just in case someone comes down. One hundred people are invited, my dear; it's hard to control them. A good girl doesn't hang her underwear on the chair!" She picked up my stuff and shoved them inside the overflowing drawer.

Then she turned toward the door, but stopped and said, "I could send you to the aunties', but I tell myself, Why should I hide her? She is feeling much better now and the boy's family has already seen her. You didn't open your mouth to say one pleasant word that day and they noticed that you were quiet. You know how people are, especially when they want to marry their son. They're curious about all the family members, even the maids and servants. The old lady was asking me who Assad was. Can you imagine? Nosy people! I don't like it at all. Anyway, thank God you're not feeling that bad, or are you? You feel calmer, don't you? Doctor Shafa believes it was just a passing crisis. Is he right, Talkhoon? Your silence worries me, Talkhoon, why don't you say something?"

The aunties had come to help but, instead, they sat at the table with their cards, a bowl of salted watermelon seeds, and cups of Turkish coffee. They saw everyone's fortune and cracked seeds. When they saw me they almost screamed. Either my hair had really gone wild or I had lost a lot of weight. So when Madame Abulian stood me on top of a chair to measure the length of my skirt, the aunties told Khanum that she had better hide me in their house. "She doesn't look that well, sister," and "What if she acts out?" they said.

"Nonsense!" Khanum said. "She just needs to fatten up a bit. I'll tell Daaye to feed her lamb stew everyday."

"Yummy!" Aunty Puran said and clicked her tongue. "I wish this lazy Daaye would serve us some lamb stew today!"

"You don't need to fatten up, sister!" Aunty Turan said and laughed.

"To be a bit chubbier than normal is always better than looking like a washboard!" Aunty Puran said. "This girl takes after her mother, that Soraya; she was a washboard. Remember, sister?"

A woman came, sat me on a chair and trimmed my hair. She made me long bangs that tickled my eyelids and left me half-blind. Through the curtain of hair the whole world went blurry, and I looked like an eight-year-old. Now with a long, white string that she moved back and forth with her fingers, she plucked everyone's facial hair. The aunties and Khanum didn't feel the pain; they sat relaxed and chatted while the woman fluttered above them like a strange winged animal and plucked off their mustaches. But when it was my turn, with the woman's first attack, my skin was on fire. I screamed, covered my face, and ran down to my room.

On May ninth, the mason and his workers finally collapsed the major part of the brick wall that had separated the courtyard from the garden. For the first time, I had a view of the whole garden and the tall, dark, brick tower from my basement window. The gardener had only a day and a half left to do something about the jungle of weeds and bushes. The speed of the work was dizzying and the three repaired clocks constantly chimed and clanked, announcing the passage of time.

There was no sign that Assad had done anything to postpone the engagement party.

Early on the morning of the tenth, Assad and his friends from the neighborhood mosque took twelve live turkeys to the fountain and chopped their heads off for the special dish he was planning to cook. All the men had bloody faces and hands and looked like criminals. Dark, red rivulets ran on the courtyard floor. Taara, who was running down to my room in her school uniform, stepped in a puddle of blood and stained her white socks. She screamed and sobbed hysterically.

"Bad omen." She dropped herself on my bed and wept. "Blood stained my white socks—it's a bad sign! Assad hasn't done anything to cancel this crazy party. Why did I trust this man in the first place? He always resented us, didn't he? Now he has brought these vagabonds to our house to kill the poor turkeys! It's like a nightmare, Talkhoon, everything is happening in a nightmare. All these clocks ticking, people working day and night, and now these poor, dead birds. They want to throw an engagement party for me and I don't even want to be engaged! I'm going to give a letter to Vahid today. It's everything that I need to tell him. But I'm not sure how he will respond. Pray for me, Talkhoon. Pray for your poor sister!"

The Ghost Did it!

When I woke up on the morning of May eleventh, a short note was next to my pillow: "I'm going to school to take my last exam. Most probably I won't come back. Let Grandmother engage herself to the General, or the General's son! T."

I felt a wild pulse in my throat and wind whirled in my head. *Didn't you think about me, Taara? How could you leave me behind?*

But the whole thing was my own fault! Assad didn't cancel the party because *I* failed to provide the fifth stack of the letters. It was *I* who caused Taara's flight.

An ear-piercing shriek shook the house—a shriek one heard on seeing corpses in the ruins of a city after an earthquake or a bombing.

"Lost! Lost! Everything is lost!" And then the *bang, bang* of footsteps, and more cries. Sensing that something had happened that might bring Taara back, I ran upstairs.

Khanum-Jaan, her sisters who had stayed overnight, Daaye, Madame Abulian and her seamstress girls who had also stayed to finish the dresses, were all either crying or covering their mouths to keep from screaming. They were in their long sleeping gowns. Assad, in his sleeveless undershirt, pulling his pants up, limped barefoot from room to room, investigating. Khanum fainted. They sat her on a recliner and Daaye held a camphored kerchief under her nose. The aunties sobbed and murmured broken sentences. The festivity had turned into calamity overnight.

"All is lost. Ruined beyond repair," Aunty Puran lamented. "The silk carpets, the carvings on the ceilings, the paintings, the curtains, all—"

I tiptoed to the guestroom where the ceremony was supposed to take place tonight and saw black spots the size of small coins all over the place—on the carpets, the freshly painted walls, the panels of antique paintings, the couches, the lace and velvet curtains, freshly washed after half a century, even on the ceiling around the chandelier, where the artists of hundreds of years ago had carved fat angels and cupids in the European Renaissance style.

Assad knelt on the floor, touched one of the black circles, sniffed his fingers, touched it again, even tasted it, then smelled it again. Now he stood up and shook his head.

"Tar!" he announced.

Everybody repeated in wonder and disbelief, "Tar?"

"Someone has left tar stains all over the place," Assad said.

"But how?" Aunty Puran asked. In her white gown and black robe, wide open in front, she looked like a pregnant penguin. She was panting. Her small heart buried under layers of fat couldn't take it anymore. "How could anyone reach the ceiling?"

"No one without a very tall ladder can reach the carvings," Aunty

Turan, who was gray in the face and shaking, said. The bangs of her Cleopatra wig had slid to the side of her head, covering her ear.

Assad inspected the little circles, measured them and compared them. Daaye massaged Khanum's neck. She came too, sat motionless, and waited for Assad to say something. The gardener, the mason, the carpet cleaners who had come to clean the last carpet and get their money were all standing by the oaken double doors, looking at the tar spots.

"We cleaned these carpets yesterday," the carpet cleaner said with deep regret.

"They're ruined. Millions!" Aunty Puran said.

"All of Khanum's inheritance," Aunty Turan said, and wept for her sister.

"It's a cane," Assad announced. "The tip of it. If you don't believe me, get a cane and look at its tip. These stains are made by a cane dipped in tar."

"Who uses a cane around here?" Aunty Puran asked.

A deep silence fell and then Khanum's voice rose, cold and remote. "Papa uses a cane!" Silence fell again, and she added, "He is upset."

"But why?" her sisters asked at the same time. "Because you were trying to restore the house?"

"No. The match. Papa is upset about the match," Khanum said, unable to make long sentences. "He came to cancel the engagement."

"But couldn't he send his message without ruining your inheritance?" Aunty Puran asked.

"Spirits live in a realm beyond matter, sister. In a realm that has nothing to do with the things that are important to us. Spirits do not care about carpets and curtains."

"But why is the match wrong?" Aunty Turan asked. "The family is from the old dynasty, our own blood. They're even related to us. The boy's grandmother on the mother's side is the third cousin of our grandfather on the father's side."

"The match is wrong because the girl is being forced to marry," Daaye said between her tears.

"Is she?" the sisters asked at the same time.

"Let's not waste time," Assad said impatiently. "Let me see if we can remove the stains."

"If these are tar stains, as you're saying," the carpet cleaner said, "nothing can remove them. Maybe benzene will make them paler, but forget about removing them."

So they brought a bucket of benzene and, with a rag, smeared it on one spot on the silk carpet; the stain spread like ink and looked even worse. They tried one of the stains on the wall. It grew larger and darker, like a black cloud. Khanum stood up and ordered her sisters to call the General and then the guests, and apologize for the cancellation of the engagement party.

"Tell them I'm severely ill. Hospitalized. Dying!" Then she retired to her room and we all heard the lock and bolt and realized that she was not going to come out again soon.

The workers gradually left the house, some of their work undone or half done. No one could pay them and they didn't dare to knock on Khanum's door. They'd rather wait until she recovered. One meter of the brick wall remained in the courtyard, like an ugly fence separating the present from the past. Madame Abulian and her girls left, all in tears, taking our half-sewn dresses with them, knowing they would never get paid. The aunties sat at the phone to call the guests. They had to make at least a hundred phone calls. Daaye and Assad went to the kitchen to find a way to do something about the two dozen turkeys that lay on the counters, legs up, bellies open, waiting to be stuffed. And they had to think about all the other dishes and snacks they had spent so much time preparing. I heard Daaye asking Assad, "But who could have done this?" And Assad telling her, "Khanum's papa. Didn't you hear what she said? Papa Vazir's ghost!"

So, why should Taara flee? Now that either Assad or Grandpa Vazir, or some other apparition, in the cruelest way (cruel to Khanum-Jaan), had cancelled the party, why should Taara run away? She could stay and continue seeing her friend on the sly as long as she wished, until they were ready for marriage. I rushed down to change. I was going to leave the house. I had to run to school and see Taara before she finished her exam and left with Vahid. If I missed her, there would be no way to find her again.

At the Intersection

I tucked my bangs into a cap and put on Uncle Vafa's shirt and pants. I had to walk by Jangi's cage and I didn't have any food to bribe him, so he followed me to the gate. As I stepped out, a white truck parked and two men took out large baskets of flowers. They asked me if the party was here. I said it was and let them take the baskets and buckets of freshly cut lilies and gladiolas inside. They asked if it was all right to leave them on the front steps behind the oak door. I said it was all right. The driver handed me a card with General Nezam El Deen's name on it.

I walked and Jangi followed me like a shadow. I ordered him to go back, but he didn't obey. After a few blocks I didn't mind his company and he felt it, sped up and walked at my side, looking up once in a while to see if everything was all right. His large almond eyes were full of wet gratitude. No one had ever taken him for a walk.

In Vafa's cotton shirt and khaki pants and a pair of thick-soled tennis shoes I felt comfortable and free. Taking long steps, the way boys did, I felt the urge to whistle or hum a tune. When I reached my old school, Mariam Catholic Institute, a flood of black-and-white-uniformed girls suddenly rushed out of the open gate. I moved back and stood behind a tree. I knew that soon the old security nun, Soeur Maria-Theresa, with her long stick would chase the strangers away from the entrance. Jangi sat next to me and we waited. It was hard to find Taara among hundreds of identical girls. I looked around and saw a man across the street, standing under the eaves of a shop. On a mild sunny day, he had on a long, white raincoat.

No doubt this was Vahid. Instead of searching for Taara, I observed him, trying to read him, to figure him out. *Let me just take a look at him, I'll tell you who he is.* Khanum's voice echoed in my head.

Vahid had a bony, cat-like face. His sea-blue eyes were wet and large, like marbles. His cheeks protruded, his hair was light and thin like a baby's. When the breeze played with its soft strands, I noticed his bald spot. He combed his hair back to cover his bare scalp. His fingers were yellow, knotty and long. He was older than I'd imagined, much older than Taara. Now he took out a cigarette and held a match under it. His yellow fingers trembled.

Taara crossed the street and approached him. She had her setar case in one hand and a black attaché in the other. A few years ago, when she began high school, Baba-Ji gave her his own attaché, the one he'd bought in London and had used for years in his teaching job. So Taara had Baba's attaché which was too big for a schoolgirl and odd to carry around. But she loved it and kept her most important papers in it.

Taara and Vahid embraced briefly, friendly but without passion. Vahid took the setar case and they walked down the street toward the intersection. I followed them and Jangi followed me like a crooked shadow. I tried not to get close to them. They slowed down sometimes, looking at the shop windows and then walked faster again. Now they were holding hands. They reached a café, "The Four Season's Ice-cream and Pastry."

Downstairs there were tables and chairs, but a narrow stairway took the customers up to a better seating area. A sign on top of the stairs said, "For families only." Taara and Vahid went up to the family section and I sat downstairs by the window. Jangi stayed outside on the sidewalk, looking at me from behind the glass. What if he started to bark? What if everyone noticed me? All the way to the cafe I'd felt invisible, and now, for the first time, I was afraid I'd be noticed.

I pulled my cap over my eyebrows and sat, waiting. The cafe was famous for its rich, oversized ice cream dishes, and my mouth watered. But I didn't have money to buy anything. People held trays full of tall deserts and took them to their tables. Soon Vahid came down, went to the counter, bought two small dishes and carried them upstairs. Taara looked calm and serene, but unhappy. I could see them holding hands and eating. Vahid murmured something and Taara nodded. I waited. I didn't go up to talk to her. I didn't tell her that her engagement had been cancelled and that she could go home now.

Finally, they descended the stairs. But Taara had forgotten her attaché, climbed the stairs again and picked it up. I watched them leave the store and then followed them. Jangi, who lay spread out on the sidewalk, woke up. On the crowded sidewalk we followed Taara and Vahid who continued to hold hands. Taara sighed now and then and nodded. She gave a pendulum movement to the attaché and adjusted her steps to the movement of her hand. At one point Vahid brought the setar case up to his chest and hugged it like a baby. As if this were my cue, I stopped following them.

"Let's go back, Jangi. Let's go home."

The dog turned and we walked back home. I hadn't told Taara that she didn't need to elope. I let her go.

At that moment I had a strange feeling that wasn't quite clear. It was freedom and despair at the same time. I hadn't played any part in my mother's leaving—she'd gone and left me behind. I hadn't played any part in my father's leaving—he'd gone without thinking about me. It wasn't I who had let Baba-Ji go—he had gone without even himself knowing. But now I had the choice of stopping my sister from leaving or letting her go, and I let her go. It was I who marked her destiny, and mine. I felt freedom and despair.

I entered Drum Tower with my friend Jangi. No one even noticed we had been out. The red and pink gladioli in the baskets and the white lilies in the buckets were waiting on the steps between the two bronze lions. These animals had been sitting here for centuries, growling and threatening the world. They had just been polished for Taara's engagement party, but no one was about to enter Drum Tower today. Their golden glow and fearsome majesty would go unappreciated.

The house was calm and I knew that the aunties were still sitting at the dining table with the endless list of guests in front of them, whispering apologies into the phone. I knew that they'd finally decided that the stars were not lined up the way they should have been, or the shape of the coffee grounds indicated gloom, and the whole thing was not meant to happen.

And I knew that Khanum-Jaan was up in her nun's room, not writing to her dead father, but lying on her soldier's bed with a camphored handkerchief on her forehead. Assad and Daaye were packing, preserving, and freezing tons of food and putting the rest in containers for the aunties to take home.

All of a sudden I missed Baba-Ji who was absent from all this commotion, forgotten by everyone. I wanted to rush up to his room, put my head on his chest and tell him that Taara was gone. But I couldn't. Instead, I went down to my room and sat on my bed, looking at the dirty courtyard and the half-ruined wall. A gust of wind blew, brick dust rose and balloons floated in the red air—some were trapped in the top branches of the trees and some gathered behind my window, sticking to the panes. It was a strange sight, balloons in the ruins and a broken brick wall—remains of a few happy days in my grandmother's joyless life.

Learning From the Spider

"It's your sister's engagement party, come out of the closet, girl! Come and look out! A ruined wall, a pile of bricks, and the stupid tower winking with red bulbs like an old whore! Come out, Talkhoon, its party time! Red and blue and yellow balloons. Look! They're all over the place. They're floating over the tower.

"You don't even wonder what happened? Huh? Or you pretend you don't? Do you wonder about anything at all? Are you really crazy? Or are you acting all the time? I know you dived from the top of the tower and then stopped talking—but haven't I heard you chatting with Daaye and Taara? So who is it you're not talking to? Me? Khanum? You put me and the old hen in one bag, huh?

"But aren't you even a bit sorry for the bitch? Don't you know what happened to her? I saw you sneak like a mouse upstairs early this morning. So you saw it. You saw how she was ruined. Finished. Do you think *I* did this to her? *I* was the one who finished her? I know that your sister told you what I promised her, so probably you think I did it. But I swear to God and all the twelve Imams that I didn't do this. You know why? Because these carpets, curtains, and paintings, and all the rest of the shit in this old, fucking fort of a house, belong to me! You laugh in your dark closet, huh? Are you laughing at me? But answer this simple question: Who has worked in this damned house for forty years? Who has kept it from falling apart? Come on, answer me! Who? Your father? Your Uncle Kia? Or your Uncle Vafa? Who?

"So, you see that the answer is as simple as the question. Why would I destroy things that belong to me? But your aunts have another theory. They say Taara has done this. You're surprised, huh? Didn't you know your sister is gone? Eloped, so to speak? Yes sir, she e-l-o-p-e-d! With that junky guy—the man with a white raincoat and nothing else. The vagabond, as your grandmother would call him. But Khanum doesn't know this. She hasn't come out of her room to know that her little Taara has not come back from school. No sir, she never returned. Stupid, blockheaded idiot! Didn't I promise her I would postpone her engagement? Didn't I? But she didn't trust me. I had a plan for tonight. Not to ruin the house, but to postpone the whole thing for six months in a quiet, respectable way, and who knows what would happen in six months? But she went and got herself ruined. She's ruined, Talkhoon. Finished! I know these guys who stand in front of the girls' high schools with a cigarette between their lips and love notes in their pockets. I know them. I've been in the streets myself. They're tramps. That's what they are. Vagabonds!

"But now the aunties think Taara ruined the house before she eloped. These old, fat turkeys don't have enough brains in their bald heads to see that no puny girl could have done this alone. So, what am I saying? That the ghost of Grandpa Vazir did it? He floated in the air in his tuxedo and marked everything with the tip of his fucking tar-stained cane? No, I don't believe in ghosts, and frankly I can't figure out who did this shit! And besides, the ivory cane is with me. How could Papa Vazir possibly possess the cane when it is in the real world and not in the fucking ghost world. The cane is where all the other stuff is and only Assad knows where.

"So, what I mean is, I don't have a clue as to how to solve this mystery. Who would ruin the priceless objects of Drum Tower, free Taara from a forced marriage, and kill Khanum-Jaan when she was gaining her youth back? The old hen is not going to unbend her hunched back. She is done for.

"So, as you can see for yourself, your sister and your grandmother are done for. Our dear Baba has been done for since the last Norooz; I don't think anybody remembers to fix his hose and feed him anymore. Your father is done for. They're arresting all the lefties and executing them without a trial. How long can he stay underground? Your Mommy is done

for, and that's a long messy story you don't want to know. Your Uncle Kia
will be done for in his own time, when this government finally falls. Your
Uncle Vafa is totally done for—they're arresting and killing these so-called
Moslem Marxists too.

"So, who remains in the house of drums, huh? Assad the servant and
Talkhoon the mad. It's a good match, isn't it? Now if you don't come out
today, you'll have to come out tomorrow. If not tomorrow, then the day
after. I'm sending Daaye back to her village to live out her old age in peace
and quiet. The poor woman has suddenly aged. So it's just you and me,
bitter herb. Assad and Talkhoon. And Assad is a very patient man. He can
wait."

I stayed up all night in the dark and looked at the tower twinkling with red
bulbs. A twisting wind circled in my head, alternately sweeping away all
my thoughts and forcing me to think about everything at the same time.
He'll get you one day, he'll get you! A voice not unlike a parrot's repeated the
phrase. *Fear is the brother of death*, Baba answered calmly. *On the balcony of
the tower I play my setar and listen,* Taara sang.

"I dreamed, I dreamed!" Khanum screamed and broke out of her room.

It was dawn and in that liquid blue the spider's web glowed. This
silver net had always been here, but now I saw it as if for the first time. I
found the spider, that tiny creature, hanging on her own web. And I sat
very close to watch.

She knew what she was doing, this spider. With a neon orange band
around her neck, with protruding eyes, she shined in the blue light,
hanging like a tightrope artist from her web. She used her silk, her own
substance, to build a house. Watching her circular movement, I realized
that the spider's web-weaving was a dance. Into the circle and out on a line,
back to the circle and out—another line. I could even hear the repetition of
a rhythm, the music of the spheres. In this way the spider wove a precise
diamond-shaped net, all along hanging on her own silk.

*Are you less than a spider, then? Can't you weave your own life, your own
home, out of the substance of your own self?*

Gently, I blew on the spider's web. It felt the breeze, stopped weaving, listened to the wind and became absolutely motionless, then went on. Into the circle and out in the line, restlessly, until the diamond was large, wide, made of many smaller diamonds and a transparent web covered the space between the two walls. The spider had made her home.

Before the sun rose higher, I set to work. I took a pair of scissors and cut my bangs and the semi-circle of a doll's hair around my face. In the mirror I saw a twelve-year old boy. Good enough. Anything but a girl! I tucked Vafa's old shirt into the khaki pants and put on the cap. Now I slipped the gold chain with the little hanging bird—my father's New Year present—into my pocket. I had to pawn it for some money. I took some dried bread, fed the dog, and while he munched sleepily, I left the house.

Before crossing the street, I turned back and looked at Drum Tower. Upstairs, behind the window, Baba-Ji lay in his old recliner. Someone had moved him back again, someone had denied him the possibility of opening his eyes and seeing the world. Now I looked at the morning sky to see if by any chance the Simorgh was coming, if she was here to see that I was leaving her house, not on her wings, but on my own feet. But the sky was cloudless and the bird was nowhere around.

Book II

Circular Flights

I am where I was: Within the indecisive walls
of that same patio of words.

—Octavio Paz

Assad's Blue Bird

Even from inside the closet I smelled his odor when he entered the room—vodka, sweat, and the grease of a lamb dish he had brought for me. He burped, sat on my bed, and called, "Talkhoon, where are you?" knowing very well where I was.

"You're a crazy little devil, you know that? Wild and stubborn, like your mother. Come out this minute, or else!" He laughed. *"Or else?* Am I going to spank you or what? No. Not when you're injured like this. Not now. But I'm warning you! I'll hit your bony ass if you think about escaping again. Now come out and eat. You haven't eaten anything for a long time. When was it I caught you getting on the train? Two nights ago? And since then you've been sitting in this closet, on strike. Like the post office and the taxis and the factories outside. All on strike! You're doing your revolution here, girl—you even broke the window and cut your hands! But I'm patient with you—am I not? Don't you think I can drag you out by force if I want to?"

Now he laughed again and burped. He was half drunk, working to get fully drunk.

"I caught you with that fucking ticket in your hand. Where were you heading? To Bandar?" he chuckled, and then talked more to himself. "Children believe in fairy tales you feed them. She was going to find her Mommy," he told himself, "because I'd told her Mommy was in the Big Sheikh's harem!"

Through the hole of the closet door I saw Assad's face, blood red, unreal. In a moment he could pull me out and do whatever he wished, or he could remain calm, act motherly, and scold me for not eating my food. He could slap me the way he did in the train station, or he could remain grumpy like an old nurse. He was unpredictable. Now he panted, talked to me, talked to himself, and drank from the bottle. Through the circle of the hole, I saw a small portion of the broken window. The parrot sat behind the shattered glass as she had the first day she guarded my room, but now she was blind and cageless, one twig of a leg chained to the metal post.

"I didn't realize you'd left. I was cleaning up the mess from the party. The party that never happened! Then I came down with a tray of dinner for you. You were not here. I panicked. The first thing came to my mind was, *She did what her stupid sister did—escaped!* So I ran upstairs and knocked on Khanum's door. She had locked herself in. I knocked and knocked, until she opened the door a crack. I told her what had happened. She didn't know about Taara, either. I told her that first Taara and then Talkhoon had run away. She just stood there, pale as a ghost and shaky, like a sick child. 'Go get them, Assad!' That was all she said. But that toughness was not in her voice. There was something else that made me feel sorry for the old hen. In spite of what she'd written in her letters about me, I felt sorry for her when her voice broke like that. I said, 'I can't get the older one, she's eloped with someone and I don't have a clue where they are. But I can guess where Talkhoon has gone. She's gone to find her mother in Bandar—the Big Sheikh's castle. If you give me some money to get on the night train, I'll go and get her for you.'

"Now listen to this, because this is when your grandmother disclaimed you. I swear to all the twelve sacred imams that this is exactly what she told me. She said, 'You don't get Talkhoon for me, Assad, you get her for yourself. She is no relation to me; you know that. And I don't have a black coin on me. I'm ruined; you know this too.' And she banged the door on me.

"But now a strange thing happened, as strange as that whole day and night. I was standing in front of the main gate, debating whether to go alone to find you, or call my friends to help me. Because I thought you'd either fled on the bus or the train; you couldn't afford a plane ticket. But I couldn't go to the bus station and the train station at the same time. I needed help. I decided to call the boys at the mosque and send a couple of them to the bus station and take one or two with me to the train station.

But as I was standing in the dark night, thinking hard, I heard a scream, a familiar ear-piercing scream. This was Boor-boor. I strained and listened some more. She cried again. Wasn't she dead? Hadn't she gone with the flood, or fled to India—as Khanum had said? I paced up and down the sidewalk and listened. The bird was calling me. I stopped by a neighbor's door. Her cry was coming from that house. I went inside and asked for my bird and they had to give it to me. You know what had happened? When the storm lifted the cage, it landed in the neighbor's yard and the parrot was there all the time. But the cage was broken and the poor bird had lost one of her eyes. So I took her home and rushed with Mustafa's van to the train station. I sent Karim and Morad to the bus station. I trust these boys; they're God-fearing men, my brothers at the mosque—we're forming a vigilante group to guard the neighborhood.

"Anyway, you know the rest of the story. I came to the train station and saw you sitting on the bench, next to this family, with a ticket for Bandar in your hand. You were in a boy's clothes—small and cute and worried-looking, sticking to this mother of seven children who sat on the bench with her kids hanging on her chador. Had you left with one of the earlier trains, I'd have had to spend money and travel all the way to the end of the world to find you. I told Mustafa, 'That's her, that's my girl, but let's wait and see what she's up to. If we approach her now she may scream and make a scene. She's a wild cat and crazy as hell.'"

Assad was right. I was crazy enough to spend sixteen hours in the streets, wasting my time. After I sold the gold chain and put the money in my pocket, I walked on the wide sidewalks, enjoying the spring sun. I took long steps, watched myself in the store windows, and whistled like a boy. I was going to Bandar to find my mother. She'd take me in, but I'd remain a boy, living in the Sheikh's castle. I walked, whistled, and fantasized about my future, but when dusk came and I heard bullets cracking in the air, I panicked and took a taxi to the train station. I bought a ticket for Bandar and sat close to a large family, pretending to be with them.

For a long time I watched everything hungrily. I hadn't seen much in my life. People rushed to their destination—families, single men, but no woman alone. I felt safe and happy in my disguise, and grateful that this family with many children was travelling with me. The train's rusty, panting body, just a few steps away from me, gave out a hot, steamy sigh, promising to take me to a new life. I sat and watched and took in the odor of the smoke and a faint scent of rose-water that was evaporating from the woman's clean chador. I didn't think of Drum Tower, my family, my past, or even Baba-Ji and his Simorgh. The present was all there was, and the yellow, blurry picture of the future lay beneath the haze of the train smoke.

But the moment I was about to climb the steps of the train, a heavy hand landed on my shoulder and pulled me down. I didn't even turn to see who he was. I smelled him—vodka, grease and sweat. I jerked my shoulders and ran, but another man, someone I didn't know, blocked my way. I screamed when the man twisted my arm behind my back. People gathered around us and Assad yelled at them and said, "What are you looking at, huh? She's a runaway. We're taking her back home." Now he came straight toward me and slapped me right and left. I burned with shame, not because of the slaps, but because he had called me a "runaway." Suddenly I felt naked and weak. I was just a little girl and all these people knew that. Assad and his friend pushed me into a black van and took me home. The minute I was in my room I waved my hands crazily in the air and destroyed the spider's house. I broke the web with my fingers, ruined the diamond-shaped patterns, and let the spider fall on the floor. Then I stamped on it. Now, in a growing rage, I put my fists through the dusty window, breaking the glass. Sharp shards tore my hands and blood gushed out. My arms were unaware of my body and acted on their own. An unfriendly wind circled in my head and ordered my hands to smash the glass. Assad rushed down and wrapped my hands in towels and took me to a nearby clinic. I sat on a tall, narrow bed and a doctor took the pieces of glass out of my flesh and sewed up the cuts.

"I'm going to stitch you up in such a way that these ugly scars stay with you for the rest of your life!" the bald doctor said. "I want you to grow up and look at these rough lines and remember how crazy you were!" He said this and looked at me as if everything that had ever happened to me had been my own fault.

The parrot behind the window fluttered her wings and Assad snored until an explosion in the street woke him up.

"Shit. I fell asleep." He looked at his watch. "It's nine-thirty. I have to leave. We have a meeting tonight. I guess when I leave you'll come out and eat. You won't starve yourself, will you?" He yawned and stretched his arms. "One of these days I'll send the witch to her sisters. That's where she belongs. Let the three witches live together and tell each other's fortunes and call the fucking ghosts. What's left for Khanum in Drum Tower, huh? I have to make a decision about Baba-Ji, too. I can't feed him his yellow water forever. I'm busy at the mosque now; I don't have time. I have to find a hospital for him. Then I'll make this basement into a shop with a window right here, where the closet is. I'll open a neighborhood store. Yes, that's what I'm planning to do. A corner store with some groceries, bread, and some plastic toys for kids. And eventually I'll flatten the garden and make apartment houses and rent them out. Then you and me will move upstairs, not to the master bedroom where your parents lived, no, not that cursed bedroom, we'll move to the bedroom next to Baba's study and land on that huge brass bed your grandparents never used. You'll be my wife and I'll be your husband and we'll produce a dozen cute children and we'll become rich! What do you say, huh? Let the witch go to her witch sisters, girly—let her go!

"But first I have to read the last stack of the old hen's letters. Ever since Papa messed up her house she's been writing to him like crazy. Now I'm sure that you're a bastard and not from my own blood. The next thing is to find the old fart's will! There must be more than Drum Tower, much more. She must have land. Acres of it." He chuckled to himself and re-peated, "Yes sir, acres—" and picked up my sleeping gown and smelled it.

There was silence for a while, then with a shaky, muffled voice, he said, "Come out, for God's sake, I need you! Don't you think I can pull you out the way I pulled you off that train? No, I won't do that. I want you to be my wife and I don't want to mess with you before we're married. But what if I did? Who'd care, huh? You wouldn't tell anyone, because you don't have a tongue!" He laughed, held the gown in front of the light, and looked through it. "Maybe we could just do it without anyone knowing, even without you knowing, while you're sleeping. Like a while ago when I slipped under your blanket and pressed myself against your bony body. You were drugged and you didn't wake up. But no, I'm a God-fearing man, His vigilante, His devotee, at His service, and I want to marry my girl and see her blood on the handkerchief the first night of my honeymoon. I'm waiting for that night and I'm trying to be patient. But my bird—my bird is crushing me under its weight—"

Now he was directly in front of the hole and I could see all of him, except for his crooked legs. He slipped down his pants and underpants and pulled his shirt up. On his lower belly, under his navel a blue bird was tattooed—wings open to either side of his waist, long tail extended down to the bushy hair of his private parts: a caricature of the Simorgh. His penis was erect, horizontal, and moved up and down. It was as if the bird's tail moved, or it was about to take flight.

I held my breath and covered my mouth to keep from uttering a sound. He buried his face in my gown and the tail of the bird kept moving. Then he dropped himself on the bed, pressed his body against my mattress, and gave out a loud moan. He was not even afraid that Khanum-Jaan might hear him. Then he turned on his back and covered the bird with my gown, crying, "I want you, I want you, I want you, damn girl! But don't you dare come out, because I'll eat you!"

Dreaming Awake

Khanum-Jaan didn't go to her sisters as Assad had wished. She knew if she left, she would lose her house. She even stopped going to the central bazaar for the regular monthly shopping, saying her eyes were bad, she couldn't see well. For the small amount of groceries we needed, she sent Assad to a nearby market.

All through the summer, I heard the clicking of her slippers upstairs, roaming the half-empty rooms, even the empty third-floor rooms, not taking inventory anymore (because there wasn't much left to make a list), but searching for her lost play room, the almond room. I heard her talking to herself, or to her dead father. I heard her dreaming while awake.

"—then the earth opened and she popped out, stark naked as Eve—her thick unnatural hair clothed her, wrapping around her like a blanket. Papa descended the tower's steps. He was in his white suit and white Panama hat, a cigar in the corner of his mouth, like the time he traveled to Mexico and came back with such a suit and a big cigar. The girl rose, spring breeze playing with the silk curtain of her hair. Papa approached her. I was on top of the tower all this time, watching, a heavy golden egg in my arms—the Simorgh's egg— and I was bent under its heavy weight, as if I was pregnant and my belly was pulling me down. I thought if Papa touched the girl, I'd drop the egg, and if I dropped the egg, the world would end—"

She dreamed this way at least two or three times a day. *Click, click, click*—she came down to the porch sometimes and I heard her dreaming aloud over my head. The evening breeze took her words to the garden, or if the day was still, the images sank into my basement room.

All through the summer, at dusk, Assad swept the courtyard, spread a small rug on the brick floor behind my window, and prayed. He said he prayed in the yard because he wanted to be close to God and to me.

Some nights I heard his slippers and woke and sat alert, but he wasn't coming to my room. He was either carrying things in a burlap sack on his shoulder, or toting heavy boxes in his arms, limping in the dark. This happened more frequently and I was used to seeing him with all kinds of loads now.

Doctor Shafa prescribed new pills for me and so I lost count of my dreamless nights and no winds blew in my foggy head. The cuts on my hands healed but many crisscross lines remained—the scars that would stay with me the rest of my life. The spider, or another spider, wove a new web between the two walls of my room, but the insect and its net didn't mean anything to me. The spider was a spider and a web, a web; there was no meaning behind them. The first autumn winds blew behind the new windowpanes and, after a long time, Boor-boor screamed, announcing the new season. She demanded a secure cage. Jangi bayed like a wolf every night, smelling the fresh snow that sat on the peaks of the distant mountains.

But as long as Khanum-Jaan was home, I couldn't go up to visit Baba-Ji. I hadn't seen my grandfather since before my failed flight. Last year at this time he was awake, working at a slow but steady pace. Taara and I spent most of our time in his room, copying his manuscript. Last year at this time Uncle Vafa hadn't married yet, Father hadn't come to hide in the pantry room, Taara hadn't left, Assad hadn't sent Daaye away. We were happy sometimes—we laughed once in a while. Now the change of season, the winter's sweet smell, brought memories of the last year back.

I sat in my room alert. I meant to hide if Assad approached. At times, I watched the spider and her mechanical dance, or stared at the web-like stitches on my hands. I thought how this year seemed like a lifetime. I measured the time, as if time were measurable.

At night, most nights, there were the sounds of gunshots in the streets and, lately, the rattle of machine guns. Once or twice the windowpanes shook because of the bombs that went off nearby. I sat still and tried to hear my father's footsteps upstairs and Khanum's scream of joy. He came on such a night last year.

One morning, Assad came down and told me that the terrorists had bombed a government building nearby. He said that Uncle Vafa and his wife had disappeared. They had gone underground.

The next morning he brought my breakfast down, shouting, "News, news!" His white apron made him look like a fat peasant cook. "I have news for you, Talkhoon. They're arresting your uncle's gang. Today they executed ten terrorists; maybe Vafa was among them."

I knew that Khanum silently grieved for her sons, Vafa and Sina, and I knew she missed Taara, no matter how hard she cursed her ungrateful soul. Uncle Kia visited his mother every Thursday afternoon. They sat together in Baba-Ji's room (the only room with some furniture), sipped dark tea and whispered. I imagined Khanum sighing, crying, and Uncle Kia advising her, feeding her his own version of the political situation, scaring her with his stories of Moslem rebels and left-wing guerrillas.

All through the autumn Assad went to the mosque every day and practiced target shooting and learned bomb making; he came back in the evening to cook and make his last prayer of the day in the courtyard behind my window. In the month of Moharram, the month of mourning, he wore a black shirt every day and let his beard grow full. He talked less, prayed more, and adopted a somber mood.

Khanum-Jaan didn't receive visitors anymore. She asked why the aunties, who were better off, didn't invite people over to their place. She wrote her father compulsively and her fifth stack of letters became thicker than the rest.

So I sat in my room all day, looking at the one-eyed, cageless parrot that was chained to my window, her head hidden in her feathers. Was anything going to happen? Was anything going to break the chain of monotonous days and nights that slowly, but inevitably, carried me toward my end? I'd given up on finding the sapphire feather, and I knew that even if I had it and burned a barb, nothing would happen if nothing was supposed to happen. The spider wove her massive web because she was a spider. Her job was simple; mine was not. She was free; I was not.

But I always knew that when nothing was happening, something was about to happen. This was the pattern of life. Jangi pressed his face against my window, his wet eyes begging for food. I gave him most of my meals and he became my sole companion.

Now I began to take long walks in the garden and Jangi followed me like a shadow. I strolled in every corner, the spots I'd never seen before. The decayed garden was wet every morning, with dew or light rain. I stepped on moist yellow leaves and found my way through tangled twigs to the dark, virgin corners. I still feared the ghost of Great Grandma Negaar, but what could the ghost of a weak, paralyzed woman do to me? So I went to the dark spots, places that even Jangi didn't want to go, and I didn't murmur, *Ghosts don't exist*, or *Fear is the brother of death*.

On one of these long walks I learned that Drum Tower had another gate on the eastern end of the garden. The sun and rain of many decades had rotted the wood, and twigs and the leaves of dried ivy had hidden it from my eyes.

Did I think about escaping? I thought about it obsessively, but didn't know how to do it. I knew that sooner or later, in their unannounced battle, Assad would defeat Khanum and she would agree to leave the house and join her sisters. Assad constantly scared her by recounting the shootings and bombings that were happening in the streets, and Uncle Kia, not knowing what a service he did for Assad, frightened her even more. Maybe one of these days she would simply die — of grief, of defeat, of bankruptcy, of dreaming awake. She would die of immense unhappiness, of loss.

I knew that one day Assad would arrange our marriage. A night would come that he would take me upstairs to my grandparents' bedroom and throw me on the bed and rip his pants open. Then I'd imagine myself, shabby-looking, beaten and half crazy, with twelve butt-naked children hanging on me, working in the hot kitchen to fill the urchins' bottomless bellies. I'd imagine Assad as the grocer and the slumlord, selling over-priced groceries to poor people and forcing the tenants of his numerous apartments to pay more rent.

I walked in the garden, pictured the future, and listened to the *squeak, squeak* of Great Grandma Negaar's wheelchair following me. She was trapped in this garden too. I walked toward the brick tower, but I never climbed the steps to the top. I knew that no bird had nested there, that no Simorgh had left a sapphire feather. All the songs and legends of the Bird of Knowledge, all the names of the birds of all the nations of the world were lost to me. All I knew about Grandfather's Simorgh book was forgotten. Since Baba-Ji's fall into silence, chaos and confusion had reigned. So I walked around the tower and thought about the Simorgh without being able to remember what the bird was.

All through the fall, hard winds blew in my head.

Father in the Closet

On a cold and cloudy morning—one of the first mornings of winter—Assad brought my breakfast and some kerosene to light my small heater. He said he was taking Khanum-Jaan to the eye doctor. She had finally agreed to get glasses—now she couldn't see what was close to her, either. He said he would convince her to stay at her sisters' for a few days until her glasses were ready. He left, and a few minutes later I heard the Cadillac pulling out. I rushed outside, peeked from behind the wall and saw the back of

Grandmother's head. Her hair was all white. She had stopped dyeing it.

When they left, panic came. Assad would convince Khanum-Jaan to stay with her sisters and I'd be left alone in Drum Tower with him. I had to escape. So I rushed upstairs to see my grandfather, say farewell, and leave. But as I reached the dim vestibule, there was the crack of thunder shaking the walls. Somewhere on the second floor or the third, doors opened and closed. Now I heard the harsh rain whipping the top branches of the trees. I had to leave in this wild weather and plunge myself into the flood that would carry me to an unknown place. But as I approached the double oaken door, the house trembled and staggered, the tall door opened by itself, and the wind gusted, sweeping someone inside. It was Father, wrapped in fog like the jinni of the magic lantern.

He asked me to hide him and I did. I took him to my room and showed him the closet. He said the secret police were chasing him. He said that nobody except me should know he was here. If anyone came down, I should stay silent.

Did Father know that this was the way I lived? Staying silent?

He squeezed his wet body inside the narrow closet among my childhood clothes and I sat on my bed, guarding the door. Outside, pistols exploded with dry sounds and rain turned into gentle snow. After a long while, Father pushed the closet door open and talked.

"I had nowhere to go. This is the worst place I could hide. But I was around here when the shooting began. Fortunately no one is home. Why didn't you go to school? Where is Taara?"

I didn't answer his first question, but I said, "Taara is gone."

"Where?"

"With a man."

"Married?"

"No."

"Ran away?"

"Yes."

He was quiet for a long time and I couldn't see his face. He was in a dark box, like a priest listening to a confession, and I was on the other side, like the sinner. I'd seen this at Mariam Catholic School and I'd always wished I could be the one in the box, listening to people's secrets. Now the one in the box, the Father, began.

"Who is the man?"

"Vahid."

"That's it?"

"Yes."

"What happened to her setar?"

"She took it with her."

He was quiet again. Taara—his favorite, his talented bard.

"How is my mother?"

"Went to the eye doctor."

"Oh, yes, her eyes. I always told her—years ago I told her to get a pair of glasses. She neglected it. And Father?"

"Sleeping."

"Now? He doesn't work anymore?"

"No."

"Who could imagine the day that my father wouldn't write anymore?" He said in a whisper to himself. "His hands must be shaking. They were shaking badly last year."

"Not anymore," I said.

Outside, the bullets whistled and someone shrieked. Then it was silence, such an absolute silence that we could hear the soft snow landing.

"They're arresting everybody. They're desperate—that's why they stop people in the streets and check their cards. I arrived last night. A mistake. I could've stayed in Baluchistan, where your uncle is—your mother's brother. He is a brave man. He has lived with a native Baluchi tribe for twenty years. I was with him in the desert, trying to organize the tribesmen. Then I lost contact with my friends in Tehran. I came to see what's happening. I didn't know they were arresting people. I should've stayed with your uncle." He paused for a long time, then asked, "How is Vafa?"

"Disappeared," I said.

"I knew it! They're underground. Foolish boy! Revolution and religion are two sides of the same coin. They'll never meet. Do you understand these things, Talkhoon? Do they teach you about the revolution at school, or make a taboo out of the word? But I've seen students sliding flyers under the doors.

"You see, religion means no change, stagnant water, water left to stink. Dogma. Revolution means change, transformation, flowing water, air, freedom. The justice Vafa is seeking remains in the pages of his holy book—if it's even written there—but my revolution has happened in the world and has changed people's lives."

He continued lecturing from the closet and I sat on the bed, watched the snow, and listened. He asked me if I would like to hear a poem he'd written about the revolution. I said I would. He read it with a voice rising from the depths of the darkness. The phrases were sad and I didn't understand them well, nor could I link one to the other, but the train of words and the pauses in between reminded me of the rhythm of my life last year—Baba-Ji falling asleep and I throwing myself out of the tower; Grandmother refusing to speak to me and I keeping silent ever since; Ta-ara leaving and I letting her go; I making it to the train station, but Assad bringing me back.

I didn't hear anything in my father's poem saying that the revolution was coming or was going to change the world. Maybe I missed those parts, maybe his voice and the train of the words took me with them, took me somewhere else that belonged only to me. Maybe I heard the poem the way I wanted.

Now he asked about everyone except me. He didn't wonder anymore why I was home or why my room was in the basement and in such chaos.

Did he love me at all? Or did he know I was not his child? (How could he not know, when everyone else knew?) Wasn't even this little attention he paid to me a favor? I was not related to him—was I? Who was I to him, if I wasn't his child? Did he love my mother so much that he loved her bastard child? Was he really *majnoon*—love crazy? He didn't seem to be. All he cared about was his revolution, and now he was explaining it. He was saying that it was happening, slowly, but eventually it would pick up pace. He said this house was not safe for us and he promised to take all of us to an apartment. He said if he survived today, next time he'd come and take us with him.

In the afternoon he said he was hungry. He sent me upstairs to bring him food and to look around to see if his mother or Assad had some cash somewhere. He needed money for a taxi to go to his friends' house.

I brought him some food—cold meat, bread and yogurt, but I couldn't find any money and I didn't have any. He asked me to lend him the gold chain—my last year's New Year present. He could pawn it across the street and get some money. I said it was lost. He became upset. I could tell this from the cold tone of his voice.

Assad and Khanum didn't come. I was sure they were at the aunties' where Assad would try to convince Khanum to stay for a while. Father would leave and Assad would come back to marry me. Father had wasted my day. I could have been far away from Drum Tower by now.

Early in the evening, when a layer of fresh snow covered the court-yard's brick floor and dusk painted everything dark blue, Father came out of the closet to leave. He said he had to walk all the way to the end of the city, so he'd better start now. His voice was cold and remote—he was sulking about the gold chain, as if that were the only thing that could save his life, as if I were responsible for his eventual arrest. He said he was going upstairs to see if he could find money or something he could sell. I told him that the house was empty. He was shocked.

"What do you mean?"

"Everything is gone."

"What do you mean, gone?" he said angrily.

"Just a few things left."

"What did my mother do with everything?"

"She didn't do anything."

"Then what happened? Can't you make longer sentences, Talkhoon?"

"They disappeared. Kept disappearing. Now they've all disappeared."

"I don't understand. Three floors full of antiques disappeared?"

"See for yourself."

He went up and came back in ten minutes, shaking his head in regret. He had taken a bottle of chilled vodka from Assad's icebox. He shoved it inside his shabby overcoat.

"Mother must have sold them. She must have needed money desperately. I saw Baba sleeping in his study, but didn't wake him up. It would be a shock for the old man to see me. But too much sleeping is worrisome. He might be depressed. He was always a little depressed. And now Vafa is in danger. Not to speak of me. And I know that Kia is not much help.

The bastard! If I had his money and position, I'd do something for my old parents. Now I have to go, Talkhoon. Give this poem to Taara. Tell her this is my birthday present for her. Tell her to read the poem carefully and try to make music for it. Tell her to practice her setar." He handed me a white sheet of paper, folded in four. Then he murmured again, "I can't believe she's gone. Did you ever see the...the boy?"

"He's a man."

"What do you mean?"

"He wears a white rain coat," I said. "Smokes."

For the first time Father looked at me carefully, as if suspecting that something was wrong with me. But he didn't have time to stay and find out.

"You've lost weight again. You look like a skeleton. Girls your age— how old are you now? Almost seventeen, huh? Girls your age are arming themselves. They're getting ready for the revolution. Haven't you heard anything, Talkhoon? At school?" Then, in a sudden rush of something like affection, he took my hands in his big hands but didn't hold them long enough to feel the roughness of the stitches, the lines that would stay with me forever. "Take care of yourself, okay?"

I didn't tell him that this was exactly what I did all the time—took care of myself. He left. I didn't follow him to the gate. I watched him from the window. He had on the same old suit and the same crooked shoes he had worn the last time I saw him. A shabby, once black, now gray overcoat had been added. His hair, once salt and pepper, was all white, like the snow on the ground. He left like a vagabond, without a penny in his pock-et, hugging a stolen bottle of vodka.

I felt sorry for him and blamed myself for selling the gold chain to es-cape to a fairytale land in search of my nonexistent mother. As the evening turned into a white night, my remorse changed to rage and then guilt. Why couldn't I help my father? He was walking in the dark, cold streets, with police on every corner. I wept and forgot about Assad's eventual arrival. Outside the sky was light gray, reflecting the snow that glowed on the courtyard's floor. Night never came. I couldn't stand it anymore, so I ran barefoot to the cold garden, toward the tower. I climbed the steps and stood on the roof. The snow was thicker here; my feet were ankle deep in it, freezing. I raised my head and looked at the ashen sky. Something told me that the Simorgh was an irrelevant notion, not worth thinking about. Baba-Ji was crazy. He was a scholar who had become obsessed with the subject of his research and made his family obsessed too. He ruined our lives, wasted our time. It was the revolution I should have sought—the real happening, the thing that was being made in the streets, and I was ignorant of it.

Haven't you heard about the revolution?

How could I have heard about anything if I was in the basement day and night? I'd just heard the bullets and the distant explosions. But I had to see it, learn it. So I came down from the tower and ran through the slush and freezing snow to my room. I had to disguise myself before Assad arrived. A boy would be in danger on such a night. I wore Grandmother's clothes, the same black shirt and skirt I had brought with me when I stole the last stack of her letters. But my hair, my damn hair again. It was neither a boy's nor a girl's. I wished I had one of the aunties' wigs. I found a scarf, put it on, and headed toward the gate. Jangi shook himself and splashed dirty water on me. I became angry with him, shoved him and chased him away. I reached the gate and stepped outside. I was about to cross the street when a blinding light made me stop. It was as if it stripped me, seeing my insides as with an X-ray. A car pulled up very close. I stepped back, it moved forward and almost crushed me against the iron gate. Assad from the driver's side and his friend, Mustafa, from the passenger's side jumped out, ran at me, and grabbed me by the arms.

"Look! She's wearing her grandmother's dress! The lunatic bastard! You can go, Mustafa, I'll teach her a lesson."

Contemplating Murder

He dropped me on the bed and slapped me on both cheeks, then grabbed the collar of Grandmother's silk shirt and ripped it down to the waist. He rolled me on my face, straddled me with his knees, and pulled the black skirt up. He spanked me with his big, rough hand and spat angry words from between his teeth.

"I warned you the first time, didn't I? I said I'd spank you if you didn't behave. Didn't I warn you, damnit?" He hit me, and cursed. "So this means I can't trust you. I have to tie you to the bed before I leave." As he said this, he pulled a checkered handkerchief out of his pocket and tied my wrists behind my back. Now he found Grandmother's scarf and tied my ankles to the bedpost. "I have work to do. I'm very busy these days. The mosque has given me a huge responsibility and I have to prove that I can handle it. They're going to give me a gun tonight, and soon I'll be wearing a uniform." He got off the bed, wiped his sweat and examined the door. "The damn lock is broken. I'll have to fix it later. I'll be back in few hours."

Just before leaving, he pulled the skirt down over my butt and laughed, not his usual, silly laugh, but a bitter, angry one. "Wearing the old hen's clothes, huh? I have to take her fancy wardrobe to her sisters'. She'll need it, because she's not coming back. Oh, by the way, first thing in the morning my Brothers will be moving in and there'll be two men guarding the gate. So don't you ever imagine running away! Are you listening to me? We have occupied this house. Poor people are occupying rich people's houses all around the city. This is my house now. I just need to find the fucking document and put my name on it. The country doesn't have any law now." He said this and dragged his booted foot behind him. "God loves me because He knows that I'm His devotee. How could I catch you both times you escaped if He didn't love me? Huh? So, don't stir because He's watching you for me!" He said this and banged the door.

Most of the long night, I lay half-naked on my belly, drifting into sleep. Then I heard long nails scratching the windowpanes. It was Jangi behind the window, his long tongue hanging out, his wet eyes begging. *Old friend, I'm tied up, I can't come out and feed you*, I whispered, and drifted into a light sleep. It had been a long time since I'd slept.

The pressure of a heavy weight woke me up. It was on my back, a tractor pressing me into the ground, burying me alive. It was dark, I couldn't see anything, but I could smell sweat, vodka, and grease. He forced my head into the pillow and cursed. He had untied my wrists and ankles, but with his weight on me, I couldn't move. His prickly, unshaven face brushed my neck.

"Damn you, damn you and your mother who ruined my life! Damn both of you!"

He pressed my head down with his right hand, pulled up my skirt and said, "No, I won't mess with your virginity now—that's for the wedding night. But how about your little ass?" He spanked me and I screamed, but into the pillow, into my own mouth.

Tearing winds blew inside me and released their old voices, but I was deaf and couldn't hear; I was blind and couldn't see. I was empty—the winds filled me and I lost all my senses.

Now I heard the sound of a spoon nervously hitting the side of a drinking glass. He dissolved something in water, turned me over, lifted my head and brought the glass to my mouth.

"Drink it! Come on!"

I took a sip.

"The whole damn thing!"

I drank the bitter water.

"It's your own stuff, your pills. Sleep! I have to take a nap too. I have work to do early in the morning." He said this and collapsed on my bed. I moved to the edge and when I heard his snores, tiptoed to the desk. There was a handgun next to his key chain. Khanum's marble box was on the desk too. I sat, half-naked, staring at the gun. The pills would cloud my head any minute and I'd fall asleep. I had only a short time to act—maybe a few seconds. I could lift the gun, wrap it in a shirt and shoot him so that no one would hear anything. But what if I collapsed and fell asleep? His friends who were guarding the gate would come in and find us. They'd throw me in jail for murder.

Or, I could shoot him first, then shoot myself. But how absurd my short life would be. Having found nothing. Having gone nowhere. Did I find the sapphire feather of the Bird of Knowledge? Did I find my mother? Did I find my father's revolution? Did I wake Baba-Ji?

It wasn't easy to kill. After death—my death or his—things would cease happening. I had to make things happen. Maybe I could get out of here somehow. Maybe I could find Taara—she'd play her setar and sooth my pains. Maybe Father would write a long poem, recite it, and say it was meant for me. Maybe I could walk on a long street, carefree, my hands in my pockets, whistling a tune. Maybe a brown-skinned woman would stop me in the street and ask, "Are you Talkhoon?" I'd nod and she'd say, "I'm your mother, Soraya! I've been searching for you!" Maybe Baba-Ji would wake up, comb his white hair, turn on his Firebird music, and sit at his lap desk and finish the last chapter of his book. Maybe he'd raise his head from his manuscript, gaze at me and say, "Talkhoon, did you doubt? Did you ever doubt the Bird of Knowledge?"

Winds howled in my head and dark clouds filled my skull. Now even if I wanted to stretch my arm and pick up the gun, I couldn't. Too much thinking. Wasted time. I lay my heavy head on the desk, thinking that everyone that I'd ever loved was frozen in time. Baba, Taara, Vafa, Daaye, Father—even Khanum-Jaan. Only us, this man and I, were still alive. This man, who was not my half uncle anymore, who was not that dumb, dirty-looking Uncle Assad anymore; only this man, who was a complete stranger, and I, Talkhoon, the bitter-blood, were moving in time. Things happened only here, in this basement room, to us.

The Vine-Covered Gate

I heard the unmistakable sound of teeth biting into an apple and opened my eyes. I saw him sitting with his back against the desk, facing the bed, eating a red apple.

"Did you sleep enough?" he asked, munching. "You slept like a stone! I have to go now. As I said yesterday, I'm bringing the boys here today. So behave yourself. Don't leave your room unless I tell you. Your grandfather is going to stay in his room until I find a vacant space in a hospital for him. Hospitals are full these days; we have to wait. But I'm checking on him regularly. He's still alive! Poor Baba-Ji. All of Khanum's antiques are gone, except for this last piece. No one wants him!"

He took another bite of the apple and threw the rest on my desk. Then he picked up his handgun and shoved it under his belt. There was a machine gun leaning against the door; he limped toward it, picked it up and stopped.

"Before the Brothers occupy the house, go up and eat something. There is still plenty of food in the kitchen and pantry. Then come back and rest. You have to fatten up. You're all skin and bone!"

After he left, I stayed in bed and looked at the courtyard. The deep, artificial sleep had clouded my head. I couldn't remember the details of yesterday—only bits and pieces. I wanted to escape, Father had come—rain and then snow. I wore Khanum-Jaan's clothes; Assad and Mustafa held my arms. Curses. Smell of vodka. Slaps. But I couldn't remember anything more. Did he touch me? I looked at myself—instead of Khanum's clothes, I had on my blue sleeping gown.

I slipped out of bed and climbed the steps to the courtyard. My knees shook. The cold air pinched my skin. The day was dry, sunless and still. Jangi ran toward me, jumped up on his hind legs and hugged me with his front legs. Boor-boor made a husky sound that wasn't quite a "Boorrr." She was excited too. I stroked the dog and examined the bird's wings. Some of her green feathers were broken.

But I didn't have much time to stay with the animals. I had to see my grandfather before the Brothers arrived; maybe this would be the last time, maybe Assad would take him to a hospital today—a third rate, poor people's hospital where he'd die.

Baba-Ji's room was bare—no furniture. The tapestry of the Simorgh was missing from the wall. The tall bookshelves were empty and in the middle of the room a few piles of books were ready to be sacked and thrown away. But he was on his recliner in the same position, half-sitting, half-lying, in a deep sleep. He was the same and was not the same. He had shrunken and I could swear that his legs in his blue pajamas were shorter and his face was thinner. My old grandfather had become a child. He was a white-haired Prince Zaal, abandoned by his family, waiting for the Simorgh to save him. Meanwhile he slept the longest night of his life, without light and with no bird in the sky.

I went to the window and looked out. Assad hadn't been bluffing. A jeep was parked in front of the gate and two armed Brothers paced up and down the sidewalk. Across the street, where Vahid in his white raincoat had slipped love letters into Taara's hand, a tank sat, squat, muddy, and ugly, but not empty. Something like the lid of a can opened and a hooded head popped out. It looked around, then disappeared inside the tank's belly.

Back at the pile of books, I searched until I found the cardboard box of the original manuscript of the Simorgh book. I pulled it out from under the books and sat down on the cold floor, recently robbed of its carpet. Leafing through the manuscript to make sure all the chapters were there, I glanced at my grandfather's small, round cursive—his little green words, fruits of half a century of steady work. I began reading the preface, first in a whisper, then louder. He must have written these lines decades ago, before his sons were born.

When he was a small child residing in the deep quietude of the mountain skirts of Azerbaijan, in the house of his father who was a knowledgeable but humble school teacher and scholar of Persian and Azeri folklore, in the harsh winter nights of the Aras River area where the scent of snow rode upon the wind, he sat by the fire next to his seven brothers and sisters, all wrapped in thick sheepskin coats and listened to Dada, their father, whose round spectacles sat on the tip of his nose, reading the old, forgotten legends that he strived to resurrect from the dust of neglect and oblivion.

The seed of the notion of the bird, the mighty Simorgh—the Ang-ha, the Rukh, the Feng-Huang, the Phoenix, the Ho-ho, the Ilerion, the Firebird, and many more, in many different lands—was planted in his small head, the head of a nine-year-old. He played with the notion, fed it with his ambition and imagination and the tales of his scholar father, and before puberty he knew what the path of his future would be.

What was this crimson, gold, purple bird, with jeweled eyes and sweeping sapphire tail feathers? Why did the Greek writers give the Egyptian bird, Bennu, a symbol of the gods Ra and Osiris, the name Phoenix and associate it with the sun? But shouldn't he go even fur-ther back to prehistoric Persia, and trace the bird's origin to the Epic of Shahnameh? Won't he find the same bird, with the same descriptions as before, now symbolic of "knowledge," restoring justice in the unjust world of the kings and warriors? Why should the wise Persian bird—that in some manuscripts was called Senmurv, or Dog-bird, and had the powers of reason and human speech—shelter the abandoned, white-haired Prince Zaal in her nest in the branches of the Tree of Knowledge? And wasn't this Tree of Knowledge the same dryandra tree in which the legendary Chinese bird, Feng Huang, built her nest? The same Feng Huang who was born of the sun and was the source of the Chinese musical scale? Sun, knowledge, wisdom, justice, music? What was the connection between these? The boy wondered.

His road was long and unpaved. The blue horizon that separated the vast sky and the sea of knowledge seemed unreachable. Little had been done; no one had linked the myth, the archetype, the legend, the poetry, the folklore, the history, the illusion and the reality of the archaeological discoveries to find the truth of the Bird. If the bird was Virtue, Justice, Truth, Knowledge, Humanity, Art, the promised Savior, one of the forms of the numerous shapes of God, no one had done much to discover this. So how could he, the young, unknown, unequipped scholar in a remote corner of an unfortunate country, at the far edge of the Near East, at the beginning of a strange century, be the one who would prepare seven iron shoes, seven iron canes, seven iron hoods, set off on a voyage through the dark and narrow passages of uncharted mountains in search of the lost bird?

But his doubts didn't last long. At age twenty-one, when he graduated from—

I pressed the manuscript to my chest and whispered, "Baba-Ji, your book will be with me. I'll keep it here, against my heart," and dashed out of the room because I heard doors opening and closing. But it was only the wind that whistled and rushed into the house and escaped from the open doors. I stood in the dim lobby and listened. Upstairs, in the third floor's master bedroom, the old springs of the bare bed creaked. Unaware of time, Grandpa Vazir and Grandma Negaar lay together on their ancient bed, whispering. Ghosts could not perceive change. For them, time did not exist.

I walked, barefoot, in the wild garden. The sun was cold in the sky, unable to warm the earth. I walked under the willows and stopped by the water storage and looked inside the black hole. Nothing could be seen in that immense darkness. A foul odor—the smell of standing water, dead animals, and rotting leaves—rose in the air. I ran toward the right edge of the garden, pulled away the tangled twigs of the overgrown trees and walked toward the depth. It was as if someone else led the way. I didn't know my destination, but she knew. She took me to that hidden gate, covered with thick vines. I stood there and remembered that once before I had walked to this end of the garden and had even thought about escape. This was the eastern gate opening onto a back street. Assad's guards were not here. I looked at the thick, tangled layer of vines and ivy covering the gate. This needed more than a day's work—many days' work. I had to cut the hard, ancient branches with a sharp knife and work my way out gradually. With the Brothers inside the house and Assad in and out of my room, I couldn't do it. I lost heart and turned away. But then I stopped and stepped closer to the gate. I touched the thick branches and dry twigs. I had to find a knife before they occupied the house. I had to hide it somewhere in my room. I'd cut the vines, twig by twig, branch by branch, whenever I had a chance.

Back in the house, I found Daaye's collection of knives hanging on the kitchen wall. I took two, in case one broke or went dull. I left the kitchen just as the Brothers' truck pulled through the front gate. When I hid the knives in the depths of my crowded closet, I realized that Baba's manuscript was still pressed against my body. My left hand had secured it so tightly against my chest that when I stretched my arm, it hurt. On my crowded desk I found my father's poem; I unfolded the old piece of paper and glanced at it. On top of the page, he'd written, "For Taara, my setar player." I smoothed the paper and lay it between two pages of the Simorgh book and hid the manuscript in the closet with the knives. Feeling a strange lightness, as if I were clean and new inside and nothing could hurt me, I took the longest shower of my life.

Now I pulled the dirty sheets and blankets off my bed and took them to the abandoned laundry room next to my room. I covered the bed with fresh sheets that Daaye had stacked in one of the closets. I picked up as many pieces of clothing as I could manage in a short time and shoved them into the closet. I cleaned up, then went to the bathroom, took all the old and new bottles of pills from the drug cabinet and emptied them into the toilet and flushed it. I lay on my clean bed and felt my body's pulsing. Heart, temples, wrists, neck—all thumped like drums. But there was a hidden pulse too, somewhere within, somewhere vague. This solitary drum tried to remind me of something that I could not quite remember— something alarming and dangerous. It told me that I had to use the knife, unveil the hidden gate and escape. When I saw Assad's boots behind the window, my pulse ceased. I closed my eyes and pretended sleep.

"Here, I brought you warm food from outside. Rice and meat. Get up and eat, before it gets cold. I know you didn't eat. Get up! Leave all the sleeping for the night. I'll be with the boys upstairs. We're storing artillery up there. Now Drum Tower is one of the most important headquarters of the Holy Revolution. Weren't Khanum-Jaan's ancestors war viziers and Drum Tower a fortress? Well then, *I'm* the war vizier now! Get up, Talkhoon, and see what a revolution means! Get up and look at Assad! He's wearing a uniform now and carrying Grandpa Vazir's ivory cane!"

The rest of the day I heard their boots stamping on the tiled floors over my head. I heard their loud voices too, but couldn't make out most of the words. Sometimes they chanted, "One party, Party of God—" in a rough, angry tone. The rice and meat sat on my desk for a long time and cold grease covered the dish. I didn't have an appetite, but I reminded myself that hard work was awaiting me and I needed to be strong. I called Jangi to the door and sat with him and we shared the cold dish. I put pieces of meat in his wide, slobbering mouth and told him, "Slow down—don't bite!" and he took the meat slowly, trying not to bite my fingers. It had been a long time since I had eaten with anyone. In Jangi's company, the cold, greasy food tasted better. Now I let him inhale the rest of the rice and lick the dish. After lunch, Jangi didn't leave me. He lay by the door, rested his chin on his paws and looked at me. I lay next to him on the floor and stroked his gray, prickly hair. He licked my hands in return and watched me with love in his eyes. Soon he fell asleep.

All afternoon I lay next to the dog's warm body and heard the Brothers walking upstairs, singing, even running. When dusk fell, Assad came

down with two large burlap sacks, dropped them on the hallway floor
next to where Jangi and I were lying down, and ordered me to get up.

"Dogs are filthy," he said. "Never sleep next to the dog again. Now get
up and sort these sacks. These are all that was left in the closets upstairs.
They're old clothes and knickknacks of God knows which fucking aunt,
uncle, or ancestor. See if you can find anything valuable. Gold buttons,
dress pins, jewelry, or money in the pockets or purses." He paused and
when he talked again his voice was different. He was excited and worried at the same time. "Tonight is the biggest night of the revolution. The
main event is about to happen." He hesitated for a second and said, "Pray
for me to stay alive, Talkhoon, because there might be a bloody battle."
His voice dropped and shook a little. "In case I don't come back, break
this clay bear and take all my savings for yourself." He handed me a fat,
heavy, clay bear. "When I was a little boy, Daaye brought me this from her
village. I've put all my money in its fat belly since I was a child—occasional tips, New Year coins…"

He said that under no circumstances should I let anyone take his savings. They belonged to me. Now he knelt beside me and murmured a
prayer. His voice was sad, as if he was sorry for himself even before anything had happened. Finally he bent over me and kissed my forehead.

"Bitter herb, baby girl, forgive me for being rough to you sometimes.
Forgive me for everything, Talkhoon!" Now he got up and limped away to
hide his tears. Using Grandpa Vazir's ivory cane, he passed the courtyard
and climbed the steps.

I sat for a long moment with the clay bear in my lap, trying hard to
imagine myself free in this world, without Assad hunting me. I fantasized
his death. I could travel with his money. I could go to the four corners of
the country—to the sea, the mountains, desert and forest. I would carry
Baba-Ji's book in a secret purse sewn inside my shirt and I'd take it out
only on the day that better people wanted to publish it. In this way, I saw
myself as a solitary traveler of remote lands, shielded with my grandfather's book, secure with dead Assad's money. I saw myself as someone
who didn't need friends, family, or even a dog. I'd be self-contained, in-
vulnerable, free, and almost invisible.

I imagined myself strolling on long streets, whistling.

But the dog woke up, yawned, and pulled me out of my daydream. Assad was not going to die tonight. If he were, I'd feel it in my guts. A vague joy would tickle me. No, I had to get up, go to the garden, and cut the vines and the thick ivy. I had to open that gate with my own bloody hands.

The Visit

Before long my hands bled. Cutting tough branches was more difficult than I'd thought. After a few minutes, blood bubbled from the old stitch wounds in my palms. I needed gloves. I returned to my room, angry and disappointed, afraid I'd get an infection. I washed my hands, poured plenty of Mercurochrome on them and wrapped them with gauze.

It was dusk now, the air outside was blue-gray and black clouds promised rain or snow. I heard distant shots from the streets, explosions, and people's shouts. The big event was happening. What was my father doing? Was he there too? Was this the same revolution he was anticipating?

I noticed the burlap sacks in the corridor and began to sort the clothes. I didn't look for gold buttons or money for Assad, but for a pair of gloves. With two fingers I fished out strange things—old, long-forgotten objects: a green, silk scarf with a flowery design, now wrinkled and pale, smelling faintly of violet perfume; a brown felt hat shaped like a salad bowl, with two black feathers sticking out, one broken and hanging loose; a little sequined velvet purse, nothing inside; a leather wallet, beaten and old, containing a yellowed invitation card: "Peace Concert: June 14, 1942. Open air Concert in the National Garden, celebrating the Tehran Conference. Guests of Honor President Roosevelt, Prime Minister Churchill and Secretary Stalin will sign the historic peace document. Entry only with invitation cards." I found an old calendar with someone's small, shaky handwriting noting certain dates with red ink: "Negaar's birthday—"

At last, I found a pair of black velvet gloves—soiree gloves. Long, and not very old. They covered my burning hands and came up to my elbows. This will do, I thought. I also found Taara's turquoise dress, the one she wore last year when the General and his son came to propose. It was all wrinkled. I brought it close to my face and smelled the warm, tropical perfume. This was the scent that drove the father and son crazy that evening. I found a deep blue taffeta evening gown and I decided this belonged to my mother. It wasn't old-fashioned enough to be Negaar's and I was sure it wasn't Taara's. It belonged to a slim woman with a narrow waist. Soraya.

In haste, I went through the rest of the clothes. I was surprised to find Khanum-Jaan's golden, strapped slippers. Why had she left them behind? I picked them up to see if she'd really hammered nails into the heels. She hadn't. The short heels were made of iron. I smiled and kept the slippers for myself.

I didn't check for gold buttons or money, but I found a white wig and put it on. Now I put on the blue gown—it fit me well, but swept the floor. I wore the golden strapped slippers too. With this strange costume I lay on the bed thinking about all the women who'd occupied this house and had not even remained as names. Forgotten ghosts. Soon, I fell asleep.

Assad didn't show up that night. I woke up early in the morning and heard the rain hitting the windows. I climbed a chair, pressed my face against a windowpane, and cupped my hands around my face to see if the parrot was still on the wall. She was. She'd die in the rain. I ran out in the wet, blue air. There was no way to unchain the parrot, so I lifted the loose brick and brought the bird inside. I dried its wet, broken feathers and for the first time held her in my hands. A small heart beat inside that green, fragile body. I set her and the brick on my desk next to Khanum-Jaan's black marble box. She shook herself once or twice and began biting on the box. Now I took off my carnival costume, put my work clothes on, and went to the garden with the other knife, the sharper one.

I cut the vines under the cold drizzle for a long time, until the rain turned to snow and the velvet gloves tore. Then I went back to my room, exhausted but happy. I had cleared one third of the gate. The cedar wood showed now. I ran up to get something to eat before the Brothers came back from their war. I found some stale bread, a jar of olives, and one wrinkled cucumber in the refrigerator. I ate them with Jangi, sat and contemplated my new project. My head was strangely calm and I had a determination I'd never had before. Everything seemed possible. If the gate existed, I would open it.

The next project was to make a purse the size of Baba's manuscript with four straps attached, so that I could wear it on my chest. If I wore a loose fitting shirt over the purse no one would notice I was carrying something. I had no problem finding the right material. I picked Soraya's blue taffeta gown and cut off the beaded front. For the back, I used Taara's turquoise dress. The purse would be the color of the Simorgh's tail feather and it would be beaded too. This was nicer than I'd imagined. Didn't Baba-Ji and his bird deserve this luxury?

When I sewed, Boor-boor stared at me with her one eye and nibbled on Khanum-Jaan's marble box. "Eat the box, birdy," I told her. "I don't have time to find sunflower seeds for you now."

It took me the whole morning to make the purse. Since my Catholic School sewing classes, I hadn't held a needle in my hand. But soon the old skill came back to me and I stitched hard and fast, like a seamstress in a sweatshop. When the purse and its straps were ready, I slipped the manuscript inside and tied it on my chest. After making sure I'd done a good job, I hid my product in the closet.

The Brothers didn't show up in the afternoon either, and I thought I shouldn't waste the time. I should go to my gate.

By evening, half of the gate was unveiled.

Early in the evening I cleaned myself up and sat on the bed looking out the window. My burning palms, red from the Mercurochrome, rested on my lap. I was hungry again and didn't have anything to eat except three olives, but I couldn't go upstairs because I was afraid the Brothers would arrive. When it was dark and I couldn't see outside anymore, someone tapped on the door. I opened it a crack and saw a tall man in khaki, a bandana covering half of his face. I knew those eyes. For a long moment I stared at him, trying to remember. He pulled the bandana down and said, "Talkhoon, don't you remember me?"

"Vafa? "

"Himself!"

"How did you get in? Are you a Revolutionary Guard too?"

"No. This is a disguise. I tricked the guards at the gate. Let me come in."

"Come in. But Assad will show up any minute."

"So he's occupied our house—"

"He's turned Drum Tower into a headquarters."

"You mean he's become a Revolutionary Guard?"

"Something like that."

"Why are you still here, then?"

"Khanum-Jaan has given me to Assad."

"What?"

"She'd always had doubts about me. Apparently Grandpa Vazir in the last seance session assured her that I'm not—"

"What are you talking about?"

"This was around the time when Baba-Ji—"

"I came here once, with my wife. Doctor Shafa and Kia insisted I should apologize. How stupid I was to listen to them. Were you here that night?"

"I was looking at you from my window upstairs."

"Why didn't you come down to talk to me? Did you come to my wedding?"

"Don't you remember?"

"No. I didn't see you."

"I guess no one saw me in those days. I was invisible."

"You can't stay here with this man."

"Where can I go?"

"I've heard that Taara has gone. Do you know where she is? Can you join her?"

"No."

"Zahra and I change places all the time. She is pregnant. We have to find a new hiding place. That's why I came here." He paused and said, "Last night we lost the revolution. I don't see any chance for our organization, or any civilized organization, to be able to play a role in this country. Suddenly an Ayatollah fell from the sky to run the country."

"But I thought you believed in a religious government."

"Not run by the mullahs! The teachings of Islam must be adapted to a modern society, in a government that is formed by the representatives of the people. Freedom, democracy, and justice are our first slogans. Haven't you read any of Doctor Soulati's books? How can a bunch of ignorant clergy run the country, huh?"

"So, they won last night?"

"They won. They shipped the old man in from Paris."

"Assad is alive then."

"There is going to be a big purge."

"And they're going to arrest you?"

"Us and the leftists. But don't worry about your father—the commies are supporting the Ayatollah."

"Are they?"

"Yes. That's probably what Moscow dictates. Listen—I came here to hide."

"You know that the house is occupied."

"I was thinking about the tower."

"I wouldn't do this, Vafa."

"Just for one night. I sent my wife to her aunt's. I'm hoping her family will find us a place somewhere out of Tehran."

"Where in the tower do you want to hide?"

"In the hollow space, where we left cinnamon sticks for the Simorgh."

"You remember?"

"Oh, yes. How can I ever forget my crazy childhood? Is Baba still sleeping?"

"Still."

"Is Assad taking care of him?"

"He wants to take him to a hospital."

"That's the best for him, Talkhoon."

In the dark room we sat on the edge of the bed, looking out the window. The vague shadow of the broken wall and beyond that, the gray tower, blended into the black night. Boor-boor chewed on Khanum-Jaan's marble box with a steady crunching sound.

"Vafa, I can't believe all this. It was only yesterday that we sat under the dryandra tree and Taara played her setar to call the bird."

"Baba's idealism drove us all insane. We're all insane."

"Vafa!"

"Huh?"

"Don't sit here anymore. Go. He's coming."

"Does he come down here to your room?"

"He does."

"Does he...bother you?"

I didn't answer. He sighed and held my hand. He felt the gauze, removed it and brought my hand close to his eyes. "What have you done to yourself?"

"He wants me to remain a virgin. He wants to marry me. Now go, Vafa."

In silence he put the gauze back on my hand and held it in his palms like a broken china plate badly glued together. After a long moment he said, "Did you know how much I hated my mother? Even as a child. All that's happening to us is her doing."

"You're sitting here blaming Baba and Khanum for everything. Go and try to save yourself and your wife."

"I'm done for, Talkhoon. They'll kill me."

"Go, Vafa, go!"

"My mother and her rotten, bankrupt aristocracy! Rotten and stinking to the core. This disaster happened in our country as the result of centuries of rotten-to-the-bone monarchy. And now that we have a republic, look! They send us an Ayatollah to run it! As if we people are a bunch of imbeciles, needing either a Shah or an Ayatollah."

"Go, Vafa, go! You're raising your voice!"

"And leave you here like this? To become Assad's wife?"

"Don't tell me you've come here to save me. You've come to hide in the tower and I'm telling you that's the worst place."

"You're angry with me, Talkhoon. You think I abandoned you."

"You were only seventeen when you left. I don't blame you. You had to save yourself from Drum Tower."

"From Baba's book."

"And Khanum's ghosts."

He was silent for a while, then he said, "It's not that I wasn't thinking about you. I thought you were safe. How would I have known?"

"Go now. He'll arrest you. He never liked you, remember?"

"I remember. Of the three of us, Assad was closest to Sina. He resented me, and was afraid of Kia. Kia was gone, and when he came back he was an intimidating bastard."

"He must be hiding too."

"Oh, he and his kind are the main target now. The mullahs are putting the monarchists against the wall. They put this woman minister in a burlap sack—a potato sack—and executed her."

"Go, Vafa, please!"

"Talkhoon, I'll find a place. I'll come back and get you. You can live with us. Then we'll see what happens. Maybe the tide will turn."

"Go now!"

We embraced quickly, then he wrapped the bandana around his face and left.

For a while I sat motionless in the dark, holding my palms up. A cold wind blew in my head, blurred my mind and confused me. Where was Vafa? Did I imagine this visit?

Grandpa Vazir's Son

When I heard his footsteps I rushed to the closet, but something told me I shouldn't go inside. Baba-Ji's book and the knives were there; if he pulled me out, he'd see them. So I took out the shorter knife and hid it under my arm. The thick handle was inside my armpit, the sharp tip tickled my waist. Then I sat on the bed, leaned against the wall and watched Boor-boor. She had seriously damaged Khanum-Jaan's marble box and was still eating.

The knife's blade warmed against my body and my heart pounded loudly.

From the corner of my eye I saw him limping into the courtyard, carrying a fat paper bag. He stopped at Jangi's cage, peaked in, and dropped some bread inside. So he wasn't in a bad mood. But he looked disheveled. His khaki uniform was muddy and torn at the shoulders. When Jangi jumped up to reach the bag, he didn't scold him. He dropped another piece of bread on the floor and came down the steps, shouting in the corridor.

"I'm alive! Hey, girl, I'm back!" He took off his muddy boots at the door and entered. "You have to talk tonight. Enough is enough! You have to start talking to me. We won the revolution! Do you hear me? We won!"

He put the paper bag on the floor, fished out a cardboard picture and rested it on the desk, next to Boor-boor. This was an old man in a black turban—an angry cleric with bushy tangled eyebrows. An old, bad-tempered mullah.

"You took some interest in your parrot finally, huh? It's a good sign. First the dog, then the parrot. Maybe now it's my turn. Did you hear what I said earlier? We won! This is the picture of the Great Leader of the Holy Revolution: The Imam. We escorted him to his holy home today. He is a modest man. He lives in a regular house, not a palace. No more Shahs in this country, hear me? No more American servants. We have a holy leader now. And this will be a holy state. But the war is not over. We have to get rid of the monarchists, the infidels, and the satanic elements. Traitors like your Uncle Vafa who claim to be Moslems but hide underground like rats, and spies such as your father who pretend they support the Revolution, but are really the agents of the East."

He babbled for a long time and his friends stamped their booted feet upstairs and sang anthems. Now he spread his wide bandana—a checkered scarf—on the floor and took all kinds of food out of the paper bag: French bread, salami, cooked sausage, olive salad, pickles, Swiss cheese, and finally a chilled bottle of vodka. He had shopped at an Armenian deli.

"We party tonight, Talkhoon. You and me! You see? I could spend my time upstairs with my Brothers, but I told them I had to go to my family. They don't know my family is down here. No one knows anything about you, except for Mustafa, and I trust him. I've forbidden them to open the doors to the porch and the courtyard. Now let's have a picnic. I can see that you've cleaned up the room. Another good sign! Come on!"

He knew I wouldn't sit with him, so he made a colorful dish on a paper plate and put it on my bed. I was too hungry to resist and I began to eat while he drank his vodka. Now he turned his head toward the desk and noticed that the old, angry mullah was staring at him. He rose up and laid the picture face down.

"This is my last night, Imam," he addressed the picture. "I swear to Allah and to your dear life, I'm going to quit. This bottle is my last and I'm going to kill one hundred Satan worshipers to make up for this."

Now, his mouth full, he described the events he had been involved in. He said he was one of the men who sat on the hood of the Imam's car, guarding it from possible assassins. He said he burned ten American flags, one effigy of the American president, and one effigy of the damned Shah. By the time he finished all the bread, meat, and olive salad, his tall vodka bottle was half empty and his face was crimson. He stood up, took off his shirt, mumbled something about mud, and cursed. He loosened his belt and let his pants fall down to below his belly button. The blue head and the open wings of his Simorgh showed. I pressed my right arm against my body, feeling the knife. I could see how his rough side was coming out. He picked up Khanum-Jaan's black marble box and sat cross-legged on the floor.

"If I don't find the damned will tonight, I'll never find it," he told himself. He fished in the box and took the stacks of letters out. He removed the rubber band from the last stack and opened the first envelope. "March 20... No, it was later, much later." He looked at me and asked, "When did Papa Vazir's ghost ruin the old fart's fucking furniture? Huh? What month was it?" He searched some more. "When did your sister run away, huh? I can't remember. Do you want to talk, or do I have to get up and slap you? When was it? It was spring. Okay. Taara's fucking final exams. All right. So the engagement party was supposed to be in May. May, May—" He opened several envelopes, took out the letters, scattered them around himself and sat amidst them, confused. He breathed heavily, sipped from the bottle and wiped his sweaty forehead with his hairy arm. He had to hold the letters far from his eyes to see the words.

"My fucking glasses are upstairs. I can't see well. May. Okay. May the twelfth. This is after the mess. It's a long letter. Two pages. It must be the letter she wrote when she locked herself up and didn't come out for a while. Let's read it. But I can't see well. I didn't sleep last night. My eyes are watery. Read this, girl, please!" he pleaded, and held the letter out to me.

I looked at Boor-boor who didn't have the box to chew on and was nibbling on the Great Leader's picture.

"No? Okay, we'll get to this later. We'll get to your silence and disobedience later. One hundred men in this neighborhood are under my command. Do you hear me? They call me Brother Sheeri now. That's my new name. Sheer, meaning lion. Assad, meaning lion. Brother Assad Sheeri. Double lion! It scares the shit out of them. Don't you think I can open your fucking mouth? But later. I need the will before they start making laws in this country. Let me see—if I only had my glasses—it says, 'Papa—' no dear, no nothing. Just 'Papa,' this must be it. It sounds sulky."

Papa, the door bell rings every minute, Daaye and Assad return the three-tiered cream cake, the one hundred red roses, the caskets of wine, the rented china and silver— Taara's engagement is cancelled. I'm here in my room, sitting in the dark, no window to allow the last ray of daylight to fall on this paper. Darkness will do.

"She's trying to make her Papa feel sorry for her. The old fart!"

I always knew that Taara was your favorite. You came to me in my dream the first night of her life and told me to name her Taahereh—the pure. So I knew that I should protect her. But what did I do, instead? I tried to sell her. Even before she turned eighteen. I tried to force her to marry a man she didn't love.

"Can you believe this shit? This is the old fart talking about love."
Assad continued reading, and as he read, his voice relaxed and became Khanum-Jaan's voice when she was sad and mournful:

But what did you expect me to do, Papa? The house, your Drum Tower, your ancestral fort was falling on our heads. The General was close to the Shah and could pull us up again. Taara would shine among the people she belonged to; we would feel happy and secure. Love would come later. But what if it didn't? But how would I know? I, who had never experienced love in marriage? So I didn't know what love was and you became angry with me. You raged at my callousness, at

my petty calculations, at my blind, rash decision—selling your flower
so cheap. Because you thought Taara must not be sold; she needed
something beyond money—what you gave to my mother, Negaar—
and while flying above Drum Tower, you dipped the tip of your ivory
cane in the roof's softened tar and ruined my property...

"You hear this, Talkhoon? This woman is a lunatic! Do you know who
vandalized the house? The Satan worshipers, or the infidels—either Vafa's
gang, or a Marxist group. They've done this to other mansions too. Now
listen to this:"

But did you think for a second, Papa, that you yourself were far
from being perfect? You who passed judgment on me and punished
me even after your death were far from being innocent. Who helped
you, Papa? Who kept your name clean? Who buried the girl at the foot
of the tower, and your sins with her? You were not here anymore to
see, to witness how I single-handedly took care of the whole damnable
job. How I alone, with my weak arms, dragged her blue body out of
the water storage, slung it on my shoulder, carried it all the way to the
tower, and buried it with my own hands. Her hair, her unnatural hair,
wrapped around my neck like wet moss and it's been choking me ever
since.

"You hear all this? Who is she talking about?"

All for you, Papa. For your reputation. What rumors would people
spread if the constables drew the girl's corpse out of the filthy water? A
fourteen-year-old servant girl, drowning herself in the water storage a
day after the birth of her child. Would your name survive the scandal?
And then I had to lie. First to Daaye, telling her that her daughter had
run away, and then a fairy tale about my husband bringing his illegitimate son from the mountains! This poor, imbecile professor of mine,
this naive bookworm! I told him that the little girl had fooled around
and had a bastard child and he agreed to be your son's father. He said
he didn't mind—the boy needed to be secure. He said he wasn't a public figure to be afraid for his reputation. He even liked my story—an

affair with a village girl, on top of the mountain, right before his marriage, bringing a baby to his bride's house. He laughed and admired
my imagination.

Then I had to raise this boy—your son, Papa—because I couldn't
bury him alive with the body of his mother. I didn't have the heart.

Assad stopped here, lost his voice, and cursed under his lips. "Damn
old hen, she is the one who should've written books, not Baba. But what
nonsense—"

He sat still, with heavy eyelids, fighting sleep. He didn't talk anymore; he murmured and whispered incoherent fragments. His mind was
so fatigued that he couldn't make sense of what he had just read. The
answer was within his reach, but he couldn't grab it. He kept repeating,
"Drowned herself in the water storage…even before Soraya…way before.
Fourteen years old… Khanum raised her bastard son. Her father's son…"

Now suddenly he dropped the box and got to his feet, swaying. He
held to the wall and tried to look at me, but he seemed not to see me. He
looked past my head at the vacant wall and shouted, "I'm him! That baby!
I'm Grandpa Vazir's son—a fucking blue blood—Khanum's brother! But
a bastard!" His horselaugh echoed in the quiet night.

"I'm the heir! I'm the sole heir to whatever is left! Drum Tower, the
lands—. The lands? Where are my Papa's lands? Where has the old hen
hidden my father's lands? I want the fucking will. I want the old bitch's
will."

He sat on the floor again and spread the letters around. He groaned,
brought the papers close to his eyes, and threw them away. Now he stood
up, swaying again, grasped the bed and approached me. He grabbed my
arm and dragged me to the floor.

"Come on! Find the will for me. Why are you just sitting here doing
nothing? Don't you know what's happened? Don't you know who I am?
I'm not Assad the servant, Baba's illegitimate son. I'm the descendent of
war ministers—Grandpa Vazir's only son! Do you get me? His only male
heir! And I want my fucking lands! Come and find my lands, Talkhoon!
I'm dying. Can't you see? Have mercy! Do you know what I've gone
through the past two days and nights? Do you think it was easy to do a

revolution?"

He sat me on the floor among the leftover food and piles of letters. I pressed the knife under my right arm to hold it secure. If it fell, Assad would stab me.

"Go ahead! What are you waiting for? Use all your fancy Catholic school education and read all these fucking letters and find my will."

I was motionless. My right arm pressed against my chest.

He slapped me and shouted, "Either you start sorting these letters, or I'll whip your little ass with my leather belt!"

I bent on the floor and picked up a bound stack.

"Leave the fucking old ones alone. Look at the last letters, the ones that are all over the floor. Pick them up one by one and read them. Look in the envelopes for a piece of paper with a letterhead and a big stamp under or above. You know what I mean, don't you? Who went to school, you or me?"

He fell on my bed and lay on his back. He covered his face with his hairy arms and moaned. The bird on his lower belly expanded and its wings grew larger each time he inhaled. Before I picked up the first letter he was snoring and the blue bird on his fat belly quivered as if carved in jelly.

For a while I looked at the letters. My grandmother's sentences ran in front of my eyes, "You were in my dreams last night...," or "You were furious when you lifted the top of the oak table..." "We bought your little Taara a diamond ring..." "I dreamed, I dreamed!"

I stacked the letters and picked up some more, hearing Boor-boor biting on the cardboard picture of the Great Leader. She was quick and agile, the way she cracked sunflower seeds. I was grateful that Assad had passed out. He'd sleep like a stone for at least five hours. He had missed two nights of sleep, done a revolution, and found out about his origins after drinking two thirds of a bottle of vodka.

I soon found the will. It was attached to the deed of the house. It was a typed letter on thick, yellowish paper—brief, less than one page, and stamped with the sign of the sun and lion of the monarchy.

...all my properties, consisting of a house—Number One, Shah-Reza

Avenue, College Intersection, known as 'Drum Tower'—an ancestral half crown, a seal and a sword kept in a safe deposit box at the Royal Bank, go to my sisters, Puran-dokht and Turan-dokht Vaziri.

An attached document showed that in 1340 AH, 1961 AD, Drum Tower's ownership had been fully transferred to Khanum-Gol Vaziri. Grandmother had bought her sisters' shares—fifteen million rials in cash.

Khanum-Jaan didn't have land as Assad had imagined, but of what she had— a decaying house, a half crown, and a dull sword—her three sons, four granddaughters, still-breathing husband, a half-brother (Assad), and a faithful maid/nurse, wouldn't get anything. We were all disinherited.

Unveiling the Gate

All night, in the light from a flashlight secured on a branch of a tree, with my bare hands—the black velvet gloves shredded in minutes—I cut the tangle of vines on the old wooden gate. My palms bled, but I didn't stop. When the sky turned light, I had finished the job and I saw a long, rusty, metal rod that bolted the gate. It was heavy and I couldn't slide it out. I would have to work on it later.

With a sense of joy I'd never felt before, I ran along the wet path. When I reached the willows around the pool, I stopped and listened. The garden was silent except for a few sleepy birds, waking, stretching their wings, chirping here and there. I glanced at the water storage on the other side of the pool, its black mouth wide open behind the trees. Now I remembered that last night Assad had murmured my mother's name when he read about his young mother's suicide in the pool of the water storage. I thought hard, but couldn't remember anything more.

The courtyard vibrated with the loud sound of a radio. This was Baba-Ji's transistor radio sitting on the edge of the upstairs porch. So the Brothers had gone into his room; any minute they'd come down to the courtyard and find mine. The volume was at maximum and would wake all the neighbors. It was a military march, interrupted every few seconds by a man who recited an epic poem in a declamatory tone. I knew this poem by heart. Baba had read it for us a million times: *Let my body perish without my motherland!*

In my room, Assad lay on his side, hands between his legs, snoring. If he didn't wake up, if he missed the rest of his revolution, he'd become furious. So I began making loud noises—dropping bottles and brushes in the sink and banging the doors. The guards would soon come down to find him. I cleared last night's trash, the leftover food and the vodka bottle, and made more noise. I lay Khanum-Jaan's will and the deed of the house on top of the half-chewed, black marble box on the desk so that he could see them. But he didn't wake up. He was going to sleep until noon, his crew would leave without him, and I wouldn't be able to go back to the gate and work on the bolt.

Now an idea came to mind. I lifted the sleepy parrot—who'd eaten all of the turban and the upper face of the Great Leader and had now curled into a green ball—and placed her next to Assad's face on the pillow. The old bird looked at Assad with one eye, then turned her head toward me in confusion. She shook her wings and looked around for something to busy her idle beak. There was nothing, so she began biting Assad's beard. Assad scratched his beard and moved a little. Boor-boor bit him again. Finally he opened his eyes, stared at the parrot absently, and jumped. He glanced at his watch, then looked around. His gaze passed over me and fixed on the morning light pouring from the window. He realized how late it was, cursed under his moustache and rushed to the bathroom.

Pulling up his pants in haste, he rushed from the toilet to the desk, picked up his handgun and car keys, but didn't notice the documents on top of the marble box. He rested one foot after the other on my clean sheet, pulled on his muddy boots and wrapped his bandana around his neck. Then he picked up his machine gun and ivory cane and rushed toward the door. But before exiting, he stopped, turned to me and said, "I'll bring some food for lunch. Get some sleep, you look like a ghost!" He left, half his brain still asleep, not remembering last night.

In the courtyard he bumped into Brother Mustafa who was heading down.

"Didn't I tell you not to open the porch door?" Assad yelled.

"We were looking for you, Brother. The liberals, infidels and Satan worshipers are all gathering in the former Shah Square today—"

"Now it's called Imam Square, idiot. So what?"

"It's getting late. We have to disrupt their demonstration, scatter them, and, if necessary, shoot them before they start to deceive people."

"Who is in command here? Huh?"

"But, Brother—"

"Go upstairs, get the boys, and don't talk anymore. And from now on, if anyone steps on this porch, I'll take care of him myself. Tell everybody this is an order! Take this fucking radio inside, too. Can't you tell it's babbling liberal junk?"

Arise! Arise!

Click, click, click—the metal heels of Khanum-Jaan's golden slippers echoed on the asphalt. I'm here, here, here, I announced and walked in the narrow alleys. It was early afternoon and the back streets were vacant, untouched by the revolution. A vender on a bicycle passed by, calling, "Cucumbers! Fresh, slim cucumbers!"

I passed brick houses with barred windows sheltering lonely housewives, their children at school, their husbands at work, themselves somewhere in the dim corners of the house, chopping onions and daydreaming. Some of the kitchen windows were open, giving out the aroma of leftover food, cold grease from unwashed frying pans and the odor of rotten vegetables sitting in overflowing trashcans. In these narrow back alleys life was as stagnant as it had always been. These houses were untouched by the storm.

An old lady like me could feel safe here. *Click, click, click*—I walked without haste, passing the row of houses. A small girl was home today. She sat on the last step of her house, drawing something with pink chalk on the pavement. I slowed down to watch her. Her mother opened the door a crack and handed her a bowl of green plums. She munched one and spat the seed out. Now she drew two stick figures on the pavement, drew a flag for each and spoke to them in a murmur. When I reached her, she raised her head and looked at me—at my black blouse (covering a heavy manuscript secured in a knapsack against my chest), at my bluish white hair frizzing out of a black scarf, at my face (too smooth for an old woman), and finally at my golden slippers, three centimeters of iron heels clicking noisily on the asphalt. This girl was only a child; she believed I was old.

What was I doing when I was her age? I thought. Burning a barb from the Simorgh's feather on the balcony of the tower, preparing her nest with cinnamon, organizing my grandfather's card catalogue. We were not allowed to play in the street or to watch television, which contained a forbidden world.

But now I roamed the streets and the winter sun tickled my cheeks. A group of swallows chased me, hovered over my head, and sat on the bare branches of an almond tree. Crows cried somewhere, telling the swallows that it was still winter, too early for games, and I listened to all this and felt an urge to whistle. Then I realized that I had better not—an old, respectable lady never whistled in the street.

When I reached a main street, I saw people, thousands of them, gathering in a mass, moving slowly like the tides of thick water, an ocean with slow-moving waves. Men, women, and children held hands, held banners above their heads and waved flags. Smaller children sat on their fathers' shoulders as if waiting for the amusement park to open. These people were quiet, just waving their flags in silence, waiting.

There was no way not to join them, not to become a wavelet in this massive sea. In my old lady's dress, I found myself among the people, and when the tide moved, I moved with it. Someone held my right hand. It was a woman. A second later, someone else reached for my left hand. It was a young man. My hands were as rough as an old woman's—the stitches, scratches, and calluses had hardened them. The woman and the boy smiled at me. I smiled back.

I'm not sure how long we slow-walked this way—hands tangled, a human chain, bodies moving in harmony, a monstrous sea. When we reached a large square, we saw a raised platform with a podium on top. Next to the podium was the statue of an old king on a horse. A group of men had tied a thick rope around the king's neck and were pulling hard. The king and his horse toppled, still attached to each other. The sea roared. There were

hurrahs, whistles, and the clapping of thousands of hands. Someone had
a trumpet with him—he blew on the horn.

A gray-haired man climbed the steps and stood behind the podium. I
saw the sudden flashes of cameras and lights; there were clicks and murmurs. "The Secretary—the Secretary—Comrade Uncle—." Before the old
man began to speak, recorded music rose from the speakers installed in
the trees. It was soft music. Some people around me wiped their tears
and tried to chant, first hesitantly, then proudly. Now everyone sang
and raised their fists. By the time the music came to an end, thousands of
throats vibrated with the song's words, "Arise, you prisoners of starva-
tion! Arise, you wretched of the world!"

Now the gray-haired man raised his fist and the crowd followed. They
shouted, "Freedom!" I shouted, "Freedom!" They shouted, "Justice!" I
shouted, "Justice!" But I couldn't understand the speech. People constantly clapped or interrupted by repeating, "Freedom!" and "Justice!" until
the man raised his hand to silence the crowd. He said a few sentences and
again the uproar of the people rose to the sky.

Time passed at a strange pace. The whole thing took only a second, but
dusk had already fallen. This must be my father's revolution, I thought. I
looked around to find him.

With darkness descending, shooting began. From the roofs of the
buildings and the tops of the trees, from behind the parked cars, bullets
flew. We all lay flat on the asphalt. My wig fell into the gutter. With my
small bare head hidden under my arms, I stayed on the asphalt and heard
children crying, people cursing and shouting. "The Party of Allah—," my
neighbor whispered. Then everyone rose up, scattered, and ran in different directions. I lost the woman and the young man who had held my
hands. I ran with my grandmother's slippers, hugging myself to keep the
knapsack from hopping inside my blouse. I followed a group of people
who turned into an alley. We were safe there and could walk peacefully
in a group again. But this was one small rivulet separated from that massive ocean. My iron heels were broken. I said good-bye to Khanum-Jaan's
golden, strapped slippers, kicked them off and walked barefoot with the
people. Soon they held my hands again.

We walked along a narrow alley, uphill in the dark.

I don't know how long we walked, but all along the way people joined us. Students handed us leaflets, women gave us candles and flowers, and by the time we reached the cemetery, I was holding a candle in one hand, a few stems of red roses in the other, and a stack of leaflets under my arm.

We lay the candles and flowers on the ground, and for the first time I noticed the graves. I'd never been in a cemetery before, and now I saw flat stones raised above the earth, around which were wreaths of flowers and large pictures of men and women. This was the Cemetery of the Martyrs of the Revolutions—the present revolution and the past, failed ones. Women opened boxes of cookies and passed them around, and everyone sang uplifting anthems. Although I didn't know a soul and had never known any of the martyrs of any of the revolutions, and couldn't even sing their anthems, tears filled my eyes. I cried for my own lost ones— Baba-Ji who slept an endless sleep; my mother who was only a scent; my father, a voice trapped in a closet; Vafa, my playmate; and Taara, whom I missed immensely.

I sat on the unpaved ground by a grave and wept as if the martyr lying under the earth was my own brother. I'd had a very long day, I hadn't eaten and my head was filled with wind.

Now the same gray-haired man whose speech had been interrupted by the shootings earlier spoke in a calm voice, without a microphone. Someone told his friend, "Can you imagine? Spending twenty-five years of his life in the Shah's prison? They just released him a few days ago." I noticed that some people called him Comrade, some Uncle, and some Comrade Uncle. They all gathered around him, just to be able to see him. I was outside the circle, but could smell the prison cell on his sweaty shirt. His voice was shaky, unused and rusty.

When the crowd headed toward town, I walked back with them. Everyone was more relaxed now, chatting two by two, discussing the day's events. I walked alone, avoiding conversation. Instead of wearing a pair of pants and a T-shirt like most of the students, I had on Khanum-Jaan's silk blouse and her long, black skirt. I was barefoot and my short hair was shabby. Embarrassed, I bent my head and looked at the ground.

But this quiet march didn't last long. First we heard a groaning sound, then the hubbub of the crowd. Sensing something ominous, babies burst into tears. When the narrow alley opened onto a wide street, we saw the tanks approaching. Their metal bodies were muddy and they crawled toward us like legless animals, seemingly intent on rolling over us. But then they stopped, blocking the way. We all stopped and the tanks, like living monsters, stared at us. Parents took their children off their shoulders and held them tightly in their arms. We waited. The city lights twinkled in the distance and a cold breeze brought the smell of the cemetery's fresh earth down the alley. I inhaled the scent of the graves, thinking that the martyrs of the past revolutions were telling us that it was our turn and we'd soon join them under the earth. Death looked us in the face with the rusty eyes of the mud-covered monsters.

Someone from inside the nearest tank said something in a muffled voice and then I heard the crack of a single bullet break the silence. People lay face down on the asphalt. I lay down too. A little girl cried next to me. Then we heard more bullets. The lids of the tanks opened and black flags popped out. On the flags was written "The Party of Allah!" Now there were more bullets and we all hid our heads under our arms. I heard screams, shrieks of pain, and hoarse voices shouting, "Stop! We're not armed; we have children with us, you fascist bastards!"

When we heard the tanks groaning again, moving back toward town, we cautiously raised our heads and stood up. People fell into each other's arms and cried. Some ran to the wounded or the dead. Children screamed and called their mothers. Men shouted, "Call an ambulance! An ambulance!" But I wasn't brave enough to stay and see the blood. I walked to the other side of the square where the National Bank's round clock showed nine and sat on a bench. There was something missing in the middle of the circular flowerbed—a statue, another king on a horse.

I realized that I'd been here before; this was the train station. I looked to my right, saw the wide steps of the station, and felt secure. Staying out in the dark night was dangerous and the air was getting colder by the minute. If I spent the night inside, the next day I could join the revolution again. It wouldn't be hard to find Uncle and his people. I had a feeling that these were my father's friends, and if I stayed with them I'd soon find him.

Mother in the Water Storage

I was only one step away from the glass door of the train station, when two men grabbed me from behind and forced me down the steps. I kicked and screamed, but they covered my mouth, pushed me into the back of a van, and closed the door with a bang. It was pitch dark inside, but someone struck a match and held it up in front of my face. It was Assad. He smiled that old, slimy smile and showed his yellow teeth. He was sober and a bit crazy, like old times.

"Did I scare you?" He tapped on the window that separated the driver's part and yelled at his friends, "Go!"

The van took off. Through the dark gray windows I saw the city's glittering lights, faded and blurred, as if belonging to another world. Smoke rose from burning tires—the remains of the riots.

"Well, well, well!" He sighed. "I found you again, and where? At the train station! You know, Talkhoon, sometimes I've had doubts about your insanity, but tonight all my doubts are removed. You *are* crazy, and crazy as hell! If you had common sense, you'd never go to that fucking train station again. Didn't I catch you here the first time? You could've gone somewhere else and I'd never have been able to find you. You're a lunatic, Talkhoon. Mad!" With his large knuckles he knocked my head so hard it hurt.

The van made a turn and pulled inside Drum Tower, now guarded by several Brothers, like a barracks.

"How did you pass through the guards? Huh? I arrested all of them. These are new ones. The ones who let you out will rot in jail."

He jumped down holding his arm out to help me. "Come on. Let me take you to your room. Now my men know everything. They all know you live down here. I told them we were engaged. You understand? I told the Brothers that we'll soon get married. These people are religious, they can't digest seeing me messing with an unmarried girl. So we're engaged. Remember! Now come down!" He pulled my hand. I screamed and crawled back into the depth of the van, as if it were a safer place.

"Don't act crazy in front of my men." He lowered his voice and said this from between his clenched teeth. "Don't make me beat you up here. Come down, I said." He crawled into the van and pulled me out. The Brothers were around us, but pretended nothing was happening. It was a family scene and they didn't interfere.

Assad pulled me out and I screamed, trying to bite him and run away. He held me like a crazy monkey on his shoulder and I was afraid that he'd feel the hardness of the manuscript on my chest. I wriggled, kicked his belly and punched his back. He headed toward the courtyard. In the basement he dumped me on the bed, but I bounced up like an elastic ball and ran toward the door. He limped toward me and grabbed my shirt collar, ripping Grandmother's silk shirt and revealing the straps of the knapsack. But in his anger he didn't notice them. Holding my chest to secure the manuscript, I ran. He caught me in the corridor. I kicked him and screamed, calling my mother out of blind instinct.

"Help! Mother, help!"

"You want to see your mother, huh?" he said from between his teeth. "Are you sure you want to see your mother?" He asked again. "Come! Let me show you where she is. I'll take you there. She's where *my* mother is!" He prodded me toward the courtyard.

"This way!" He pushed me to the other side of the pool where the water storage was. "She is right here. Let me take you down to see her! Go on down! Your mother is here. Go and see for yourself!" He prodded me with his hand and followed me down the tall stone steps. Now he took a big key ring out of his pocket, selected a key and opened the old iron door with an annoying squeak. I thought he was going to lock me in and I screamed.

"Didn't you call your mother? She's here! It's my fault that you didn't know this before. All these years I wanted to protect you. I didn't want to shock you, I didn't want you to become crazier than you were. I didn't tell you because I cared for you. Look now!" He struck a match and in the dim light showed me an empty pool at the bottom of the steps. It was a small, square hole, deep as a well. I'd heard that water was stored here in olden times. Taara and I had always been scared of this place. The smell of mud, rot, and mildew turned my stomach. Assad struck another match.

"Do you see? Look closer. By the pool! Do you see the bones? Look at that white piece of cloth. It's not white anymore; it's gray now. That's her dress. It used to be her dress. Her skull must be somewhere near."

I didn't see bones, white cloth, or a skull, but I screamed from the bottom of my lungs. He pressed his wide hand against my mouth. "Shut up! You scream one more time and I'll spank your little ass. The brothers know that you're crazy, but I don't want them to think I torture you. So no more screaming!" He kept his hand on my mouth and I kicked him with my sharp, bony knee. I hit him below his belly where his tattooed bird lived. He let go of me and bent forward as if he'd been shot. His bad leg gave way and he fell down the stone steps. I ran up to the garden and toward the tower. Anywhere but my room! I knew he was hurt, because it took him a long time to reach me. I was already on top of the tower when I heard him calling me from the bottom.

"Talkhoon!" His voice was desperate. "I didn't mean to scare you. I'm an idiot, okay? I know I frightened you. We have to sit down and talk about your mother. I was mad at you, because you left me again. Because you keep running away from me. Talkhoon, you know what the problem is?" He paused. "You hear me? The problem is that I care for you more than anyone in this world. Think about it for a second. Who else cares for you?" He paused, letting me think. "Name one person in the whole world." He paused again. "No one. You're all alone. Except for me. I want to take care of you!"

I stood on the balcony of the tower, looking at the night sky. The smell of burnt rubber filled my nostrils. Somewhere in the west, greasy smoke curled up and formed a black cloud. A cold breeze from the north removed the odor of burning rubber and spread the scent of fresh earth. I remembered my day—the people, the banners, the cemetery, the candles, the songs, the bullets, the screams of children, and the smell of earth and blood.

I heard him climbing the steps, panting and cursing under his breath. Any other day, I'd have thrown myself off the tower, taking care not to fall on top of the tree again. But now I couldn't. I didn't want to die. I wanted to go on. I wanted to see things. I was burning with a thirst to be where things happened.

At last he reached me, encircled me with his arms and put his head on my back. He wept for a while and mumbled sweet things, "My bitter herb—my baby girl. How many times did I change your wet diapers?" He sniffled. "After she died—after she drowned herself in that smelly pool—I rocked you on my chest. You were a motherless child and I loved your mother. She went and killed herself and I witnessed it. Why was I the only one in this damned house who saw it? Because I was around her all the time. I was her shadow, Talkhoon. I always followed her."

He pushed me down on the floor of the tower, sat me next to him, and curled his arm around me. My knees were weak and I couldn't resist. He sniffled and said, "I saw her—oh, I wish I had something to drink now. I'm so fucking thirsty.

"When she plucked star jasmines and put them between her breasts, inside her laced bra, I saw her. She didn't know I was watching. First she smelled the tiny blossoms one by one, then squeezed them between her breasts. When she strolled in the garden these little white flowers fell from inside her dress, as if she was a fairy raining star jasmines. I picked up the warm blossoms and kept them in my shirt pocket all day.

"You don't need to hear all this, but I just want you to know, wherever she was, I was there—at the pool when she lay in the sun, half naked, her dark skin getting even darker, or on her bed, the door wide open, lying lazily reading a book, then falling asleep. I saw her legs when her skirt hiked up and her thighs showed. She stretched her long, tanned legs and I watched her, memorizing her lines, to be able to dream about her at night.

"It was around this time that I tattooed the Simorgh on my body. Maybe I thought Baba-Ji's bird would bring me good luck. No, I didn't have any hope of ever possessing her. She was in love with your father. Khanum weaves nonsense when she says Soraya was loose. The witch lies and lies, then believes it's the truth. Soraya wasn't unfaithful. Ask *me*! I know the truth! I'd seen them together. I'd eavesdropped. I'd peaked through the crack of the door. They were in love. Have you seen that tapestry of Leili and Majnoon on the wall of the Tea Room? Your parents were more in love than the fairy tale lovers.

"Then she went and killed herself—just like that." He snapped his fingers and paused. "The voices in her head... Everybody knew she heard voices—" Assad sighed and the winds gathered in my head.

"I was spying on her that night when she went to the water storage—all the way down the steps and inside the dark, stagnant pool. That was the worst kind of death. A fairy should kill herself in the clear water of a spring, not in that poisonous water. But I just stood there, behind the trees, watching. I knew—I mean I sensed what her intention was—but I didn't move to save her. Now you're going to hate me, Talkhoon, even more than you do now. But I can't explain this. Why didn't I run down and pull her out? Why? I've asked myself a million times.

"The next day, they began to search for her and I searched with everyone else. Khanum said since she was a loose woman, something had happened to her in the streets where she walked all night. After a few months, I spread the rumor that she was in Bandar—she'd become the Big Sheikh's wife. I wanted to end the gossip, to shut Khanum's and her sisters' damn mouths. I said my friends had seen her in Bandar. They're stupid, your grandmother and her ugly sisters. They believed me. They wove more stories and added to mine. They believed their own tales. At the Shah's Coronation Ball, the Arab sheikh fell in love with her, they said. One said the Arab kidnapped her, the other said she went of her own will. Fantasies. They cooked them. I added salt and pepper.

"Sina stayed for a while, a few months, in the hope that she'd return. We drank together every night, Sina and I. In the rose arbor we cried. We grew very close to each other. Then he left. I knew he didn't believe the Sheikh story. I don't know what he believed. He never talked much. He scribbled poems on small pieces of cigarette paper and read them for me. I didn't quite get them, but they brought tears to my eyes. When he left, Khanum said he left because of his wife; he went crazy, became Majnoon of the deserts. But this was not the whole truth. Sina was involved with the leftists. Even then he was doing underground work—in a radio station or something. But I kept his secret because I liked him. I liked your father because Soraya loved him. I saw the world through her eyes."

Assad sighed, then continued. "Years passed. I never removed her body. The contaminated storage was a problem now. Mosquitoes for one thing, and snakes. All the neighbors who had water storages had emptied them and filled them with cement. It was three or four years after Soraya's death when Khanum talked about emptying the pool. I was scared. It was stupid, but I was frightened, as if I had killed her. I thought if they pulled her corpse out, they'd accuse me of murder and I'd spend the rest of my life in prison. How can I explain this? I felt I'd killed her. I believed it, and suffered from guilt and remorse. So, one night, before the workers came to pump out the water, I pulled her out. Don't ask me how—I couldn't explain this to you even if I wanted to. It wasn't her anymore. I kept telling myself, this is not Soraya. I buried her. This is a damn big garden. I buried her near the tower, not far from Baba's herb bed.

"They pumped out the muddy water and found some bones at the bottom. They said they were the bones of people of past centuries—a miserable servant girl of one of the viziers, or a poor harem woman. Years passed. I never married."

Assad wiped his face with his bandana and tried to continue. Now that his arm was not on my shoulder, I slid back.

"I saw her in you for the first time when you were thirteen. I saw Soraya in your face and growing body—in the lazy way you walked and the quiet way you did everything. When you lay on your side, studying, when you listened to your grandfather's stories, your black eyes wide and shining. You were nothing like your sister who was rude and bossy, and spoiled like a pet. I said to myself, *I've raised this girl; I'll wait for her to grow ripe. She'll be my Soraya. She'll be mine.*"

There was silence for a while. Assad stayed in the depths of his past, reminiscing in his head. My brain pulsed and my guts sensed danger. He was going to marry me tonight. He was remembering all this and he was going to marry me.

Now a huge explosion shook the city. It was so strong that I feared the tower would collapse. Assad jumped to his feet, hit himself on the head with both hands and said, "They killed my Imam! They blew up his holy house. The infidels!" He pulled my hand, ran with me down the steps, and said in delirium, "Stupid ass that I am. I should've been there, but I sent Mustafa instead. We knew something was going to happen tonight, but I didn't go. All because of you, Talkhoon! You ruined me."

He took me to the basement, picked up his cane and machine gun and went to the door. "I don't know what's happened and I don't have any idea when I'll be back. But a guard will be behind this window all the time, watching you. And some are at the gate. So there is no way out. If you get hungry, tell the boy behind the window to buy you some food. Here, keep this money for food. Don't break the clay bear before I die." He threw a bank note on the bed and rushed out.

Two Letters

A short while after Assad left, the lights went out and my room sank into darkness. A young man came down to the courtyard and sat on a chair, his back to my window. I lay on my bed, breathing calmly, relieved that Assad was gone. I didn't want to think about his story—true or not. I still liked the old tale, the one I'd been raised with: Once upon a time, there was a sheikh who fell in love with the beautiful Soraya at the Shah's coronation ball. He kidnapped her and took her to his castle in Bandar; he made her the flower of his harem and she was happy to be loved. I had lived so long with this fairy tale that I was not able to replace it with another one.

The next morning I opened my eyes to the hoarse voice of an adolescent boy repeating, "One party, party of God! One party, party of God!" Boor-boor was on the half wall, one of her legs tied to a loose brick. The guard—a boy of thirteen or fourteen—with shaven head and a machine gun on his shoulder, sat on Grandmother's folding chair, facing the parrot. He was teaching her to say, "One party, party of God!" and repeated this so many times that Jangi came out of his doghouse and barked at him.

I rolled over on my side. I felt heavy. I'd slept with Baba-Ji's manuscript strapped to my chest under Khanum-Jaan's torn silk shirt. My stomach burned. I tried to remember my last meal. It was the night before, when Assad had read Khanum's letters. I sat up and glanced at my desk. The will was not there. The half-eaten picture of the old Ayatollah lay against the wall—the turban and frown gone. What if the Leader was dead? What if he had been killed in the explosion? I picked up the bank note and looked at it. It still had the Shah's picture, but someone had drawn two sharp horns on top of the monarch's head. Now I looked at Assad's clay bear. It was still sitting on the desk, but at the far end of it, on the verge of falling.

If the courtyard were not guarded I'd take all this money and escape out the back gate. I would avoid the train station. I was mad at myself, not because I was crazy, but because I didn't have experience. I lacked judgment and made rash decisions. I hadn't seen anything in my life, hadn't done anything. I even half-believed in ghosts! How could I know better? How could I know he'd find me in the train station again? I had to become wise.

I could escape again. What if I sent the child-guard away? I wouldn't starve, would I? I tapped on the window. The boy squatted on the floor, cupped his hands around his face, and tried to look inside. I'm not sure if he saw me, but he motioned with his hand, inviting me out.

I changed into a shirt and a pair of pants and went up to the courtyard.

"Listen—I'm hungry."

"So?"

"Brother Sheeri said you'll buy me some lunch."

"I can't leave my post," he said.

"You disobey your boss?"

"He's not my boss. We don't have bosses anymore—he is the head of the Committee."

"What committee?"

"The Revolutionary Committee Number One. Our mosque opened the first committee in the city. Other mosques are following our example."

"I'm hungry! Take this money and buy me some bread and cheese. Please! I haven't eaten for two days."

"I said I can't leave this place."

"I'll report you to Brother Sheeri!"

"He'll praise me for not listening to a crazy girl like you. And you're a dirty aristocrat too."

"Who said that?"

"I wonder why Brother Sheeri wants to marry you."

"If I'm related to Brother Sheeri, then you have to respect me. You're a rude boy."

"Don't call me 'boy,' my name is Brother Hassan." He lifted his gun, aiming at my chest. He was agitated; he could shoot me.

"Okay, okay, put your gun down. I'll wait for Brother Sheeri to come back. Then we'll see."

I went back to my room, fell on the bed and wept.

An hour later another boy came to the courtyard and handed Hassan a long barbari bread. I saw a bunch of green grapes and a big piece of feta cheese on top of the bread. The boy had a small paper bag full of sunflower seeds too; he emptied it in Boor-boor's cage and left.

Hassan sat on the folding chair to eat. Now he turned and glanced at my window. He ate some more and once in a while said to the parrot, "One party, Party of God!" He looked at my window again and finally tapped on the glass. I went out. He tore his bread and gave me half. With his dirty fingers he broke the big square of the feta cheese.

"You want grapes?"

"No. Just bread and cheese. Thank you."

I grabbed the food and ran toward my room.

"You can stay here and eat in the fresh air, if you want."

I lingered.

"Sit on the chair. I'll sit on the floor."

I sat on the folding chair and ate. Each bite that rolled down my throat gave me immense pleasure. The mild winter sun tickled the right side of my face. My hands shook.

"Your hands are shaking."

"I was sick."

"What sickness?"

"Asthma."

"If you have such bad asthma, why did you run away? There is a war outside; they burn tires and set off dynamite."

"I'm sure you want to be in the streets and do all of these things."

"You're right—that's all I want."

"Then why don't you go?"

"My shift ends at five."

"All sorts of things are happening between now and five—explosions, everything."

"I know. These infidels blew up a mosque last night. Three leaders were killed."

"The Great Leader?"

"Oh, no. Thank God. Not him. Three ayatollahs—very important ones. We're going to wipe out these infidels."

"But you're here all the time," I said, chewing my cheese sandwich. Jangi sat at my feet and, like old times, begged for scraps. I threw a little piece of bread to him.

"This is a nasty dog. Barks all the time," Hassan said. "I almost shot him this morning."

"This is Brother Sheeri's dog."

"No!"

"Yes. Brother Sheeri kept him since he was a little puppy."

"It's good you told me. I was going to shoot him."

"You want to shoot real bad, huh?"

"How do you know?"

"I just know."

"What is your name?"

"Taara."

"What?'

"Taara!"

"You look like a boy. It's like I'm talking to a boy."

"Why?"

"Girls are different. They're shy. They blush when they talk to a boy," he said. "They're pretty—"

I laughed and enjoyed his comments, and this way we sat and chatted for a while. He asked me questions about the house and I told him horror stories—my great grandmother's ghost roaming in a rusty wheelchair, bones and skulls at the bottom of the water storage, the hollow space on top of the tower where the Simorgh once landed and left one sapphire feather. I told him about my grandmother's séances, ghosts turning the tables, talking and whining, flying and smearing tar on the walls and carpets. The more I said, the wider his eyes became, until he stopped me and said that I was lying. I said I was not. He made me swear on the Great Leader's dear life. I did and he believed me. At the end, he was very friendly and showed me how to hold the machine gun. When I went back to my room, all I thought about was to find a way to send Hassan away and escape.

Later that day, I was taking a nap when Hassan tapped on the window and woke me. When I went up he handed me a stack of letters.

"Hey, the mail just came. I thought maybe you should hold it for Brother Sheeri."

"Thank you, Hassan."

"I'm leaving now. It's five. Brother Morad has the next shift. Listen, I'm going to the Imam's house. He's speaking tonight. Poor Morad has to listen to the Imam's sermon on the radio. 'Bye."

He ran, his machine gun bumping against his back.

I sat on my bed looking at the letters. There were several from the light, water, and telephone companies. The last ones were from Khanum-Jaan and Taara. With trembling hands I hid Taara's letter inside my shirt, to postpone the joy or the grief. I opened Grandmother's envelope. She still used a fountain pen and her small cursive danced shakily.

Assad,

This is my third letter to you. What has happened? Why don't you bring me home? I can't come to that part of the town by myself, and the phones are disconnected. Please, son, I'm waiting for you! I don't want to die here away from home.

I dreamed that poor Anvar had finally awakened and I was not with him. He woke up and went into the garden, all the way to the tower, to his dryandra tree; he sat under it and waited. Guess what he waited for? The Simorgh? No, son, no. He waited for Taara to come and play her setar, but she didn't. Anvar sat and sat and sat. He cried and pulled his hair, but Taara didn't come.

Take me away from here. My eyes are terrible and I can't go any-where alone. My sisters are tormenting me with their stupidity—their tarot cards and ghost calls. I don't believe in this nonsense anymore, Assad. I'm not writing to Papa anymore. Papa died forty-six years ago and his spirit died with him. I want to come home and burn all those silly letters I wrote him. But Anvar is alive and will wake up any mo-ment. I know that. The thought that I've neglected him is tormenting me. Come and take me home, Assad. I've dreamed....

Khanum

I read the letter several times and heard Grandmother's voice in my head. Her worry for Baba made me uncomfortable. What if her dream was real and Baba woke up, saw all these guards, panicked, and died? But what if he was dying now? I paced my room. How could I see my grandfather, just for a few minutes, to make sure he was fed and sleeping sound and safe? There was no way to go upstairs. I could hear the Brothers stamping their boots above my head. There were many of them now and I was sure all three floors were full of bearded guards. I lay on the bed, thoughts and worries circling in my head, twisting and tangling with the wild winds. I caressed Taara's letter, but didn't dare open it. Postpone! Postpone her news!

All afternoon the Leader's sermon blasted through the small speakers of Morad's transistor radio. "The West must go! The East must go! This is the government of God!" He sermonized angrily, with a villager's accent. Late at night, Morad left with his radio and a third boy came with a gas lantern and a book. It was blackout again. I lit a candle and opened Taara's envelope.

Through the Ash Trees: A Letter to Talkhoon

Talkhoon,

At last I'm writing to you, on this bus, on this shady road, and I'll mail it at the next town, hoping that Assad won't hide it from you. I also hope he won't give this to Khanum-Jaan. She'll die of grief.

This is my story: Vahid takes me to his room on the second floor of a two-story tenant house. Men occupy all the rooms. Most of them are addicted to drugs. The ones who smoke opium consider themselves healthy. They hold some kind of a job. Those who shoot heroin are the hopeless. They buy the drug by selling it to the younger kids. Hashish and marijuana, rolled in cigarette paper, are ordinary things. They smoke them between the hard drugs. The men bring women, their drug companions, to their rooms.

Talkhoon, there is a beautiful college girl with large green eyes and the husky voice of a movie star who shares needles with Vahid. She passes out on the floor and I have to drag her to bed. This is repeated like all the rituals that repeat themselves here—the foggy music, the broken, nasal conversation—dialogues in a dream.

In our room, there is a squeaky metal bed that sinks and touches the floor each time we lie down on it. Vahid and I seldom have privacy, but even when we do, we don't make love. He kisses me and sometimes when he wants more, he falls asleep. But why am I saying this to you? To my little, innocent sister?

In spite of this, my belly is growing and it gets bigger every day. Marriage is not even an issue here. These people are beyond these matters. Besides, who is going to work? Vahid doesn't really work, but he goes out every day and comes back with a bag of food and some liquor and a little money that he keeps in a drawer for my needs. He says he adores me; he calls me his golden muse and writes poems about my beauty. Sometimes, when we're alone, he sits me in a chair in front of the window and brushes my hair. He murmurs his poetry and runs the brush slowly from the top of my head to the ends of the long strands with the rhythm of his verse, and this takes a long time. I sit quietly, feeling the blood running under my skin and his poems pulsing in my veins.

Every morning I roam around the house and inhale the burnt, bittersweet aroma of opium. There is this jobless actor who invites me to his room. He never sleeps and his eyes are wide and hollow like an owl's. He wears this small, black velvet jacket that smells of smoke and old sweat. His hair stands up, stiff and unwashed. He shows me an oval mirror on the mantle place, covered with the dust of years. He writes TAARA on the dust with his index finger, and smiles. Now without a word he lies down on his dirty bed and opens his arms for me. That's when I leave his room and roam around some more.

Sometimes I go out, but I never leave the neighborhood. I'm afraid of getting lost. I stroll to the nearby market and buy myself a pair of cheap earrings from an accessory store, or a blood-red nail polish for my nails. The dangling earrings and my red glossy nails make me happy for few hours.

We party every night. Tenants from the different rooms get together, drinking and smoking. Some of these people are very intelligent—they discuss art, philosophy, and politics. There was a movie director here once, a famous poet, an actress, a small girl with long black hair who talked about the French philosopher, Sartre. And my belly is rising by the minute, not letting me enjoy myself. If it wasn't for my growing belly I'd do everything everyone does. But this baby is always present. She presses herself against the wall of my womb and stares at me through the transparent skin of my belly. When I stand in front of the mirror looking at myself, I see her, small and imprisoned, as though a hundred years old, pleading with her wide-open eyes to come out into this world. Its dark here, she says, it's dark, let me out! I see her full image when she turns toward me, and I know that I have to save her.

One afternoon Vahid leaves the house, and I go to the window and look out. It's late autumn and the red maple leaves float above the ground. The street looks clean and wet, as if swept and hosed down. I smell the scent of the damp earth and feel happy. I feel happy because I think of the possibility of not being here. A few children play at the door of their house. I raise my head to the sky and see a bird, or rather the shadow of a bird. I can tell that it has four wings, two smaller, two longer, extended toward the earth. I see the shadow of its talons. They are big and strong, and could lift a person.

I say to myself, Real or just a shadow, this is a good omen. I take the stack of money from the drawer and leave the house. I say to myself, I'll follow the bird and go wherever she leads me. I walk. I keep looking at the sky. The street is full of people. There is a demonstration going on. Men and women walk slowly with banners, shouting, asking for freedom or food. They act as if someone will listen to them and give them what they need.

And I find myself among them. It's impossible to avoid. They have filled the street from corner to corner. I walk and chant what they chant, absently, looking up at the sky. The shadow of the bird hovers above me. It's a good omen and I follow. We pass Shah Reza Avenue,

College Intersection, Drum Tower. The bird doesn't enter our garden. I know that. I know that the Simorgh would never take refuge in a war tower. Baba picked the wrong place to look for it. Baba was where the bird belonged at first, in the mountains, but came to the city to look for it in the house of the war viziers. What a mistake our grandfather made. So I feel that I have had a vision, or whatever you may call it. The bird resides on top of the Black Mountains of Azerbaijan, where Baba-Ji was born and heard the Simorgh story from his father. I buy a ticket and go to Ahar.

Now Vahid, the gloomy house of the tenants, the actor with the dusty mirror, the parties, the smoke, the haze, the drunken girls, are all behind me. I don't even remember very much. My belly is growing and I'm going where I think the Simorgh is.

I'll make this long story short, Talkhoon, and skip the door-to-door search, the narrow uphill streets, the blind alleys, the houses of Baba's relatives now occupied by strangers, the house where he was born now a ruin. I'll skip all this and get to the point where someone tells me about an Angha family, the only one left of the tribe, living out of town at the skirt of the mountain. This is Baba-Ji's cousin's house. But the man, the cousin, is dead, and his wife and son live in this shack at the foot of the Black Mountain. I take this as a good sign.

The son is forty years old and has red and yellow hands. He dyes wool. They are poor. I pay money in advance and promise more. The man, Zafar, takes me every morning with his donkey to the mountain. (Yes, with my big belly I sit on a donkey, climbing the unpaved mountain roads!). He leaves me there in a shepherd's shack for hours. I tell him I'm an ornithologist, looking for a rare bird. I always take my black attaché with me. When Zafar leaves, I sit on a rock in front of the shack or walk around, looking up at the sharp, snow-covered peaks, or gazing at the silvery stream running along the rocks. Cold wind hits my face and powder snow settles on me. I remember some passages of Baba's book word by word:

"The mysterious bird was called Phoenix by the Greeks. It also means 'purple-red,' 'crimson,' 'date,' 'date palm,' and 'Phoenicia.' The date palm continually renews itself. All these words suggest that the bird is associated with red and purple and comes from the East, the land of sunrise. The Simorgh is the Bird of Fire."

I keep going to the mountain until it gets too cold to stand the harsh winds—even with the sheepskin coat that I borrow from the old woman. At last, I give up when there is no sign of the red purple wings or even that pale shadow I'd seen in the skies of the city. My belly is growing; the old woman and her son get less hospitable and whisper behind my back in Turkish, thinking I'm another crazy Angha with a bastard child inside me. I feel that it's time to go.

It's a twenty-hour bus ride to Tehran. But I'm planning to stop in Tabriz and stay in a hotel. I need a few days to gather my thoughts. Then I'll go to Tehran and start a new life. But I have to find a place in the big city. Khanum-Jaan won't have me in Drum Tower with my enormous belly and I can't go back to Vahid's house. I don't want my daughter to know him.

I'm writing this letter to you, Talkhoon, while the bus is traveling on a narrow road curtained on either side by ash trees. These trees are not green, Talkhoon, they're gray. The breeze plays with the long, gray branches, waving them in the air, like some old woman's long hair. My fellow traveler, a middle-aged man from Azerbaijan, who wears a brown fedora, explains to me that ash trees bear small, yellow fruit like olives. People of this area dry the fruit and eat it. It's sweet and full of nutrition and it's called senjed. I tell him that I've eaten senjed before at the Norooz table and he smiles with joy, as if he is the one who has created the fruit. So this way we pass between the ash trees and I write to you on the hard surface of my black attaché and my kind neighbor takes a noisy nap with his head resting on my shoulder.

Black Uniform/ White Gown

Someone had decorated the table: a glazed blue vase, a thick, hard-covered brown book (I knew it was Baba-Ji's Simorgh book in print), and a chestnut-colored, polished setar whose neck was much longer than a real setar's. These were all arranged on a small table, covered with a white, laced cloth. I sat, watching them, thinking how good it would be to cut a few long branches of star jasmine and put them in this blue vase. A gust

of wind blew in from an open window and brushed my face. I stretched
my hand to pick up the book, but an annoying sound—a hammer hitting a
nail—stopped me. I pulled my hand back. I can open this book only when
there is peace and silence in the world. Absolute silence. Because I have
to read it aloud. The hammer hit the nail harder and harder, repeating the
same nerve-wracking bangs. It went on for so long that the bright room,
the table, and I all disappeared.

I opened my eyes and saw Assad standing on top of a chair, banging nails with a hammer. He was hanging a curtain—a dark gray fabric
the color of ashes under burned coal. He was in his old threadbare house
pants and yellowish undershirt that stretched across his round belly and
had sweat rings under the arms. His khaki uniform hung on the back of
the chair and a tall bottle of vodka stood on the desk.

All my senses rang and my nerves vibrated as if an electric current ran
through my body. He was in his house clothes and his bottle was on the
table. He was going to stay for a while. I held my breath, thinking about
the knives. They were still in the closet among my clothes. I could hide one
under my arm the way I'd done before. Baba's manuscript was safe in the
knapsack, now as always strapped on my chest. Taara's letter had joined
the pages of the bird book. But Khanum-Jaan's letter lay open next to me
on the bed. Let Assad read the letter and know that Khanum wanted to
come home. Let him remember to feed Baba.

I closed my eyes to keep from seeing him, but then I opened them
quickly, thinking that if I pretended sleep he would slip under the blanket. So I ran to the closet, picked up one of the knives, and rushed to the
bathroom.

"Woke you up, huh?" He said from the top of the chair. "I have to put
this curtain up. All these boys are outside all the time and tomorrow a
bunch of workers will come to cut the trees. We need privacy."

Which trees? I wanted to ask. But I couldn't talk with this man. In the
bathroom, I secured the knapsack on my chest and held the knife under
my arm. Now I came out to creep into the closet and sit there like old
times, but Assad blocked my way; he had a large white box in his hand.

"This is for you, Talkhoon. Sit here, let me open it." He had one of
those wide, yellow-toothed grins.

I stood by the bathroom door and didn't move. He put the box on the bed, opened it, and drew out a black gown. It was something like a long raincoat. Then he took out a large black scarf.

"This is your uniform. It's not as pretty as the dresses you've always had, but from now on you have to wear it. Not only you, but all the women in this country should wear uniforms. This is the Imam's order. You women must cover your hair and body. I've really come to believe in this. It makes sense. It reduces temptation and prevents lust and adultery. Later, I'll buy you a couple more so you can wash and change."

Now he shoved his hand inside the box and laughed. "Did you think that was all? There is something prettier here. Very special. Let me see—aha!" He pulled out a white gown. A wedding gown. It was so long that it took him a while to take out all of the skirt and its train. Layers of lace over lace, gauze over gauze. "I want you to put this on and climb the chair. I know it's too long for you. I'll measure the hem and fix it. Come on, put it on."

I didn't move.

"Are you shocked? Did you think it wouldn't happen? There is no other way, Talkhoon. It's not good for my reputation to spend time alone with you while we're not legally wed. We have to finish the deal. Next month, when the whole country celebrates the first Sacrifice Day after the Great Revolution, we'll have our wedding. How about that? But we need to fix this. It's too long for you. I took it off of a wooden manikin in a fancy department store. We occupied the store and turned it into a mosque. Come on, I want to measure the hem. Hey, I'm tired, Talkhoon. You don't even care if I've slept the past thirty-six hours. I just have the morning off."

He approached me with the gown in his hand, but I moved back, slipped into the bathroom, and shut the door behind me. I pressed my back against it because it didn't have a lock.

"Now, what the fuck is this again?" he yelled. "Why are you acting like that? Open the door and come out. If you don't want to wear this now, don't wear it. To hell with you!" He grumbled from a distance now. "Why do you have to poison everything? Why do you ruin my mood all the time? I'm telling you I'm exhausted and I need to rest."

I heard him drop himself onto the chair and take something out of a paper bag. He opened the bottle of vodka.

I stayed in the bathroom for a long time, pressing the knife against my body. When I didn't hear him anymore, I opened the door a crack and saw him on the bed, flat on his stomach, snoring. He'd drunk some of the vodka, but hadn't touched the food. Four long sandwiches lay on the desk. I smelled fresh salami, pickles and sliced tomatoes. I picked a sandwich, tiptoed out of the room into the corridor, and sat on the floor next to the two large burlap sacks full of old clothes. I leaned back against the laundry room's wall and ate with appetite. From the window I could see part of the courtyard. It was Hassan's shift again. He sat on Khanum's folding chair, teaching Boor-boor to say, "One party, Party of God." Three workers hit the low brick wall with stone hammers. The old flowerbed and the fountain were full of pieces of broken brick. The few pansies left in the bed had been crushed.

Seeing the men, I remembered what Assad had said about building apartment houses. He wanted to tear up the tower, the trees, and the bushes—the climbing star jasmine—the one from which my mother plucked its tiny blossoms and put them between her breasts. He wanted to uproot Baba-Ji's dryandra tree under which we held our breath and waited for the bird to come; my father's rose arbor where he wrote poems on cigarette papers. He was going to flatten the garden, run a tractor over Baba-Ji's herb bed, cut the weeping willows behind which Grandma Negaar's ghost had hidden for half a century. Then the eastern gate would be revealed and I'd be trapped here forever.

The bite of sandwich turned to stone and tears blurred my vision. If Assad uprooted the trees and flattened the garden, there would remain no hope.

"One party, Party of God! Come on, you stupid aristocrat! Aren't you a parrot?" Hassan was mad at the bird.

Boor-boor's emerald green feathers glistened in the bright daylight. Having been fed by different guards, and enjoying the spring sun, she looked completely recovered. Now she jerked her neck and stared at Hassan with her only eye, puzzled. But Jangi was sulky and sat by his cage, panting nervously. He didn't like the men. The one phrase the boy insisted on teaching the parrot irritated the dog. Now he saw me, or smelled my sandwich, and came down the steps and sat in front of me. I gave him my leftovers and he ate greedily. Looking at Jangi, I remembered our only walk together, following Taara and her friend. I remembered that busy intersection where I lost my sister, or decided to lose her. I wondered how the course of events would be different if I'd brought Taara home. I realized that I had been responsible for my own entrapment and for Taara's misery. Where was she now? In a third-rate hotel in Tabriz, gazing at her growing belly, "gathering her thoughts"? If Taara were in this house, Assad could never trap me here. Taara and I would think of a way to confront him. So was it true that I was crazy?

At five, when Hassan's shift ended and Morad came with his transistor radio, Hassan tapped on the window to wake Assad. A few minutes later, Assad came out and saw Jangi and me sitting together in front of the laundry room. He was wearing a clean uniform and a black bandana around his neck. His eyes were bloodshot. He hadn't slept enough and he was in a bad mood.

"Get up!" He said angrily. "I have people out there. Get inside and put on your uniform. If I see you one more time with bare head and bare feet, I'll start to do what I should've done before. I'll make you black and blue. Understand? And wear a pair of black pants and black socks under the uniform. No more barefoot around hear. You are a woman—do you get this? Crazy or not crazy, you have to cover yourself."

He limped toward the steps, using the cane to climb. He left without saying when he'd be back.

Another Disguise

I waited a long time for the night-shift boy to fall asleep. I knew he would. These were children after all, not grown men. This one didn't look like a street boy. He was literate—always brought a book and read in the light of his gas lantern. Outside, there was curfew and the city lights went off at ten o'clock.

In my dark room, I wore Assad's dirty khaki uniform and secured the waist with a tight belt. The shirt's stench turned my stomach, but I had no choice. This was my most dangerous flight. It was curfew outside and I had on a Revolutionary Guard's uniform, many sizes too large for me. I lit a candle and looked at myself in the mirror to make sure my appearance was convincing. It was not. Even if the rolled-up pants legs and the baggy shirt passed notice, my hair was suspect. It was longer now, and although I'd combed it back with gel, it looked girlish. I picked up the scissors and cut my hair short. But the haircut was lousy; it looked crooked. So, with Assad's razor, I shaved my head. My scalp bled and burned, but there was no way back—my head was half shaved and I had to finish the job. When I was done, I smeared some hand cream on my bald skin to stop the burning. In the mirror, I saw a sexless lunatic fresh from the public asylum. Searching for a long time in the crowded closet, I finally found my black woolen hat. One cold winter Daaye had woven it for me. I put it on and sat down and waited.

The boy kept reading. I waited for so long that I thought I could kill the bastard. I could get out, attack him from behind, and stab him with the knife I'd hidden in the knapsack. I could kill the boy because he didn't stop reading, wasting my precious time. The unusual quiet of the night added to my anxiety—no gunshots or distant explosions. I could hear Jangi snoring in his doghouse.

At last, I heard a thud. The boy's book fell on the brick floor. Then he spread his bandana and knelt on it. I thought he was going to take a nap, but he prayed instead—knelt and bent and rose, knelt again and murmured to himself. I could kill him while praying and send him to heaven where his Allah and his dead ayatollahs were. But at last he lay down on the floor, curled up like a fetus, and slept. He was exhausted.

When I was about to leave the room, I saw the clay bear on the desk. But how could I break it without making a sound? That would wake up the boy. I should have broken it before, when the sound of the workers in the yard would have covered the bear's explosion. Again, I hadn't planned well. That money could make me secure for a long time.

There was no way to take the bear, so I left Assad's money and tiptoed upstairs to the courtyard. When I reached the boy and his lantern on the brick floor, I almost tripped over his book. *One Hundred and One Prayers and More*. So this was what the idiot read. Quietly, I climbed the steps and went upstairs. I had to see Baba-Ji before leaving.

The vestibule was bare. Once a large Kashan carpet had lain on the floor and a crystal chandelier with eighty candle-shaped lamps had lit the large panels of Persian miniatures. Now, along the walls the guards had piled boxes of ammunition, boots, rifles, machine guns, and handguns. The smell of men's sweat, cigarette butts, and the residue from fired weapons hung in the thick air. I turned to the right, entered Baba-Ji's study and turned on my flashlight. The room was empty. I moved the light's small circle all around. Baba and his recliner were gone. My heart sank. My knees buckled and I sat on the floor.

The bastard had taken him to a hospital—or he had died. Assad had killed him by not feeding him.

But I had to move on.

Move, stupid girl! He'll kill you too. You have to run away, before the boy wakes up.

I got to my feet, fighting to suppress a scream forcing itself out of my throat. Before I left, I opened the small closet room—Khanum-Jaan's cell— and threw the beam of light ahead. Baba-Ji sat opposite the door, staring at me. He was in his recliner, eyes wide open.

"Baba, it's me, Talkhoon." I approached him. "Are you awake?"

But he was asleep with his eyes open. Did he open his eyes one day, wake for a minute, and fall asleep again? Did he wake, trying to call us, but seeing the bare room and no one around, panic and fall into the dark hole again? There was no way to know. I checked his IV bottle; it was full of the transparent liquid. I cast the small circle of light on my grandfather's head and face. His hair and beard had grown long, as if he was still alive. Daaye was not here to trim them. I brushed his dry, lifeless hair with my fingertips and caressed his white beard. Oh, how far away he was, how far away and inaccessible. But Assad had cleaned him, fed him, and put him here, in this closet—until a bed in a hospital became available. He hadn't disconnected the tube. How could he? Wasn't Assad Baba's son?

"Baba-Ji, if you're going to wake up at all, now is the time. I'll take you to the back gate, and we'll fly off together. Where, you're asking? I don't know. Maybe the Simrogh will see us and pick us up. Maybe you'll burn a barb of the sapphire feather and we'll both disappear. Baba, wake up, please!"

My childish words surprised me. Whenever I was around Baba-Ji, I spoke as if I believed in the Simorgh and the miracles of its blue tail feather.

"Baba-Ji, wake up! Please! It's me, Talkhoon!"

He didn't wake up. I assured him I would make his manuscript into a real book. I also told him that he shouldn't worry about the last chapter. Who could tell? Maybe I'd be able to write it some day. This surprised me. Why was I committing myself to such a huge task?

Before I left, I told my grandfather about my dream—his book with its hard brown cover sitting next to Taara's setar. If Baba could speak, he would say, *A bright dream! Both the book and the instrument are signs of promises. Unread words and unheard songs.* I could even hear his voice interpreting my dream.

I kissed his forehead, said farewell, and left.

In the vestibule I heard moaning. I stood still and listened. Were these the ghosts of Khanum-Jaan's ancestors mourning the loss of Drum Tower? I concentrated. These were real voices echoing in the empty second floor. People were in pain up there.

On the dark porch, I held my hand to the wall to keep from falling. The boy was still sleeping in the courtyard. A half moon swam smoothly beneath the dark clouds, now and then throwing light on the boy's prayer book. I could easily bypass him and run into the garden to the eastern gate. But Jangi would bark. I should have brought a piece of bread for the dog. Lingering for a few seconds, not knowing what to do, I heard voices from the direction of the pool. It was Assad, giving orders in a loud whisper.

"This way!" he said. "Move, or I'll shoot you right here!"

"Where are you taking me?" Someone said. "I'm not going with you!"

This voice was muffled, as if rising from behind a thick cloth. It was hard to tell if this was a man or a woman.

"Shut your fucking mouth!" Assad ordered. "Mustafa, you know where the laundry room is? Here, take this key. Now be careful, I don't want the girl to wake up—I have to go back to the van and get something."

From behind the wall, Mustafa appeared, prodding someone with the tip of his machine gun. He kept saying, "This way, watch out!"

Now I could see a head hidden in a brown paper bag and a pair of black pants and tennis shoes. This person was either a girl or a young man.

"Go down the steps!" Mustafa pushed his prisoner.

"No!" the prisoner protested.

"Shut up! There are people sleeping here. Shut your mouth, or I'll beat you up!"

The boy in the courtyard woke and picked up his bandana and book. He was startled. His lantern was out and he couldn't see much. He looked around, trying to figure out where the voices had come from. Mustafa returned from the basement and noticed him.

"Sleeping, huh? Is this the way you're serving the Holy Revolution? There is a prisoner down there. An infidel. Brother Sheeri wants to do the interrogation himself. If I tell him you'd slept on your shift, he'll shoot you on the spot. Understood?"

"I'm sorry, Brother Mustafa. I was praying, and suddenly I passed out. I haven't slept for two nights in a row."

"Sheeri is coming back. He has a few hours off to get some sleep, then we have an important meeting at the Leader's house. It's your responsibility to keep this prisoner quiet. You know that Sheeri's girl is nuts. She may wake up and make a commotion. Here, get the key." Mustafa handed the boy a key and left.

I stood in the shadow of the porch, not knowing what to do. If I ran into the trees, the boy would chase me and the secret gate would be revealed. No hope of flight would remain. If I just walked down to my room, he'd still see me and report me, but at least the gate would remain hidden. So I went down the steps to the courtyard and casually walked toward the basement.

"Hey, stop! You're not allowed to go down there!" The boy shouted after me. He thought I was one of the Brothers going down to the basement.

I ignored him, went down to my room and closed the door. I knew that
he wouldn't dare open that door.

"Hey, come out!" He ran upstairs, calling, "Brother Sheeri! Brother
Mustafa!"

Meanwhile the prisoner in the laundry room banged crazily on the
door, "Open! Open!" This was a woman's voice.

I ran to the bathroom, took off Assad's uniform and hung the knapsack
behind the door. I didn't want him to see me in his dirty clothes. I was
about to jump into the shower and draw the curtain when the door flung
open and Assad aimed a machine gun at me. I tried to cover my body with
my hands.

"Is it you? They said a guard came down here—" He saw the uniform
piled under my feet. "You wore my uniform, huh? To run away again?"
He waited for my answer. Someone was knocking violently on the door.
Assad yelled, "It's okay, Brother. Go back to your post!" They knocked
again. Assad went out and sent the worried guards away. Now he came
back and stood in the frame of the bathroom door, gazing at me. I was
shivering. He pulled the woolen hat off my head, saw my clean-shaven
scalp, and broke into a horselaugh.

After laughing enough, in a good humor and in one of his caressing
tones, he said, "Talkhoon, Talkhoon! Crazy baby!" He hugged me and
rubbed my bald head with his hand. "You little cantaloupe! But you don't
look ugly at all. Anyone else would look horrible. Look at you, you silly
girl!" He turned me toward the mirror, embraced me from behind, and
made me look at myself. "You shaved your hair, put on my clothes, and
tried to run away again. But where? And how? How could you get past all
these men?" He knocked his knuckles on my bare head. "When will you
get some sense, huh? Maybe I'll have to get some pills for you again—the
kind that used to make you easy to handle. But I don't have a prescription
and your doctor has fled the country. I'm too busy to find a brain doctor
for you. Come now, let me wash you. Now that you're naked, let me wash
my stinky sweat off your body. You know? It's nice that you wore my
stuff. Doesn't that mean that you don't hate me anymore?" He turned on

the hot and cold water, and then the shower. He led me into the bathtub and began to soap my back, mumbling broken sentences.

"This is all I want in the world—is it too much to ask? I just want to wash you, girly. I want to care for you, protect you, and you keep running away from me as if *I'm* the one who has hurt you. Have I ever hurt you, Talkhoon? Oh, God, look at your thighs; I can't believe I'm finally running my hand inside your thighs. God Almighty, have mercy on me, give me strength just for a few weeks, help me to wait. I'm touching Talkhoon's slippery body, the way I did when she was only a baby and I changed her diapers."

I shut my eyes and heard deafening drumbeats from beyond the whirling winds in my head. This was the prisoner, banging crazily on the door. Now a storm gathered in my brain—*Hoo! Hoo!*—and dry winds blew and washed the insides of my body. Was I all body? Or was my real self somewhere else? Could he touch that self? Could he take that away? *Hoo!* the tearing winds answered.

Now the parrot screamed, the dog barked, the prisoner banged, and someone tapped on the windowpane. A thin voice shouted, "Let me in! This is my own house, bastard! Are you asking me who I am? Who are *you*, vagabond?"

Assad dropped the soap, cursed, and went out. A few seconds later he came back, and in a controlled rage, said, "Turn off the shower and stay in the bathroom. Your grandmother is here!"

It's Dark! It's Dark!

"What is going on here, Assad?" I heard Khanum's voice from behind the bathroom door. "There are guards at the door of my house! I said I'm Assad's mother. They said, 'You mean Brother Sheeri?' Have you changed your name?"

"Calm down, Khanum. Sit down and catch your breath."

"Catch my breath? This puny little bastard kept asking who I was. What is going on? Tell me, or I'll die this minute and you'll be responsible for my death! What is this uniform you're wearing? Are you a Guard? Have you let these vagabonds stay in my house?"

"Sit down, Khanum, let me explain everything—"

"First tell me, what are you doing in the girl's room? I can smell her. Is she here?"

"No. I put her in a hospital."

"Oh, Assad. You took the girl to a crazy house? This is an awful thing to do. I dream all the time—I dream she has long black hair, all tangled around her neck, choking her. She is a fragile girl, Assad, only fourteen—"

"Talkhoon is seventeen, Khanum."

"Seventeen? I thought she was fourteen. But what difference does it make? Anyone would perish in a crazy house. Now they call it clinic. But it's really the same. And she wasn't that crazy in the first place. Now that the whole country is going crazy and everybody is acting like lunatics, she could be out too. But tell me, why are you here? Are you using her room?"

"They've occupied the house—"

"What?"

"Temporarily. They'll leave. I'll take the girl out, soon—"

"Who has let them occupy my house?"

"This is a revolution, Khanum. Haven't you followed the news? Don't your sisters have a TV or a radio?"

"To hell with them. I'm fed up. They're vain and stupid. That's why I came back. I can't stand them anymore. I want to live in my own house and die here. I want to go upstairs, where Anvar is."

"Baba is fine. I feed him everyday. I clean him."

"Oh, Assad, Assad, how could I do this to him? To my own husband? How could I just leave him like this? He's alive, Assad. Do you understand?"

"If I didn't understand, would I feed him and clean him and take care of him? But this can't go on forever. We have to find him a good hospital. He'll get weak like this. Nurses have to take care of him, give him vitamins."

"Nonsense! I won't let him out of my house. I'll take care of him myself. I'll get vitamins or whatever he needs from Doctor Shafa."

"Doctor Shafa has escaped the country, Khanum—haven't you heard?"

"Without even saying goodbye?"

"Many have left without saying goodbye."

"What happened to Kia, Assad? They shot my son, huh? Tell me the truth. Did they shoot him?"

"I don't think so. If he was executed, I'd see his name in the paper."

"He is hiding somewhere. And Vafa—"

"If they catch Vafa they'll torture him to death; they won't just put him against the wall. He is an infidel."

"Whatever that means. I hate these names. I hate all these ugly words they're using these days to label people. That mushroom head, that Imam—the butcher—"

"Hey, hey—watch out, Khanum! These boys out there are all devotees of the Great Leader. If anyone hears you talking like this, you'll lose your head."

"Do you think I'm afraid of a bunch of vagabonds?"

"Okay, you're not. Say whatever you want. I'm just warning you. You've got to understand the changes that have happened in this country. There is no Shah anymore. You know this, don't you?"

"To hell with the Shah. He and his illiterate father ruined our country. If England hadn't ended the Ghajar dynasty, these disasters would've never happened. Sons of bitches, traitors, all— they sold our land to a bunch of ignorant shitheads."

"Okay now, don't hurt yourself over nothing. Let me take you home."

"Home?"

"To your sisters. This place is occupied."

"Have you done this?"

"Done what?"

"Given away our house?"

"I didn't give away anything, Khanum-Jaan. The Revolutionary Guards occupied the house."

"And you cooperated with them. You're wearing their uniform."

"They forced me to wear it."

"Nonsense!"

"Let me take you to your sisters, Khanum. It's dangerous here. There are bombs and ammunition upstairs. You have to leave."

"Is Anvar sleeping among bombs and ammunition?"

"I said I'm trying to find a vacant bed."

"No way! I'm staying. I'll go up by myself, and if this little vagabond stops me, I'll teach him a lesson!"

"Listen, Khanum. Upstairs is full of men. It's not a house anymore. All I'm trying to do is to chase them out."

"You?"

"Yes. Why do you think I'm staying here? I could've left. Do you think I like to live in a barracks? I'm trying to do my best to chase them out. But I can't do it by force. You understand? They're armed to the teeth. They're dangerous. I have to be careful with them and trick them. I'm working on it. I promise you it won't take more than a month. You'll be back home and I'll bring Talkhoon, too."

"How about Taara?"

"Taara is gone, Khanum."

"Gone?"

"She's married, Khanum. Now don't start crying!"

"Married to a junky? Did you say he was a junky?"

"How would I know? It's almost a year now, Khanum. If she was unhappy, she'd come back."

"She may still come back, Assad."

"She may. She may. Now wipe your eyes and let me take you home."

"Let me see him for a minute, Assad. Please! I beg you, son. Let me look at Anvar for a minute. He's all I have. I dreamed about him. Didn't you read my letters?"

"No, Khanum, I didn't receive any letters. It's a revolution. Letters don't go through."

"I dreamed he had woken up—"

Their voices faded away. In the corridor, Khanum said, "I can't see anymore, even with the glasses you bought me. The whole world is dark. It's dark—"

Charcoaled Shish-Kabob

Between the day Khanum-Jaan visited and the day men began to cut the trees, my hair grew a bit. After hanging the gray curtain, Assad put a lock on the door, and now whenever he left he locked me in. Drum Tower was now officially a Revolutionary Committee center, a jail, and a barracks in one. Through the crack of the curtain I could see a black flag waving on the roof of the tower. When the spring wind blew hard the flag slapped itself.

I sat all day in my uniform and slept in it. The black shroud and the scarf enveloped me, securing me like a coffin. When Assad was in my room, I moved into the closet and stayed there. He came whenever his revolution was on pause, or he was too exhausted to do more revolution and needed some rest. He sneaked bottles of vodka in and hid them inside my desk, and when he drank, he lay the half-chewed picture of his Imam face down, so that the old man wouldn't see him. He was too tired to bother me, but he hadn't forgotten that we were supposed to marry on Sacrifice Day.

So he cut hours from his sleep, sat cross-legged on top of the bed, spread the multilayers of gauze, satin, and lace around him, and stitched the hems. The white gown had many layers. Each gauze, lace, or satin skirt needed to be trimmed and hemmed. In his yellowish undershirt and old pants, he sat Buddha-style on my bed, sewing. His beard was now full and beginning to show gray. His belly was bigger and his fleshy breasts rested on top of it in a grotesquely feminine way.

The gown was taking him forever and Sacrifice Day was approaching. So he swallowed a gulp of vodka, filled his mouth with salted chickpeas, cursed, and stitched. If I was in the bathroom, he raised his voice so that I could hear him; if I was in the closet, he talked in a low voice as if I was next to him. If by accident he caught me out of the bathroom or the closet, he cast his blood-shot eyes on me and cursed me for not helping him fix my wedding gown. Once in a while, when he was in a good mood, he told stories of his revolution—how millions participated in the Friday mass-prayer and how the Great Leader stood on the platform and led it. The moon was full and the crowd raised their heads to see the image of their Imam on the surface of the moon. "He's so holy, Talkhoon," he concluded. "The moon reflects his image."

Or, "We occupied the Opera House today. The house of sin and blasphemy. You can't imagine what strange things we found there. A whole warehouse full of tiny gauze skirts these little whores wore—the kind of skirts that show all of their naked legs. We burned them. We burned their satin dancing shoes and their half-naked pictures on the walls. We broke their mirrors and destroyed all the pianos. On the second floor, the symphony floor, the boys smashed all the instruments. They were out of control. I couldn't stop them. I told them not to destroy the instruments, but they didn't listen to me. They said this was the center of sin and the house of Satan. So bang, bang, bang, they broke the violins, took hammers to the pianos, and tore up the drums. It was a sight. It made me a little sad, because I like music. In a few hours they turned the seven-story building into the Central Mosque. The damned shah had spent millions on that fancy opera house."

In a good mood, Assad told stories, swigged vodka, and collapsed with layers of white lace covering him. When he woke up, he hurried to rinse his mouth, prayed, and asked his imam to forgive him. Then he put on his uniform and left in haste.

In the next room, the prisoner pounded on the door and cursed the guards.

When a crew of twenty men came to cut the trees, Assad was not home. I saw them from the crack of the gray curtain. They had chain saws and axes. The Brothers gathered in the courtyard, watching. They began from the left side, the western edge of the garden, and moved to the east. It would take them a few days to get to my gate. My stomach twisted and dry winds circled in my head.

Boor-boor, who didn't have anywhere to sit, stood right behind my window, one leg chained to a loose brick. She screamed as the men sawed the trees, "Boorrr ... boorrr ..." The bird called Khanum-Jaan and her ancestors to rescue the trees. Jangi barked incessantly and the girl in the laundry room banged on my wall, thinking I was a prisoner too.

Twice a day Brother Mustafa entered the laundry room and beat up the girl. I heard smacks and slaps, screams and curses. The girl cursed back.

They cut the ancient trees of Drum Tower one by one and I sat on the edge of my bed, weeping. When the girl next door heard me, she knocked on the wall in sympathy. Now a knot opened in my stomach and I threw up green bile. It was as if the winds were now loose in my guts, trying to clean my insides.

Assad came early that evening and saw me sitting on the edge of the bed, looking at the garden, vomit all over my uniform. I was so weak that I couldn't hide in the closet or the bathroom. There was no energy left in me. He put the package of food on the table, washed my face, and sat talking to me.

"Crying for the trees?" He paused as if I would finally speak to him, as if I would choose this very moment to begin a conversation. "Crying for these fucking trees, huh? These are the damned ministers. Each tree is one of my fucking ancestors. Now wipe your eyes and look at this."

He stretched his arm toward me. Two pieces of paper were in his hands. He held them in front of my face. One was a typed document and it looked like Khanum-Jaan's will—the one I'd found among her letters. But instead of "—all goes to my beloved sisters—," the document said, "—all goes to my beloved brother, Assad-Allah Vaziri, the only son of my deceased father, Hessam-Mirza Vaziri." The second letter was the ancient, hand-written document of the house. Khanum's name was erased skillfully, but the space was blank.

"I forged a will. Now I need to find someone to write my name in cursive on this document. Then I'll be the sole owner of Drum Tower. I had to change my last name from Angha to Vaziri, because that's what I really am—I'm Grandpa Vazir's son." He said this with a mixture of pride and disgust, then paused for a long moment and added, "It's a shame, isn't it? Nowadays no one attaches himself to the aristocrats, especially someone in my delicate position. But I had to do this for us. For us, you hear me? This revolution and the war won't last forever. I'm not flattening the garden for the guards to practice shooting. They can do that anywhere; I'm following my old plans. Remember what I told you? I want to build apartment houses here and make money. I'll furnish the whole three floors of Drum Tower for you. Not with old, rotten junk, but with the best furniture you can imagine. I'm confiscating land too. Soon we'll own villages, with farms and cattle and businesses you can't even fathom. One, for example, is a carpet-weaving business. I'm putting some money in it until the day that I can buy the whole operation. I'll have five hundred skillful weavers. I'm talking about fortunes, girl, fortunes!" He paused, lowered his voice, and continued, "But I'm the same Assad, your loyal devotee, Talkhoon. My love is deeper than you can ever imagine. My love for you and your poor mother are mixed together in one huge lump, here in my chest." He hit his chest with his fist to show the lump of love. "Come and eat now. I brought your favorite dish. I'm sorry that I can't cook for you these days, but this won't last long. I'll cook for you and our kids. Come now. It's charcoaled shish-kabob—it'll get cold."

Into the Gray Alley

That rainy March day when the crew reached the dryandra tree, the old winds sang strange, harsh and stormy songs in my head. I looked at the men through the curtain of the rain, chopping down the silk trees around the dryandra. When they secured the saw on the thick body of the Simorgh's tree, I took Assad's clay bear and thrust it toward the window. The bear and the glass pane broke with an explosion—gold and silver showered into the courtyard.

"Not that one, not the dryandra!" I screamed like a wounded animal and climbed a chair. I pulled myself out of the narrow hole of the broken window and shouted, "Not that tree!"

It was Hassan's shift. "Stop! Stop, or I'll shoot you!" He yelled.

"Shoot me! Shoot me!" I ran toward the men who had stopped to watch the commotion.

"No, no! Not this one—keep this one tree, please!" My black uniform was wet, the large scarf had slipped off my head and I was barefoot in the mud, pleading for my grandfather's tree. Jangi joined me, barking. He showed his fangs and circled around the men like a hungry wolf. Boorboor shrieked and the prisoner in her windowless laundry room, sensing chaos, pounded on the door and yelled.

The men looked at me as if I were a lunatic. The knife I waved in front of their faces and the layer of prickly hair on my scalp didn't leave any doubt that I was dangerous. Without a word, they distanced themselves from the dryandra and went toward the other trees.

"Couldn't you just ask them not to cut that one tree?" Hassan asked. "Do you always have to act crazy? No wonder Brother Sheeri locks you up. Get inside now. I hope he doesn't punish me for the broken window."

All night I sat in my wet uniform on the edge of the bed, looking out at the Tree of Knowledge. It stood tall and solitary, the top branches forming an open umbrella, protecting the dry ground beneath. This was where we used to sit. Taara played the setar, Vafa and I held our breath and waited for the bird to come.

Wind blew in from the broken window and sprayed rain on my face. The night-shift boy sat on the folding chair with his umbrella in one hand and a prayer book in the other. The parrot sat on his shoulder, craning her neck as if reading. Under the umbrella, the dim light of the boy's lantern flickered now and then.

I sat for hours, motionless, listening to my neighbor's quiet sobs. It was more than a month now that she had been locked up. Once a day, they fed her stale bread and cheese. Brother Mustafa interrogated her and beat her, and nothing changed. They neither took her to a different jail nor released her. Now I knew which part of the day she screamed, when she kept quiet, and when she sobbed. She always cried from midnight until dawn.

Some time after midnight, the girl was quiet for a short time and I heard the squeak of Grandma Negaar's wheelchair. The young guard raised his head too and glanced at the pool where once ancient weeping willows bent over the water. The girl, who'd stopped sobbing to hear the noise, cried louder—like a child who stops crying, listens with hope, then, disappointed, resumes wailing.

I sat still until the sky outside became gray.

Assad came and saw the broken window. He was not in a good mood, but he was too tired to make a commotion. He dropped himself onto the chair and held his forehead in his hand. He was still for a while, then asked, "What happened?" as if we had always conversed and I had always answered his questions. "You broke the window to run away—with the guards and all these men out there. Do I have to commit you? Do I have to cancel our wedding and lock you up instead?"

I sat motionless, staring at the dryandra and the tower. The girl in the laundry room was quiet, trying to hear our conversation. Assad talked with long pauses between his sentences. He didn't have food or vodka with him. His voice was scratchy and I could hear the dryness of his mouth.

"Tomorrow is Sacrifice Day. It was supposed to be our wedding. But look at our life! Your gown is not finished. You're crazier than ever, and I'm a corpse. They needed me for the security of the Imam's house. And I'm responsible for this place too. It's a month that I've kept this bitch down here and a bunch of bastards upstairs, but I haven't had time to interrogate them. I'm overwhelmed. Mustafa is doing my job and he is an ignorant imbecile. And you constantly torment me."

He kept quiet for a long moment, his head bending. I thought he was dozing, but he raised his head and said, "I saw your father today." He knew I would react, so he paused and studied my face. I didn't turn my head or utter a sound. But my heart ached. "It was a mass demonstration to support the Holy Republic. He and his buddies were there. I saw him. For an instant I thought I'd missed him. We hugged. Then I told myself this bastard is a communist, had always been. But then he was Soraya's husband. Only he knew who Soraya was, only he loved her. Then I thought he was a goddamn hypocrite who pretended he supported the Government of God. An atheist was supporting the government of Allah. Then I remembered that for forty years I thought he was my brother and I loved him. But again, I told myself, he was cheating—his party was cheating. They were the servants of Communist Russia. Spies. So to make a long story short, we hugged like brothers and he asked about the house. I told him everything. The truth. That Khanum was with the aunties. The house was not a house and I was the head of the Committee. He asked about you and Taara. I said Taara was still missing and you had run away too. This last part was the only lie. I couldn't say you were here and I wanted to marry you. It was crowded and we were in the middle of a noisy demonstration. Then I lost him in the crowd. But he is fine. A bit wind-beaten and aged, but not much."

Assad said all this and took off his boots. Then he stood, undressed, and with only his underpants on, lay down on the bed. Now he crawled toward me like a slow-moving spider. He reached me and pulled my sleeve the way a child pulls his mother's. I didn't have a knife with me. I'd lost one in the garden yesterday, when I threatened the men, and the other was in the closet with the knapsack.

"All I want from you is to sit on this bed and let me put my head in your lap. That's all. You can stroke my hair, the way women do to their children or lovers; you can sing for me, but even if you don't do these things and just let me put my head in your lap, I'll be content. Just come close. I feel so lonely, Talkhoon."

I went to the bathroom and sat on the toilet seat for a long time. When I heard him snoring, I came out. He was on his back, the massive wedding gown covering his face and torso. On his hairy belly the blue Simorgh breathed silently. The layers of satin, lace and gauze formed fluffy clouds around the blue bird.

From the crack of the curtain I looked outside—the rain had stopped. The boy closed his umbrella, looked up at the sky and yawned. I sat on the chair next to the desk and looked at Assad's gun, his belt, his key chain, his flashlight, Khanum-Jaan's black marble box, the Great Leader's half-chewed picture, still face down from Assad's last drinking binge. Instead of the clay bear, a paper bag sat on the table. Hassan had collected the coins in this bag.

I sat and stared at these objects, then I looked around the room—my room—my cell. The familiar spider web, the orange-headed spider tangled in her own web. Slowly, I went to the closet and took out the knapsack. In the bathroom, I took off the black uniform and threw it in the bathtub. I wore the knapsack on my bare chest, then put on a pair of pants and a baggy shirt. I wore my boots and my woolen hat and slipped the flashlight into my deep pocket. I picked up Assad's handgun and shoved it into my other pocket. The paper bag full of gold and silver tempted me, but it was too heavy and noisy and the bag was thin and could fall apart easily. The money had to stay. Instead, I took the deed for the house, folded it and put it in my pocket. A few pieces of dried bread were left from the other night's dinner. I took a piece for Jangi. I picked up the key, stepped into the corridor, and locked Assad inside the room.

In the courtyard, I approached the boy from behind his chair and aimed the muzzle of the handgun at his head. In a whisper, I said, "Give me the key to the laundry room." He bounced. I pushed him down and pressed the gun against his temple. "This is not a toy, this is Brother Sheeri's handgun. You don't want to die now, do you?" He shook his head. "You know that I'm crazy, don't you?" He didn't answer. "I'm crazy enough to shoot you. But you want to live and do your revolution, your Holy Revolution. Don't you?" He nodded. "Give me the key." He handed me the key. "Now get up!" He got up. His machine gun was on the floor next to the lantern and his prayer book. I pressed the tip of the handgun into his back and pushed him down the basement steps. I opened the laundry room and pushed him inside. He fell.

"Get up!" I commanded the girl. She was shocked—she couldn't move. "Tie your scarf around the boy's mouth! Come on!"

She was panicked and her hands shook. They had put a long black uniform and a wide scarf on her. She tied the scarf over the boy's mouth and made a straight jacket out of the uniform and put it on him and tied the sleeves. She stepped outside.

I locked the door and told the girl to run behind me and keep running if the dog followed us. We ran toward the eastern gate and I heard the girl's labored breathing behind me, then before long Jangi caught up with us, barking. I called his name and dropped a piece of stale bread for him. He caught it in mid-air and swallowed it while running. When we opened the gate and stepped out, I told the girl to turn right and keep to the narrow alley. In a few minutes the curfew would be over and she could mix with the city crowd. Having no doubt that I was an important revolutionary and more experienced than herself—a guerrilla fighter perhaps—she looked at me with admiration, shook my hand with a firm, comradely grip, and turned right.

"Well, do you want to walk with me like old times?" I asked Jangi. He looked at me as if considering the offer. "Hurry up, dog! Decide! Do you want to go back, or come along with me?" I left the gate open and took a few steps away from it. The dog stood for a second, looking at me with large, desperate eyes, then dropped his head and walked back to the garden. I shut the gate, turned left, and stepped into the gray alley.

Book III

The Last Circle

The wind blows to the South,
And goes round to the north;
round and round goes the wind,
and on its circuits the wind returns.

—Ecclesiastes

At the Teacher's House

A block away from Drum Tower, I found myself whistling in a wet, narrow alley. This was the same alley I'd passed through a month ago—the same row of old brick houses, the same barred kitchen windows giving out the smell of stale food. A door opened—an arm extended and put a garbage can on the steps. Birds woke and chirped in the top branches of an almond tree.

Gray clouds rapidly shifted and made room for the sun. I felt dew on my skin, inhaled deeply and let every moving limb of my body enjoy the wet dawn. More birds chirped and crowded the sky. Now I heard a car's groan intruding on the peace. A jeep approached from the far end of the alley. I pressed myself against the brick wall of an old house. If they caught me I'd end up in Drum Tower—the Revolutionary Committee Number One, my permanent jail. The jeep crawled slowly and the guards looked around, searching. I slid back and hid in the hollow space of the entrance. The jeep approached. These were Assad's men.

On the surface of the narrow sidewalk I saw some drawings in pink chalk. I remembered a little girl playing here last month, drawing stick figures. Her mother gave her a bowl of fruit and she spat out the seeds as she ate. What if I knocked on this door before the jeep got closer? But the door opened by itself and a woman, the same one, looked out from the crack and said to someone, "No, not now. They're here. Let them pass."

Before I could show myself and say something, she shut the door. My heart sank. I had lost the opportunity. The jeep was closer now, reaching the almond tree. Soon they would see me. I should have knocked on the door.

While debating whether to knock or run, the door opened again. This time, a young man's head appeared. "They're still here," he reported. "They're moving slowly. Must be looking for someone—" Now he turned his head to the right and saw me in the corner against the wall.

"Who are you?"

"Who is it?" the woman asked.

"A child," the boy said.

A child? I blushed and felt smaller. I hadn't thought losing so much weight would shrink me into a child.

"A child?" the woman said and came to the door. "Who are you, son?"

"Please let me come in," I pleaded.

The woman glanced at the jeep that was only two houses away. Two armed guards stood looking around, a third one drove.

"Are they searching for you?" she asked.

"I'm not sure. But if they see me, they'll arrest me."

She looked at me from head to foot and said, "Come in!"

I slipped inside the house and she shut the door.

"Are you a girl?"

I nodded. Hearing this she relaxed, shook her head, and circled her arm around my shoulder. "You've run away?"

I nodded again.

The young man, who was eighteen or nineteen, stood by the door, staring at me. A girl in cotton pajamas came out of a room, her black hair covering her shoulders like a woolen shawl. The family circled me, looking at me.

"Sit down," the woman said.

We were in a small hall they used as a living room. The floor was bare cement and the house felt cold. A few cardboard boxes sat against the wall. An old couch was the only comfortable seat. There were several wooden chairs, hard and narrow. All of a sudden my body felt tired, drained of life, and I sat down on the couch.

The woman was middle-aged and had the same shiny black hair as the girl, but rolled in a bun behind her neck. Her eyes were strange. One looked at me and the other didn't. She wasn't cross-eyed, but one eye seemed not to be alive. She sat down beside me. The boy sat too, and questioned me with his dark eyes. The girl kept standing.

"Why don't you make some tea, dear?" the mother said to the girl. "And you can take your stuff and go—the jeep must have passed," she told the boy. "But be careful! Don't go too far."

The boy picked up a stack of papers and opened the door a crack.

"Have they left?" the woman asked.

"They just turned onto the main street. I'll be back."

The boy left and I could hear the girl in the kitchen making tea. The woman bent forward on her chair and looked at me with her one good eye.

"Who are you?"

"Please let me stay until the streets get crowded. Then I'll go."

"Don't you want to tell me your story?"

I didn't answer.

She got up and went to the door, opened it and looked out. "He's going too far," she told the girl who was back in the living room. "I told him not to go so far."

"Don't be worried, Mother. He knows what he's doing," the girl said.

"Are you hungry?" the woman asked me.

I nodded.

"Bring some bread and cheese for all of us. I'm hungry too. Wash some grapes. We'll eat an early breakfast today."

When her daughter went back to the kitchen, the woman asked how old I was. I told her. Then she asked other questions—what was my name? why was I running away? who were my parents?—one question after another. She didn't give me a chance to speak.

Now her daughter came with the breakfast tray. She'd changed into a skirt and a blouse. She had Taara's tall, proportioned body. Large breasts, narrow waist, rounded hips. She could never disguise herself as a boy the way I did. The mother was still asking me questions.

"When exactly did you leave your house?"

"Mother, leave her alone!" the daughter said. "You're interrogating her!"

"I'm sorry, child. I'm under strain myself." She said this, rose, and opened the door again. She looked worried. "I'll go after him," she said.

"Are you crazy, Mother?" the girl said.

"I can't see him anymore. The boy is reckless. They'll arrest him."

"Calm down and have some tea." The girl poured tea for all of us. I was thankful she didn't speak to me.

"Eat, child!" the mother ordered me.

We ate in silence. I drank the warm tea and instantly felt better. Toward the end of our breakfast a little girl in her pajamas appeared from one of the rooms and hid in her mother's arms. She was half-asleep. The woman stroked her uncombed hair and rocked her in her arms. She was the same girl I'd seen playing in the street. She looked younger than I remembered—four or five.

"Where are you planning to go?" the woman asked me, and this time she paused, waiting for my answer.

"I don't have any plans," I said. "Not yet. I just need to get far away from here. Maybe I'll go to the eastern border where I have an uncle, my mother's brother. He lives with the Baluchi tribe."

"Sounds very adventurous," the woman said and sighed. "Do you know what is happening in the country?"

I nodded. Who knew better? I lived in the house of Revolutionary Committee Number One!

"You won't make it to the east like this," she said. "And I think you don't even know if your uncle is there."

I didn't say anything.

"Now do you want to tell me the whole thing?"

I nodded. There was something both soft and strong in her voice. She caressed her daughter until she purred like a kitten and laid her face on her mother's chest.

"Get Grandmother some breakfast dear," she ordered the older daughter. "She must be up."

She said this to dismiss her and encourage me to speak. But the door opened and her son came in.

"I won't let you do this again!" she said. "Why did you go so far?"

"I dropped one at each house. I had some extra, so I went to the next alley."

"Is the curfew over?" she asked.

"Yes. That's why I went to the next alley."

"Okay, get some breakfast from Minoo. We have a lot of work to do today."

The boy glanced at me and left.

"Well? I'm all ears!"

When I told the story, my voice shook and I sounded like a small beetle under a kitchen sink. I was afraid she wouldn't believe me. Mother's suicide in the water storage, Father's wanderings, Grandfather's bird book, the tower, the dryandra tree, Grandmother's letters to her dead father, the ghosts, the garden, the lame uncle-servant—in fact, Grandmother's brother and now the head of the Revolutionary Committee—Taara's elopement, the endless hem of a multi-layered wedding gown, a jail in the house, my circular flights, and, finally, releasing another prisoner in my last flight. How could she believe any of this?

Several times, the son or the daughter opened the kitchen door, saw their mother still listening and pulled his or her head inside. When I finished my story, the woman sighed and didn't say anything for a long moment. She just rocked the small girl in her arms. Now she began talking about herself.

"I'm still mourning. My husband died last year. He was an activist twenty-five years ago—nationalization of oil. We both participated in the uprisings. Look!" She pointed to her left eye. "It's a shame. In the middle of a demonstration a thug, hired by the Shah's police, hit me in the eye with a sling. I was not shot by a bullet, but a pebble! I never recovered from the shame of not being shot in a heroic way! But now I'm much older and I don't ask for trouble. Of course, I'm continuing my political work, but I don't wish to get shot!" She looked at me with her one good eye and smiled. When she smiled I felt that she trusted me. She said. "Some kind of fascism is taking over this country. What is happening here is unique in the world. Do you understand what I'm saying?" I nodded and she continued. "The elections are near. My children and I work very hard to inform people about the real nature of these incidents. Our neighbors suspect us; we have to leave. This is where my children were born and my husband died. But we have to move." She paused for a second, then said,

"There is no way I can keep you with us. You'll be in more danger. Now that you're finally out of that tower, you have to be very careful not to get caught. Did you say the house is only a few blocks away from here?"

"The first house on the south side of the College Intersection. Drum Tower."

"Oh! That dirty looking fort!"

"Yes."

"I didn't know people lived there. I thought it was a neglected historical building. A ghost house."

"It is a ghost house," I said. "Do you think I can sleep here just for a couple of hours before I leave?" As I said this I felt dizzy and grabbed my forehead. I hadn't slept for a long time.

"Yes, you can, dear. You can sleep a few hours, and meanwhile I'll think about what to do. I'll check on a few places for you."

She called her daughter and told her to take me to her room and let me sleep. Minoo smiled at me and I followed her. When we passed a narrow hallway, a very old woman with a large, white scarf covering her head and shoulders entered from the backyard. Against the strong morning light she looked like a small, transparent angel. A breeze from the open door played with the wings of her scarf.

"Grandma, this is my friend! What is your name?"

"Taara."

"This is Taara, Grandma."

I said good morning to the old lady and she stood watching me.

Her spine was bent. She came up to my chest. Through round, thick lenses she observed me and said, "Welcome, dear!" She made smacking sounds as if tasting something, and asked, "What happened to your hair?"

"Nothing, Ma'am. It's just too short."

She shook her head, walked away and mumbled something.

"She is ninety-eight years old," Minoo said. "My mother's grandmother. Come in. You can sleep in my bed. Here, wear these pajamas. I'll see you later."

I hung my clothes and knapsack on a hook behind the door. Without my burden and in Minoo's cotton pajamas, I felt light and comfortable. When I slipped under the blanket and closed my eyes for a few seconds, the image of the white-winged grandmother filled my head. Then I fell into a deep sleep.

At the Bus Station

The smell of cooking meat woke me up. I found Minoo on the carpeted floor, lying on her belly, reading a fat book. On my right, a tall window framed the backyard. At the center of the yard's brick floor, a square flowerbed lay under the spring sun. Yellow tulips glowed on green grass. Minoo smiled, rose and led me to the bathroom. She showed me the shower and gave me one of her dresses to wear. She said her mother believed that if I was disguised as a boy, I'd attract more attention. So I showered and wore Minoo's summer dress. The flowery cotton dress was large for me and the wide collar showed my bony chest.

In the living room, food was on the table. Mother, her grandmother, Minoo, and her little sister, Mina, and I sat around the table and ate meat broth with fresh bread. The boy was not around. When I glanced at the clock on the wall, I realized I had slept for six hours. This was lunch.

"Today is Sacrifice Day, we're all off," Mother said. "The mullahs have slaughtered a thousand cows. There is a big feast at the university. They're all going to pig out, pray, pour into the street, and scream their fascist slogans. They will harass people—especially women." She paused, bunched her eyebrows in a frown, and with a lower voice said, "Yesterday, in front of the post office, this bearded guard hit a pregnant woman with a baton and knocked her into the gutter. Why? Because she wasn't wearing a scarf!"

"When I was a young girl," Grandmother said, "Reza Shah ordered his soldiers to pull women's scarves off their heads; if they resisted, they'd hit the women and unveil them. The old Shah wanted the women to dress like Europeans."

"It's so funny!" Minoo said. "Once they beat up women to unveil, now they beat them to wear veils."

"Because we're a bunch of minors, my dear. We can't decide for ourselves," Mother said. "First we have to free ourselves from oppression, then see who dares dictate to us what to wear!"

The door opened and the boy came in. He had some newspapers with him.

"What's happening? Did you put the flyers in the stores?"

"In stores, restaurants, and bus stops," he said proudly. "The cabinet has been dissolved. The Prime Minister has resigned. An army general has been shot in his car." He reported the important news. He was panting slightly.

"Give me the papers! Which army general?"

Mother began reading the headlines and the boy sat down to eat. He tried hard not to look at me, but he couldn't keep his eyes away. Our gazes tangled in mid-air. Something strange was happening. My heart ached with pain and pleasure and blood rushed down into my belly. There was an invisible bridge between us.

"Oh, this is General Nezam-El-Deen." Mother said. "One of the shah's military advisors. His U.S. liaison."

I knew General Nezam-El-Deen. He almost became Taara's father-in law.

"The Party of God dragged him out of his car and executed him right there by the wall. They shot his chauffeur too." She paused and added, "An unidentified terrorist group is burning the movie theaters."

"They want to close all the restaurants and movie theaters," Minoo said.

"A bank is robbed by masked people. A group of youth are vandalizing mansions and smearing tar on the walls and carpets," Mother read.

"When the revolution for the constitutional monarchy happened," Grandmother said through smacking lips, "I was just a little girl."

"Do you remember anything, Grandma?" Minoo asked.

"Nothing."

The children laughed. The old woman laughed with them, showing a few yellow teeth.

"Come, girl, follow me!" Suddenly Mother dropped the newspapers and stood up. "Things are getting worse by the minute. We have to talk. Come."

She took me to the room next to the kitchen and offered me a seat. This was a dim room with one of those small, barred windows overlooking the street. It was crowded with stacks of leaflets, newspaper clippings, papers, and an old typewriter. She sat at her desk and I sat on the other side, like a student having a conference after class time.

"I called my sister. She lives in the north, by the sea. I'm going to send you there. You'll be safe with her. When things calm down here—if they ever do—you'll come back. By that time, we'll have moved, hopefully, and you may want to live with us. Fine?"

I nodded. Then I said, "I can't travel by train."

"Oh, I know. The bastard searches the train stations. I'll send you by bus. Farid will take you to the bus station with his motor bike. He'll buy you a ticket. Get up now. I'll give you my grandmother's chador to wear. If you wrap yourself in a long veil, you won't have any identity. You'll become invisible."

At the door, they all hugged and kissed me as if they'd known me for a long time. The old woman slid her crooked index fingers behind her round lenses, and pressed her red eyes to stop the tears. Mother gave me a small change purse containing her sister's address and some money. I sat behind Farid on the motor bike but the chador slipped off my head. Farid told his mother that the wind would blow the veil off, so they decided I should put it on at the bus station. Mother assured me that she would call me tonight and Farid took off. I almost fell off the bike and screamed. "Hold me!" he yelled into the wind. I encircled his chest with my arms and as he sped up the alley I turned back to see the three women and the child waving at me. If I had not seen this little girl playing by the door one day, I would never have sought refuge there. I couldn't imagine where I'd be now. Back in my closet, holding my breath?

The wind blew in my face, almost blinding me. I hid behind Farid's back and held him tightly. I didn't want this ride to end. He sped up and passed all the cars. When he pressed the hand brake at an intersection, I slid forward and my chest touched his back. My blood froze and my fingers became conscious of the flesh on his hard belly. His muscles moved when he pushed the gas again, responding to my fingertips, playing with them. When we reached the bus station, I was dazed and I didn't want to get off.

"Got dizzy, huh?'

I nodded.

"Come in. Be careful, you're tripping over the steps. Let me hold your hand."

He helped me up the few steps and at the counter bought me a ticket for the Northline, which departed at two p.m. The big clock on the wall showed one o'clock. He handed me the plastic bag containing the chador and told me to put it on in the restroom. In a minute I came out with the long, pale blue veil hanging all over me. I tried hard to hold it under my chin the way I'd seen Daaye holding hers when she went to the mosque. Farid laughed quietly and shook his head.

"You look funny!"

"I know."

"You look better with your boy's clothes."

"I know."

"But this is safe—I don't know your name."

"Taara."

"This is safe, Taara." His voice quivered a little. He coughed to hide it. "Don't take it off. Even in the bus." His pleading tone left me no doubt that he'd eavesdropped. He knew my story.

"I won't take it off."

Now we stood for a long embarrassing moment. We didn't have anything else to say. It was only five past one. I looked around—all the benches were taken.

"Listen," I said. "I can get on the bus by myself. Why don't you leave? I know you're very busy."

"I have a few stacks of flyers to take to the university, before the ceremony starts."

"Then go. I'm fine. I'll wait here for my bus and I'll be at your aunt's tonight."

"When my mother calls, I'll talk to you."

"Yes."

"Take care."

"I will."

He lingered for a second, then left. I expected him to turn back and look at me, and he did. Our eyes met again and he smiled. My muscles went slack. But he was out now, moving his motorbike onto the street. He glanced up the steps at the glass door, but I stepped back, to avoid seeing him again. His bike coughed and groaned and I heard it sputtering for a short time. Then I heard nothing but the confused hubbub of people's conversation in the large waiting room. I sat on the first empty bench I saw and my heart ached with pain and despair.

Through the thickening crowd that rushed into the waiting area from the outdoor garage, I saw the Northline arriving. I tried to secure the damned slippery chador on my head and went out to the dusty lot to sit in the bus and wait. But the driver, who stood by the door, told me that I needed to wait half an hour. They were cleaning and fueling the bus.

When I went back inside I saw a dozen Committee Brothers standing behind the glass door, peering inside the sitting area. I recognized Mustafa, Hassan, and Morad. There were others I hadn't seen before. Their black van was parked in front of the bus station. I pulled the veil over my face and rushed into the restroom. My heart thumped in my throat. There was no bench in the restroom and the smell of the toilets was revolting. I stood for a long time, blocking the way of the women who went in and out. The winds blew hard in my head and confused me. I could barely hear the voice of the man announcing something in the speaker. Maybe it was time for the Northline's departure. I didn't have a watch so I asked the time from a woman. It was fifteen minutes to two. From the fear of losing the bus, I stepped out. The guards were not behind the glass door anymore.

I found my way among the rushing crowd, stepped out in the lot, and headed toward the Northline. The Northwest had just arrived. The passengers were stepping down from the bus with stiff legs and walking sluggishly toward the building. I stood for a second to see the driver help a pregnant woman down the steps. The woman's belly was big and she tried to find her balance between a heavy handbag, a black attaché, and a long instrument box that kept bumping against the driver's leg.

Taara and her setar!

Taara

I could not move. People passed me in a rush and the Northline panted heavily, ready to depart. I stood in the chaos of the crowd and the rising dust. Taara wore a shapeless brown maternity dress and her dark golden hair flowed like waves of honey behind her back. I looked at the way she hugged her setar, resting its belly on her own, forming two round hills. My eyes burned. The Northline was full and ready to take off. But now Taara entered the building and I had one second to decide: Should I ignore my sister and travel to the north where a kind family waited for me, or join Taara and stay with her, no matter what her plans were?

But what were Taara's plans? Where was she going? To Drum Tower? Didn't she know what had happened to our house? Or maybe she didn't know where to go—maybe she hadn't been able to gather her thoughts. What if she needed me? I heard the last announcement for the Northline and the driver honked as if to alarm me. A strong wind rushed through my head and I ran toward the building before Taara went through the other door.

"Taara!"

She turned quickly, but didn't find anyone she knew. She resumed walking toward the exit.

"Taara, it's me!" She turned again. I pulled the veil down and smiled at her. She looked at me absently for a long moment, then tears filled her eyes. I fell into her open arms and pressed myself to the two mounds—her warm, hard belly and the setar's wooden head. Weak and shaky, we sat on the closest bench and let all the buses, people, and noise fade and vanish.

Taara didn't have any intention of going home. She was looking for the Simorgh and she was sure that the bird wouldn't nest in Drum Tower.

"The bird lands in a pure place, where there is no crime and corruption. Baba-Ji wasted his life, looking for the Simorgh in a war tower," she said. "The Simorgh is the bird of peace, the bird of knowledge. Why didn't Baba think of this, it's so obvious?" She told me that she had dreamt that

the Simorgh resided on top of the Black Mountain of Azerbaijan, where
Baba-Ji was from.

"In my dream, the bird told me, 'Your grandfather was where I was,
but he moved to where I was not—' So I went all the way to that part of
the country alone, to find Baba's relatives, to stay with them for a while,
just to find the bird. I went to Ahar, a small town at the foot of the Black
Mountain."

"I know, Taara. I read your letter."

"Oh, you did? So you know."

But like people who mutter in their sleep, she told me the whole story
again with half-closed eyes. Her voice was dreamy, as if her journey to
Ahar in search of the bird had happened in a delirium.

Now she opened her eyes wider to see me better; she held my hand,
squeezed it, and for the first time asked me what I was doing with an
old woman's chador in the bus station. When I told her my story—from
when she left nine months ago and I let her go in that busy intersection,
to the moment Farid brought me here on his motor bike—her golden eyes
opened with wonder.

"Nothing happens for many, many years," she said in the same delir-
ious voice, "then all of a sudden everything happens." She paused for a
while, thought hard and asked, "So, Assad is not Baba-Ji's son?"

"No. He's Khanum-Jaan's half-brother, Grandpa Vazir's illegitimate
son, Daaye's grandson."

"Still a bastard!" she said this from between her teeth. "He hurt you!"
She held my hands and caressed them as if making up for all the caresses
I'd missed.

"He says he loves me."

"He loves himself, Talkhoon" she said. "And Khanum—just imagine,
she'd kept this secret from everyone."

"After Assad's mother, who was Daaye's daughter, drowned herself in
the water storage, Khanum buried her body under the tower."

"Where? Where under the tower?" she asked, as if it mattered.

"I guess in that empty space between Baba's dryandra tree and the
tower. You remember that patch of dirt where a honeysuckle grew at its
left side?"

"How do you know?"

"I read Khanum-Jaan's letters."

"Oh, yes, you told me." She paused and thought some more. "I can't believe it. So Assad is the real heir to the crown."

"He took what belonged to him before he knew he was Grandpa Vazir's son."

"Thief!" Taara said from between her teeth. "He lied to me. He didn't have any plan to cancel my engagement party. He tricked me." She said this, closed her eyes, and leaned her head against the wall. Her white, graceful hands rested on top of her belly.

To have such a big mound in the middle of her body and look so beautiful.

"Taara!"

"Hmm—"

"Where were you going?"

"To find her—"

"Who?"

"The bird."

"Don't joke, Taara. Please! In few hours it will be dark. There will be a curfew. We have to think where to go."

"I'm not joking, Talkhoon. I didn't just dream of her, I saw her. No, I didn't see her, I saw her shadow and heard the flap, flap, flap of the wings—long wings, and not just a pair, but two pairs, one pair hard like an eagle's, but ten times bigger, the other pair soft and flowing, twisting down to the ground like a rainbow of feathers waving in the wind."

She didn't say any more and I let the silence fall between us. It wasn't easy to extract words from her. She wasn't feeling well. What if the baby was coming? A sharp pain moved down my spine. Taara was helpless, and no one was around but me. The burden bent my back.

"Taara, when is the baby due?"

"Whenever I find the bird. I'm going to give my baby to her, to raise her like Prince Zaal. I want the Simorgh to raise my baby."

I ignored her and said, "I know that in some cases the baby comes sooner than expected—doesn't it? What if it comes sooner?"

"It won't. I'll tell her not to." She said this and raised her head, looking at me. "Here, give me your hand."

When she placed my left hand on the side of her belly, a lump suddenly grew under my palm and moved playfully. My heart sank.

"The baby—"

"It's her foot. It's kicking!"

"Taara, are you all right?"

"I'm weak. I haven't eaten anything for a long time."

"Let's go out and eat."

"Then what?"

"Then?"

"After eating—"

We sat and thought for a while. The clock on the wall showed ten minutes to three.

"Let's go to the sea, to the teacher's sister. They don't mind if you join me. We'll stay there until things calm down here."

"No, Talkhoon, things won't calm down until she arrives."

"Taara, the Simorgh is in Baba-Ji's book," I said impatiently.

"All our grandfather tried to say was that the bird is real."

"How do you know? He didn't finish the book, Taara—"

"I know. I copied the whole damned thing with my own hand. I know some passages from memory. '*Aepyornis maximus* was a gigantic bird whose bones and fossilized eggs were discovered on the island of Madagascar. This sixteen-foot-tall bird is the same as the Rukh of *The Arabian Nights*. Sindbad used his turban to tie himself to a talon of the gigantic bird—.'"

"Taara—the guards might come here again and find me. We have to get out of Tehran. It's dangerous here."

"But how?"

"Do you remember what Father said about our uncle on the eastern border?"

"Our mother's brother, who lives with the tribesmen?"

"The Baluchi tribe is on the eastern border. Our uncle can help us."

"But we don't even know him," she said.

"It's not so hard to find people in small towns. We know our mother's last name."

"What is it?"

"Pardis."

"Maybe the guy, our uncle, has changed his name," Taara said.

"Even if he has, we can mention our father who lived with him not long ago. People in small towns don't forget visitors."

"Maybe Father is still there."

"No. Father is here, doing his own revolution. Assad saw him a few days ago in a demonstration. We have to leave this city—even the country, Taara. Our uncle can help us cross the border."

"Tribes live in tents," she said, and closed her eyes. "I can't give birth to my baby in a tent where native women with their dirty hands deliver—"

"Where else can we go, Taara? Do you want to go to the aunties, where Khanum is?"

"With you?"

"No. I can't go back. Assad will get me. He wants to marry me."

"For God's sake, Talkhoon. Stop this nonsense! Why are you weaving these horrible stories together?"

"Weaving? So you really didn't believe me when I said he stole a wedding gown and sewed the hem every night?"

She didn't answer, but wiped her tears and murmured, "I'm tired. I'm tired and hungry. Confused. And someone kicks me from inside."

"Then let me decide."

"Decide, Talkhoon, decide—I can't."

Taara's baby had filled her whole body and her head was full of cries. She had suffered. Whatever I'd decide, she'd do. I had a few seconds to choose between the north and the east. I went to the counter. A sleepy old man sat inside the booth. Soon several people formed a line behind me and I was pressured to decide.

"Excuse me. I was late—my bus left. Can I still use this ticket?"

He looked at the ticket and said, "The next Northline will leave at seven."

I could have bought another one for Taara, but I asked, "Can I exchange it for one on the Eastline?"

"Why not? But the Eastline leaves late—at ten."

"I need two for the east, please. How much do I have to pay for the second ticket?"

I took some money out of the teacher's small purse, paid, and returned. We were going to the eastern border to find our unknown uncle. He'd help us leave the country.

In the Basement Restaurant

After eating platefuls of rice and Kabob in a dim basement restaurant smelling of cold grease and damp towel, we chatted the way we used to in the old days. The yogurt drink we had with the meal was a tranquilizer, and we yawned, wiped our wet eyes, and spoke sluggishly. Taara lit a cigarette (she didn't smoke before), blew the smoke away from my face and murmured sleepily, "Mother didn't drown herself in the water storage. I don't believe this. She didn't have any reason to kill herself."

"She heard voices, Taara. The house talked to her. She wanted to move out, but Father couldn't leave his mother."

"Nonsense!" Taara said with Khanum-Jaan's tone. "It's all his work."

"Whose?"

"Assad's."

"But why? He loved her."

"Don't call it love. He was hopelessly lusting after her. It was an impossible and ridiculous desire and everyone knew it."

"How do you know everybody knew it?"

"Khanum told me, once. She said, 'This crazy Assad was in love with your mother. He followed her in the dark streets where she met her lovers.'"

"Taara! What are you talking about?"

"It's common knowledge, my dear. Our mother sneaked out of the house whenever she could. Khanum said, 'She itched for men!'"

"How dare you repeat Khanum-Jaan's words! How can you believe someone who hated our mother and made her miserable. It was Khanum who pushed her to suicide."

"Hey, why do you get so upset when you hear our mother had lovers? Does this make her a bad person in your mind?"

"It makes her a bad mother," I said, trying to be calm. "I saw a mother yesterday, Taara. Her little girl was in her arms. She rocked her and stroked her hair for a long time to get her to go to sleep. Do you have any such memory of our mother?"

"I still remember something—she hugged me once when I was two and squeezed me so hard that my bones almost broke. Maybe this was the last time—"

"But she didn't even give me that one hug. She left when I was three days old. Assad hugged me, instead. He raised me."

"Nonsense!"

"Who raised me, then?"

"No one!" Taara said, and broke into wild laughter. Fortunately the restaurant was empty and the only person who heard her was the mustachioed waiter who cleaned the tables and watched us from beneath his eyelids. "I'm sorry," she said, and dried her eyes. "It's cruel, I know. But it's true. No one raised you, Talkhoon. You just grew up like a weed. Khanum loved only me—played with my hair all the time and put ribbons in it. Your hair was never combed. No one even bathed you regularly."

"Baba-Ji loved me."

"But he didn't wash you or feed you. Never tucked you in bed. Now that I think about it, I realize that I never saw Baba-Ji doing anything that was not related to the Simorgh book! Did you ever see him doing anything else, or talking about anything but the bird?"

"He did some gardening. He had an herb bed."

"But that was related to the Simorgh too."

"Taara."

"What?"

"Do you know why they didn't raise me? Because I'm not our father's child."

"Nonsense!"

"That's the reason Khanum-Jaan treated me differently."

"No, that is not the reason. Do you know what the reason is?"

"What?"

"You looked like our mother and Khanum hated her."

"But if Mother didn't sleep with Father and had many lovers, as you say, then it's very possible—"

"Shut up, Talkhoon!"

"Assad wants to marry me because he is sure I'm not related to him. He is absolutely sure. You know how religious he is!"

"Assad is religious? What a big lie!"

"Oh, yes. You don't know him. You don't know how he prays and whispers stuff to his Allah and rinses his mouth and fasts till he collapses."

"Assad the alcoholic?" Taara asked. "He is faking the whole thing, Talkhoon. He wants to get somewhere in this regime."

"He has. He is the head of Revolutionary Committee Number One!"

Taara laughed. "What a title. He is a war vizier!"

"He is, Taara! He has turned our house into a barracks!"

"Bastard!"

"We have to go now. Let's go, Taara! The longer we stay in the city, the more we're in danger. He can send one hundred men, even more, to search for me."

"Our bus leaves at ten. It's only five. Let's go to the movies to kill time. No one will find us there," Taara suggested.

The Knapsack

Even in this busy, central street, the honeysuckle perfumed the sidewalk and clusters of purple jasmine hung over the tall walls of old gardens. These were the scents of Norooz, only two days away, mixed with the aroma of snacks sold by vendors on their moveable tables—fresh walnuts, roasted beets, grilled liver and heart of lamb. Small boys fanned ears of corn on burning coals and called out in their thin voices, "Roasted corn, soft and salty—buy before it's cold!" Then other vendors in competition advertised their own products with louder chants.

"Grilled liver and heart, I have—stop and have a bite!"

"Fresh, salted walnuts! Buy a bag, get another for free!"

It was a festive holiday, Sacrifice Day, the day of killing lambs, cows, turkeys, or chickens—according to one's class—roasting and eating them, celebrating the end of the fasting month. This afternoon there were more people in the street, trying to enjoy their freedom, before the curfew sent them back inside their dark houses.

Taara and I, as carefree as schoolgirls, found our way through the crowd, chatting nonstop. We'd left her heavy handbag and the black attaché at the bus station, and the only thing we carried was the setar which I hid under my chador. I told Taara what Assad had said about the Brothers smashing music instruments.

Letting the heavy veil slip on my shoulders, I told Taara more about my past year's adventures. I told her how Assad ran toward the tower, lamer than ever (because I had kicked him at the water storage), pleading with me not to kill myself. Now I imitated the way Assad limped and shouted, "Talkhoon, I love you!"

Taara held her belly and laughed. When we resumed walking toward the theater, I limped on purpose, and made the *lek, lek, lek* sound with my shoes, repeating, "I love you, baby. I love you, bitter herb," to entertain her.

Spending time with my sister in that sunny street, I found a joker in myself. I could make her laugh. I could take any incident, a sad one or an absurd one, and make it into something hilarious. This comic side of myself had been unknown even to me. Now Taara laughed so much that she needed to rest on the stone steps of a shop.

"Stop now!" she said, wiping her tears. "They say if you laugh too much, you'll end up crying afterwards!"

A long line extended and curved along the wall of the theater and behind the building. Taara planted me at the end of the line and went to buy a pair of black shoes from a vendor. She threw her old pair, which didn't look old at all, in a garbage bin. Then she bought a pair of sunglasses, put them on, and looked at herself in the vendor's small mirror. From a distance, I looked at my sister with disbelief. I should have been on the bus, heading toward the sea. A few hours later the teacher would call her sister's house to talk to me. Farid would want to talk too. My heart sank and I felt a hollow space in my chest. What had happened? Why was I in this line to get tickets for a movie? And was this my sister Taara, buying ice-cream sandwiches from another vendor?

When I heard a tall iron wall collapsing somewhere, I came to myself. "Explosion!" someone said. "It's in the south," another man said. We all turned and looked toward the south. A cloud of greasy smoke rose from behind the tall buildings. In a minute, helicopters began circling over us. It was chaos now and people ran toward the south as if they could do something. The carefree holiday afternoon had changed into a violent scene. Tanks appeared out of nowhere and a group of fifty or more black-shirted, bearded Brothers hit their chests, screaming slogans familiar to my ears, "One party, Party of God. One leader, chosen by God!"

Taara stood close to me, holding my hand. Her ice cream melted, running down. She wasn't happy anymore and looked around in confusion.

At the box office when she opened her handbag, I saw a thick stack of green hundreds rolled and stuffed in her small change purse. She pulled one out. When she noticed my gaze, she said:

"I worked all of last year."

"Where?"

"Around here. In this area. I taught music. Setar mainly. Sometimes guitar."

"Vahid didn't work?" This was the first time I'd mentioned him. I regretted it immediately.

"No, he didn't," she said. Now she corrected herself and added, "He couldn't."

The movie was about a dolphin that had feelings like a human and could even talk. The mean guys wanted to kill him. The dolphin cried like a baby. Someone, a woman in our row, wept.

"Do you remember chapter three of Baba's book?" Taara whispered in my ear.

"No," I said.

"He mentions dolphins. There is a list of intelligent animals in the chapter."

I thought that the moment we got to the first comfortable place, I'd take Baba's manuscript out and find the passage. Now I touched my chest to feel the manuscript and my heart almost stopped. I wasn't wearing the knapsack. For how long had I not been wearing it? When I reviewed what I'd done today, every pulse in my body slowed. I remembered that this morning I had changed into Minoo's summer dress. I must have forgotten to put on the knapsack. So it was still hanging behind her door.

I had lost the handwritten draft—the only draft—of my grandfather's bird book, the pages that contained his entire life. Now I remembered that Father's poem and the document of the house were in the bag too.

"Taara!" I whispered. "We have to leave this minute!"

"But why? I like this movie!"

"Come out, I'll tell you everything."

People complained and some cursed us when we stepped on their feet or tried to keep the setar above our heads, and banged it on theirs. Outside, in the lobby, I told Taara about the knapsack. I was surprised that all the while I'd been telling Taara different stories of the past year, I'd missed this one story—how I'd used her turquoise dress and Mother's sapphire gown to make this knapsack to carry Baba-Ji's manuscript under my shirt.

"You took Baba-Ji's original manuscript with you?" She was overjoyed.

"Yes, but I lost it. Stupid, damned, dumb imbecile that I am."

"But it's not lost. It's in your friend's room. Let's go and get it."

"But I can't go there again. I've placed them in so much danger helping me, and now I'm still in Tehran."

"When they see me they'll understand everything. Come on, let's get a taxi. It's only six-thirty."

In the taxi, Taara talked excitedly. She said that having Baba's manuscript would change everything. It would definitely help us to find the Simorgh. She said in some chapters there were specific signs as to where and when the bird would appear. She thought that leaving the country from the eastern border would make it possible for us to go to India and live there. She said she was sure that Garuda, the flute-beaked Indian Simorgh, could be found there. She didn't make much sense and again all she said sounded like feverish delirium. She was dreaming aloud. But I couldn't ask her anything. I was anxious about seeing the family and Farid again.

From the taxi's dirty windshield I saw how the darkening city changed shape. Within an hour the peaceful, festive afternoon had turned into menacing night. Now darkness added to the horror. Piles of burning tires flamed here and there, and people ran, shouting slogans or screaming for help. The rattle of machine guns came from the distance and the crack of dynamite or bullet broke the peace. Five blocks away from the movie theater a massive explosion shook the ground and traffic stopped. People got out of their cars to see what had happened. We saw tall flames rising to the sky. When the driver came back, he said, "They blew up the theater! People are trapped inside, burning alive!" Taara closed her eyes and held my hand. Her fingers were icicles.

The taxi and a thousand other cars had stopped. There was no way to move on. The driver told us to get out and walk. He said traffic wouldn't move for hours. "Women should go home now," he advised. We got out and looked around. It was a long way to the teacher's house and an even longer distance to the bus station. So we began to walk in the chaos on the sidewalk towards the College Intersection—toward the walls of Drum Tower.

"Let's take the back alleys, Taara. There are too many Guards here and I can't walk well with this chador on top of my head. In the alley I can take it off."

She didn't say anything, just followed me across the street where we zigzagged through the parked cars and sought refuge in a back alley. Now I took off the veil, folded it, and dropped it on my shoulder like a shawl. I took the setar and let Taara walk freely. But she walked slowly and the teacher's house was at the end of the alley, at least two kilometers away. It would take us a long time to get there. Taara's watch showed seven-thirty—we were two and a half hours away from the curfew and the departure of our bus.

Finally I suggested that Taara should sit somewhere and wait for me. Without her I could run, get there in few minutes, pick up my knapsack, and return. But where could she sit? This was a narrow alley onto which the back doors of shops opened. No one was around to help us, to take her in. We walked another block until we reached a small, dingy shop—a smelly, neighborhood deli selling old feta cheese swimming in a jar of gray water, dried rolls of salami, and stale bread. The whole store could accommodate two people standing in front of the counter.

An old Armenian, with shabby gray hair and long, fuzzy whiskers said in a thick accent, "We're closing."

I pointed at Taara's belly and told him she couldn't walk anymore. I had to find a taxi. I pleaded with him to keep her inside until I came back. Through a door the height of a child he went to a place in the back, bending so as not to knock his head against the frame. We waited for more than five minutes, inhaling the sharp odor of pickled cucumbers and sour yogurt. Taara was nauseated and her face had become gray like the block of feta cheese floating in the murky salt water. I looked around—there wasn't even a stool or a stone step for her to sit on. At last, the shabby man came out and a chubby, middle-aged woman followed him. The traditional Armenian chignon was coiled behind her neck like a snake. She told Taara she could go inside and rest until the taxi arrived. We thanked the old couple. I handed the folded chador to Taara and waited for her to pass through the small door beyond which nothing was visible. Then I stepped into the alley and began to walk fast, thankful that Minoo had given me a pair of canvas shoes, not something with straps or high heels. I was alone, I was unburdened, and I felt strangely light. I ran into the darkness, penetrating the thick wall of the night.

Night in the Vacant House

Farid's motorcycle lay on the sidewalk like a dead corpse, its front mirror shattered. I looked for a bell, but didn't find one, so I knocked with the brass paw, but the door opened by itself. Hesitant to raise my voice to call the family, I stepped into the darkness and ran my hand along the wall. I found the switch and turned it on. A yellow bulb lit the living room, the same room in which I'd eaten two meals with the family. The table, the old sofa, and the six wooden chairs were broken, the boxes they had packed for moving were open, odd objects scattered around. In the teacher's room, the desk had been tipped over and all the drawers opened. Papers, leaflets, books and clothes were strewn everywhere. I ran to Minoo's room and turned on the light. The same chaos. I looked behind the door—my shirt and pants still hung on the hook and my knapsack was under the shirt. I unzipped it—everything was there. The guards had not looked behind the door.

Now I took off the summer dress and put the knapsack against my bare chest. I thought I'd be safer looking like a boy, so I put on my cotton shirt and slipped into my pants. Both pockets were heavy. I found the flashlight and Assad's handgun in them. How could I ever forget this gun? What an imbecile I was. How could I survive with such a numb mind?

In the corridor I saw the great grandmother's white scarf on the floor. I remembered how this morning a light breeze had lifted its corners and the ancient woman had looked like an angel.

Next to Minoo's room was another door. I entered and turned on the light. The first thing I noticed was Farid's black cap on the floor. The room was an earthquake scene. They had broken his desk into pieces. I picked up the cap and found a wallet under it. It was empty, except for a motorcycle license with Farid's picture. I learned the family's last name: Royaie, meaning "from the dream." Had they been real, or images of a dream?

I put the wallet in my pocket, placed Farid's hat on my head, and left the house. Outside, in front of the door, I panicked. What if I was being watched? I stood in the dark and checked either side. A couple of yellowish bulbs on top of the posts poured dim light into the dark alley. Only when I shut the door behind me did I realize I shouldn't have closed it. It had been open before. And I had left all the lights on. There was no way to undo what I'd done, so I ran toward the Armenian deli, the knapsack hopping on my chest. I wasn't light and free anymore and the old wind howled in my head.

I couldn't think coherently while I was running—only fragments of thoughts dashed through my mind. I should have taken Taara's change purse from her. What if the old couple robbed her? Carrying all that money and stepping through a short door, entering an unknown place? I kept looking back to see if anyone followed me. I was out of breath and couldn't run anymore. A sharp pain knifed into the lower side of my belly. As I slowed down, I became aware of time. Was it nine? Could we find a taxi and get to the bus station by ten? Hadn't I told the Armenian man that I was going to find a taxi? Maybe I should find one first, then get Taara. She

couldn't walk. We would be left in the streets and the curfew would begin.
The guards would arrest us and send us to the closest jail—Drum Tower.

Fear is the brother of death ... fear is the brother of death— I repeated Baba-Ji's old mantra and ran. It had been a mistake to go for the knapsack. It
had been a mistake to waste the time. We could be sitting in the bus station
now, waiting for our bus. But the manuscript—oh, how I hated it. I hated
the bird and the book.

I burst into tears and slowed down again. I had cursed Baba-Ji's book,
his breath and blood, the years of his life. *Baba*— I whispered and walked,
weeping and panting. *Baba-Ji, are you alive? Are your eyes open? Is Assad
feeding you?*

I cried like a lost child and forced myself to run again. The damned
alley seemed much longer than before, as if its length had expanded. At
last, I reached the deli and found its double wooden door closed, a big
lock hanging on it. I could run to the street, find a taxi and bring it here, or
I could find a way into the deli, get Taara, and walk with her to the street.
This was the hardest decision of the whole day. My brain was tired and
I couldn't weigh the advantages and disadvantages of each option. Oh,
how badly I wanted to take a warm shower and go to bed.

I had to get Taara first. What if they had taken her to a hospital? What
a mistake to separate from each other. I muttered all of this to myself and
walked crazily in front of the shabby shop, trying to find another entrance.
There was none. On the left, an old vacant house with broken windows
sat in darkness, stray cats screaming inside. On the right, a soot-covered,
four-story apartment building stood in absolute silence. I pressed the button for the first floor, and waited. Now I rang all eight bells, two apartments on each floor, but no door or window opened. I looked up—all
the rooms were dark. The building was vacant. I paced up and down the
sidewalk, looked at the closed deli, kicked and banged on the door and
showered it with stones. But no one opened it. Time passed with the speed
of light. In the distance, traffic on the main street was thinning. It was close
to curfew and I stood in this vacant alley, not far from Drum Tower. Had
I ever visited a family in this alley? Had I ever found Taara? Or was this
whole day a long dream, confused visions in a distant mirage?

I went to the dark, vacant house and sat in a broken plastic chair on the porch. A dusty fig tree with branches extending from either side con-cealed the porch from the alley. I could see small green figs among the leaves. Where would I be in a month or two, when these figs ripened into juicy, golden fruit?

Soon I realized that this house had sheltered homeless people before the revolution. Empty beer bottles and cigarette butts were scattered around and cats screamed in the dark rooms, mating or fighting. Once, when they were quiet, I heard shouting. It was a familiar cry, something like, "Boorrr!" The blood almost froze in my body. Did I imagine it or was it Boor-boor crying a few blocks away to inform Assad that I was nearby? I was going mad now. Wasn't I the crazy Talkhoon, after all? The fool, the runaway, the wind-headed girl? Why did I ever think that I was sane or smart?

I held the gun with both hands and aimed at the fig tree's dark shadow on the asphalt. I kept holding it until my heartbeat slowed and the winds in my head settled into a breeze. I would have to spend the whole night in this broken chair until, early in the morning, the old Armenian opened his smelly shop. Then Taara would bend her big body and step out of that short, wooden door and we'd go to the bus station and change our tickets again. We'd travel to the eastern border where our uncle would help us leave the country.

I repeated this hopeful scenario in my head in a state between sleep and wakefulness. This one night—one night among wild alley cats in this filthy place—wouldn't kill me. I pulled the hat down over my brow and leaned my head against the metal frame of the chair. With the gun pressed against my chest, I fell asleep.

Sometime in the middle of the night the groan of a jeep and a blinding light woke me. Through the branches of the fig tree I saw it crawling through the alley. One Brother with a flashlight searched the houses on the right side and another threw his beam on the left side. I thought about creeping into the house, but I couldn't move. The column of light was on the fig tree. Could they see me? I aimed the gun at the shadows of the tree.

Now a dog barked and I thought everything was over. I thought they'd brought Jangi to find me. If I hadn't been so stupid as to change into my own clothes, I might have survived. I thought that in a minute or less I'd be in my basement room and Taara and the baby inside her would be buried somewhere near here, in a hidden hole on the other side of a short door at the end of a dingy shop.

But the dog was not Jangi and the bark was not for me; it was for the gang of cats inside the house. When the jeep passed, the dog ran toward the house and cats flew from every direction and leaped into the darkness, crying jungle cries. The stray dog stood in front of me, panting. His thick slobber hung from the sides of his wide mouth. I didn't move. After the panic of seeing the jeep, after the flight of the cats above my head, this miserable, undernourished dog couldn't scare me. I assumed the pose of a statue and the dog, which suddenly seemed exhausted, fell flat on the floor and slept next to my feet. Dogs liked me.

Close to dawn, I heard Taara's setar. Her songs penetrated soot-covered brick walls to reach me. How could she play so late, or so early? Were the Armenians awake? She played and I felt the lightness I'd lost last night. The dog snored, Taara played her melodies, and I smiled and waited for the dawn. Happy to be awake and out of the darkness, I waited for the old man to open his shop.

"Where is my sister?" I asked, pressing the gun in my pocket.

"Is it you?" the Armenian asked. "You've changed."

"Where is she?"

"Where have you been?"

"In that vacant house, all night—because I couldn't find a way in."

The old man burst into laughter, showing two rows of tar-stained teeth. Then he coughed and spat somewhere behind the counter. All the while, he weighed a yellowish piece of cheese on a small brass scale, picking it up and putting it down with his nicotine-stained fingers. Someone was in the shop, standing behind me, waiting for his cheese. He was a sleepy house servant, a boy my age.

"You should've gone to the other alley, the one parallel to this. That's where the door of my house is."

I was puzzled.

"Come, come, lower your head and come in. Be careful, don't knock your forehead on the top."

The shabby man was in a better mood early in the morning. He let me through that ominous door and, without telling me where to go, closed it behind me. I was in a shady yard, square and small, but full of trees. Old metal tables and chairs sat rusting under the trees. The plastic, red-and-white-checked tablecloths had lost their gloss. This had been a café.

I followed the setar's melody and looked through a wide glass door. On a long couch, Taara sat, her legs stretched out before her, resting on the glass top of a coffee table. The setar rested on top of her round belly. She hit and strummed the four strings, now frowning, now closing her eyes, biting her lower lip. Her long hair cascaded down around her.

The glass door was the sliding kind and when I opened it the strong smell of coffee made me dizzy. Before I could say anything, the chubby woman came in from another door, carrying a tray in her hand.

"Oh!" She was startled. "You scared me, child! How come you changed into a boy?" she said this with a heavy accent and laughed.

Taara kept playing as if I wasn't there. Or maybe she was away in her own head and couldn't see me.

"I came last night, but the door was locked. I couldn't find the entrance."

"Ah, child! All the front doors are in Jamshid Alley, back doors in Farshid Alley. Your sister waited and waited, and finally she fell asleep."

"Why is she playing this early? Is it okay with you?"

"Oh, it's okay with me and Avaak. We love music. Look! Look out! This was our restaurant. We served dinner. We had live music—balalaika, accordion, mandolin. My cousins played. The Guards closed our business. Now it's just the little deli. Before, most of our income came from the homemade vodka, wine, and cherry liqueur. No more of that! Just cheese and bread and some bologna. They don't let us sell ham. We're broke!"

Taara finished her piece, looked up and smiled. Her face was pale but radiant. She put her setar in the case. She didn't even ask where I'd been all night.

"Here!" the old woman said. "My coffee is famous in this neighborhood! Sit and have some. And the cake. I baked a dozen last night. Now that's what I do. I bake marble cakes and sell them to stores. See if you like it."

"Yerjanik! Yerjanik!" the man called from the shop.

"Oh, excuse me, Avaak is calling me. I'll be back. Don't let the coffee get cold."

"They're angels!" Taara said. "They fed me last night. Guess what? Veal cutlet and fried potatoes and a heavenly red wine Yerjanik has made. I drank half the bottle and played for them. We partied until midnight, and then I fell asleep. Did you stay with your friends?"

I said neither yes nor no, but sipped my thick, bitter coffee and looked at the shady yard through the wide glass door. Swallows had gathered in the top branches of a pomegranate tree, chirping crazily. Large grape-shaped clusters of purple jasmine had climbed the small dome of a wooden trellis and hung over the sides, creating a flowery pyramid. Farther back, a small stone fountain gurgled against the brick wall. A narrow, silvery stream poured from a hole in the wall and rolled over the rocks that lay at the bottom of the fountain. A couple of fat, gray pigeons drank from it.

This was all I needed in my life. A room at the end of such a yard, where I could grow old and die. But we had to move on. We were too close to Drum Tower.

To the East

Taara, wearing the blue veil, enjoyed pretending to be an older woman. I pulled the black cap over my brows and walked behind her, carrying her luggage like a porter. It was dusk and the Eastline sat in the dusty garage, panting.

"Hey, boy, take the lady to the back seat," the driver told me and tore the tickets. "The last bench has more space. Let her be comfortable."

At last we were sitting in the back of the Eastline and the bus was leaving the garage. The street was calmer than yesterday; it would look like any street in the world if a group of black-veiled women hadn't suddenly jumped in front of the cars, blocking their way. They carried gigantic pictures of the Great Leader and chanted through their veils, "You are my soul, Imam! You are the breaker of idols, Imam!" And "O' God, O' God, until the last revolt, keep our leader safe and sound!" They looked like a colony of penguins, but penguins with submachine guns slung on their shoulders. It was half an hour before they left.

"The devotees of the Holy Revolution!" a passenger said.

"Black ravens," someone else added.

"Death squad!" a woman said louder.

Taara and I looked at each other. Apparently no one from the Party of God or its sympathizers were on this bus.

As we left the city, the sporadic shootings, distant explosions, and hysterical chants of the black ravens faded out. The tall pictures of the Great Leader and the angry graffiti on the walls, cursing the infidels, were behind us now. With the land opening ahead of us, the driver turned on his radio and a military march filled the bus. He turned it off and inserted a cassette. The thin voice of a prerevolutionary popular singer rose in the dim bus, "Even when I'm drunk, this damned pain stays with me—," she whined. Taara's head fell on my shoulder and her warm breath brushed my neck. I sat still and watched the night descending on the dry land until darkness was complete. We were approaching the desert and I wanted to hear the barren earth sighing. All I wished for now was silence.

Taara raised her head and muttered something in dream language. I covered her body with the blue chador and looked out the window again. The driver had turned on the lights so that people could read. All I could see in the windshield was myself: thin face, big sunken eyes, and the shadow of the black cap darkening my brows. *Who are you?* a tiny wind in my head asked in a small voice. I touched the tip of my cap in the mirror of the window, felt the gun in my pants pocket and looked at Taara from the corner of my eye. Her golden hair brushed my cheek. I glanced at the ball of her belly and the tiny wind repeated in my head, *Who are you? What is all this about?*

Taara raised her head and whispered in my ear, "Si means thirty, morgh means bird; Simorgh means thirty birds."

"Hush— you need to sleep."

Only to contradict me, she sat up and began to talk.

"Long ago, these thirty birds became one. The Mother Simorgh hatches one single egg every thousand years."

"Some legends say every five hundred years," I said.

"Does it matter?" she looked at me, annoyed. "In my dream—not a new dream—in an old dream in that tenant house, I saw her. She whispered in my ear. She told me to search for her. If I seek, I'll find. And that was when I left."

"Taara—"

"Listen! Listen! Don't interrupt me. I'm not through with the dream. She had two normal wings. By normal, I mean the way Baba-Ji has described them in his book, eagle-like, huge. But she had two extra wings— curling and twisting, as if they had life of their own. They were not quite like serpents, but similar, or maybe they were streaks of rainbow—red and blue and purple. These wings were like roots reaching for the earth. With these she picked me up."

"In your dream."

"In my dream. But I woke up and didn't see where she took me."

"Probably to the top of Mount Ghaf, where she takes everybody else."

"You're being sarcastic, Talkhoon. I'm serious."

"The bird is just in the books, Taara. Baba knew it too."

"You don't know Baba. I know him."

"Sleep now. It's a long night and everybody else is sleeping. It's an eighteen- hour drive. Just three hours have passed. I don't want you to have a bellyache in the middle of the trip."

"I won't. How many times do I have to tell you? I know when my baby is due."

She was quiet and sulky for a while and didn't sleep. The driver turned off the lights and lowered the singer's sad song. His assistant began a conversation with him to keep him from dozing off. What reached the back of the bus was not clear.

When I saw the desert in the gray light of dawn, I touched the window-pane. The cold penetrated. A warm gush of heat rising from somewhere under the seat felt pleasant. I was sleepy, but I wanted to see the dawn, when daylight defeats darkness. I blinked several times and rubbed my eyes. Yesterday at this time I was sitting on the porch of that vacant house waiting for the long night to end. I thought I'd lost Taara until I heard her singing. Now she sat next to me eating a piece of marble cake the Armenian woman had wrapped in a napkin for her.

After finishing the last crumb of her cake, she turned to me and said, "I left Vahid."

"You wrote to me—"

"He was hopeless and I left him. I didn't want my baby to know him."

She looked at the dark window. Outside, the sky was the deepest shade of blue.

"I think I didn't love him enough to stay, to endure." She pulled her hair back, separated a bunch and tied it around the thick pony tale behind her neck. "What I told you about the Simorgh was true. She came to me in my dream and that was my cue. It was as if I was waiting for someone to tell me that the whole thing was hopeless and I had to leave that house. And she came and lifted me up." She rubbed her eyes the way children do, with her fists.

"You have to seek it, then you'll find it. The thirty birds sought her, they became her."

"This is in Attar's book," I said. "*Conference of the Birds*—twelfth century."

"Attar was a Sufi. Baba-Ji was a Sufi too. But he hid it from everybody. It was his big secret. I've become one too. But you don't believe in divine unity," she said. "What do you believe in, anyway?"

I didn't have an instant answer. She waited for me for a long moment, her stare burning my cheek.

"In survival," I said. "I try to survive."

"This is not a belief."

"Yes, it is. The eastern gate was there at the far end of the garden, hidden under decades of vines and weeds—thick, like a tangle of frozen ropes. I had to cut them with a kitchen knife. I had to do this in rain and

sun, midnight, dawn, at any time I could find for it. I had to use my bare
hands—look!" I showed her my palms.

"What are these stitches?"

"I broke the window after he caught me once."

"There are new cuts too."

"These are from the vines. My palms have more lines than anyone
else's," I said. "I've added new lines to my destiny. Look! My lifeline is
longer now, extended by a cut. My love line is distorted, scratched out."

She held my hands and looked at them closely. "You opened that
gate—"

"But he found me on the steps of the train station, took me back to the
basement, brought me a black gown to wear and a white gown to wed in.
The gown had multiple layers of gauze, lace, and satin. It was too long for
me; he had to stitch the hems so that I could wear it and he could marry
me on Sacrifice Day."

"Stop this!"

"I used the gate again. This time I had to steal his gun and put someone
in jail and release someone else."

"You've told me this already. But it sounded funny, the way you said
it at first. It's not funny now. I can't believe you did all this. How could
you? I mean all alone, by yourself?"

"I didn't think I could either. But there was no other way. No bird
came to my rescue. Once or twice I looked up at the sky—nothing. Baba-Ji
didn't wake up either. I went up and pleaded with him. Khanum didn't
save me. Taara didn't remember that I was all alone in the basement. Father didn't stop his revolution to save his own daughter. Mother didn't
come back to life. Vafa forgot me."

"Stop now," she said. "I get it. I think I know what you believe in.
Don't say any more and don't make me feel guilty either. I had to save myself, too. My story is different from yours, but I survived too. Now let's not
talk about these things. Maybe sometime when we're settled in a room, I'll
open that black attaché and read a few things to you."

"You wrote?"

"I've always written. And I've kept everything. Even the composition
assignments I wrote at school. I wrote two dozen songs in that house—I

wrote letters that I didn't mail. For you, for Father, for Khanum, and Baba-Ji."

"Father has something for you too," I said. "When he came a few
months ago and hid in my closet, he read this long poem and said it was
for you. It's here."

"You brought it?"

"Of course. It's between the pages of the Simorgh book."

"Give it to me. Now! You should've given it to me the first minute you
saw me."

"My knapsack wasn't with me."

"Okay. Where is it?"

I had to unbutton my shirt in the dark, unzip the knapsack and take
out the whole manuscript. Under the yellow night light we leafed through
the pages to find the poem. A tear dropped from the end of Taara's chin,
smearing the green ink on one tiny word so that it reformed into the shape
of a miniature butterfly. We found Father's poem. Taara snatched the yellow paper and moved away from me. She read by herself, in a whisper,
sniffling all through it. People were waking up. A baby cried. The driver turned on the music. The same tape. The thin-voiced singer lamented
about another love affair. "I've been left alone, so utterly alone —"

Taara returned the poem.

"What do you think?" I asked.

"About what?"

"Father's poem."

"It's good. Different from Vahid's style. Father uses a lot of symbols.
When he says the woman with hyacinth braids will arrive one day, he
doesn't mean a real woman, he means the revolution."

"Oh, I thought he meant our mother. That's why I didn't get it when
he said it was about the revolution."

"I wonder why he's dedicated this poem to me?"

"Maybe you're the woman with hyacinth braids?"

"Nonsense. Where was he when I was growing up?"

"Maybe he dedicated the poem to you because he misses you."

"How did he react when you said I'd run away with a man?"

"He became sad. Very."

Taara sighed and put her hands on top of her belly and looked into vacant space.

"The revolution is an excuse," she said. "Khanum-Jaan was not always wrong."

"What do you mean?"

"I mean Khanum was right when she said our mother's disappearance drove him crazy."

"Do you think Father is crazy?"

"This obsession with the revolution is crazy. He abandoned us."

"Shouldn't all the revolutionaries be obsessed with the revolution?"

"But this is not even *his* revolution! Is he a religious fanatic?"

"He supports them now. Assad saw him."

"Nonsense. Father is a communist. Did you know this?"

"He told me. Indirectly. Assad told me too."

"I've seen a lot of them. There is more than one kind: Russian, Chinese, Cuban, guerrilla fighters, bookish types, extremist, terrorist, anarchist, academician—. They came to that house. Talk, talk, talk."

"Was Vahid one of them?"

"Oh, no. Vahid worships a rose petal, a piece of rock—"

"Father's poem made you sad."

"It reminded me that he exists."

"Sometimes you wish he were dead, don't you?"

"How do you know?"

"Because it makes it easier to mourn him. Doesn't it? But when he is alive and not present, you don't know how to mourn."

"You've changed, Talkhoon."

"Look at the sand, Taara, like a yellow sea. Tides are moving. It's dawn."

"This girl kicked me all night, you know? Right here." She put my hand on the right side of her belly, close to her thigh.

"How do you know it's a girl?"

"I know it. Once, in that house, I dreamed that I'd named her Soraya. But I woke up with horror. I said no, this woman, this mother of ours is too scratchy."

"Scratchy?"

"Exactly. She's like a book written in bad handwriting and with a messy pen, and then scratched all over. It's impossible to get what she's about."

"People's stories distorted her."

"What she really was—"

"What she really was got lost."

"That's what I mean by scratchy. No, I don't want to name my daughter Soraya. I would call her 'Negaar,' except—"

"Except she is even more scratchy."

We laughed and waited, as if for a name to descend from the roof of the bus.

"How about Talkhoon?" she said.

"Oh, no! My name brings bad luck."

She laughed. "How silly you are! You are even more superstitious than I am."

"But this is not even a name. Assad made it up."

"Nonsense. He didn't. He lies. Baba-Ji named you because you were cute, because he loved his herb bed—his basil and tarragon. I always envied your name."

"You did?"

"Oh, yes. It was unique. Mine was ordinary. If I used the full name—Taahereh—it sounded like an old lady's name; if I used Taara, it sounded too common. Grandpa Vazir's ghost named me."

"Assad named me."

"He didn't."

"He did!"

We sat for a long time and watched the yellow tides giving the illusion of movement, repeating the same shape and color. I touched the window-pane. Heat penetrated.

"Vahid will die," she said.

At a Caravansary

We reached a courtyard covered with sand. In the middle, a mud and clay caravansary sat. Two outhouses were behind the building and the vast desert spread all around. Men and women formed lines in front of each outhouse. I had to stand in the men's line. In the women's line, Taara covered her face with the blue veil and laughed.

The morning sun burned. Its rays penetrated my skin like hot needles. Native men who worked in the caravansary wore turbans and puffy black pants. Their skin was dark leather, toughened under the lash of sandstorms.

There was a wooden bed outside the building, covered with a threadbare rug. An old native sat on it, smoking a water pipe. When I reached the old man's bed, I saw a pink rose petal floating in the glass container at the base of the water pipe. The native took a deep drag, water made a gurgling sound, and the rose petal danced. A gust of wind threw dry sand at my back. Farid's black cap was covered with a white powder. I touched the pocket on my chest and felt Farid's wallet. I touched my pants pocket and felt Assad's gun. I would protect my sister. I would take care of her.

We drank two large glasses of dark tea and ate freshly baked bread mixed with crunchy sand. As we ate, we chased the flies away. A tiny one found its way into Taara's ear, buzzed, and stayed there. She tried to get it out, rubbed her ear, hit her head, but the fly kept buzzing inside her head. The breakfast was ruined. We went inside the bus and I looked into her ear with the help of the flashlight. I couldn't see anything. The fly was buzzing inside her brain, Taara said.

We sat for a long time in the bus, trying to take the intruder out. I didn't dare poke anything into her ear. If it was true—if a fly was inside, alive and buzzing, or even dead—we needed a doctor. I went back to the caravansary and talked to the driver, hoping a doctor would be among the passengers. He laughed and said doctors didn't travel by bus, they took the plane and got to Zabol in two hours.

Taara came in, holding her head, hitting it, and shoving her forefinger into her ear like a mad woman. She had forgotten her veil. She was in the same brown maternity dress, made for the fifth month. Her belly was full now, a huge beach ball moving ahead of her, forcing the dress apart and setting itself free. Now all the passengers noticed. Each said something. They all had suggestions. A young man looked into Taara's ear and said he couldn't see anything. A woman tried. No result. "It's buzzing! It's buzzing!" Taara kept saying. No one finished his breakfast.

Some native women in colorful dresses—layers of silk skirts, green and yellow kerchiefs around their heads—sold knickknacks in the courtyard. Zinc bracelets, earrings, hand-made bead necklaces, charms, talismans containing beaded prayer books inside tiny velvet purses—all were spread on a carpet in front of them. When the women saw the commotion, one of the elders, whose henna-treated braids came down to her waist, approached Taara and said something. The driver said the old woman wanted to look at Taara's ear. Taara was reluctant. I told her that since everybody else had looked into her ear, the old woman could try as well.

She took Taara to the carpeted bed and said something to the old man with the water pipe. The ancient man moved himself with much effort and mumbled something. The woman helped Taara lie down on her side. The male passengers moved away, as if this was a surgery bed and she was going to get undressed. The women circled around the bed. The native woman bent over Taara and pressed her ear against hers, trying to hear the buzzing fly. Now she put her mouth on Taara's ear and sucked. Taara gave out a broken scream. The woman took a hairpin out from under her scarf, dipped it in the ear and took out a small fly. Like a magician, she beamed with triumph and showed the little insect to the audience. Now she laughed loudly, revealing a few long, yellow teeth.

The passengers clapped and the native women made a loud catcall, trilling their tongues. Taara hugged the old woman, thanked her, and bought the most expensive item she had in her merchandise—a necklace made of zinc coins. She wore the jingling necklace and with the help of the driver climbed the bus. When she walked and jingled in the aisle, all the passengers clapped and whistled. Women looked at her belly with affection, weaving different stories in their minds—a lost husband, a husband waiting for her in a remote station, a husband left behind to join later, a husband dead, killed, martyred. She was such an angel that no one wove a story that didn't contain a husband. All through the long trip, fruit, juices, sodas, pastries, salted nuts, cold sandwiches, and even carefully cleaned pomegranate seeds traveled to the back of the bus for Taara, the jingling angel.

Four Directions

In small towns there is always a square with four major streets branching
out, offering you a choice of the four directions. You mark your destiny
depending on which road you take. Who can tell which way is the right
one? Does west take you to security? East to freedom? Is north where fear
hides? South where your death awaits?

When our bus reached Zabol's square, it entered a dusty parking lot
and stopped. It was five-thirty—two hours before sunset. We stepped out
in a cloud of dust and stood in the middle of the lot. None of the passengers who had earlier fed us fruit and snacks said goodbye. It was New
Year's Eve and all of them rushed home to their families. No one offered
us a ride and the kind driver and his assistant vanished.

We walked to the street beside the lot and waited. At any minute a taxi
would arrive, we'd check into a motel, pick up the phone book, and find
our uncle. But the street was vacant. There were no cars. The other side
looked as if a battle had taken place there—half-ruined, soot-covered brick
walls and broken windows. This must be the wrong street. We walked
toward the square. Taara wore the blue veil and carried the attaché case.
I walked behind her—a younger brother, or a servant carrying her heavy
bag and the setar. At the square we picked the street to the west, the one
with the sun sinking behind its tallest building. We stood waiting. There
was no taxi. A pickup truck passed; a few leather-skinned natives with
bandannas around their heads and faces sat in the back, dozing. A gust of
wind blew dust into our faces. I pulled the cap down to protect my eyes.
Taara wore her sunglasses. The air was getting colder by the minute.

"What have we done?" Taara murmured. "What if there are no taxis
in this town?"

"Don't panic. Remember what Baba always said, 'Fear is the brother of
death!'" I said this in good humor to cheer her up, but my voice gave me
away. I was afraid too.

Taara was tired. She sat on the curb and spread her bags around her. I
paced up and down the pavement, then walked back to the street where
the dusty parking lot was—but our bus was gone. We should have stayed

by the bus and waited for the driver to come back and help us. Mistake. Mistake. The sun that was now behind the wall of the four-story building would soon melt into the desert sand and the chill would come. Taara didn't have a jacket. What if her baby came? I walked to a tall building on the corner. The lower part was a shoe store—closed. The top floors were vacant. Next to the dingy shoe store there was a dusty fabric shop, a dustier stationery store, a carpenter's shop—all closed. They close early in small towns.

Taara sat awkwardly on the curb, holding her belly in her arms, rocking back and forth.

"Pain?"

"No."

"Do you want something?"

"I want a room and a bathroom. I want to take off my damn clothes and take a shower. My ankles are swollen. My shoes feel tight. I want real food with chunks of meat. A glass of wine. A cigarette."

"Wait. I'll knock on all these doors."

"No. Let's go to the other side of the square."

"Wait! A car is coming. Get up, Taara. Let them see your belly." I helped her to stand up. She removed the veil and showed her big, round belly. An old American car, a once blue Dodge, now gray with powdery dust, approached. A woman rolled down the window. She was unveiled and wore make-up.

"Excuse me, where can we find a hotel around here?" I asked.

The woman stared at me as if I were from another planet. Now she glanced at Taara and fixed her eyes on the middle of her body. But the man driving was full of smile, showing his tar-stained teeth, wide gaps between them—the bad teeth of a six-year-old.

"Hotel?" he asked.

"Or a motel," Taara said.

"There are a couple of lodging places on Shah Street, oh, sorry, Khomeini Street," the man said, and laughed. "But I wouldn't exactly call them motels."

"You must be from Tehran?" the woman said.

We nodded.

"You have family here?" the man asked.

"We've come to look for our uncle," I said. "We don't have his address. But we know his name. My sister is not well—"

"I can see that!" the woman said. Now she turned to her husband and whispered, "She's due!"

"Be our guests! It's Norooz, after all!" the man said and smiled. "Get in. We'll find your uncle. I know everybody here!"

We squeezed into the back seat with our luggage. The man was laughing.

"Hotel!" he said. "These caravansaries are for seasonal workers and truck drivers. But don't worry. You're my guests."

"I'm sure we'll find our uncle tomorrow," Taara said. "It's a small town."

"I'll find him for you," the man said. "What's that back there? An instrument?"

"Oh, this is my setar," Taara said.

"You play it? Excellent! Maybe you can play for us tonight. We have a few guests at home."

Taara held my hand and squeezed it. The man was too friendly. He laughed all the time and drove recklessly, turning left and right in narrow, dirt alleys, raising a cloud of dust. But the woman was somber, looking out the window as if she was sulking. I could see her profile, the round circle of red rouge on her cheek, not quite blended, a thick black line around her eyes, sticky mascara. The eye that I could see was unblinking, staring out through its charcoal frame.

"We are not from here, either," the man said. "But we live here. We have to. I mean for now."

"People are rude and wild here," the woman pointed out the window. There were some turbaned men walking along the dirt road with two donkeys and a camel. "It's not easy to live here. I can never take a walk outside."

"Just a few more months, dear!" the man patted her leg. "Be patient. We have to wait till this business ends." Now he half-turned and said, "I'm a contractor. I'm building a barracks at the border."

"At the border?" Taara asked.

"There!" The man pointed his index finger toward the passenger window. We were almost out of the city and the blazing sun was sinking behind the red line of the horizon. "That's the border of Afghanistan," he said, pointing at the thin line.

"You mean a barracks for soldiers?" Taara asked.

"When I started six months ago it was supposed to be for the soldiers of the Imperial Army, to protect the border. You know, there is a lot of drug traffic here. But now our work has almost stopped. We have to see if the Islamic Guards are coming here, or what."

"That's why I'm saying we shouldn't stay any longer," the woman said. "We can't wait. What if this shit in Tehran lasts forever?"

"They haven't paid me for what I've done, dear. I have to wait and get my money. If the big Ayatollah is in charge now, he has to pay me."

"To hell with all of them!" the woman said bitterly.

"Here they do other illegal business too," the man said. Now the road and the desert around us were dark. Taara squeezed my hand again. "These drug smugglers take fugitives over the border."

"Really?" Taara asked.

"Really," the man said. "It costs though. Thousands. They're ripping off these fat generals. It's dangerous too. An air force general and his family were trying to cross the border into Pakistan, a mine blew, the general went up in pieces. One of the kids was blown up too. The smugglers returned the wife and the other kid."

"The poor general," the woman said. "Fucking bad luck."

"Now you know why they need my barracks?" the man half-turned again and looked at us. "They need my barracks even more than the Shah's regime did." He said this to the woman and patted her thigh again. "It won't take long. They'll send someone from Tehran with the orders to continue the work."

"Are we going there now?" I asked. He was still driving, and except for a few huts in the middle of the sand, there was nothing left of the town.

"To the barracks? Oh, no. We're going home. It's a bit outside of town—a deserted area. But it's not a bad house. Spacious, for sure. It's one of a kind in this desert." He said this, chuckled, and repeated it. "One of a kind!"

At Master Memaar's

"Here! Welcome to our resort!" the woman said, and stepped out of the car. She was short and plump and wore a tight black skirt and a tight red blouse, its buttons on the verge of popping off her large bosom. Her hair, fixed with spray, was wine red and curled down below her ears. She unlocked the narrow, wooden door and we entered. The man and the woman took their shoes off in the dark corridor. We did the same. There were more than twenty pairs of shoes behind the door.

The couple led us into the first room on the left and turned on the light. The room was almost bare, but fully carpeted with a cheap hand-woven rug. In a corner, mattresses, quilts, and pillows formed a little mound, covered by a bedspread. We put down our load.

"Be comfortable, please!" the woman said. "Take that chador off!" she told Taara, "I know you're not used to it. You just wore it for the trip, huh? The minute I saw you two, I told my husband, these are city kids. Let's pick them up. They'll get lost here. This is a dangerous town, I'm telling you! A few nights ago they cut a man's throat from corner to corner, just behind the wall of the garage where you got off. I told you earlier, they're a bunch of wild people. Nomads. Uncivilized."

"Okay now, you don't need to scare them," the man said. Out of his car, he looked small and boyish, but his sideburns were gray. He had an old-fashioned, thin mustache, carefully trimmed. "Make some tea for them," he told the woman. "I'll go and get some dinner."

"Buy some kebob," the woman said. "The inn is open till nine. I'm starving!"

"You better give me a hand with these bottles in the trunk," the man told her. "We had to drive twenty kilometers to a Jew's house to buy some wine for Norooz," he explained to us. "Rest now. Make yourselves comfortable. We'll be back soon."

The woman left the room, but the man stood in the frame of the door and said, "Oh, how absentminded we are! My wife's name is Mehri, and everyone calls me Master Memaar, the house builder. Drop the Master please, Memaar is good enough." He showed his cavitied teeth and left.

We stood in the middle of the room, listening to the clinking sounds of the bottles being carried inside. Then the car took off and Mehri opened and closed cabinet doors in the kitchen. Feeling weak, Taara melted onto the floor and I sat next to her and rubbed her swollen knees and ankles. She lay her head against the wall and closed her eyes.

There was a window above our heads covered on the inside by a bamboo shade. Another window, opposite us, looked out over the dirt alley. That one's shade was rolled up. The room was chilly. Taara pulled the veil over herself and shivered. I pulled the shade's string and looked out. There was a big backyard and a square pool, glittering with dark water. A dusty tamarind tree grew crookedly by the pool. An outhouse was at the left corner of the yard. I saw several rooms along a long porch on the right, all opening to the yard. The lights in some of the rooms were on. The building had a second story too, most of which windows glared in the dark.

"This is a big house, Taara."

"How big?"

"Many rooms. Like an inn."

"They said they had other guests."

"Are they letting their rooms?"

"Wouldn't they tell us, then?" Taara asked. "They volunteered to tell us everything."

"You mean all these people in these rooms are their guests?"

"How do I know? Are you afraid of Master Memaar?" She opened her eyes for the first time and looked up at me.

"He's too friendly and generous. I wonder what's hidden under his generosity."

"Ah, stop this, for God's sake. You've become so cynical."

Now the woman came in with a small kerosene heater and a kettle. She put the heater in the middle of the room and placed the kettle on top. The kettle began to hiss. She went out again and came back with a china teapot. After taking off the kettle's lid and placing the pot carefully on top of the kettle, she sat cross-legged on the floor and relaxed. She had changed from her tight skirt into wide transparent pajamas.

"The tea will brew in few minutes," she said. "Did you pull up the shade? It's okay. But make sure to drop it when you want to change," she told Taara. "There are men out there. They get water from the pool."

"There is no running water?" Taara asked worriedly.

"Not for them, dear. But for us, there is. The people on the other side of the yard don't have plumbing, but we do. There is one inconvenience, though—we have to share the outhouse with them. Whenever you need to use it, go to the kitchen, fill the plastic pitcher with water and go out. Don't use the pool water."

"One toilet for all?" Taara asked.

"I told Memaar a million times when we first came here, 'Build a toilet inside the house, you're a house builder, for God's sake!' He kept saying we're staying here for just a short time. Now look! Six months have passed and we're stuck. God knows how long we'll have to stay in this hell."

"What do you do all day, when your husband goes to work?" Taara asked.

"Nothing!" she said. "I'm bored to death. There is a puny, dirt-covered bazaar two kilometers from here that I prefer not to go to. I catch a ride from one of the men and go all the way to Zabol to do some shopping. At least the bazaar is bigger there. Sometimes they sell neat stuff too. All smuggled. We'll go shopping tomorrow. You can buy three yards of Indian silk for nothing! Twenty-four-karat gold earrings and bracelets for nothing. Leather bags, belts, American cigarettes. Whisky! But they've become cautious about that last item recently." She sighed and said, "That's my only fun. I go shopping some days. We can buy you some clothes tomorrow. You need to change. I don't think you have much in that small handbag."

"No. Not much," Taara said. "But I need to wash first. Do you have a shower in the house?"

"We have a bathhouse at the end of the yard. It doesn't have running water, but we take a few buckets of water with us and it's not that hard. First thing tomorrow we'll warm up some water for you."

"It's nice of you," Taara said.

"Oh, with pleasure. I don't really see many city people here. You guys are very welcome. Hey, why don't you take off your dusty cap?" she told me. "Air your head a little!"

"I'm okay," I said.

"Keeping your sister company all the time, eh?" she said while pouring tea into small, narrow-waisted glasses. "What is your name, by the way?"

"Farid."

Taara pierced me with her eyes.

"And you?"

"Taara."

"Where is your husband, Taara?" She asked what she was dying to know.

"He's dead."

Now I gave Taara a burning look. She smiled, winking. This was a lying contest.

"Oh, I'm so sorry," Mehri said. "It must have happened just recently, a few months ago, maybe," she pointed to Taara's belly.

"Very recently. Did you hear about that movie theater that was bombed in Tehran?"

"No. I don't read the newspapers. Was your husband...?"

"Yes," Taara said, and bent her head.

"Horrible! Horrible!" She said this and slid the tray of tea toward us. "Have some tea. You're tired. It's refreshing. So horrible," she said, and left the room.

When I came back from the outhouse, which was just a bit cleaner than the ones on the road, Master Memaar was spreading a long, rectangular tablecloth in the middle of the room. Mehri kept bringing different dishes of appetizers—fresh herbs, garlic pickles, yogurt and spinach, four-seasons salad, olives, sliced lime. It was obvious that this amount of food was meant for more people. At the end, she brought some candles and a shaving mirror and planted them in the middle of the cloth, saying that these were the only items she had for the Norooz decorations. We should at least light some candles.

I sat next to Taara and looked at the cheap candles that burned fast and made a whizzing sound. In a minute three men entered, nodding politely. They sat at the other side of the tablecloth. Two of them were in some kind of native clothes—baggy pants, embroidered vests, and dark turbans, an extension of which hung on their shoulders. One man was in a regular gray suit, but wore no tie. He was middle-aged and avoided eye contact.

"These are our guests," Memaar said, "Mr. Amaani is from Tehran, too. And these brothers are our Baluchi friends, Safdar and Samandar." He introduced us to the men and added that there was another gentleman who stayed upstairs, resting.

"We eat together every night," Mehri said, sitting cross-legged on the floor. "Otherwise it feels so lonely. We're all foreigners here, so to speak; it's better to keep each other company. I hope you don't mind?" She said this to Taara.

"Oh, no. I'm so grateful for the food," Taara said, and ate greedily.

"Enjoy it!" the house builder, said. "Eat as much as you can. There is more in the kitchen. As you can see, they don't make bad kebobs in our desert, do they?"

Now he poured vodka into small tea glasses for everyone and passed them around. Mehri asked Taara if she drank. Taara said she did, and with a quick jerk of her head, emptied the vodka into her mouth. The men noticed, bent their heads, and pretended they hadn't seen her.

Mehri poured some Pepsi for me without asking what I liked to drink. The men began a broken conversation. It was about the latest news in Tehran. The bombings, assassinations, resignations. Master Memaar and the older Baluchi man talked more than the others. The younger Baluchi gazed at Taara and ate slowly, barely looking at his food. Mr. Amaani, the Tehrani man, was silent.

After dinner, everyone, including Mehri and Taara, smoked cigarettes, drank vodka, and talked about the desert weather. Taara's cheeks were pink and her irises danced playfully. I wanted to talk to her, to urge her not to drink any more, but I couldn't even whisper to her. Five pairs of eyes stared at us—at her. Taara took her setar out of the box and began to play.

When the house builder's wife started to clean up, I got up to help her. In and out of the room, I saw Taara playing, her eyes half-closed and the dark-eyed Baluchi, the younger one, staring at her, mesmerized. Whenever Taara came back from where the music had taken her, she opened her drunken eyes and responded to the young man's gaze with a faint smile.

I was the only person in the room without alcohol in my blood, but I was the most confused. I had lost the sense of time and place, and wasn't sure what exactly had happened that I was here and not somewhere else. I remembered the town's intersection—the four streets extending from the only square—and I wondered where we would be now if we'd taken another street and another car had stopped for us? All this and Taara's music, which crept into my soul and summoned all the ghosts of the past, disoriented me such that the old winds in my head whistled once again.

The moment I sat down, my eyelids felt like iron curtains and closed shut. When I heard the young Baluch's voice rising, I tried to look at him, but instead drifted on the slippery surface of the yellow desert tides. Was Samandar singing along with Taara, or was I dreaming? I fell into a dark abyss and didn't hear, see, or smell a thing.

A Nightmare

I woke up with the unmistakable shriek of the old parrot shouting, "Boor-rr!" The scream came from somewhere above my head and not far away. I sat up, my blood cold, my pulse slowing to a near stop. The room was dark, except for a faint red light penetrating the holes of the kerosene heater. When my eyes became used to the darkness, I saw Taara's body next to mine. We were each on a single mattress, under goose-feathered quilts. Who had put me to bed? I tried to see the rest of the room. Someone slept on the other side, close to the door. It was the house builder's wife.

I sat for a while, holding my breath. I thought I heard the flapping of wet wings, a bird trying to dry itself. I shook Taara; she half opened her eyes.

"What?"

"Did you hear that?"

"What?"

"Boor-boor."

"Who?" she asked again, her eyes wide open now.

"The parrot. I heard her screaming. Assad must be here."

She sat up, looking at me. In the faint red light of the heater she looked unreal, a creature of imagination. Her hair was all around her, as if on flames.

"What are you talking about?" she asked.

"I woke up with Boor-boor's shriek—"

"You were dreaming, Talkhoon. How can Assad be here? Use your head!"

We sat and listened. The house builder's wife began a rhythmic snore. We listened to it for a while, then we heard men's voices behind our window. Someone struck a match. Taara said, "Sleep now."

"Who put me on this mattress?"

"Mehri did. They wanted you to sleep in the men's room. I told them not to bother you."

"Why is she sleeping here?"

"I guess all the men sleep in the other room. She doesn't sleep with her husband."

"Strange."

"I know."

"That boy sang. Didn't he?"

"Oh, yes. Samandar. He has such a warm voice—and hot eyes!"

"Taara!"

"What?"

"How is the baby?"

"Kicking all right."

"Regular kicking?"

"The same old kicking."

"Did you ask Master Memaar about our uncle?"

"Yes. He doesn't know him."

"Then what are we doing here in the middle of nowhere?"

"He said he'll inquire."

"But didn't he say he knew everybody? Our uncle has lived in this area all his life. Our father visited him not long ago."

"Maybe our uncle has changed his name. If he has, then there is no way to find him. We're in the desert. They don't have a newspaper here to put an ad in."

"What are we supposed to do now?"

"Let's wait till Memaar inquires. It's not such a bad place here, after all. They're nice people."

"Who are all these men out there?"

"How do I know, Talkhoon?"

"Who are Safdar and Samandar?"

"Safdar is a real Baluch, but his brother is just visiting him. He is from Tehran. He is a mechanic."

"That's what he told you?"

"We talked a little. He works as a mechanic and goes to night college. He's wearing Baluchi clothes because he's visiting his tribe."

"And what is his brother doing in the house builder's house?"

"Shut up, Talkhoon! You wake me up in the middle of the night to ask stupid questions? I want to get some sleep now." She lay down, turned her back to me and pulled the quilt over her head.

"Taara!"

"Now what?" She uncovered her head.

"Where would we be if in that intersection we'd stood on the other side?"

"Where would we be if you hadn't stayed at your friends' house that night and we'd come to Zabol one day earlier?"

"Where would I be if I hadn't seen you in the bus station the day before?"

"Where would I be if I hadn't met Vahid at all?"

"You'd be General Nezam-El-Deen's daughter-in law."

"Oh, yes."

"They killed him."

"The old General?"

"Yes. They pulled him out of his car and shot him."

"Where is the boy with the big nose—my fiancé?"

"Who knows? Maybe arrested. You'd be in prison too."

"So things didn't turn out that bad, Talkhoon. We're together and we're safe now. Either we'll find our uncle here or we'll return to Tehran."

"What a bright future!"

"Shut up now! I thought you were tough!"

The rest of the night I lay on my back, listening. I didn't hear the bird's scream or the flapping of her wet wings any more. But I heard the men outside in the dark courtyard, speaking in whispers. They struck matches and poured something into glasses. A while later I smelled a bittersweet odor, so strong that it nauseated me. Taara raised her head and murmured, "I know this smell. Opium."

Bathing

When the buckets of warm water were ready, Mehri and I carried them to the bathhouse. The morning heat was intense and we had to walk a long way under the blazing sun. Mehri walked in front of me, her wide transparent pajama pants showing her legs and the shadow of her dark panties. As a top she wore a tight, sleeveless shirt—red again—and her braless breasts hopped with each step.

Now that she had washed off all her make-up, she looked older. She hadn't brushed her hair either, and her sticky, disheveled curls stood up on her head. She said she had a bad headache; I thought it was a hangover. But in spite of the heat and the headache, she carried the heavy buckets for Taara all the way to the bathhouse.

The bathhouse was a spacious, windowless room with a couple of cement platforms in the middle facing a small, empty pool. A round hole the size of a serving plate was on the ceiling. A column of light entered through it, lit the floor, and created a spotlight. Taara was in the middle of this spotlight, getting undressed. Her naked belly was huge and unreal, her breasts swollen, her dark nipples like ripened figs.

"Hey, boy, get out of here!" Mehri pushed me out. "Do you always look at your sister?"

I had forgotten I was a boy. Taara covered her breasts and I left the bathhouse.

"Let's go and warm up some water for you," Mehri said. "Two will be enough. You're little and you don't have much hair."

In the kitchen, she asked all of a sudden, "Now tell me, sugar, what are you guys doing here, huh?"

"We're looking for our uncle."

"Why are you looking for an uncle you don't even know?"

"We need his help." This honest answer popped out of my mouth and surprised me. It was too late to take it back.

"You guys are planning to cross?"

"Cross?"

"You know what I mean. Cross the border—to the other side. You must be planning to cross."

I didn't say anything.

"If you're here to cross, this is the place to negotiate," she said. "And it costs. Whether your uncle helps or not, it's going to cost."

I decided to get as much information as I could. "How much?"

"Government people pay thousands. In dollars. They give their houses and villas, their cars. What do you guys have?"

"Our uncle won't charge," I said.

She laughed, loud and hard, slapping my shoulder. "Your uncle won't take you across, sweetheart. We will."

"You?"

"Master Memaar."

"So he is not here to build a barracks?"

"Of course he is. But he's got himself involved in this business too. Now he is nose deep in it. He's making money, of course, and he doesn't want to quit. Besides, how can the others let him quit?"

"Because he knows everything."

"You're a smart boy, aren't you? Now tell me what happened in Tehran? Was your sister involved in politics? Her husband?"

"No, ma'am."

"Don't ma'am me. I don't like it. Call me Mehri. So, you're running away. She got herself pregnant and took you with her." She ran her hand over my hair. She said, "What a precious brother you are!"

Before she could get further with her scenario about Taara and stroke my hair again, her husband called out. He needed to unload the trunk.

From the kitchen window I saw Taara, flushed, rolling toward the building, her wet hair piled on top of her head. She had washed the blue chador and was trying to hang it on a rope that ran across the yard. She looked around to find me. I went out and before Mehri caught us again, whispered in her ear.

"Master Memaar smuggles people over the border," I said.

"Okay. I got it. Go inside now."

"Don't hang your panties here."

"They're under the chador."

"They won't get dry."

"They'll dry in five minutes. Don't you feel the heat?"

We walked toward our room. All those whispering shadows had vanished, but I felt their burning stares on our backs. In the room, Taara sat down and leaned against the wall and closed her eyes. Her breath came heavily. The heat and bathing with the buckets had tired her. Mehri brought a fan and planted it in the middle of the room. Taara lay down, moaning faintly. Soon she was asleep.

I sat on the wet cement platform with two buckets of warm water at my feet, enjoying the breeze that blew through the hole in the ceiling. The remains of the night were still cool in the air. My naked body had never been exposed to a breeze and I wanted to extend the pleasure. I wanted to let my skin breathe. I touched the column of light as if it were something tangible and ran my hand through it and played with it. I'd wash myself and save some water to rinse my shirt and pants, I thought. Then I'd wear the wet clothes and sit in the sun for few minutes to dry. I felt a tickling joy. All of these were privileges I'd never had before. My body and soul were free.

First I filled a small metal bowl with water and poured it over my shoulders, then I covered my body with the suds from a cheap, green, hand soap and inhaled its sharp, grassy smell. I sat, soapy, listening to the winds of the desert—strong, steady winds that originated here and traveled all the way to Drum Tower, pounding on its heavy gate. I listened some more and heard the voice of the wind rising from the faraway horizon where a pencil line marked the end of the earth.

Where am I? Where am I going?

The iron door of the bathhouse creaked open, as if in answer.

"Need help to wash your back?" Mehri stood in the frame of the door against the sharp light.

"No. Please go out!" I covered my chest.

"Come on! I just want to help you," she came forward.

"Please don't. I'll scream."

She laughed. Her voice echoed in the bathhouse. "Go ahead and scream! No one will hear you, anyway."

I bent forward, my chest touching my knees. She picked up a bucket and poured the hot water on my back.

"Don't waste my water! Please go!"

She laughed. "If you don't sit up straight, I'm going to tickle you." She ran her fingers over my arm, reaching my armpit. I screamed, rose and ran into the dark shadows around the column of light. She was like a wild cat, a leopard, chasing a fawn in the dark, circling her prey. Her red hair was frizzled in the damp air. She almost groaned and leaped toward me. My soapy feet slipped on the wet floor and I fell on my face. She was still laughing, saying silly things.

"You shy little boy! See what you did? Did you hurt yourself? Get up!" She extended her arm.

"Go!" I screamed. I was angry.

"Don't shout at me, you little brat!" she was serious now. She took her blouse off and bent over me. Her breasts were so large that they touched my back. "Turn now!" she whispered. "I said turn! How can I fuck you if your back is to me! Let me see how little your thing is!" She giggled.

I stayed hunched over on all fours, hiding my breasts. She ran her hand between my thighs to find what she was looking for. Not finding anything, she grabbed my shoulder and, with a sudden surge of strength, turned me over. Now she sat on me, as if to ride. She looked at my chest, my small, girlish breasts, and moved her gaze down to my underbelly to make sure. She froze for a long second, defeated. Now she moved away from me and broke into a hysterical laughter.

"Devil! You're a devil! Aren't you?" She wiped her tears. "You were a girl all the time. All the fucking time!" she sobbed.

"Hey," I sat up. "I'm sorry —"

"Sorry for what? For being a fucking girl?"

"If I were a boy, I'd definitely desire you. You're so…charming."

"Shut up now! I should've known that…so close to your sister…too mature to be a teenage boy…" She cried some more, then sobbed into her palms.

I put my shirt and pants on my wet body and lifted her up. We both sat on the platform. I rubbed her shoulders, comforting her.

"It's all right," she said. "I'm just lonely here. It's a fucking hard life. All these rough men around—and Memaar is busy all the time."

"You never sleep together?"

"Fuck him! We're not married. I'm his mistress. But I guess he is tired of me or something. Not that there is another woman. There is no other woman for thousands of kilometers in all directions. Unless you count those stinky, dirty, nomad women with their callused skins. Greed has blinded this man. He's lost interest in sex. All he thinks about is money. And his smoke."

"Opium?"

"That is his undoing. I keep telling him, you've made enough, let's get out of here before something bad happens. But the damned smoke has taken away his judgment. He is deaf and blind."

"Why don't you leave?"

She raised her head for the first time and looked at me in the dim light. Last night's mascara ran down her cheeks. "Leave? After all these years? Either he has to marry me, or give me my share of everything. I've spent nine years of my life with him. I've worked for him like a housemaid. He's dragged me all over the country to different fucking construction sights. Just leave?"

"Let's go in, Mehri."

"If I'd stayed in my own town and married one of my suitors, I'd have my own family now. I left with him because he said he'd marry me. But now I'm sure he won't."

"Maybe he will, after this business—"

"Oh, I don't care anymore. I just want my money. Some savings for my future." Suddenly she paused and stared at me. "Why are you pretending to be a boy?"

"I feel safe this way."

"I envy you."

"Envy me?"

"Yes." She buttoned her shirt, went toward the door, and stopped. "I won't tell anybody. Stay a boy. Good for you!" Now she laughed. "Did I make a fucking fool of myself? Trying to seduce a little boy?"

"I'm not little. I'm seventeen," I teased. "Don't think about it anymore. And keep my secret. I'll keep yours."

Politics in the Desert

The tall, rotating fan was in the middle of the room sending waves of hot air toward us. Mehri taught me how to splash water on the bamboo shade from outside to cool the room. Passing through the wet bamboo, the hellish breeze turned heavenly. All afternoon Tara slept in the cool current.

So this was my job—every half-hour I filled a bucket from the pool, splashed water on the bamboo shade, poured some on my head and came in. Once, I felt so hot that I stood in the middle of the yard and poured the whole bucket of cold water over my body. A bearded man looking down from a window on the second floor laughed and said something in a language I did not understand.

When Taara woke up, she had some hot tea and lemon with Mehri, who insisted that steaming tea was the best cure for heat. Then they squeezed into the passenger seat of a truck that belonged to the same bearded man who'd laughed at me earlier, and went to Zabol to shop. I tried to take a nap, but it was too hot. Besides, how could I sleep and splash water on the bamboo at the same time?

So the rest of the afternoon I sat in the empty room, wrestling with fragments of disturbing thoughts, waiting for Taara to return. If Taara wouldn't talk with Memaar, then I had to do it. Either the man would find our uncle or we'd leave. But where to? Back to Tehran? I thought about the deed for Drum Tower. Was it valid? If Assad could erase Khanum's name, then a smuggler could put his own signature there. Could we use this document instead of money and cross the border? But the dim vision I had of the other side was something I did not want to think about.

And what if Taara became comfortable here and spent her days in a daze and her nights at opium parties? And then the baby would come and we wouldn't be able to move. I had to talk to this Master Memaar.

At dinner, Mehri was quiet and somber. I knew now that she had two moods: talking and sulking. Taara drank again. I warned her that she was feeding alcohol to the baby—it would be crippled. She laughed and told me to shut up. Samandar with his charcoal black eyes drilled holes in her. Either Taara's belly didn't matter to him, or he liked big-bellied women. Master Memaar and Safdar discussed politics, cursing the revolution, praising the old regime, the safety and security of the twenty-five-hundred-year monarchy. One of the guests, who had been absent last night, joined the dinner. He was chubby and bald and wore a short-sleeved shirt. Memaar never introduced him and he didn't even glance at us.

Now when Master Memaar praised the fallen monarchy, Mr. Amaani, the gray-haired man who had been quiet last night, raised his head for the first time and spoke in a calm voice.

"Imagine a pressure cooker, water boiling in it. The lid is tight. The water expands and pushes against the lid; the lid bursts open and hot water overflows. It's a law, isn't it? If the Shah and his American advisors were wise enough, they'd leave the lid open a crack. They wouldn't censor the poets' books or arrest the university students for reading Jack London or Maxim Gorky."

Memaar and Safdar looked at the man, puzzled. They didn't know who Jack London and Maxim Gorky were and what they had to do with the revolution. The bald man pretended to be deaf.

"Are you saying the revolution was inevitable?" the younger Baluch, Samander, asked.

"Obviously. If it wasn't inevitable, it wouldn't have happened," the gray-haired man said, and smiled.

"But why all these mullahs?" Memaar asked. "Where have they been? Where were they hiding all this time?"

"They were around us all the time—in the dark chambers of their theology schools in Qum, in our neighborhood mosques. The Shah exiled their leader. He fanned their rage. He created the Islamic movement."

"You mean the Shah is responsible for the Ayatollah's power?" Memaar asked.

"He and his masters," the man said. "Yes. They caused it. Again, they didn't leave the lid of the pressure cooker open."

"What is to be done now?" Safdar asked.

"The secular organizations are weak," the gray-haired man said. "They're out of practice. The monarchy never gave them the freedom to exist, to be among people, to spread their roots. People are used to tyranny. In this country, one tyrant replaces another. People don't know the concept of democracy. Every single man in Iran is a little shah in his own house, dreaming of a big shah to control him and save him. That's all they know: tyrants. Our history is full of them. People worshiped the bloodsucker kings. Now they worship the ayatollahs. The tyrant is the same; the crown has turned into a turban. Liberal and leftist organizations cannot gain much power. People don't know them. Some of them have just arrived from exile. Twenty-five years in Europe. They even speak with a funny accent!"

"So you're saying the rule of the clergy is inevitable?" Samandar asked.

"They were here. They've spread their roots in the commercial sector. They're popular among the shopkeepers of the bazaar. And the poor are ignorant. The government of the Shah, or the government of Allah, it doesn't make any difference to them, as long as a savior is up there—a savior who doesn't need to save them. Just an idol, a father figure. The ayatollahs are playing with the people's deepest emotions—their blind faith."

"What about those who understand?" Taara asked. "Those who are not blinded by religious faith?"

"This country is not their place anymore, my dear. They had better leave. Some have already left."

After the tablecloth was cleaned up, shaken and folded for the next meal, the mysterious bald man returned upstairs. Mr. Amaani, as if embarrassed by his long lecture, vanished too, and everybody else went to the yard to sit in the cool breeze and smoke. Taara was wearing a loose-fitting maternity dress she'd found in Zabol's Bazaar. The dress was a native gown with glittering green sequins all over it. It was a color she would never wear in the city—the hot pink of a strange evening sky, dotted by stars. She held her setar in her arms and followed her belly to the porch. The zinc coins of her native necklace jingled on her chest.

They had cleared the porch of all the faceless men, and had spread a carpet there. Mehri, Taara, Memaar, and the two Baluchi brothers sat drinking, smoking, and chatting. I wanted to speak with Master Memaar, but he was busy trying to refute Mr. Amaani's earlier comments in his absence. I couldn't interrupt him and besides, he considered me a child. I needed Taara's help, but she couldn't see me. She was absorbed in herself and conscious of the young man's attention. She was acting like a soloist, sitting majestically on a stage ready for her concert. As she began playing and Samandar singing, I left the porch.

Since they had brought us here, I'd never opened the front door of the house, never seen the outside. Now I sat on the steps looking at the narrow dirt alley. A dusty, yellow bulb on top of a wooden post cast a dim light and moths flew around it. I saw a few other houses in the alley, much smaller and older—poor people's hovels. The alley was short and its end lay in darkness. A gust of cool wind brushed dry sand onto my face. I ran my hand over my head and felt the grains.

If Memaar kept drinking and smoking, I would never be able to talk to him. Had we come all the way to the end of the earth to linger in this strange house and get drunk?

"Upset? Or alone?"

First I saw the red spot of his cigarette, then he emerged from the darkness. It was Mr. Amaani. I didn't say anything. He sat next to me on the stone step.

"It feels lonely here, especially at night. There is something about the desert, I don't know what, that makes one feel orphaned, abandoned. Maybe trees keep us company in Tehran—all those tall maples—our old friends."

"Are you a poet too?" I asked.

"Too? Who else is a poet?"

I realized that ever since I saw this man I'd been thinking of my father. Father could have made such a speech about the revolution.

"Are you?"

"What?"

"A poet?"

"Oh, no. But I do write."

"Are you here to cross?"

He laughed. "You're already using their terms. 'To cross!' Yes, I'm here to cross. What else would bring me here? This is the end of the world."

"That's what I thought."

"I don't want you to tell me what you're not supposed to, but how come you and your sister are planning to leave the country? Where are your parents?"

"We don't have parents. I mean, not in a normal way."

"I see."

"And we didn't come here exactly to cross. I learned about the crossing business here. We came because of our uncle."

"Where is he?"

"Somewhere around here. Master Memaar said he knew everybody; he'd find him. But now he says he doesn't know him."

"Be careful."

"About Memaar?"

"Everybody. Everything. You should have stayed home."

"No home was left."

"I see."

"Why are you trying to cross?"

"I guess I already told everybody at dinner. Oh, damn! I shouldn't have talked so much. And in front of that man. I regret it."

"I don't think they know who you are."

"They know what type of person I am. A cowardly intellectual." He laughed bitterly.

"Why do you say this?"

"Because everything I said was a justification for what I'm doing."

"I don't think so."

"You're kind."

"You're neither a political activist, nor a religious believer," I said. "So you should leave."

"Some people believe that every single person who understands what is wrong is responsible."

"For what?"

"For staying and fighting. So that the catastrophe won't happen. Have you read about the rise of fascism in Germany in your history classes?"

"But aren't these matters beyond the power of individuals?"

"Individuals, yes. But they're not beyond the power of political organizations. Sufferers of the World Unite! Haven't you heard such slogans?"

"I've seen them on the walls. Once I walked with a group of people all the way to a cemetery where their martyrs were. They sang their anthems. Their leader was called 'Uncle.'"

"Oh, really?"

"I joined them accidentally."

"Then what happened?"

"The Guards shot at them."

"I know. Criminals are gaining power by the minute. Cowards and realists are leaving."

"Where is your family?"

"I don't have one."

"Oh—"

"I don't want you to tell this even to your sister—I was a political prisoner in the former regime. When the revolution opened the doors of the Shah's prisons, I walked out."

"Just recently."

"To be precise, six months ago. I spent fifteen years there. 'Uncle' was my cellmate."

"Really?"

"Yes. My wife divorced me before my trial was over. I don't blame her. We have two children. I haven't seen the older one since he was two, the younger I've never seen. They must be around your age now."

"No contact?"

"Nothing. They live in England. Their mother didn't want them to know me."

We sat for a while, listening to the sound of the wind blowing in from the desert, brushing sand against the clay walls of the houses. From inside, setar music was rising. Taara's fingers had warmed up and she played the way I'd heard only a few times before. Inspired.

"Your sister is a real artist."

"I know."

"Why does she drink?"

"I have no idea."

"It's not good for the baby."

"I know."

He got up and paced along the wall, then stood facing the vacant end of the alley, where the dark desert lay. He tried to light a cigarette, but the wind didn't let him. He turned toward the wall, cupped his hands and tried again; he lit the cigarette and came back.

"Well, I'm supposed to leave tomorrow or the day after. Depending on when the border is safe. We're waiting for a messenger to bring news. I spent all I had for this trip. If the whole thing turns out to be a trick and they bring me back, I'll be homeless. I gave them the small house and a little inheritance money my father had left me. I could've stayed in Tehran, lived in that house, and watched the show to the end. But I'm leaving. I fought once; I was young then. They put me in prison. I came out old. I can't fight anymore. I can't even watch the fight. Let Uncle do it. He is an optimist, an idealist. I'm a pessimist. A realist. They'll shoot them all. Remember this, kid! They'll shoot Uncle, his people, and all the rest of them. I can see the black tyranny. I'm surprised no one else can see it!"

Jack of Spades

A minute before Mr. Amaani and I went back inside, a jeep pulled up in the alley and two men jumped out in a cloud of dust. They rushed inside and soon there was a meeting in the room where the men slept. Mr.

Amaani whispered, "These are my messengers," and joined the meeting. Men sat on the carpeted floor in a circle, smoking and waiting for Master Memaar. I had underestimated the Master's importance. But how could he discuss serious matters when he was drunk or drugged? He entered the room and, before closing the door, asked me, "Are you here for the meeting, too?" He was teasing me, of course. He pinched my cheek and shoved me out.

I found Taara alone, sitting in the backyard with an old deck of cards, arranged in four rows, in front of her. She was staring into the dark, thinking. I crept close to her, but she didn't notice me. She was somewhere far away.

"Napoleon?"

"Is it you?" she asked. "You startled me. Look! Two cards didn't come out. Two obstacles." I looked at the cards that were still facing down. "Queen of hearts," she said, and picked it up. "A good-hearted woman. A romantic. That must be me. Jack of spades. A mean man." She picked up the second card.

"Taara, listen. This is extremely important. We didn't come all the way here to eat and drink and shower with buckets, did we?"

"What do you mean? Get to the point."

"I don't think this man, this Master Memaar, will find our uncle. I don't think he'll even make an effort. He's busy smuggling people out of the country. Why did he bring us here? Have you thought about it?"

"We were possible customers?"

"He told his wife to find out if we wanted to cross."

"Do we?"

"That's what I want to ask you, Taara. Do you want to leave the country?"

"How can we pay him? Do you know how much I have? Almost nothing."

"I have Drum Tower's deed with me."

"They won't take it."

"If we tell them what kind of house it is and where it's located, they may take it. They can put their own name on the document. The country doesn't have any law now."

"We can try—"

"But do you want to leave?"

"What is on the other side?"

"Afghanistan."

"What will they do to us?"

"They have a Communist government. Maybe if we say our father is a Communist they'll let us pass through and go to India."

"Where Garuda is—"

"Leave Garuda alone. I'm serious."

"I'm serious too. Maybe the whole thing was meant to be this way. Maybe when I saw the shadow of the bird and left Vahid's place to search for her, she led me in the right direction. Maybe we took the right street the other day."

"The bird didn't lead you here, Taara. She led you to the Black Mountains, to find Baba-Ji's's crazy family. She misled you!"

"I thought she'd be there. But there are many other places she could be. India is one. An important one, too. The flute-beaked Garuda with scarlet wings. Remember? 'In India lives a bird that is unique/ The lovely phoenix has a long, hard beak. ...'"

It wasn't easy to talk with Taara; she couldn't focus. She dreamed aloud, drifted in and out of reality, and finally sought advice from the old deck of cards. I realized I had to decide alone and the moment was now. It was as simple as this: we didn't have a home in Tehran. We couldn't seek refuge with Khanum and the aunties. Our grandmother had become senile; she would hand us over to Assad. The aunties were crazy from the beginning. Living alone in the chaotic capital, jobless, with a new-born baby was impossible. We had to leave. I had to convince Memaar that he could put his name on the document and claim the house. I had to tell him that the house was an abandoned historic sight, ready to be occupied.

I sat in the dark, shivering. Where was I? What was I about to do? Cheat the cheaters? Mislead the dealers? Outsmart the crooks? Give them a house that was a barracks now and contained dozens of the devotees of the Holy Revolution?

Taara set out four rows of cards.

"This is the most accurate," she said. "This is what Napoleon did the night before Waterloo."

"And you know what happened to him."

"Look! All came out except one."

"The mean man!"

"This is not Memaar," Taara said. "He is not mean. This is Safdar. I'm scared of him. I think he hates me."

"Why should he hate you?"

"Because his brother loves me."

"Samandar loves you?"

"I think so. He is the one who can do something for us. I'll talk to him."

"Who is *he* in the middle of all this?"

"He is Safdar's brother and it's Safdar, not Memaar, who is the main guy."

"What else do you know?"

"Just this. Without Safdar, Memaar cannot do anything. They work together. Memaar recruits the customers and Safdar knows the local smugglers. Safdar's men take the people across. Let me talk to Samandar."

Everybody was up all night, except Mehri who washed and dried the last tray of glasses and slept in the women's room, next to the hissing kerosene heater. Taara and I sat in the backyard waiting for the long meeting to end, wondering where all those shadowy men who were whispering last night had gone.

Around two-thirty Samandar came out. I gave him my space on the carpet.

"Going to bed?" He patted my shoulder.

I ignored him and went into the corridor. I lingered behind the door of the meeting room, waiting. I didn't want to go into the room where Mehri slept, and I couldn't stay in the yard where Taara wanted to be alone with Samandar. Muffled sounds came out of the meeting room. They were either drawing a map or studying one. They were talking about directions, routes. "The horses can't cross the ditch," I heard. "Take the left path," Memaar said. "That's the worst one. Minefield," one of the messengers said. They were debating by which route they should take Mr. Amaani.

Tired of standing in the hallway, I went out and sat on the steps facing the dark alley. I heard Taara's laughter in the backyard and the men murmuring in the meeting room. A cool, dry breeze, a breeze full of clean sand, swept my face. I closed my eyes and let my body lighten, drifting somewhere on the border of sleep.

When I woke up, my back was stiff and my legs hurt. I limped inside and found the door to the meeting room open. The men had already left; three ashtrays full of cigarette butts lay on the floor. I went out to the backyard. Taara was not there. Her four rows of cards sat in the same way, a jack of spades facing the sky. Back in the corridor, I opened the other door and found Taara asleep under her quilt. Mehri snored loudly, her naked leg sticking out from under the blanket. The men had disappeared. I entered the backyard again and looked up at the second floor. Only one light was on. I sat down on the carpet and waited. I had to keep myself awake; I had to speak with Memaar tonight.

A while later, I heard the men—the bearded tenants—descending the stairs. They all had rifles on their shoulders. Some wore black, puffy pants and turbans, and some city clothes. Behind them, Memaar, Safdar, Samandar, and Mr. Amaani came down the steps. I pulled myself into a dark corner, watching. Safdar and Samandar were armed too, but Memaar and Amaani were not. They all passed without seeing me. I almost called to Mr. Amaani to say goodbye, but I didn't. I let him go. Memaar stayed behind, squatted beside the dark pool and splashed water on his face. This was my last chance.

"Sir—"

"Is it you? Why are you still up?"

"I wanted to talk to you."

"Now?"

"Now."

"I'm in a rush now. Tomorrow."

"Did you find our uncle?"

"What uncle?"

"You said you knew everybody here, remember?"

"Did I say I knew your uncle?"

He was either confused or he was playing with me.

"Why did you bring us here?"

"Are you having a bad time?"

"Thanks for your hospitality, but—"

"If I hadn't picked you guys up that evening, you wouldn't be alive now."

"But how long can we stay here?"

"It's up to you. People stay for months sometimes."

"But why?"

I wanted him to mention crossing, but he wouldn't. The conversation was absurd.

"Listen, son, I have to go. People are waiting for me."

"Are you taking Mr. Amaani?"

"Where?"

"To the border."

"Who told you this?"

"No one. I'm guessing."

"Don't make any more guesses, okay? Mind your own business. Go to bed now." He said this and went toward the corridor.

"Master Memaar!"

"Tomorrow. Tomorrow—" He waved his arms and left.

You stupid bastard! You dumb, blockheaded idiot! You fool! Why didn't you put it in plain and simple language? "Let's talk about crossing the border, Master Memaar—" What kind of foolish nonsense was this? Didn't you stay up all night to talk to him?

Now I heard Memaar's Dodge and the messenger's jeep groaning. How did all these bearded men fit in two cars? A horse neighed, then more horses. I heard them galloping on the sand. My question was answered.

I should have said goodbye to Mr. Amaani.

The Headlines

The next morning passed in stupor. Dry heat, pure as fire, crept in through the walls and cracks of the windows. We splashed water on the bamboo shades, but there was no breeze today. Taara slept in a corner all day, fever-ish. I sat above her, fanning her with the advertisement page of last night's newspaper. Mehri sat next to a transistor radio listening to a scratchy song travelling through space from a remote land. She mended a pair of nylon stockings, as if in this temperature she could wear nylon or there was any place she could dress up and go. The fan rotated, but didn't cool the room.

Around noon the bald man, the one who didn't say a word at dinner last night and then disappeared, came in and asked if he could sit with us. The heat was intolerable upstairs, he said, it penetrated the ceiling. He sat by the door and opened his newspaper.

Mehri brought some bread, cheese, and watermelon for lunch. She had dropped the melon in the pool last night and now it was cool. I woke Taara to eat. Why did she sleep so much? We all ate in silence and listened to the hum of the fan. Mehri gave up on the transistor radio. She wanted West-ern songs, she said. She hated the local stations. They all slept. The bald man lay on his back, his arms crossed over his forehead, snoring. I took his newspaper and looked at the headlines.

A special-mission group named the Black Flaggers, formed by a for-mer Revolutionary Guard, was arresting the corrupt elements of the rev-olution and purging them. Ten revolutionary guards had been executed for corruption. The Black Flaggers had found imported liquor and video tapes of foreign movies in their headquarters.

At the northwestern border a family was fished out of the Aras River. They had been trying to enter the Soviet Union. The man was identified as one of the leaders of the infidels.

The central prison, containing monarchists, former secret service agents, infidels, Maoists and Trotskyites, was full now. An old prison, outside Tehran, was being renovated.

The pro-Soviet Communists supported the Great Leader. There was a picture of "Uncle" lecturing at the university about the necessity of freedom in the new republic. The lecture was attacked by two separate groups: the Devotees of Islam, a branch of the Revolutionary Guards, and the Black Flaggers. The second group shot at the Communists and the Devotees of Islam.

Another movie theater was burned.

A woman burned herself to death to protest the veil. The picture showed a flaming bush in the middle of a public square, arms extended, the bush dancing. The woman was a physician.

There was a possibility of war in the Persian Gulf.

I read all this and listened to the uneven breathing and muffled snores of the sleepers. It was a long time till evening, when Master Memaar's house would come to life again.

Negotiations

Soon after sunset, Memaar, Safdar, Samandar, and the two messengers arrived, covered with white dust. While they washed at the pool, Mehri spread the dinner cloth and ran in and out of the kitchen. Taara brushed her long hair in haste and wore her starry, scarlet dress.

Evenings were happy times at Master Memaar's. The men had brought rice and turkey from the restaurant or the inn, as they called the place. Mehri added her usual appetizers—salads, fruits, yogurt and, of course, bottles of chilled beer and vodka. We all ate and the dusty men chatted about this and that without mentioning the border.

Taara played. Samandar sat next to her and sang. Mehri, who was in a good mood and had painted her face carefully, clapped and snapped her fingers. The bald, frowning man smiled for the first time and, after a couple of glasses of vodka, opened a conversation with me. What grade was I and what was my favorite sport? I told him I was a chess champion at my school district and my favorite sport was baseball, which we didn't have in our country, but I'd learned in America where I'd spent a year visiting my mother. Your mother? he asked. Yes, I said. She had moved to the U.S. many years ago and was a scientist researching dolphins. She had an American husband and my sister and I had two American half-brothers. We visited them last year in Miami.

I'm not sure why I enjoyed lying to the bald man. He listened carefully and I fed him images of the dolphin movie, half of which I'd seen a few days ago, before the theatre burned. Now he expected to hear more about America where he was planning to go, but I denied him the pleasure and joined Mehri who had begun cleaning up.

When the men rose to leave the room, Memaar looked at the bald man and said, "Mr. Sadiq, it's your turn, come on." Then he said to Taara, "Samandar said you wanted to talk to me. Why didn't you tell me the first night? Come now. Let's see what we can do for you."

With much effort, Taara rose to her feet and her native coin necklace jingled as she moved. She looked heavier and paler than ever. I stood by her side.

"You stay here, son," Memaar ordered me.

"I have to be in on this," I said.

"No way, my boy. We can't talk about dangerous operations in front of a kid. These are confidential matters."

"I'm not a kid," I said.

Taara looked desperate. She didn't know what to say. I pinched her arm, meaning, Say something!

"Master Memaar, I really can't decide about anything without my brother."

"I don't understand—"

"He has to be with me."

"Do you want to leave the country or not?" he asked.

"As soon as possible. I don't have much time left. I have to be on the other side when the baby comes."

"Then what are you waiting for? We can't talk in front of kids."

"He looks younger than he is," Taara said.

"I'm seventeen!" I said.

Samandar laughed. I gave him a dirty look.

"Let him, Master Memaar," Taara pleaded. "He has something in his possession that we need for the deal. I don't have it. He has it. It's a long story, a family thing. I can't explain it here. My brother has to be at our meeting."

Memaar looked at Safdar. He shrugged and left the room. Memaar said, "Okay, what can I say? Huh? If one word, one single word goes out of this house, we'll all end up against the wall of the prison, understood?"

This ultimatum was addressed to me.

So we followed Memaar and Safdar to the meeting room. Samandar stayed behind. I heard him playing Taara's setar. I almost returned to snatch the instrument out of his hands. But I controlled myself.

"He's touching your setar," I said.

"It's okay," Taara said with a sweet smile that was meant for the young Baluch.

Safdar sat down, leaned against a cushion and lit a pipe. The extension of his black turban hung loose on his chest. He had a long nose, broken at the bridge, thick eyebrows, and a thin mustache above his lips. He looked like the picture of Aladdin's mean uncle in the storybook I'd read as a child. As he smoked, he stared at Taara with his penetrating eyes, then turned his head toward the window and looked out.

Memaar gave an introductory lecture about the dangers of this operation, the desert, the distance between the two countries, the minefield, and how brother Safdar was risking his life for desperate people like us. But then he added that the right time was now, when there was chaos in the country and the soldiers at the border were confused. He looked at Safdar and asked him to be honest, as he'd always been, and make his offer.

"Half a million," Safdar said. I looked at Taara, but she was somewhere else again, in a daze.

Mehri came in with a tray of tea. Memaar waved his hands nervously, commanding her to leave.

Mehri bit her lower lip and winked at me before leaving.

Safdar and the bald man bargained.

"Three hundred thousand is all I have," Mr. Sadiq said. "I'm neither a general nor a minister. I'm an ordinary civilian. A clerk."

"Impossible," Safdar said.

"My house is occupied. They've bombed my car. This is all I had in my bank account."

"Can you arrange four hundred?" Memaar interjected. "It's not just Safdar and me— the men do the real work. Without them we can't do anything. Safdar has to pay their salary. How about three hundred-fifty?"

"Don't I need to have a little left in my pocket when I arrive in a foreign land?"

"Four hundred thousand!" Safdar said, and stood up. He went to the window and blew smoke out through the cracks in the bamboo shade.

"Take it, sir," Memaar told Mr. Sadiq. "You don't have a choice, do you? If you go back to Tehran, they'll kill you. I don't know what your position in the Secret Service was, but believe me, sir, even the lowest rank of SAVAK, even a typist, will go to the wall. Think about your life."

"I should've left six months ago when my family left," the man said, more to himself. "I didn't know it was this serious. My wife and children flew to Europe, then went to America. Just like that." He snapped his fingers. "It was so easy then. Why did I stay?"

"Maybe you had patriotic feelings," Memaar said sarcastically.

"Bullshit!" The bald man said. "I just didn't quite believe it. I didn't believe there was such a thing as a damn revolution. How could things that had been stable for thousands of years crumble?"

"We learn more every day, sir." Memaar said. "But one needs to survive. Sometimes I think about those fat ministers and officials who partied all their lives, built castles, shopped in Paris and London, vacationed on the Riviera, and now sit in burlap sacks against the wall, having had or not having had a quick trial. Boom, boom, boom!" He pointed his finger at Mr. Sadiq's heart.

"I offer all I have and all I have is three hundred fifty."

"Safdar!" the house builder called. "Come, brother, and finish this deal. This man is desperate. We're all human beings. Come now!"

Safdar, who was sulking at the window, came back hesitantly. He sat and knocked his pipe against the ashtray. "I take your three hundred fifty only for Master Memaar's sake. God is my witness that I make one trip to the other side and back, without carrying dangerous people, and I make a million. You get it? I'm doing this just because Memaar says we're all human beings."

"Okay, the deal is done," Memaar said. "Go, sir, and enjoy your drink. Have a smoke in the backyard if you want. Everything is on me. I'm a generous man. We'll talk about the date and other details later. Now let's see what we can do for this young lady and her brave brother."

Mr. Sadig left and there was silence for a minute. Then I said, "We don't have money with us. We offer you our house."

"Your house?" Memaar said, frowning.

"It's the biggest and oldest house in Tehran. It's a historic site. You may have heard about it. Its picture is in schoolbooks."

"It's almost a castle," Taara said timidly.

"Its garden used to be a national park," I said.

There were a few seconds of silence, then Safdar burst into laughter. This was the first time I'd seen the smuggler laugh. Some of his teeth were gold, some tar black.

"You've come all the way here to offer us your house?" Memaar asked.

"This house costs several millions, Master Memaar," Taara said calmly. "It's fully furnished. Historic furniture. Antique."

Taara didn't know that Drum Tower was empty now. She didn't know the garden had been flattened either.

"How do you want to give us this house?" Memaar asked.

"Like this!" I pulled the deed out of my pocket, unfolded it and laid it flat on the floor. "Now is the best time to occupy it—before other people do."

"The owner's name is erased," Memaar said, squinting his near-sighted eyes.

"So that you can write yours," I said. "Believe me, it's chaos out there. There is no law."

"I can't put my name here. This is not in the line of my work," Safdar said, and stood up. He was sulking again. He went toward the door. "I'm through with this, brother," he told Memaar. "You said you had two juicy deals for me. Now it turns out that you had only one half-ass deal. These kids are joking with me. Send them back to Tehran—to their castle."

"You're losing a fortune," Taara said, but the smuggler gave her such a dark look that her voice broke and she dropped her eyes.

"We're not secret service agents or government officials," I said. "If you don't take us, we'll go back home tomorrow. Then you'll regret it. Just the silk carpets, paintings, and gold and silver are worth ten times more than what Mr. Sadiq just offered you!"

"Where are your parents?" Memaar asked.

"Our parents are dead. Our grandmother lives with her sisters," I said.

"The house is empty."

"Hey, Safdar!" Memaar called the Baluch. "Do you want to give it a thought? It's worth thinking about, brother."

"How do I know this house really exists? I've never been to Tehran and I haven't been to school to read schoolbooks."

"It's easy!" Memaar said. "First thing tomorrow I'll send Ebrahim to Tehran to check out the house. If it's really there and it's not already occupied, we'll accept the deal."

My breath caught in my chest. We were finished.

"I can't forge names," Safdar said.

"Leave that to me," Memaar said.

"Send someone, then we'll talk," Safdar said. He glanced at Taara again, and left the room.

"I'll send my man first thing in the morning."

"How long will it take?" Taara asked.

"One day going, one day coming back—two to three days," he said.

"I can't wait much longer," Taara said.

"Can you afford a plane ticket for my man? Then it'll take him one day."

"I'll pay for his plane ticket," Taara said.

"So we leave it at this, young lady. Food, refreshments, lodging, and smoke—all are on me. I do this because I care for my fellow human beings. I can't see people suffering. Look at you now! A young, pregnant woman. I don't want to stick my nose into your affairs, but I tell myself, She must be in deep trouble; she has to go somewhere else and start a new life. I'm not stupid, my girl—my wife is, but I'm not. I know you're not married. I know no husband got blown up in no movie theatre. You have to go, dear, and God willing, you will. Let's hope your Drum Tower is still there." He said all this and left the room, but then he popped his head in and said, "But this boy is worth a million. This brother of yours." He grinned, showing his rotten teeth.

Taara and I sat for a long moment, breathing in the stinking odor of the overflowing ashtrays. Safdar's tobacco smoke curled above our heads like clouds of vapor. In the other room Samandar tried to play Taara's setar, awkwardly.

"Didn't you say Assad and his men have occupied Drum Tower?" Taara asked.

"Yes. And there is no furniture. All gone. No garden, either."

"So we're wasting our time and this plane ticket money. I need money for the baby."

"I didn't know he'd send someone to check."

"Were you trying to outsmart a bunch of smugglers?"

"Let's not argue now. What can we do? Can we go back?"

"My bridges are burned," Taara said.

"I read in the newspaper that a new group called Black Flaggers are arresting the Revolutionary Guards."

"Now you're hoping they've arrested Assad and his men."

"Who knows?"

"But then the new group will be in Drum Tower."

"Anyway, we won't lose much. Only the ticket money. If the guy comes back and says the house exists, but it's occupied, we'll say, well, it happened in our absence."

"You're counting on a thin chance," Taara said, "One percent. Assad and his men may never get arrested by Black Flaggers and the smugglers will never take us to the other side for free."

"No, I don't count on that."

We sat in silence for a few seconds, then I said, "Is Samandar really in love with you?"

"That's what I feel. Why?"

"If the house doesn't work, then—"

"But the baby will come."

"When?"

"My belly is falling down, Talkhoon. I feel the pressure."

"Pain?"

"Just pressure. Now she's knocking downwards."

"A regular knock, or an angry knock?"

"A regular knock."

We both smiled.

The New Deal

The next evening we were eating saffron rice with lima beans, lamb shank and yogurt when we heard a car pulling into the alley. Memaar wiped his mouth and left the room. A minute later he stuck his head in and announced the arrival of new guests. Could they join us for dinner? Mr. Sadiq said he didn't want to meet any one. Memaar told him it really didn't matter, because he'd be leaving early in the morning. But the secret service agent left his food half-eaten and went upstairs. We heard Memaar talking to the guests behind the door. He sounded courteous, trying to please.

"Come in this way. Leave your shoes right here. Forgive us for your discomfort. We eat on the floor—temporary situation—more like camping. Here you won't need to wear a headscarf, Madame. Feel free. It's your own house!"

Now the door opened and Uncle Kia, his wife, and their twin girls came in. Uncle had grown a bushy beard and with his Khaki shirt and pants looked like a hunter on safari. His wife and daughters wore thick scarves and long uniforms. When they saw us, they froze.

"Hello, Uncle!" Taara said, faking excitement.

"Is the gentleman your uncle?" Memaar asked, puzzled. "What a coincidence! You were looking for one uncle, another one showed up!" He laughed and said, "Your nephew and niece have been our guests for the past few days. What a small world! Please join us!"

Our uncle and his family sat awkwardly. They'd never eaten on the floor before. Uncle's wife glanced at my black cap pulled down over my brow, then stared at Taara's bloated belly. Reluctantly, they moved toward us to exchange cold and polite kisses.

After dinner, when we sat in a corner to talk, Uncle Kia asked what on earth were we doing here, and Taara said, we were doing the same thing they were.

"But where did you get the money?" Uncle put it in the most straightforward way.

"We're traveling for free," I said before Taara could tell the truth.

"Free?" Uncle's wife asked.

I pointed to Samandar, who had lost his special spot next to Taara and was sulking. "Taara's husband is taking us," I whispered.

"Is he your husband, Taara?" Uncle's wife asked. "You've married a...a...native?"

Uncle was silent. He had crimsoned, then gone pale.

"He is not really a native," I explained before Taara could find an answer. "His brother is, but he is not. He is an engineer," I said.

"How much do they charge?" Uncle asked in a whisper.

"Do they know you were the Minister's counselor?" I asked.

"I'm not sure, maybe—"

"The more important your position, the higher their rate."

"Damn!" Uncle said. "He should've told us," he said to his wife. "I shouldn't have trusted Assad, anyway."

"Assad?" Taara asked.

Sweat burned in my armpits.

"It was Assad who told us about this place," Uncle said. "He took my house and car. Everything! Didn't he send you here?"

"No, not Assad," Taara said. "My husband brought us here."

"I see," Uncle said. "Anyway, you know that Assad's hands are in everything nowadays. He's with the Party of God; he has a gang of hooligans. They have occupied the house. They steal people's cars and property. They've started to arrest people and lock them up in Drum Tower. Now his new business is to take money from the monarchists and send them here to the border."

"Did he know where we were?" Taara asked, looking at me with concern.

"I'm not sure. He said you were both missing." He paused. "Khanum-Jaan is ill."

"Where is she?" Taara asked.

"She's with the aunties. She's very ill."

"What is it?"

"Who knows? Everything. Worries. She suffers. She talks to the ghosts."

Uncle's wife knocked her knuckles against her temple, rolled her eyes and said, "All up here!"

"Where is Baba-Ji?"

"You may not believe this," Uncle said. "Assad has kept him in the house. He feeds him and cleans him and won't let the aunties take him to their place."

"The bastard son proved to be kinder than the real sons," Uncle's wife said sarcastically.

"Very kind, indeed!" Uncle said. "He has stolen all the furniture in the house. He is keeping Baba in a closet!" He sighed and rubbed his beard for a long moment.

We sat in silence. Everyone except Samandar had gone to the porch to drink and smoke.

"Now, Taara," Uncle said. "Do you think your husband can do anything for us?"

"What do you mean?"

"Arrange our travel."

"I don't think so," she said. "His brother is in charge of everything. He's just visiting."

"But since he's doing this for you two...I thought—"

"He may be able to get a discount for you," Taara said. "I'll talk to him."

She moved to the other side of the room and whispered something in Samandar's ear. The young man beamed and joined us.

"Nice meeting you, young man. Are you electrical or mechanical?"

"Mechanical," Samandar said and smiled.

"I like your costume," Uncle's wife said. "Do we have to wear costumes too?"

"We'll get you native clothes," Samandar said.

"I won't wear native clothes," one of the girls said sleepily.

"I won't, either," the other one echoed.

"Hush," their mother said. "You'll wear whatever the gentlemen tell you to wear. Can't you see where we are?"

Memaar called Taara into the other room for a short conference and I followed her. Safdar stood by the window, smoking his pipe. No one sat this time. Memaar announced that Safdar had changed his mind. He didn't want us to send anyone to Tehran to inquire about the house. He was not willing to accept the deal.

"The best thing, my dear children, is to go back to Tehran first thing in the morning and forget about the whole thing. More people are about to arrive. This house is getting crowded. You better give your space to people who are really in danger. People like your poor uncle."

"How much do you want to charge our uncle?" I asked.

"One million," Safdar said without looking at me.

"But why?" Taara burst out. "You took only three hundred-fifty from Mr. Sadiq."

Safdar didn't say anything, but drilled Taara with his piercing eyes.

"That gentleman is just a petty clerk in the SAVAK," Memaar said, "but your uncle is a big shot. We could charge him even more. But we're all human beings—"

"Charge him a million and a half," I said. "For them and for us."

There was silence for a second, then Safdar and Memaar burst into wild laughter.

"What a boy!" Memaar said and slapped my back with his wide palm. "What a shrewd boy!"

"But don't tell him that he is paying for us," I said in the most serious tone. "Tell him the rate for a Minister's Counselor is two million, and you're giving him a discount."

The deal was accepted. We all went to the porch where Taara played her setar into the night. Her fake husband accompanied her, and Mehri, who was drunk, got up and danced. She wriggled her round butt and shook her shoulders like a cabaret dancer. She had on a long silk skirt and the same tight, red blouse. Her curls were freshly rolled and sprayed, bouncing up and down.

Uncle watched Mehri's moving butt with eyes and mouth wide open. She sensed the attention and added more flavor to her dance—winked, shook her shoulders, and bit her lips in a seductive way. Uncle's wife became upset and took her daughters inside. A native man brought a brazier and arranged the charcoals for opium.

Some time after midnight, Memaar and Safdar called Uncle Kia inside for negotiations. He looked at me like a sheep on his way to the altar. I whispered in his ear, "We've talked to them. Don't worry. You'll get a big discount. But if I were you, I'd take my watch and rings off." He took them off and put them in his shirt pocket.

Around two o'clock the same two messengers came from the border with the news that everything was clear and the passengers should be at the shepherd's house before dawn. Memaar suggested that everyone sleep for a few hours. Uncle Kia asked for a telephone. He said he had to make an urgent call to Tehran; he offered some money to Memaar for the long distance call. Memaar didn't accept the money and led him upstairs where the phone was.

When the men and women were separated, they put me in the men's room. I couldn't say no; after all, they knew me as a smart young man. I lay next to Uncle Kia who fell asleep immediately, murmuring meaningless words in his dreams. Once he even gave out a muffled scream, as if a dull knife were sawing through his neck. I watched the spasms of his fleshy face and tried to find traces of my father's features.

Safdar and Samandar performed a duet of snoring. Memaar moaned in his dreams and constantly tossed and turned. I'd never slept in a room with many men. They were noisy and restless and gave out odors of stale nicotine, alcohol, sweat, and gas.

I was awake all night. I was uncomfortable. Just the mention of Assad's name had been enough to ruin my day. Could he possibly know where we were, or was this another coincidence? One thing was sure: he was in Tehran. Uncle had seen him yesterday. I turned on my right side and the deed to the house crunched in my pocket. I should've put it in Taara's attaché, where I'd put the handgun. I tried to sleep, but the minute I closed my eyes a tearing wind whirled in my head. So I opened my eyes and looked at a patch of pale light on the wall. I tried not to think about Baba-Ji, but I couldn't get his image out of my head. The knapsack was on my chest. I wore it every night to keep my body warm.

I thought about finishing the last chapter of the manuscript. Learning all I needed to learn to be able to end the book. I fantasized living in a shady courtyard in an Indian town, somewhere resembling the Armenian grocer's courtyard, reading and writing. I closed my eyes and saw the image of the published book, luminous gold print with miniature pictures of the Simorgh in the margins of each page. On the jacket, Baba's full name appeared in large print and my name, smaller, underneath, as the editor. The book was on a lace-covered table, next to a blue vase and a polished setar. I picked up the book and opened it. Baba-Ji's preface was on the first page: "As a child living in the mountains of Azerbaijan..."

A few sentences ran out of the whirlwind, my head calmed, and my eyelids felt heavy. But I slept only a minute. Rustles and whispers woke me up. I opened my eyes and saw Safdar getting ready. He was trying to wrap the long turban around his head. I was surprised to see he was bald. Without hair and without his turban, he looked smaller and weaker. Now he shook his brother and Memaar to wake them up. Soon, all the men were up, putting their clothes on, yawning. Uncle shook me and said, "Talkhoon," but before he could utter my name again I sat up and put my finger on my nose, to keep him quiet.

When Safdar, Samandar, and Memaar left the room I told my uncle that my name was Farid and he had to be careful about these matters here. He looked pale and had yellow bags under his eyes. Unable to control his anxiety, he asked how far the border was from here. I told him what I'd heard from Memaar. He asked if they'd give him Baluchi clothes to wear, and then he asked if he had to walk or ride on a horse. He wore his thick overcoat over his khaki shirt, and when he buttoned it up his fingers shook. He said he had a cold, coughed, and turned his back to me. He didn't want me to see his tears.

I wanted to tell him that the distance we had to walk was through a minefield, but I changed my mind. The poor man would pass out.

At the Shepherd's

It was cold and dark when we reached the shepherd's hut. Master Memaar said if it weren't for the darkness we'd see the half-built tower of the barracks on our left. From the barracks to the ditch that marked the border, it was twenty minutes' walking at a fast pace. He would work on top of the unfinished tower and watch us cross the ditch. There were a dozen demoralized soldiers inside the old barracks, uncertain as to what the new regime expected of them. They slept through the night and sometimes even the day. Memaar gave them free opium.

Women and children, shivering from the cold, took shelter in the shepherd's small hut. Men lingered in the dusty front yard around the warm mouth of a stone oven. A few horses tied to the wooden fence exhaled foggy breath, lifted a heavy leg off the ground, waited impatiently. All the dark, whispering men, Safdar's crew, were in the yard, sitting in the dust, smoking cigarettes or pipes. Mr. Amaani was here.

"I thought they took you across," I said.

"They decided I should wait one more day so that we'd all go together."

"I was worried for you."

His beard had grown a little. The prickly gray made him look sad and old.

Taara sat on a thin blanket on the hut's cold floor. The shepherd's wife, a native woman with leathery skin and many zinc bracelets that jingled with the movement of her hand, wrapped another threadbare blanket around her. Taara was pale and quiet, in a daze again. She had on her old maternity outfit, now very tight. I could see what she meant by a falling belly.

Uncle Kia's wife and her daughters in native clothes looked as fake as guests at a costume party. The twins constantly cried and their mother threatened them. She wouldn't buy them this or that or she'd take this or that from them. The woman had forgotten that there were no shops around to buy or not buy and the children didn't have much left to lose.

Mr. Sadiq, the SAVAK agent, unable to hide himself in the vast desert, stood behind a horse, smoking. Uncle Kia calmed himself by asking questions of Samandar, who patiently played the role of Taara's husband. Mehri had come with us. She told me she wanted to watch the show — this was the first time they would take a big group across.

The shepherd ran around serving hot tea, apologizing for his poor shelter. We heard sheep and goats bleating, but we didn't see them. They were in a fenced yard behind the hut. The sky was moonless, a smugglers' sky, but the stars were low, as if falling on us. The desert extended all around, slept in the dark, breathing calmly and giving out the scent of cold earth. A gust of wind swept invisible dust into our faces. I felt sand between my teeth.

Mehri came out of the hut and called me in. Taara wanted to talk to me. The shepherd's wife sat on the floor, rubbing Taara's back.

"Let me be alone with my brother," Taara said.

Mehri motioned to the native woman to follow her out. Uncle's wife and her daughters were squeezed into a corner, asleep.

"Talkhoon."

"What is it?"

"I'm ruining everything. The whole goddamn thing."

"What do you mean?"

"She's coming."

"The baby?"

"Yes. And there is no way to stop her." She hugged her belly and bent. "I'm all wet. And it hurts."

"Bad?"

"Bad."

"Taara, don't panic—"

"It's not panic, it's pain. The damn thing chose this very moment to come."

"Don't curse her, Taara."

"Damn, damn, damn!" she screamed and burst into sobs. She lay down on her side, grabbed my hand and squeezed it hard. Her nails bit into my flesh. Tears ran down her face and she bit her lips to avoid screaming. Finally she sat up as if thunder struck and hollered, "Someone call a doctor! Please!"

The men became quiet at once. Even the horses, goats, and sheep were silent. I left the hut to see what they would decide. Mehri suggested that one of the men should drive to town and bring a midwife here. No one could handle this, she said.

"Bring a midwife here?" Memaar asked angrily. "Have you lost your mind?" He yelled at his woman as if the whole thing was her fault.

"She has to go back to Zabol," Safdar said.

"I'll drive her," Samandar suggested.

"You're not driving anyone." Safdar raised his voice to his younger brother: "There is work to do here!"

Uncle's wife came out of the hut with a blanket hanging on her back. "What about us? We have to leave the country now! Before sunrise!" She looked at her husband and said, "What if they send soldiers from Tehran to arrest us?" Then she told Safdar, "We have to leave, sir!"

"You stay out of this, lady!" Safdar said angrily.

"Get inside! Get inside before the girls whine!" Uncle told his wife.

"Mehri can take the boy and his sister back to Zabol with the jeep," Memaar said.

"Are you crazy?" Mehri screamed. "You want to send me into the desert with a woman who is about to burst? Do I know anything about childbirth? And besides, it's more than an hour's drive. She's in labor now. You get me? Now!"

"What do you want us to do? Huh?" Memaar yelled back at Mehri. "Get arrested because she's in labor? Let it come in the desert. You'll be with her. Women know how to deal with each other." He said this and dismissed his woman with a crazy wave of his hand.

For a while everybody quarreled and talked at the same time, one suggesting something and another rejecting it. Then Ebrahim, one of the messengers, arrived on a horse and reported that the soldiers in the barracks were all inside, overdosed on opium—this was the best time to move. Safdar asked for his horse. A native brought a red horse with a blanket on its back. The sleepy horse had socks on, his eyelids looked heavy and his large nostrils quivered. Safdar removed the blanket, stroked the horse's back, and scratched its skin with his calloused fingers. He held the horse's head in his arms and rubbed his own face against it. It was strange to see Safdar being affectionate toward the animal.

"We'll take the two men and the family," he said to no one in particular. "The brother and sister will stay."

"This is the best way to do it," Memaar said. "We'll take the first group, then we'll see what happens."

"I'll stay with Farid and his sister," Mr. Amaani said.

"I think you better go now, Mr. Amaani," Memaar said. "We don't even know if—"

"I've agreed on one trip," Safdar said coldly, mounting the horse.

"But we've paid!" I burst in.

Uncle looked at me suspiciously. We'd told him we were going for free.

"We'll talk about it when we come back," Memaar said. I caught him winking at Safdar. "Go, Safdar Khan! Don't waste time. I'll go to the barracks and start to work on top of the tower. When you cross the ditch, fire one bullet in the air."

"I will," Safdar said.

"Let's go, Mr. Amaani!"

"I'll stay with the kid. His sister is in pain. They need a man here."

"Mr. Amaani!" Memaar said impatiently. "Don't make a mistake—"

"I'll go with the second group."

"There is no second group," Memaar said in a hushed voice.

"There ought to be. They've paid."

"Okay, you want to stay, stay! I won't insist," Memaar said, and turned his back to Mr. Amaani.

Safdar on his red horse looked taller. With his long arms, he lifted the twins like a pair of rabbits and put them on his saddle—one in front, one behind. He told the one behind him to hold on tight while they were riding. He told Uncle, his wife, and Mr. Sadiq to walk in a single file behind Samandar and not let him get out of their sight. They should put their feet in Samandar's footsteps; the ground was a minefield. Uncle's wife uttered an "Ah—" and wiped her tears. The girls, who had been cooperative for the past few minutes, seeing their mother's tears, burst into loud sobs and wanted to get down. Uncle urged Safdar to take care of his girls.

"I'm not going to gallop, sir. I'll be right in front of you to show you the route. You'll see your girls all the way."

Uncle went in the hut and kissed Taara's forehead in haste. She moaned like a wounded animal and didn't even open her eyes. Now Uncle kissed my cheeks and said, "Pray for your poor uncle! Pray for all of us!" His voice quivered. In native clothes, Uncle Kia was stripped of his importance. Now he was neither a counselor to a minister nor a hunter. He resembled an old villager, a house servant who worked in the minister's house, unnoticed. Uncle's wife, without her make-up and European clothes, in baggy native pajama pants, looked sexless. She was too scared to say goodbye.

Just before the party left, Samandar rushed inside, knelt next to Taara, and held her hand.

"You're leaving us here, huh?" Taara said, moaning.

"I'll come back and take you, Taara," Samandar said. "I promise!"

"Your brother won't make the trip again," Taara said.

"*I* will. I know the way. I'll take you and stay with you. We'll go to India. I'll be your baby's father."

"Don't say you'll do things that you won't."

"I swear on my honor—"

"Ouch! Hurts!"

"Be strong! I'll be back. In less than two hours."

Mehri and the shepherd's wife sat on a blanket next to the stone oven having a picnic. Their breakfast was hot tea, fresh goat's milk, and bread just out of the oven. Taara took a nap, but I didn't move from her side. Mr. Amaani came into the hut and sat next to me.

"You shouldn't have stayed because of us."

"I thought that would make them take another trip."

"What if they don't? Safdar said he won't go twice."

"He has to. We've paid."

Now we heard Mehri laughing with the shepherd's wife. It wasn't long ago that she'd called the natives "wild," and "uncivilized." Now she chatted with the Baluchi woman the way she chatted with us. Mr. Amaani and I sat silently, and through the hut's open door watched the dawn. The desert dunes, gray in half-light, were like a frozen sea. The air was indigo now, and the sun was rising, but hidden from us.

"They must be close to the ditch," Mr. Amaani said and left the hut.

I followed him out. We both wanted to see the tower of the barracks and Master Memaar on the top. Mehri poured some tea for us and showed her man on top of the tower. He was the size of a toy soldier. The native woman insisted that I should try some goat's milk and fresh bread. I said I'd rather sit inside with my sister. Now she and Mehri talked in the native language and laughed at me.

"Talkhoon!" Taara hollered.

Mehri looked at me, puzzled. She didn't know my real name.

I ignored her and rushed inside.

The bone-breaking pain had invaded Taara's body. It was coming every five minutes. The shepherd who had galloped on his fat donkey to the neighboring village half an hour ago came back with an old woman behind him. The woman, he said, was a midwife, an ancient, one-hundred-year-old creature, stooped and wrinkled from head to foot. Her toothless jaws were set forward and she chewed constantly without having anything in her mouth. I looked at her dark, callused hands, the hands that in a minute would touch the most delicate skin in the world.

In the intervals between pains, Taara murmured in delirium, demanding the Simorgh story.

"She was on top of Mount Ghaf," I said absently, watching the old woman boiling water on a pile of wood.

"You mean the Simorgh?" Taara asked.

"The Simorgh."

"Say it well, Talkhoon. Say it the way Baba-Ji used to say it."

"She was on top of Mount Ghaf, the tallest mountain in the world, far, far away."

"Then what?"

"And the world was in chaos. Nothing stood in its place. There was wind everywhere, blowing hard and cruel. If you lay something down to rest, the wind picked it up. If you screamed from anger or pain, the wind covered your voice—"

"You're making this up, Talkhoon. But I like it. Go on."

"No one could hear anyone else's voice. Everyone was in the same place, but deaf to one another's screams. And this was all the wind's work."

"And the Simorgh?"

"She was on top of Mount Ghaf, the tallest mountain in the world. She didn't know what was going on. She was there and she wouldn't come down."

"Why?"

"Why? Who knows? Maybe she demanded love. Absolute love. Undivided. But no one could give it to her."

"How could they?"

"Good point. How could they? With the wind and the muffled screams and everything in the air, never settling, and people at the end of their nerves—who could even think about loving the bird?"

"Loving the bird!" Taara smirked. "Strange!"

"Who would think about giving absolute love and devotion to a bird who had four wings?"

"Two of them hard and two feathery, touching the soft tops of the hills as she flew—"

"Yes. And she was up there on Ghaf, and wouldn't fly to the cities."

"Until—"

"Until, one day—"

"Help!" Taara screamed. Her nails dug into my hands again, and her wild shout echoed in the desert.

The ancient woman slowly approached, as if nothing urgent was at stake. She sat on the cold floor at Taara's feet, and gently opened her legs. The shepherd's wife and Mehri brought the pot of boiling water and began cutting our blue veil into squares, then soaking them in hot water. Taara screamed again and clawed my hand. Now everything blurred and I lost my wits and became all animal senses.

I heard the winds of the desert and thought they were in my head. I heard the goats bleating, the donkey braying and the shepherd's dog, now awake from a long sleep, barking and howling. I smelled blood, sweat and dust. I heard an ancient language I didn't know. We had moved back into biblical times. The earth had flooded and Noah was calling all the animals of the world into his ark. The old woman ordered something in Noah's language. Mehri said, "She says push! Push as hard as you can." I closed my eyes to keep from seeing the old woman pull out the baby. All I could do was give my hand to Taara to tear to pieces. My right hand with its many stitches in its palm was now bruised and scratched on its back too.

The baby cried out three times and the goats outside bleated, as if in response. The donkey brayed, reacting to the goats, and the dog barked back. The old woman stood, held the baby upside down and laughed, showing the empty cave of her mouth. It was a red-skinned boy. The shepherd's wife and the old woman trilled their tongues and hit their lips with their hands to make their voices quiver.

"This is the way they celebrate a boy's birth!" Mehri said.

The shepherd's wife picked up a tambourine from somewhere, banged on it and bounced up and down, dancing. Her zinc jewelry jingled as she hopped and kicked the dust. The ancient woman danced in her crooked way, making that quivering sound with her tongue. Mehri laughed and, like a belly dancer, wriggled her shoulders and butt. This unexpected birth, birth of a male child, had made the women happy.

"Bring the flour and butter," Mehri told the shepherd's wife. "Let's make a hot kaachi for our little mother."

In less than five minutes the bittersweet smell of burnt flour and sugar filled the hut, then a bullet cracked in distance.

"They're across!" Mr. Amaani said.

Taara closed her eyes and fell asleep.

Taara's Dream

The brothers arrived in mid-afternoon, covered head to foot with white sand. Safdar went behind the hut to feed his horse. Samandar sat down next to me in a small patch of shade by the hut's clay wall. He stared at the yellow dunes—a hot ocean under the blazing sun.

"The baby was born?"

"Yes."

"Sleeping?"

"Both of them."

"Look, Farid, I want to talk to you—"

"You can't take us," I said.

"You'll go, but not with me." He sighed. "I convinced my brother to take you, Taara, and Mr. Amaani first thing tomorrow. He wouldn't agree.

He kept saying the contract was for one trip."

"Then how did you convince him?"

"When I told him about my plans—moving to India with Taara—he got mad. He said he needed me here. I couldn't just leave in the middle of the operation. He said I had to wait till the business was over, then I'd be free."

"So you can't—?"

"No. I argued with him, but he doesn't understand. He's forty years old and hasn't married. All his life in the desert. When I insisted, he laughed at me. He said he thought I was just flirting with a pregnant girl. When I said I was serious, he laughed even more—he was angry."

"Then he made a deal with you, huh?"

"He said, if I obey him and stay here, he'll take you. If I go with you, he won't give me my share. Where in the world can I go with empty pockets?" He looked at me as if waiting for an answer. "I'll make some more money and join you and Taara."

"Then why are you so upset?"

"He has another condition." He paused. "He wants the deed to your house."

"Drum Tower?"

"Is this what it's called?"

"Yes."

"He says your uncle paid for one trip. Now that there's a second trip, you need to pay more. He'll accept the deed. He knows you don't have cash with you."

"He sent you to bargain for him."

"There is no bargaining, Farid. Everything is fixed."

"Are you really a mechanic in the city, or are you a smuggler too?"

"Do I look like a smuggler, or talk like one? I have a shop in a good neighborhood in Tehran, repairing Mercedes Benz."

"Why only Mercedes?"

"Because I have access to the parts."

"Across the border?"

"What are you talking about? Now you don't trust me anymore, huh?"

"Go on. You have your little shop, then...?"

"Safdar called me a few weeks ago and said he needed my help here. He said I'd make some quick money. Who'd reject that offer?"

"You came and the very first night you fell in love with a pregnant girl."

"You're laughing at me, too. You're sarcastic. You make me feel like a cheater or something. I really fell for her. Who would fall for a pregnant woman? Huh? So it's love. She is so special. Her music, her long, red hair—"

"Red?"

"It's reddish. Haven't you noticed? Like real gold. Gold is not yellow, it's red. Farid, my heart jumps in my chest when I talk about Taara. But I can't say no to my brother. Do you know anything about our culture?"

"No."

"An older brother is like God. He can kill the younger brother."

"So, he'll go all the way to India and kill you."

"You don't get me. It's hard for me to explain. I have to obey. You understand? But after this business, I'll be a free man again. I know the way; I'll join you in Afghanistan. Wait for me. Then we'll all go to India together."

"Well, go and tell all this to Taara."

"I can't. She's sleeping. I don't want to upset her. Besides, I have to go now. I have to rush to Memaar's house and receive some more guests. Please tell Taara to wait for me on the other side. I'll join you soon. With a lot of money!"

He stood up and extended his hand. I hesitated, then shook it. He wasn't lying. And I could understand his culture. It wasn't much different from ours; it was harsher, but it was basically the same. Their elders cut their throats for disobedience, ours disinherited or abandoned us. The hierarchy was the same.

"I had the strangest dream, Talkhooh. Disturbing." Taara's hair curled down in waves around her body. The late afternoon light illuminated her profile. It was true—her hair had a reddish glow. The boy had noticed it within three dark nights.

"Khanum-Jaan was dead, but she was holding my hand. Her hand was dry and stiff like a piece of wood and she had grabbed me tightly and wouldn't let me go. I said, 'Are you dead, Khanum?' She said, 'Taahereh, my light! The light of my eyes! Everybody left me, even my ghosts, and then I died.'"

"It was just a bad dream, Taara."

"Ghosts exist, Talkhoon. Ghosts exist!"

"Look at your son. He's sleeping peacefully. Tomorrow we'll leave the country."

"Is Samandar back?"

"Not yet. Sleep now."

"Do you know what Samandar means?"

"What?"

"You don't? It's in Baba's book. It's a mythical animal that can endure fire. Like the Firebird."

"You're joking."

"No, I'm not. Look at the coincidence! No, look at my fate—I should marry a man who is a firebird!"

"Rest now. You have to gain your strength back. I'll sit here and fan you."

"But why are they so late? We heard the bullet in the morning. So Uncle Kia and the rest have crossed the border. What if on the way back—"

"If they'd stepped on a mine, we'd have heard a huge explosion," I teased her. "They must have stayed in the barracks with Memaar."

"Talkhoon—"

"What?"

"Khanum-Jaan had a soft heart. I know that. But she did everything to hide it."

"Sleep now."

"Her heart stopped today. Her ghost held my hand."

Crossing

To celebrate the crossing of the first group and the birth of a male child—a good omen—the shepherd killed a lamb and grilled it on an open fire. His wife cooked rice in the same pot she had boiled water for the old midwife. We all sat on the cold ground around the long tablecloth, chewing the half-cooked lamb and the crunchy rice. Sand had found its way into the food. The bearded crew sat around a separate cloth, eating and whispering. After dinner they left for Zabol. Safdar said they were not needed anymore.

I hadn't told Taara that Samandar was not going with us, so while eating and feeding her baby (whose name was not decided yet), she constantly glanced at the narrow dirt road that ran into the desert and blended with the dark night. I absorbed myself in the boy whose small, jerking hands hit his mother's breasts while he noisily sucked.

Mehri pulled a bottle of vodka out of her purse and offered it to everyone. Taara didn't drink. The men drank and chatted, relaxed. The cool, earth-smelling breeze brushed my face. Invisible sand penetrated my ears and sat on my tongue. The desert gave out the scent of virgin earth. Taara asked Memaar if it was all right to play her setar, if the sound wouldn't travel to the barracks. Memaar said that no sound would reach there because of the strong wind and the thick barracks walls he had made.

I took the baby and Taara held her setar with the same care and caution she'd embraced her child earlier. She wound the strings of the instrument, then began to play. She tilted her head, closed her eyes, and ran her fingers over the strings. Her music didn't seem to belong to the here-and-now, but drifted back to the past, somewhere I alone among her listeners was able to recognize. Her red locks hung around her and quivered before her face. We were all staring at her, unable to look away. Her fingers ran madly over the taut strings and I feared that her fingertips would bleed. My sister's music that night covered the sound of the wind and the howl of the remote storm through which we had to pass.

Before midnight, the house builder suggested that we should sleep for a few hours because we had to get up at three. Now Safdar told us that Taara and her baby would sit with him on the horse and Mr. Amaani and I would follow, single-file, on foot.

"How about Samandar, then?" Taara whispered to me.

"He'll join us," I said.

The women went inside the hut and the men lay on the cold sand in the courtyard. I lay beside the hut's door to watch Taara and the baby. The chill of the soft sand penetrated my bones, and I shivered and gazed at the falling stars. The desert took a deep breath and a breeze brought the scent of fresh earth. The men snored, except for Mr. Amaani who, unable to sleep, smoked one cigarette after another.

I couldn't sleep, either; this was the third night. My head felt light and fragments of reveries twisted in my brain. Had the baby waited one more night, we'd be on the other side now. They were sending us with one man; no guide would walk in front of us to show the way. But I had the feeling that I was not going to step on a mine, that my end was not meant to happen so fast and easy. I looked at the palm of my right hand in the dim light. The line of my life extended far and long, with a break—an intersection—around age sixty. But even that was not the final cut. I laughed at this tidbit of superstition I'd inherited from my grandmother. Nothing was meant to happen. No one had written my destiny on my palm. These stitches and bruises were my fate, not the lines I was born with. If a mine were hidden where I walked and I stepped on it, I'd die; if I stepped half a centimeter away, I'd survive. Chance was the god and it was blind and it was indifferent.

At three, Safdar, who had slept with his turban, woke up as if a clock were planted inside his head. He sat on top of the cold oven and put his boots on. Now he lit his pipe and gazed into the dark desert. From the corner of his eye he saw that I was awake, but didn't say a word. He didn't put a hand on my shoulder, didn't give me an errand to do, didn't send me to fetch his horse. Wasn't I a boy, after all? Why did he treat me with such deliberate coldness? Did his strong male animal instinct, the brute in him, tell him that this skinny city boy was not to be trusted, because he had hidden a female under his shirt? Had Safdar smelled the woman in me?

Shortly, the shepherd brought the red horse with his hoofs in socks. Memaar, who had awakened with a bad headache, pulled me to a corner and told me that this second trip was not what Safdar wanted. He was only doing this for Memaar's sake and Memaar was doing it only because he was a human being and could feel how distressed my sister was with an illegitimate baby on her hands. After telling me that they were doing us a favor, he took the deed to our house and put it in his pocket.

The shepherd's wife brought hot tea in tin cups. Taara sat on the cold oven and brushed her long hair in the wind. In the flickering glow of the lantern hanging on top of the hut's door, she looked ethereal. She separated one part of her long hair, brushed it from top to bottom absently, then took another section. Safdar watched her for a long moment. Then he pulled his bandana off his neck and threw it at her. Without a word, Taara covered her hair with it. The baby cried. I brought him out and rocked him in my arms. Safdar said that if the baby cried while we were moving, Taara would have to feed him to quiet him.

I stood with Taara's weightless baby in my arms, watching her tie the bandana behind her head. Then I looked up and saw the stars almost touching the earth, giving the illusion of their falling. I registered the image in my head, knowing that I wouldn't see anything like this again.

Finally Taara was ready. Safdar mounted the horse, bent, and lifted her up the way he'd lifted Uncle's little girls earlier. He sat my sister sideways on the horse, knowing she couldn't sit with her legs open. I handed the baby to his mother and she asked me to carry the setar and the black attaché for her. We were not taking her handbag with us. The last thing she said before Safdar slapped the horse, signaling it to move, was, "So when will Samandar join us?" Her question hung in the air. No one answered. She looked at me as if I was the one who had betrayed her. I registered this, regretting that my sister's last look at me before we started was not filled with love.

When our small caravan moved, Mehri, who had overslept, ran out of the hut and embraced me tightly. Her face was wet with tears. She muttered absently, "Pray for me! Pray for me!" as if she was the one who would be traveling in the dark. Mr. Amaani ground his last cigarette under his shoe and offered to carry the attaché. Memaar jumped in the jeep and rushed to the barracks to make sure the soldiers were inside. The shepherd's wife stood by the hut's crooked door, holding a small dish in her hand. Smoke rose from the dish and a bitter scent filled the air. She'd burned wild rue for good luck and a safe trip. Now, at the last minute, she ran toward us, holding the smoking rue above our heads, circling it around the baby and murmuring prayers. The last thing I saw of the native woman was her wiping her tears with the hanging corner of her colorful scarf.

I told myself that as long as I walked next to the warm belly of the red horse, as long as I could see my sister, everything would be fine. And I walked for a long time, glancing from time to time at Taara's black shoes, the pair she'd bought on that happy day of leisure in Tehran. I remembered that exactly a week ago I'd slept in the teacher's house, in her daughter's room. I tried to remember the girl's name, but I could not. That day I woke up and ate meat broth with the family. A very old woman, a great grandmother, was there. Her white scarf waved in the breeze and when Farid took me on his motor bike to the bus station, the old woman cried. On the bike, my chin rested on the boy's shoulder and I thought my fate was tied to his, but I was wrong.

I touched my chest pocket. Farid's wallet was there. I tried to imagine the cell he was imprisoned in. Did they whip him with a leather belt? Now, like an apparition, he disappeared from my mind, and all the people of my past became phantoms too. They became transparent like Grandma Negaar and all vanished with her behind the blurred image of the weeping willows. The only thing that was real was I, myself, walking in a dark desert on the eastern border, stepping on ground I could not trust, heading somewhere I did not know. I held the setar tightly against my chest, pressed against the knapsack that contained my grandfather's book. I recalled these images to keep from getting lost in the dark, to keep from forgetting why I was leaving my land. I recalled all of this so as not to go out of my mind.

I'm going where I can live in peace—the corner of a shady yard. Peacocks will sit on the wall and monkeys will play in tamarind trees. I'll walk in the wet streets and whistle. I'll complete the bird book and wake Baba-Ji. I'll bring him and his book to life.

The horse trotted faster and Mr. Amaani walked behind me. I heard him saying something in a whisper, something like Speed up! And I sped.

What neither Memaar, nor Safdar had told me about was the thorn bushes. They didn't tell me I would need a pair of boots. My thin canvas shoes tore to pieces and thorns cut my feet. The horse broke into a trot now and we had to run. Safdar hadn't told us about this, either. He had not mentioned that he might speed up and that we would have to run on the thorn bushes. I was trying hard not to lose sight of the horse's long tail swaying in the wind. I looked back to find Mr. Amaani, but I didn't see him.

A bullet cracked somewhere. The horse galloped.

I held the setar tightly against my chest, but it kept slipping and slowing me down. The shoes were shredded. I screamed in my head, begging Safdar to slow down. I swallowed my scream because not even a whisper was allowed. It seemed like fifteen minutes now. They'd said twenty minutes, so we were not far from the ditch.

I won't die with thorns in my feet. I'll feel pain, but I won't die. My life extends smoothly to my sixties.

Now I thought I saw Taara's scarf—Safdar's black bandana—billowing, then flying like a bird in the wind. I thought I saw her hair rise behind her like a flag, then become the flapping wing of a red bird. Then a strong gust blew sand into my eyes and I didn't see the horse anymore.

Bullets cracked somewhere. I heard the horse galloping.

When I reached the dry ditch, I saw the horse for a second. It headed down and without effort climbed the other wall. But I tripped on a bush, slipped and rolled like a ball of thorns toward the bottom. Taara's setar gave a hollow bang, the case opened and the instrument tumbled out and stopped beside a bush. I slid my body toward it, but stopped moving when I heard another gunshot. Only one, but very close. I held the setar's long neck and froze, knowing that the red horse had carried Taara and the baby farther and farther away from me. They were on the other side now. But this bullet must have hit someone. I saw the black attaché slide down the bank of the ditch, hit a rock, and stop.

I lay motionless, like a desert plant that belonged on the bottom of the dry ditch.

It was dark. I didn't see their faces when they bent over me. But I tried to look at their uniforms. Two had soldiers' uniforms, one the khaki uniform of the Revolutionary Guards. The soldiers called this one "Brother." They lifted me and carried me to a jeep. They tossed the setar and the attaché inside the jeep. Then they pushed a body inside. Dark blood formed a small puddle under Mr. Amaani. They drove us to the barracks.

The ride didn't take more than two minutes. In the barracks' courtyard I raised my head and saw Master Memaar on the half-built tower, laying brick on brick. He saw us in the jeep, but kept working.

The man in khaki was not friendly to the soldiers. He accused them of slacking off instead of guarding the border. He threatened them with arrest. Now he raised his head and yelled at Memaar.

"You know these people?"

"Never seen them," Memaar said.

"A boy and a man," he yelled again. "We had to shoot the man."

"Never seen them, Brother."

The guard searched my pockets and took the wallet out. He yelled at Memaar again, "Farid Royaie. You know him?"

"Never heard of him, Brother," Memaar said.

He asked the same question of the soldiers and they said they'd never seen us before. Now he took me to a black van and pushed me inside, but didn't close the door. He left Mr. Amaani in the back of the jeep. I lay down in the van for a long time, listening to the men talking. A minute later they tossed in the setar and the attaché. I held the setar by its neck.

The soldiers claimed us, but the Brother wanted to take us to Tehran. They argued. The Brother said if he and his commandant hadn't come all the way to the border for an investigation, the soldiers would never have found us. Finally, they decided to wait for the commandant who was at the shepherd's house, interrogating him and his wife. He would solve the problem. But the quarrel didn't die. The soldiers kept insisting that legally we were their prisoners, but they didn't argue forcefully. I sensed fear in their voices.

When the Brother Commandant arrived, everyone became quiet. I heard his voice saying from behind his bandanna that he had the necessary papers to arrest people who attempted to cross the border. There was a long silence while the soldiers looked at the papers. The commandant ordered the soldiers to take Mr. Amaani to the only hospital in Zabol; he was still breathing. Then the commandant climbed into the back of the van where I was lying with Taara's setar at my side.

I tightened my grip on the wooden neck.

He closed the door. It was pitch dark inside. I wanted to take a last glance at Master Memaar on top of his half-built tower, but I couldn't. I ran my hand over the neck of the setar but couldn't find the strings. The instrument was bare. The commandant knocked on the window between himself and the driver and the van took off. A strange, muffled cry, the whimper of a small, wounded animal, twisted in my throat but didn't rise. I wept, not because I was caught, not because I'd never see Taara and her son again, but because I hadn't taken good care of her setar.

A setar without strings has no music. It was nothing but useless, hollow wood.

The man clicked his tongue, "Tch tch tch," and struck a match, "Wake up, you lazy bird! Wake up, you old bitch! Talkhoon is here!"

I sat up and in the flickering light of the matchstick saw the one-eyed parrot sitting on Assad's shoulder, staring at me. A gust of wind flung the desert sand against the dark windows and shrouded the van.

Mirage

I knew we were in a dust storm and I prayed we would die. The driver circled around—he had lost the road. Boor-boor cried and when the sand hit the windows, Assad cursed.

"Look what you've done to me! I wish Kia hadn't called me the night before, telling me that you and your sister were here. I wish I'd lost you forever." He was quiet for a while, looking out the window at nothing—at the gray curtain of sand. "I left my revolutionary duties, took my best men with me, and came all the way out here to take you back. Now look! We're stuck in a sandstorm!"

He cursed some more and looked outside, banged on the window and yelled at the driver, "Stop the car! We better wait till it calms down!" Now he looked at me and said, "If I'd been a few minutes late, you'd be gone forever. I'd have lost you just like this!" He snapped his fingers. "But you know? You're my destiny, Talkhoon. Your name is written on my forehead!" He slapped his forehead and chuckled. Then he said, "That ditch you fell into was the fucking border. Had you gotten up and climbed the damned hill, you'd be out of my hands! Your stupid sister is gone. A young woman with a baby on a smuggler's horse! People are wild on the other side. God knows what they'll do to her. What the smuggler will do to her! You're lucky, girl! You're always lucky!"

He laughed, the parrot cried, and the sand hit the windshield.

My toes had swelled with infection. Assad poured some vodka on them, found a safety pin in his pocket and tried to take the thorns out. The van sat in the middle of the desert. I prayed we'd get buried. Assad cursed and nagged like an old woman.

"Look what you've done to yourself! How can you wear your wedding slippers now? Wearing canvas shoes to travel on foot? Where is your common sense?" He knocked on my head. "You're crazier than ever, Talkhoon!"

When the storm passed, the driver saw the main road and the van roared again. I knew the road was long and the day was endless, so I tried not to think about the time. I freed the old winds in my head and let them shriek. Assad nagged, Boor-boor cried, and the hot wind whistled. The van stopped in front of a caravansary. Was this the same caravansary in which a little homeless fly sought shelter in Taara's ear? Did Taara wear her jingling necklace today, the one she bought from an old woman here? Did she wear it under her clothes so as not to let it jingle while she was on the horse? What was she doing now? Breast-feeding the baby in an identical caravansary on the other side of the border? Was she wondering where I was? Was Safdar telling her that I'd soon join her, I was just a little slow? Did she believe it? Did Safdar desire her? Did he want her for himself? Had he wanted her for himself from the first day, and was that why he'd dismissed his brother?

Assad left the van's back door open so that the light would pour inside. He squatted in front of me with a spoon and tried to force me to eat.

I neither ate nor uttered a word. The van moved again and I saw the desert and the long road that extended like a white snake. I saw a mirage—silvery water, a fresh mountain stream, glowing a short distance away, within reach and not within reach. I kept hearing the swish of other cars passing, until the heat became unbearable and the knapsack on my chest became wet with sweat. I was thirsty, but I didn't say a word.

Assad took his shirt off and loosened his belt. The top part of his blue bird showed—an angry head, long, curved beak, thick neck with layers of skin. All blue. The wings were inside his pants. He fanned himself with an old newspaper, wiped his face with his bandana. Cursed.

I napped. Dreamed while not quite asleep. Dreamed of the grocer's courtyard, the tamarind tree, the stone fountain at the very end of the yard by the wet wall, the narrow rivulet of water pouring down from a hole in the wall. Shade, clear water, and the hum of an air conditioner somewhere in the distance, cooling a dim room with a narrow bed. A snow-white sheet. The pillow—soft and puffy, like a piece of cloud. The whole room, shady and cool and the window open, letting in the breeze. A woman calls, "Talkhoon! I've made some lemonade for you!" Ice clicks in the tall glass. A small boy runs in the yard. The woman calls, "Come inside! Talkhoon is working. Don't make noise!" A monkey bounces from branch to branch. The smells of sandalwood, curry, and red pepper rise in the air. On top of the wall a peacock opens its wings—shimmering green, gold and silver, a crown on its head. The peacock cries and flies away. Music ripples like clean water in a spring. Taara plays her setar; the boy claps and giggles. I see all this. Hear all this. Smell it all. Asleep and not asleep.

Assad opened a trunk and pulled out the wedding dress.

"You remember this? I'm going to use my time here. It's a long drive. There is one skirt left to stitch."

Like an old, plump woman, he sits cross-legged with his sewing glasses on the tip of his nose. He stitches and chats, nags and gossips. His khaki uniform, his beard, his sunburnt face, his military appearance are all in contrast with his womanly manner and gossipy voice.

The van bumps up and down, but he keeps stitching and chatting.

"Khanum has gone mad. She's blind and mad. Her sisters have to watch her day and night because she leaves the house. One day they found her walking barefoot in a busy street, stopping people to tell them her dreams. Poor old hen. Big sister. The fucking liar. The bitch. One of these days she'll go where our dear papa is. Hell!"

Now he sings. Keeps repeating this phrase from a wedding song: "The bride is out of the bath, bring the groom, bring the groom."

"I'll give you a warm bath. I'll soak you in soapy water. I'll pour rose water in the tub. I'll wash you—bring the groom, bring the groom—" He whistles the rest.

"I won't delay this time. We'll wed when we get home. Tonight! I've told Mustafa to put chairs in the garden, to decorate Baba's dryandra tree with those little bulbs we used for Taara's engagement party. The dryandra tree is standing there alone. I didn't let them cut it. For your sake, my little herb. I know how much you love that tree. I told Mustafa to put our chairs under it. I told him to order some food."

The van bumps up and down. He wipes his sweat with his sleeve, stitches, stitches. The desert is gone. Slogans in red paint stain the tall gray walls of the factories like thick blood: "Death to the East and the West! Long live the Holy Jihad!" We're getting close to Tehran.

"Once, when I went to clean up your grandfather, he opened his eyes. I swear to God, I was scared to death. The old man was staring at me. His eyes were wide open. So I decided to keep him. Besides, no hospital will take him. A war has broken out in the Gulf. Hospitals are full. Who will take an old man in a coma? I'll keep him. If he opened his eyes, then he may wake up too. I'll let him live in that little room. Khanum's old closet. I'll buy him a little desk. Maybe he'll write another book. Let him write!"

He whistles, stitches, and hums. Now he says, "I'll put him in his old wheelchair and bring him down to our wedding. The boys have fixed the elevator. We'll bring Baba down in the ghosts' elevator."

Chaos

He dresses me in lace and satin and tells me to smile. He whitens my face with powder and smears green on my eyelids. He draws a pair of long eyebrows for me and frames my eyes with thick black lines. All the while he looks at a colorful magazine on the desk and follows directions. Like a fussy hairdresser, he pulls the strands of my hair to one side, then to the other. He combs them all back, now brings them all over my forehead. He steps back, looks at me in the mirror and smiles. He wants me to smile too. When I stare at him with hollow eyes, he sighs. He drops a gauze mosquito net on my head and hides my painted face behind it. He kneels down and puts a pair of white silk stockings on my legs; he does this gently so as not to tear the silk. He takes a pair of white shoes out of a box.

He whistles. Sings the wedding song.

He lifts me up and stares at me. He calls me his bride and sings for me. "Flower has come out of the bath—bring the groom! Torches and candles are burning—bring the groom!" He makes me climb up on the chair, turns me around, and studies me. My fingernails catch his attention. They're like boys' nails. He sits me down again, places my hands on his lap and paints my fingernails with shimmering red enamel. He blows on them to dry them. When I'm perfectly done, he sprays perfume all over me, *puff, puff, puff*— He claps his hands and whistles a long whistle.

There are the sounds of explosions outside, many of them—one after another, then all at once. Missiles whistle in the air, fall somewhere, boring deep holes, swallowing people. But he is deaf and blind to the screams and shouts, to the sound of boots stamping on the pavement behind the walls. The sound of rifle butts hitting Drum Tower's gate. He is deaf and blind tonight because he wants his wedding to happen.

He leads me toward the only tree in the barracks—the solitary dryandra tree by the brick tower. Small twinkling bulbs wink on the leaves. Two chairs sit side by side under the tree and many in a circle on the muddy ground. His Revolutionary Guards are coming to our wedding, he says.

An ayatollah is going to recite the prayer. But rifle butts hit the eastern gate, and missiles tear through the air like shooting stars.

Before we reach the chairs, a gun goes off behind our backs. It's loud and near. He stops, turns back and sees a man in black, then many more. Their faces are masked; they carry black flags. They handcuff him and aim their submachine guns at him. They take him to the end of the barracks, to the brick wall. He hollers, curses, and says who he is and where this place is.

"This is Revolutionary Committee Number One! I'm Brother Assad Sheeri, head of the Committee! I'm the Great Leader's Devotee. I'm a Revolutionary Guard!"

But they treat him as if he is no one. They take him to the wall as if he is a traitor to the Great Leader, a Communist, an infidel!

Now more people pour into the barracks. People of the streets enter as if Drum Tower is a public park. They are running around in confusion, as though mad. The dark night is fully lighted by the green and blue and gold of the shooting stars whizzing through the air like something otherworldly, magical. The stars fall, dig fiery holes, and swallow men, animals and other objects. People run in, crying, cursing, holding their hands over their heads to protect themselves. Babies cry in their mothers' arms.

"So, where is the shelter?"

"They said the barracks had a basement."

"Where is the basement?"

People run, fall and step over each other. They've gone mad. They lift up the wedding chairs and hold them above their heads like umbrellas.

I run back to my room and grab my knapsack. I run out toward the tower and step on the ground that has the hidden roots of a garden. The roots pulsate and grow under my feet. I run for my life, but I trip over a body and fall in a puddle. My long dress is stained with filth. I run barefoot and tear the layers of muddy gauze and lace off my skin. I reach the tower and climb as fast as when I was a small child. One hundred thirty-five steps. I stand in the balcony of the tower with the four arched openings on its four sides. I press the bird manuscript to my chest and watch the people fighting in the treeless garden. Soldiers, guards, Black Flaggers, civilians all fighting, each against all. A group of native Baluch enter the barracks. They are on horses. They have scimitars in their hands. Safdar's whispering men. Safdar himself, on his red horse, holds the deed to Drum Tower in the air, waving it. He claims the barracks. A tank enters. People panic and open the way for the monster to roll on. Its hatch opens and a black flag pops out.

I see Khanum-Jaan, as transparent as her mother, Grandma Negaar, running inside the bare garden, her white hair long and disheveled. She screams, "I dreamed, I dreamed—my almond room is upstairs, on the second floor, next to Papa Vazir's study!" Crazy and blind, she climbs the steps and enters the house. I see her opening a window on the second floor, screaming to the world, "I found my room! I found it!"

The shooting stars travel through the air and fall. From a distance, I hear men, women, and children crying.

Now the Black Flaggers pour out of the tank and stand in a line facing Assad and his men who are blindfolded against the wall. A rattle rises, the sound of thousands of iron walls collapsing. Assad, Mustafa, Hassan, and all the urchin boy-guards of Revolutionary Committee Number One fall in the dust. They're all in their khaki uniforms, except Assad who is wearing his groom's suit, rose water glittering on his beard. He dies in a pair of shiny black shoes, the tune of the wedding song circling in his confused head, "The bride is out of the bath, bring the groom! Bring the groom!"

I keep tearing the layers of gauze and lace and satin off my body. *Tap, tap, tap, tap*—this comes from the sky. A thick column of light circles the city, lighting the barren garden, then leaving us in the dark. I open the small storage room and take out the biggest drum. I face north and bang on the drum. I face south, east, and west. *Bang, bang, bang, bang.* I keep drumming. I bang the war drum, I bang the time drum, the drum of history—the drum of revolution and death.

Khanum-Jaan's face is framed in the arched window of her almond room. She screams, "Fire! Fire!"

Boor-boor shrieks somewhere, flaps her old wings and cries, "One party, Party of God! One Leader, chosen by God!" The parrot talks for the first time.

Jangi barks, bites a Black Flagger's thigh. The masked man goes mad and shoots the dog. A rocket falls on the wall behind the tower. The earth swallows the wall and the corpses of the Revolutionary Guards. A Black Flagger calls, "Allah-O-Akbar! God is Great!" People in unison repeat, "Allah-O-Akbar!"

I face all four directions, one after another, banging on the ancient drum. I tear off the last layer of the wedding gown and wear the knapsack on my bare chest. I stand in the wind and feel the heat of the rising flames on my skin. Fire stretches up from the roof of Drum Tower. Khanum-jaan screams, "I dreamed. I dreamed. I dreamed—"

Now, slowly, Baba-Ji descends the stone steps of the balcony. His deliberate pace works against the mad, spinning motion of the battlefield. He walks toward the dryandra tree. He slides his right hand inside his blue pajama shirt and takes out a long sapphire feather. He strikes a match and burns, not a barb, but the whole feather. It flames like a torch. Baba-Ji looks up at the sky and laughs.

As if this has calmed everyone, they all stop screaming, shooting, and stabbing. The battlefield stops spinning, the rockets stop flashing. All the winds settle. Silence falls. Baba looks up. We all look up. Above our heads, a huge bird opens its wide silver wings. I listen to hear the sound of flapping, but instead I hear a roar. The bird's wings are iron hard. She splits the cloud of dust and smoke and descends as if to smash into the earth. The metallic wings reflect the red and yellow of the flames that stretch up from the roof of Drum Tower. The bird descends, too close to the earth, its body too large for human eyes to grasp. A hole opens in its underbelly as if an egg is about to drop. People lay down, arms crossed over their bare heads. No one breathes, except for Baba-Ji, who laughs with joy and claps his hands.

"The Bird of Knowledge! The Simorgh!"

A Black Flagger raises his voice above the old man's, calling to his god, "Allah-O-Akbar!"

People echo in unison.

Iranian-born writer Farnoosh Moshiri was a published playwright, translator, and fiction writer when she fled her country in 1983 after a massive arrest of secular intellectuals, feminists, and political activists, most of whom were executed by the Islamic regime in 1988. Ms. Moshiri lived in refugee camps in Afghanistan and India for four years before immigrating to the United States in 1987. Her books include *At the Wall of Almighty* (to be reissued by Black Heron Press in 2016), *The Bathhouse*, *The Crazy Dervish and the Pomegranate Tree*, and *Against Gravity*. Among other awards and fellowships, she is the recipient of two Barbara Deming Awards; two Black Heron Press Awards for Social Fiction, and a Valiente Award from Voices Breaking Boundaries, for artists who have taken risks to speak out and act as advocates. She has taught literature, playwriting, and creative writing in universities in Tehran, Kabul, Houston, and Syracuse. Currently she teaches creative writing at the University of Houston-Downtown.